A HARD DAY'S MONTH

Ian Snowball & Mark Baxter

NEW HAVEN PUBLISHING LTD

First Edition
Published 2017
NEW HAVEN PUBLISHING LTD
www.newhavenpublishingltd.com
newhavenpublishing@gmail.com

Cover design©Pete Cunliffe
pcunliffe@blueyonder.co.uk

newhaven
publishing

Dedication

To Mum with all my loving

Thanks to Loz for the keen eye and edit, Teddie for giving the novel a chance and for Bax for sharing the vision. To Katie Town and Niamh Francis Smith for being our models and for Becki Morgan for taking the pic and Josie you are allowed to read this one. Love you.

And to Dad, I've still got you're a Hard Day's Night album, we used it on the front cover. I think you would have liked this story. And don't worry, Mum is being looked after x

-Ian Snowball

Dedication

'When I was around six I discovered a pile of 45's owned by my dad. Among all the Nat King Cole, Sinatra, Tony Bennett and other easy listening greats was a copy of 'I Am The Walrus' by The Beatles. Looking back, it was a surprise that the old man had bought that single, but I suppose it shows how much the Fabs were part of the fabric of life back then. I played that single to the point of wearing out its grooves. I had no idea what they were singing about, but I loved it, and the band so much, that I didn't care. We'll never see the likes of them again.

My thanks go to Teddie and all at New Haven for believing in the book, to Adam Smith, Simon Wells and Mark Lewisohn for my 'Fab' education, to Lorraine 'Loz' Prescott for the sterling work on this book and to Snowy for inviting me in on the project, which was a joy to be involved in.

And finally, I dedicate my work on this book to my Lou in her 50th year, who I simply love more than anything else.'

-Mark Baxter

Content

Chapter 1
Yesterday

29th November 2001 - Wimbledon

The alarm bell erupted into life for the third annoying time. Its sole purpose was to stoke up the weary body and mind of fifty-three-year-old Cynthia, whom had been lying peacefully beside it.

'Oh…for Christ's sake,' Cynthia groaned, reaching out her arm and feeling with her fingertips for the machine that had declared war on her. Having found it, she slammed her fist down hard on top of the alarm. She sighed deeply, relieved that the irritating buzzing from the alarm had now ceased.

She lay still and motionless on her back, refusing to unfold and unwind herself from the deep slumber she had been enjoying, and of which she was in much need. It was Thursday, her day off, but she had once again forgotten to turn off her alarm clock. The bed felt nice and warm; it was only seven thirty and far too early to get up. Besides, she didn't need to as there wasn't much she was intending to do.

A few more minutes passed before Cynthia reluctantly resigned herself to the fact that she wasn't going to be able to doze back off. She sucked in a deep frustrated breath and threw back her duvet. Thankfully the heating had been on for over an hour and her bedroom felt the benefit of it. She slid herself out of the bed and in a well-practiced and effortless motion, slipped her feet into her slippers and her body into her favourite silk dressing gown, all without really opening her eyes properly.

She took her first steps and winced, feeling that nagging twinge in her back that had been hanging around for a couple of days. Cynthia straightened herself, doing her best to ignore the pain. She then made her way over to her bedroom window and lifted one of the corners of the beige and blue striped curtains. This act contributed to Cynthia's daily morning routine; she was always curious to know what the weather was going to be like on any given day. The weather revealed itself to be that of a typical British November morning: cold, grey, windy, wet and generally grim.

She pulled the curtain down and then shuffled off around the room, picking up discarded clothes, plonking them down onto an old white painted, chipped and battered wicker chair that she had purchased from a junk shop in Lewisham. The chair was sandwiched between an even older chest of drawers which had seen better days and a tall, heavy-looking wardrobe that she had inherited from her grandfather. She loved the wooden beast that stood tall and proud like some old soldier from some distant war. Cynthia would never, ever part with the old wardrobe.

Before leaving the bedroom, she opened her eyes wider and glanced briefly at the antique wooden framed mirror that hung beside the wardrobe. The mirror had also belonged to her for many years; too many in fact to even recall how it came to be in her possession. She sometimes wondered why she held on to it; in truth, she had never liked it.

She sighed as her thoughts turned to her recent holiday in Ibiza. It had only been a few months back, in what was laughingly called the summer, but this morning it felt like a long, long time ago. Her suntan and the memories of hot sunny days and warm evenings washed down with tequilas were now fading fast.

Plus, since that holiday, so much had happened. In the space of a matter of weeks, Cynthia had found herself once again out of a long-term relationship and living alone in her house again. This had left her feeling sad and disappointed with herself. She cursed her obvious habits, the ones that defined her turning her into a hard person to live with and love, or so it seemed. Habits such as preferring to sit at home night after night, drowning in a world of reality TV and cooking programmes, rather than going out and enjoying the world. How she had developed such damning habits, she wasn't too sure, and she found herself asking that question aloud as she entered her bathroom.

Five minutes later, Cynthia was settled on the sofa with a steaming hot cup of coffee in her hand and a plate of toast on her lap, half watching breakfast television. Several times she glanced at the pile of ironing that had been staring at her since the weekend, and each time she quickly diverted her gaze back to the TV. She certainly wasn't in the mood for housework and long before she had finished her coffee she had decided it could wait at least another day.

It was nearer eleven by the time Cynthia eventually got herself motivated enough to get dressed and leave the house. She was heading off into town, if only to idle away a couple of hours. She walked briskly to the nearest bus stop, passing one of her old haunts on the way that in her teenage years had once been a popular café. Sadly, now it was yet another fast food fried chicken outlet.

The weather turned out to be bitter cold and Cynthia constantly pulled up the collar of her pale blue Aquascutum trench coat, trying to fight it off. Thankfully the wind and rain had eased off, so Cynthia didn't have to unfurl her brolly, but she kept it in her hand just in case.

In the near distance, Cynthia noticed the bus she was waiting for heading her way. Spotting a muddy puddle near to the bus stop, she swiftly took a step back from the kerb. Quickly climbing aboard, Cynthia paid her fare and sat on the nearest available seat. She glanced around and was greeted with several miserable looking people, staring blankly into space. All had a look of general disinterest in life in general and their immediate surroundings in particular. Cynthia sighed quietly. 'God,' she thought to herself, 'how depressing.' She couldn't wait to get off and get on the tube.

A few minutes later found herself showing her ticket to a tube station employee as she entered the platforms on Wimbledon tube station. The face emerging from the neck of the blue uniform looked exhausted as it strained a weak smile in her direction. In fairness, she tried to reciprocate, but it was even weaker than the half-hearted effort she had just witnessed.

Anyway, she had no time for smiles; she was too busy being swept along in the rush of her fellow tube dwellers racing to catch their respected trains. Suits, students, and mums with kids, all rushed around her as she passed towards the down escalator of her choice. Her nostrils quickly filled with the aromas of aftershaves and perfumes, leaving her with a feeling like she wanted to sneeze.

The metal staircase led the way to her platform. A train was already at the platform and only a few more passengers got on it, Cynthia being one of them. Although there were plenty of vacant seats some passengers simply chose to stand by the doors, whilst others sat.

A few produced chunky mobile phones and set about fiddling with them. One woman spread a copy of the Metro across her lap and started to read some article about WAG's, and a young black male wearing a hoody was plugged into some new-fangled device; the likes of which she had never seen before. The male had the volume turned up so that everyone else could hear the tat-tat-tat of the repetitive drum beat that the song produced.

Cynthia studied each of her fellow passengers, all seemed consumed in their unique and individual worlds. No-one engaged with anyone else; every one avoided eye contact as best. In truth, no one seemed to care...

The train passed through Putney Bridge and Fulham Broadway and most of passengers, including Cynthia, alighted at Earls Court. On arriving, she broke out into an involuntary smile. Her first of the day. This was Cynthia's favourite tube station. In her mind the station hadn't changed that much since she first started to become familiar with it back in the 1960's. She always felt at home here and actually enjoyed passing through it. Cynthia climbed the steps towards the light that eventually led to the streets outside. She turned a sharp right outside the station and walked down Earls Court Road towards one of her favourite cafés.

As she pushed open the door, Cynthia was met with a warm smile from the Italian guy who worked behind its counter. This was a fairly swanky café with modern décor and large black and white photographs that depicted life on the streets of 1930's Paris and Rome.

She smiled back and then remembered she didn't know his name. Mind you, he didn't know hers, but they always recognised one another and Cynthia liked that. He was every bit the kind of man that Cynthia felt attracted to - tall, dark and he evidently looked after himself. Basically, nothing like any man she had ever had a relationship with.

Noticing her favourite seat by the café window was vacant, she rushed towards it. Before sitting down, she removed her coat and hung it on the back of the chair. As she did so, she mouthed the words 'hot chocolate please' to the familiar face with no name. He nodded back approvingly.

Looking out in front of her, she noticed Earls Court Road was its usual chaotic self. People of all shapes, sizes and nationalities hustled and bustled their way along it, darting in and out of shops. Cynthia considered herself seasoned and skilled in the art of people watching. It amused her to think that as much as she watched others, she too was probably being watched. The thought lightened her mood. A wonderful smelling hot chocolate soon arrived accompanied with an even warmer smile from the man from behind the counter.

10

'Hello. Nice to see you again,' he said.

'Hi, and you,' Cynthia replied cheerily.

'Day off, yes?' he continued.

'Er, yeah and I found I was in much need of one of your famous hot chocolates, so here I am.'

It tickled Cynthia to hear the way the words fell out of her mouth. She enjoyed the flirty behaviour which the two of them engaged in week after week. She smiled to herself to as she noted, once again, that he was at least twenty years younger than herself.

'Ah my world-famous hot chocolate, yes, yes. Enjoy it! And how will you be spending your day off today? Maybe you do a little shopping in the Kings Road? Maybe you go and spend some cash in Harrods?'

They both chuckled, him confidently, and Cynthia just like a schoolgirl. Cynthia noticed that some customers hovered by the till. He shrugged his shoulders indicating his services were needed elsewhere and then he snaked his way around several tables towards the counter, greeting the new customers as he did so.

Cynthia's eyes followed him. He had a marvellous physique, with even more impressive bum! Her thoughts began wandering onto delights she hadn't known since one especially drunken night back in Ibiza, but she soon snapped out of that when she felt the buzzing of her mobile phone, coming from inside her bag. She reached down, rifling around in her bag blindly, pushing aside a pack of travel tissues, a box of Tic Tacs, her everyday purse with its contents bulging and which hadn't been sorted out the months, and finally…finally, she found her phone.

She looked immediately at the name on the screen. It was her mum. Sighing, she reluctantly answered it, noticing at the same time, she had four missed calls from her oldest and closest friend Sandra. 'That's odd,' she thought. Mum first though.

'Hi Mum,' Cynthia said mustering as a cheery tone as she could.

'Hello Cynthia, it's mum.'

'Yes Mum, I know,' she said a little irritated, 'how are you?'

'Oh, I'm okay!' her mum replied, 'I just thought I would let you know what the doctor said.'

Oh shit, oh shit, oh shit…Cynthia suddenly realised that she had forgotten about her mum's doctor's appointment.

'Sorry Mum, I was going to ring you this afternoon. I thought you said the appointment was at three,' Cynthia lied.

'No, it was an early one, eight thirty this morning,' snapped back her mum.

For the next few minutes Cynthia quietly supped her hot chocolate as she held her phone to her ear, listening intently as her mum gave her every detail relating to her appointment, which included what the doctor had said and who she saw in the waiting room and what they had said. Cynthia swallowed the last dribbles of her hot chocolate and felt a little cheated that she hadn't been able to enjoy it in peace.

Suddenly, and with a sense of being saved by the bell, she was alerted to another in-coming call. She looked to see who it was and sighed with relief; it was Sandra trying again. Good old Sandra! This wasn't just a case of being saved by the bell but saved by Sandra; something her closest friend had done a few times over the years.

'Mum…Mum…sorry…Mum,' Cynthia said, cutting across the non-stop flow of talk pouring into her ear. 'I've got to go. I've got an important call coming through. Sorry. Look, I'll ring you tonight, eh?'

'And then Edna said…oh, oh okay,' said her mum, somewhat startled. 'Oh, okay then love, yes you do that, but just after Emmerdale please, not before. You know how I can't concentrate on anything else when that is on.'

'Yes, yes,' Cynthia was rapidly losing patience and interrupting her again. 'Okay Mum, I'll time it to miss Emmerdale, I know that's not a good time to call. I'll speak to you tonight then alright? Bye then, bye.' With that Cynthia shut down her mum and hit the button receiving the call from Sandra.

Before Cynthia had a chance to say anything Sandra had already begun to speak.

'Cyn? Cyn…that you? Bloody hell! Finally, oh Cyn, where have you been all morning? Have you heard the news? Have you?' Sandra was babbling twenty words to the dozen, all with the sound of a tear in her voice.

That very tone in Sandra's voice alerted Cynthia that something was wrong, very wrong. She hadn't heard that tone in her friend's voice since December 1980. And she remembered the event behind that occasion like it was yesterday.

12

'Sand, Sand...Sandra! Whoa for Christ's sake. Slow down, slow down will ya... whatever is the matter?'

Sandra gulped some air and then continued after taking a further deep breath... 'You...you haven't heard have you? I mean you don't know, do you? You haven't...heard...?'

Sandra could hardly form the words. Cynthia rolled her eyes and again tried her best to calm her friend down. And then, after a small silence as Sandra composed herself one more time, the words rolled from her tongue. Words which hit Cynthia like the big red London bus she had alighted half hour ago.

'It's George,' she gulped, 'It's George...George is dead.'

Cynthia was silent. Her mind raced, trying to take in the news. Then it quickly emptied of all thought. She felt numb.

She didn't even have to ask 'George who?' She knew immediately, because there had only ever been one important George in their lives.

There was a few moment's silence before another word was spoken. Cynthia needed a few seconds to digest what she had just been told. Gradually, and cautiously, Cynthia emerged from her state of shock. She spoke very quietly and slowly.

'George dead? My...our, George...dead? When? How?' Cynthia was frantically trying to make some sense of the news.

'It's all over the news love. Have you not seen any TV today?' Sandra continued.

'Yes, I have, but, well I wasn't really concentrating. Really, George has died?'

Sadness was enveloping Cynthia.

'It was the lung cancer,' Sandra said slowly. 'It finally got the better of him Cyn...'

Cynthia felt the tears welling up inside her.

'No, not him. Not my George. George was my Beatle...'

George Harrison had indeed been her favourite Beatle ever since she had first discovered them back in 1962, when she was 14. '*Love Me Do*' was the first record she had ever bought and it was that record which set her on a path that would mean following The Beatles EVERY step of their way until Paul announced he would be leaving the band in the April of 1970 and thus, in turn, breaking up the greatest pop band of all time. They were HER band, George was HER Beatle...

13

After a few seconds of silence, which felt like hours, Sandra spoke.

'Cyn? Cynthia, are you there?' Sandra was trying to make sense of the silence that was now coming her way down the phone. 'Can you talk?'

Cynthia composed herself well, the best she could manage.

'No not really. Not really, no Sand. I need to get home. I just need to…'

Cynthia had a sudden compulsion to head home immediately. There was something she felt she needed to do. She simply told Sandra she would call her later. Putting the phone in her bag, Cynthia left the café, forgetting to pay for her hot chocolate. She was intent on getting home. Home was where she needed to be. There was something waiting at home for her…

The journey back seemed to take forever, not that she was really taking much notice of what was around her. Cynthia changed from tube to bus, without giving it any thought; she was on autopilot. She didn't even notice the now torrential rain. Cynthia just walked on as it drenched her; tears mixing with the raindrops on her face. Her umbrella was still folded up and in her hand. She was oblivious to everything going on around her. Getting off the bus, she began to walk very quickly and then started to run.

Cynthia fumbled around trying to get the keys into the locks, and dropped them in her haste to get inside. She picked them up angrily, cursing under her breath as she finally managed to get her front door key to work in the correct lock.

Finally, the door opened. Stepping over the small pile of letters the postman had dropped through her letterbox whilst she was out, and which now lay scattered across her wooden floor, Cynthia headed straight for the stairs, removing her coat as she raced up them and pushed open her bedroom door. She fell to her knees beside her bed and peered underneath. She had to remove a few items to get to what she was looking for - a suitcase and a sports bag, which hadn't been used in years, and some photo albums. Then, with an extra stretch, she reached out and grabbed an old Quality Street sweet tin.

'Ting…ting…ting…' The sound of the rain slowly dripping from her wet hair and hitting the top of the tin slowly woke her up from her dazed state. She grabbed a towel she had left on her wicker chair and roughly dried her hair on it the best she could. Her clothes were wet through, but that didn't seem to matter now.

14

Cynthia then dragged the tin towards her, noticing as she did so that the old-fashioned tins were much bigger and rounder than the modern-day ones. She pushed herself up and sat crossed legged with her back resting against her bed. She dug her finger nails under the tin's lid in an attempt to remove it. It took Cynthia a few frustrating attempts, but finally she prised off the lid. A smell that reminded her of a dozen Christmases wafted under her nose, but she was in no mood to be reminded of those happy and joyful holidays. What she kept stored in the tin now was of far more importance.

Cynthia slowly reached in to the tin. She couldn't remember the last time she visited the contents, but everything appeared to be there; all safe and sound. She breathed heavily and removed the first item that caught her attention. The Bibby & Sons Cidal soap was still intact, safe in its wrapping. She lifted it to her nose and took a long sniff. The soap smelled as good as it did from the day she got it back in 1964. As she smelled the soap she could picture a sixteen-year Sandra telling her that it was Bibby & Sons soap that The Beatles used to wash themselves with, and they did so because the company was a Liverpool based soap manufacturer. Cynthia smiled as she remembered that she was never entirely convinced of this story, but had gone along with it anyway.

Next, she touched a small bottle of Old Spice Lime aftershave lotion. The bottle was still virtually full, just missing the few drops that Cynthia had squirted onto her pillowcases many years earlier. The smell of the aftershave - the aftershave she was told George Harrison used - instantly triggered a flood of memories. Once again, she felt more tears welling up. In truth, she wasn't shocked or surprised at the impact the news of George's death was having upon her. She always knew the day would come when George would die. She had read that he was gravely ill. News of his cancer was in the public domain, but Christ, now it was here, the news bloody hurt.

Cynthia sat with the soap in one hand and the bottle of aftershave in the other and closed her eyes. Image after image of George, the shy one, with his band mates - the sad eyed Ringo, the cheery Paul and the cynical and quick-witted John - flashed through her mind, carried in a ferry full of wonderful memories.

The feeling of the weight of the Quality Street tin resting on her lap re-focussed Cynthia's attention. She placed the soap and aftershave

15

carefully on the floor beside her and then tipped the remaining contents of the tin out on to the floor in front of her.

Copies of the Beatle Monthly magazine fell out first. She noted the price, one shilling and six pence. Cynthia placed the palm of her hand on the pile and spread them out. One copy dated July 1964 had a picture on the cover of John Lennon playing the piano. He was grinning away like a Cheshire cat. Cynthia smiled back at John before gently pushing the copy to one side. Revealed beneath it were two more copies. One was a February edition of the same year which had a front cover picture of the Fab Four all wearing big smiles; and the other was a copy from March which had a front cover with only Paul, John and George on it. In that photo, George had a camera swinging around his neck.

Cynthia flicked through the pages, noticing articles by Neil Aspinall. Aspinall was an old school friend of Paul and George who was also employed as their road manager and personal assistant, along with Mal Evans. Cynthia recalled that both men had regular features in the Beatle Monthly, as did Bettina Rose and Anne Collingham, the two national secretaries of the official Beatles fan club. Noticing the two women's names instantly triggered the feeling of being insanely jealous, a feeling that took years to leave her, because she considered them to have the best jobs in the world at the time.

It had only been after the Beatles split up that Cynthia had learned that Anne Collingham wasn't even a real person; she was just someone who had been invented to help the fans feel like that they had a mate and someone who acted as a contact between them and the band.

Seeing their names also reminded her of a certain special letter which she knew she had also kept in the tin. Cynthia searched through a pile of unsent fan mail letters intended for George's eyes only, until she found what she was looking for. She removed it from its envelope and laid it out flat across her knees.

The top of the letter had on it the year 1964, but the rest was smudged and illegible. Directly below it was an address: The Official Beatles Fan Club, First Floor, Service House, 13 Monmouth Street, London, WC2. The letter was Cynthia's confirmation from the fan club that her postal order had been cleared and that she was now a member. Cynthia suddenly felt the same warm glowing sensation inside her as she had done on the day it had arrived; the day after her sixteenth birthday when it simply outweighed every other birthday present she had ever received *up to that point.*

'We're pleased to tell you that you have now been enrolled on our enormous list of more than 45,000 Beatle people and you will find your membership card enclosed herewith'

Signed

Bettina Rose and Anne Collingham (Joint national secretaries of the official Beatles fan club).

To be formally told that she was now an official Beatles person in that moment was the second most important thing in her life. George was, of course, the first. Cynthia could hardly contain the excitement she felt building up inside her as her mind recalled two other items she just had to see again.

She dived into the pile of things scattered out in front of her. 'There you are!' she exclaimed to herself. In her left hand, she held her very own Beatles fan club membership card. She didn't need to read the words on the card because she still knew what they were off by heart. She spoke the words out loud in a voice mimicking how she imagined Bettina Rose would have sounded.

'This is to certify that Cynthia Jefferies is an officially enrolled member of the fan club and has become Beatle person number 122369'.

Cynthia made herself laugh then turned her attention to the letter she held in her right hand. In her hand was a tatty, dog-eared letter. The postmark was now unreadable but she knew it was dated September 1964. The letter was a handwritten reply from Louise Harrison, George's mother.

Cynthia recalled hearing through the Beatle grapevine that the parents of The Beatles also received lots of fan mail that often asked them questions about their sons. Feeling confident and optimistic one evening, Cynthia had written a letter to Louise. In fact, she scribbled down fifteen drafts until eventually deciding on the one she felt asked the most important and not too personal questions.

Questions like: Do you think George is enjoying playing concerts in places like New York? Was New York a place George dreamed of visiting? How many suitcases did George take? Is it true his favourite toothpaste is Crest? And when was the last time he had his haircut?

Louise Harrison had done her best to reply and, although the letter was brief, it was handwritten which meant the world to Cynthia; after

17

all she had communicated directly with the person who had brought the second most important man, besides Jesus Christ, into the world, namely George Harrison. Cynthia had read that letter countless times and on several occasions, had slept with it placed under her pillow as she went to sleep.

It was her way of feeling as close to George as possible and she even convinced herself that the letter could act in some kind of a magical way and serve as a vehicle in which her dreams would pass through the paper on which it was written and find their way to George, and then they could both share the same dream at the same time.

Now, all these years later, the recollection of those nights that she slept with the letter made her feel silly, but in all honesty, at this precise moment, she didn't care. She found herself smiling at the memory.

The tin provided one memory after another. Beatles concert ticket stubs from Brighton and Blackpool, which she had attended. Ticket stubs which Patricia, her American Beatles fan pen pal, had sent her for performances in Atlantic City, Washington D.C and Indiana State Fair. There was even a poster from the Washington Sports Arena concert dated 11th February 1964, once the very poster that had once been pinned to her bedroom wall.

Cynthia also found her membership card from the Cavern Club. She remembered how she had found it laying in the gutter in Mathew Street, Liverpool. It was a junior membership card made of thin pink card. On the card was an image of an arrow and, inside the arrow, was a drawing of the cavern walls with its archways. The words written on the card said The Cavern-Liverpool 'Mersey beat' and 'expires December 1964 and Not Transferable'.

There were more letters, a couple more copies of the Beatle Monthly, a flexi pop record that had been issued by the fan club at Christmas 1964 which announced in bold writing 'Another Beatles Christmas Record'. And, finally, an assortment of fan club promotional cards with photos of the Fab Four with their facsimile autographs.

Most of those were of George. And all, at one time, had been pinned to the walls which surrounded her bed. Not a night went by when Cynthia didn't fall asleep gazing dreamy eyed at the face of her favourite Beatle.

In those final moments before the sand man finally took control, easing his subject into sleep, Cynthia had studied everything about George's face. She knew every feature and detail completely. She loved the shape of his nose, his eyes and prominent cheek bones, which she felt gave him a hungry post-war look. Cynthia adored the way his thick hair rested on his forehead. She loved his bushy eyebrows and the way his eyelashes seemed to reach out at her.

But most of all she loved the way the look in George's eyes always seemed to have a far-away look in them. It was as if George's soul gazed out into the world but looked out further, much further than most people could ever achieve. Cynthia somehow just knew George was a deeply spiritual being and had been destined for higher things, from the moment he had taken his first breath in that bedroom at 12 Arnold Grove on 25th February 1943.

Suddenly pools of tears formed in Cynthia's eyes as her thoughts turned once again to today's news about George. She clutched one of the photographs of him and held it to her chest. The news was gradually beginning to sink in.

George Harrison of The Beatles was dead.

An hour or two later Cynthia woke up with a jolt and startled herself. It took a few moments to realise where she was. Rubbing the sleep from her sore eyes, only then did she notice that the telephone was ringing.

'Shit,' she mumbled thinking it was her mother again. She made her way downstairs to answer the phone. To her relief, it wasn't her mother at all, it was Sandra.

'How are you?' asked Sandra in a hushed caring tone. 'I tried ringing you again a few times this afternoon. Where have you been? What have you been doing?'

Cynthia glanced at her watch. It was five o'clock. She looked into the kitchen and out through the window. It was now pitch black and she realised that she must have been asleep for the past two hours.

'I fell asleep after...' she began.

'After what?' Sandra butted in.

Cynthia explained to Sandra what she had been doing before she had fallen asleep. Sandra listened sympathetically without interrupting. Only when Cynthia's account came to a natural pause did Sandra speak, and, when she did, it was to offer a suggestion.

'I got an idea,' said Sandra. 'We should play *A Hard Day's Night*, tonight. It will bring back so many memories. Look, how about I come over, we crack open a bottle of wine and we toast George and listen to the album. It will be, well FAB!'

She shouted the word fab, sounding like a teenager again.

Cynthia thought this was a great idea and told her to get over to hers as quickly as her old Ford Escort would let her. Cynthia put down the phone and headed for the fridge. She was now intent on getting legless and, not feeling patient enough to wait for Sandra, decided she would open a bottle of white vino immediately.

She filled a glass, took a few sips and then made her way into her living room where she kept her CD and record collection. Her vinyl copy of *A Hard Day's Night* was stored safely there alongside every other Beatles album.

She knew exactly where to find it and removed it from its position, nestling in between *With the Beatles* and *Beatles For Sale*.

Cynthia stroked the album cover and the faces of each of the Beatles on the cover. Her eyes lingered on George the longest.

She removed the record from its sleeve and placed it gently onto the record deck of her ancient music centre. Switching the machine on, the speakers made a hissing sound as they were kick-started to life. Cynthia picked up the needle and placed it carefully onto the record. Before the first strum of the guitar that introduced *A Hard Day's Night* had faded, Cynthia was already falling like Alice In Wonderland, down the hole into her own cherished memories of being a teenage Beatles person back in the July of 1964.

It was the 10th; the day the *A Hard Day's Night* album had its UK release. Cynthia slumped down into the nearest chair. She was going to enjoy the next thirty minutes and forty-five seconds and she was going to enjoy being fifteen and in love with George Harrison all over again.

Chapter 2
I Should Have Known Better

July 1964

The Moka was bustling with the usual suspects. All a collection of teenagers from around the local Wimbledon area, who had outgrown the nearby youth clubs and who now preferred to spend their money on frothy coffees made from the imported Gaggia machine. Cynthia adored the aroma which hung around the café, although truth be told, it didn't always mix that well with the smell of Old Spice and Brut coming from the still pimply boys.

Cynthia and Sandra had strutted through the front door and headed directly for the counter, where they perched themselves onto the red plastic-coated stools which lined up alongside it. The remaining stools were all vacant and, upon closer inspection, had seen better days. As had the entire café's décor if truth be told. The pictures on the walls of old advertisement posters for soaps and teas from around the globe had been pinned to the peeling paint of the café's walls for years. The ceiling which had once been a bright white was now a nicotine colour brown. Stains of all sorts were engrained in most of the surfaces and god alone knows what unsavoury delights lurked in the dark corners and underneath the counter, clanging pinball machine and the flashing jukebox. But, whatever the condition of The Moka, it was still our girl's preferred choice of place to hang out.

A large mirror hung on the wall behind the counter. Both girls stole a moment to check themselves. Cynthia had an innocent, naïve looking face with clear skin. Her hair was long and blonde which covered what she considered her tiny pixie-like ears. Her eyes were a deep, piercing blue that sucked people into them. She had a slender figure, with slender fingers which wrapped themselves around the cigarettes that she chain-smoked.

Sandra was a couple of inches shorter than her best friend and she carried several extra pounds in weight. Her face was round, her eyes big and brown and her brunette hair was styled in a bob, which made her face appear even plumper. Her fingers were short and stubby and she chewed on her fingernails constantly. Her parents were always telling her off for doing so, but it was a habit she was finding hard to break. Whereas Cynthia always carried a small mirror in her handbag, Sandra preferred to carry a packet of pear drops, which were her favourite sweets, consuming at least a packet of on most days.

The two girls had known each other since they were five years old and had started primary school together. They had been paired up on the first day and then sat side-by-side for the duration of their school years. In truth, neither girl especially liked school and, like most their peers, couldn't wait to leave. Happiest days of your life apparently. These two weren't having any of that. Upon leaving however, they didn't spread their wings too far.

Cynthia started working in her granddad's corner shop that overlooked Wimbledon Common. Not that exciting, but Cynthia loved her granddad Nobby and was only too pleased to help him whilst she worked out what she really wanted to do with her life. Sandra fell immediately into a typing pool and became a faceless keyboard smasher all day long for an agency at various locations in central London, which had her travelling from one end of the Central Line to the other each day.

Together they had been through thick and thin. They had been there for each other during the time of their first boyfriends and the resulting heartbreaks and a whole host of other issues which blighted their teenage lives. Sandra was especially grateful for Cynthia's continued support, as she navigated her way through the stormy relationship with her parents. She had never really 'got on' with them, but couldn't really understand why. Sometimes living at home was unbearable, with them nagging at her about this or that and, when it got too much, Sandra would pack an overnight bag and go knocking on Cynthia's front door. And Cynthia's door was always open. She had two smashing parents, William and Dorothy, who supported their daughter every step of the way, or that's how it looked to Sandra and they never turned her away. She longed to have such wonderful and caring parents like these two, but she didn't and she had carried that sadness inside for as long as she could remember. Sandra was an only child and would sometimes wonder why, often suspecting that she was a mistake and that her parents never really wanted any children at all. Unwanted was certainly how she felt much of the time.

Cynthia, on the other hand, had two older brothers. John was nineteen and Andrew, twenty-two. John was very much into his music and loved going to see bands, riding a Lambretta and being a first-class mod. He had even been involved in the mods versus rockers riots in the May of that year. Sandra bought a copy of the Daily Express on the 19th May, its front page screaming 'Mods v Rockers Battle Again!' It had a picture of a bunch of mods putting the boot into a poleaxed rocker. She had only bought it because someone told her that her John was in the photograph. As it turned out she couldn't see him at all. Sandra really held a candle for John, but she tried her utmost not to show it.

Cynthia's older brother Andrew, however, was a completely different character to John. He was a mild-mannered young man and he possessed a cool presence. Whenever Sandra visited Cynthia's house and walked passed his bedroom, she always noticed that he had Bebop and Hard Bop jazz records playing. It was a sound she knew little about in truth. But Andrew, he loved his records by the likes of Cannonball Adderley and Freddie Hubbard, and Ronnie Scott's Jazz Club on Gerrard Street was his favourite place in the world. Actually, during the whole time Sandra had known Andrew, he had barely spoken more than a few sentences to her. He had an aloofness about him and she couldn't understand him at all, so decided it was best to keep her distance.

She and Cynthia had literally grown up together and therefore had many shared memories. They had played on the rubble-strewn wastelands left behind by the Luftwaffe and they had walked hand-in-hand to the local cinema for the Saturday morning pictures. For a short time they had even sung in the school choir together, but that didn't last too long and they got thrown out for messing about too much. They had also tried the Brownies but quickly found out it wasn't for them.

From the day they turned into teenagers all they wanted was adventure. They would take themselves off into London's West End and marvel at the sights and sounds before them. They loved to see the fashionable women dressed to the nines and the men looking stylish and important. Like Sandra, Cynthia too had little time for Andrew's jazz records, instead she felt drawn to the type of music that John liked and she secretly borrowed his singles when he wasn't at home.

By 1964 however, the most important thing for Cynthia and Sandra, besides their friendship, was their common love and total obsession with The Beatles. They considered themselves true Beatle people - reading, watching and listening to ANYTHING to do with the now world-famous pop group. Like most of their peers, they both had their favourite one. For Cynthia, it was George and only George. For Sandra, it was 'her' Ringo - not just Ringo, but HER Ringo. The Liverpool mop tops consumed the girls' thoughts and invaded their hearts night and day. The simply adored them, no other word for it.

At The Moka, the owner Sammy was out the back, so the girls had to wait to be served. Cynthia searched within her handbag and produced a packet of Woodbines. She smoked this particular brand and sometimes 'Kent' because that was what she heard The Beatles smoked. On such detail was now how she lived her life.

She popped one of the cigarettes into her mouth, then nonchalantly offered Sandra the box. Her best friend also plucked one from the carton and now held it between her lips whilst she fished around in her handbag for a box of matches. Having found them, she lit her cigarette first before offering the still burning match to Cynthia. They both inhaled deeply and blew out the smoke in unison as if rehearsed.

Cynthia took a moment to scan the room; she recognised nearly everyone. In the corner, furthest away from the counter and nearest the pinball machine was Danny, Tommy and Spike. They were three boys she had known from school, although they were two years older than herself and Sandra.

Danny was a hard-looking young man, who strongly resembled The Who's front man Roger Daltrey in almost every way from his build to the piercing blue eyes. He was manning the pinball machine whilst his two pals eagerly watched on. Danny had a growing reputation for being a real scoundrel and a king mixer. It seemed they were so engrossed in what they were doing, that they didn't notice the girls' arrival.

Sitting on another table and nearer to the main window were three more slightly older boys: Kenny, Pete and Eric. Unlike the others, these boys were fully aware of Cynthia and Sandra's presence, especially Kenny who had taken a keen interest in Cynthia and had done since she had become a Moka regular. He managed to catch Cynthia's attention and nodded his chin, trying to remain as cool as possible as he did so. He had been impressed by the way cowboys did that in the westerns he had seen at the cinema and had adopted it himself as his greetings for the girls that he liked. Cynthia, being somewhat startled at this exhibition, sent him back a polite smile. She noted he always had neatly-combed dark hair) and she thought his most striking features were his bushy brown eyebrows and long eye lashes, both of which helped to soften his face.

Near to them, a larger group of around ten teenagers had pushed three tables together so they could all huddle around them. Some of the boys had draped their arms across the shoulders of the girls and virtually all of them had a cigarette on the go. It being a beautiful summer evening, light, casual and colourful clothing was being worn, many with sweaters tied around waists and shoulders for later, for when the weather would cool a little.

One of the boys suddenly stood up and jumped across his mates. He did this accompanied by everyone cheering and some of the girls pinching his bottom as he climbed across them. Once free, he ambled over to the jukebox. Only seconds earlier *Glad All Over* from the Dave Clarke Five, a firm favourite of The Moka crowd from the previous year, had just finished and now the boy was feeding the jukebox with some more money. He knew exactly what he wanted to hear and rapidly pressed the buttons C6. A few seconds later *'Can't Buy Me Love'* burst into life and spilled out from the jukebox's speakers.

Cynthia and Sandra's ears pricked up immediately and they turned to observe who had selected one of their faves, tapping their feet along to the song's beat as they did so.

A lone voice cried out, 'Oh for gawd's sake, not this bleeding racket again.'

Cynthia smiled as she recognised the familiar dulcet tone of Sammy the owner. He emerged from the back of his café as he spoke, dressed in a pale blue shirt with its sleeves rolled up, revealing now fading tattoos on his forearms and a sauce stained apron hanging over his large belly. Still, he looked like a man content with his life and happy he had dealt with all it had thrown at him.

Sammy was born and bred on the streets of Wimbledon. He was now in his mid-fifties and had owned The Moka since 1958. For years he had worked in other people's cafés, mostly around Soho in the West End of London. By the late fifties, he had been cute enough to squirrel away a few bob as he observed the increase in coffee bars and the increasing interest from teenagers going into them and decided to open his own. He had tried to find a spot in Soho but nothing really came up and, besides, he found he was always getting hustled out by the Italians in 'Froth Street' so he turned his attention to the familiar surroundings of Wimbledon, nearer to where he lived.

The building where The Moka was located was an old tearoom, so fit for purpose. It was available for a reasonable price, so Sammy didn't think twice. He took it and within a few weeks he was running his own café.

Soon after opening, Sammy witnessed the arrival of the Teddy boy phenomenon. The boys wore their greased hair with a long curly quiff at the front and combed into a 'DA' at the back, so called because the style resembled a duck's arse. To complete their 'look', they donned Edwardian inspired drape jackets, drainpipe trousers and crepe shoes, soon nicknamed brothel creepers. The Teddy girls or 'Judies' as the boys called them were always nice, but they knew how to stir the boys up. Sammy liked the way they dressed in their circle skirts and wore their hair in ponytails, but he knew full well that any chatting up of them could be hazardous to his health. Sammy often saw the boys flashing their knuckle dusters and flick knives about, so decided the skirts were well off limits.

During the reign of the Teds, the café had been filled with the sounds of Gene Vincent, Elvis Presley and Eddie Cochran, but slowly, by the turn of the early sixties, tastes were changing and a younger, newer breed of teenager who called themselves Mods had replaced them. They had an edge to them too, but it was somehow different. Some were known to dress smartly in mohair suits all the time, even on a week night, but most preferred to dress more casually in jeans, polo shirts and desert boots and then make the extra effort to sharpen up at the weekends.

Their choice of transport was the scooter instead of the heavy, clumpy motorbikes favoured by the Teds and then later favoured by the rockers who spun off from the Teds. These Lambrettas and Vespas were imported from Italy and the bikes went hand in hand with their image. Sharp, smart and clean. Most nights there would be a handful of scooters lined up outside The Moka and it was an impressive sight.

Subsequently the sounds of the café jukebox had also changed radically and now contained almost everything that came out of the Liverpool music scene around then, The Beatles, Gerry and the Pacemakers and Billy J Kramer and amongst them some Bo Diddley, Muddy Waters, Ben E King and Sam Cooke.

In truth, Sammy preferred the music that the Teds had listened to, which was more of his generation, but he never let on though; not good for trade to do that. So, he welcomed the Mods and their friends and did his best to keep the jukebox up to date for them.

Both girls smiled when they saw Sammy appear and ordered their espressos. Cynthia and Sandra liked him, even when he confessed that he didn't like The Beatles and despite him moaning and groaning about the noise and the mess 'the youngsters' made.

'Hello Sammy,' said Cynthia, 'two of your finest frothy coffees please. Nice to hear your favourites are on the jukebox, isn't it?'

Sammy tutted and turned his back to them to place the clear glass cups on the Gaggia behind him and pour the coffee from the machine. The girls began to hum along to *Can't Buy Me Love*, upping their volume as they got into it. Of course, they knew it would wind Sammy up, and it certainly seemed to be doing the trick. He turned and placed the girls' drinks on the Formica counter top in front of them, then theatrically threw a striped red and blue tea-towel over his shoulder, tutted once more and retreated once again to the back room, where he based himself most of the time, only venturing out occasionally to see if a customer needed serving.

Sandra smiled, as she took a small sip of her hot drink. 'Ooh I needed this Cyn. I've had a right day of it down at that office. The agency has had me working for some firm who have offices above some shops down Shaftesbury Avenue and only half the windows are allowed to be opened. Christ, it was so hot and stuffy in there.'

'I can imagine,' said Cynthia. 'It's been like an oven in the shop today too, but still we shouldn't complain, it'll soon be bloody winter and dark at four in the afternoon.'

'Ooh, don't, I hate that. I suppose you're right though,' Sandra nodded. 'Mind you, it doesn't help having a boss who just lurches over me and most of the other girls all day either. Looks right down my blouse he does, bleeding perv. He must love his job being able to spy on us young talent all day long. I'm always catching him staring at this girl or that girl. Filthy old sod!' Both the girls laughed at the thought of it.

''Ere, nearly forgot,' continued Sandra excitedly, 'I'll tell you what I did see though when I was on my lunch break. Some workmen rolled up in a van outside the London Pavilion Theatre and started measuring up the area above the entrance.'

The mention of the London Pavilion Theatre prompted Cynthia to sit bolt upright.

'No! Do you think...?' she began.

'Yes, you've guessed it. I know because I crossed the road and asked a workman what they were doing. He told me that they were going to be hanging up the advertising for the *A Hard Day's Night* premiere next Monday.'

Cynthia smiled. 'Did you...?'

'Yeah of course I did,' continued Sandra, 'I said asked him if he could get hold of any spare tickets, but he just laughed at me and called me a silly little cow.'

'Charming,' said Cynthia.

'I know. I gave him some lip, flicked him two fingers and walked off with my head held high.'

Cynthia smiled at her feisty mate. 'Good on you girl.'

Sandra smiled as she sucked hard on her cigarette and blew out a large puff of smoke. She tried to look unconcerned that the workmen had made fun of her. At the time, she knew the chances of the workmen having any tickets was virtually impossible, but it was worth a try, well she thought so anyway. But, they didn't need to mock her.

Sadly, she was used to people making fun of her. It had been like that as far back as she could remember. To some extent she only had herself to blame because she was the one often bold enough to put herself in the firing line. But then, she had also taught herself that if you don't ask you just don't get. So, she often took a gamble and every now and again the gamble paid off.

'It doesn't matter Sand,' Cynthia said kindly, 'we will still be going down there next Monday anyway wont we? And you never know George or Ringo may spot us in the crowd and invite us in to see the premiere. Wow, how wonderful that would be?'

Sandra smiled and gently shook her head at her girlfriend, 'Keep on dreaming Cyn. You just keep on dreaming.'

Both girls fell about giggling and were still giggling when Kenny joined them. He hovered between them, arms crossed and shifting one foot to the other, looking nervous. Both girls ceased giggling, then looked at him as they sipped their drinks. They waited for him to say something. After a few moments filled with an uncomfortable silence, Cynthia sensed his terrible unease and decided to help him out.

'Alright Kenny. How are you?'

He continued to shuffle his feet on the spot, exposing his obvious crush on Cynthia. His attraction to her had been growing at an increasing rate over the last couple of months and she was well aware of this. She also knew that she didn't feel the same about him.

Cynthia liked Kenny and, in many ways, she admired him. He was kind, simple and, well, he liked The Beatles! But he wasn't a Beatle and she wasn't going to let any boy come between her and her George - not yet anyway. After all, there was always hope that she and George may meet someday, and she was certain that if they did, he would fall madly in love with her. And it was that dream she clung to from one day to the next.

'I'm ok thanks Cynthia. Hello Sandra,' Kenny answered, his cheeks flushing and small beads of sweat forming just under his hairline.

'Kenneth!' Sandra replied cheekily. She liked to call him by his full name.

There was more silence as Kenny looked at Sandra and wished for all the world that she wasn't there.

He gave a small cough as he cleared his throat to speak. 'Yes, hello Sandra. Erm...I...I wondered if you two will be heading down to the London Pavilion next week?'

'Us? Yeah, of course!' Cynthia exclaimed excitedly. 'We plan to get there early and get a good look at the boys as they arrive. Sandra is even thinking of making a banner to help grab their attention, ain't you Sand?'

Sandra nodded, 'S'right Cyn.'

'Now, that's a good idea,' said Kenny feeling relieved he had got the conversation flowing. 'Tell you what,' he said helpfully, 'if you need any paint I've got loads down the yard. They won't know if any goes missing.'

'Okay Kenny, ta,' said Cynthia, 'we'll let you know. We're really excited about it actually. Been ages since we did anything like this. It'll be just like when we went to Heathrow to welcome the boys back from abroad and that time at the Royal Command Variety Performance...'

Kenny was now struggling to know what to say, as his opening line was all he had in his head. Once again Cynthia decide to bail him out.

'Where are you lot going tonight?' she asked helpfully.

Kenny shrugged his shoulders. 'Eh? Tonight? Not sure yet. There's a band playing down in Fulham that I want to see but the other two want to go into Soho. I don't really fancy a club in town tonight though.'

'Not in the mood for a dance then Kenneth?' Sandra teased, knowing full well that Kenny wasn't a dancer.

Cynthia glared at Sandra and she quickly got the message.

'Well, look you have fun whatever you're going to do Kenny,' Cynthia said in a tone indicating it was probably time for him to be on his way. Kenny shuffled on the spot some more before getting the point.

'Oh right, yeah, right you are then. I had better be going anyway; I reckon the other two will want to be getting out of here soon.'

And with that he gave the girls a half-hearted wave, glanced longingly at Cynthia and walked away to re-join his friends. As he reached their table they stood up, said something to him as they looked over in Cynthia and Sandra's direction and then they left. Kenny's two friends had their scooters parked outside The Moka. They fired up the engines and a waft of two-stroke soon filled the café. Kenny leapt onto the back of one of the bikes and then they were gone. Everyone in the café had tuned in to the 'pop pop pop' sound of the scooters' engines before they faded into the distance.

'Ah poor Kenneth. He really fancies you, don't he?'

'Shut up you,' Cynthia replied smiling, 'I should really put the poor sod out of his misery.'

'You leave him be love. I think he likes the suffering. Come on,' continued Sandra, 'let's sit down over there, these stools always hurt my bum.' They headed for the table that Kenny and his friends had vacated. As they sat down, Sandra noticed that there was no more music spilling out from the jukebox.

'Not having that,' said Sandra under her breath, I'll be back in a mo.'

As Sandra stood poised to slot a coin into the jukebox, a hand appeared from out of nowhere and covered the slot. Sandra recognised the silver bracelet dangling from the boy's wrist. It was Danny, dressed in his recently purchased Fred Perry polo shirt, blue Levi's and desert boots that he had dyed a greenish colour.

He had obviously finished playing the pinball machine.

'Awright Sandra! You awright girl?' Danny spoke in his usual upbeat, cocky manner.

Sandra tried her best to look dismissive and uninterested. In truth, she and Danny had a bit of history. On more than one occasion had they had a fumble about in the dark at someone's house party, but once he had got what he wanted, he was off and wouldn't speak to her for a few weeks. This pattern was repeated time and time again and recently Sandra had begun to beat herself up for falling into his trap over and over again.

'Here you go,' Danny said, dropping some coins into the jukebox, 'You can choose whatever discs you want. You can have *Love Me Do* or *Please Please Me*...there's a ton of Beatles songs on here...'

Sandra cut him off mid-sentence, 'And what do *you* want Danny Francis, eh?'

He looked her straight in the face. 'Me? Me, Sandra? Nothing mate...nothing at all.' As he replied, he leapt up onto the stool beside the jukebox and crossed his legs. 'But, err...you may want something from me.'

'Ha!' Sandra laughed. 'Really? I doubt it Danny, seriously I do.'

'Yeah? I wouldn't be so sure. You might change that mind of yours, once you know. In fact, I know I've got something that you would want, something that I know every girl...well, every Beatles girl that is, would want.'

Sandra suddenly froze, mid dropping her coins in the jukebox. The word Beatles had definitely caught her attention. Suddenly she was interested. Very interested indeed. 'My God Danny, you ain't got tickets for the *A Hard Day's Night* premiere, have you?'

Danny looked confused and then screwed his nose up.

'What? No!' he said shaking his head. 'What I have got is even better.'

And with that he leaned closer and whispered something into Sandra's ear. A few moments later Sandra was sitting at the table again beside Cynthia. Before she had time to tell Cynthia what Danny had just told her, Cynthia started to tell Sandra that she wanted her to go with her to the hairdressers Saturday morning. She explained that she had decided to get her hair styled in the same way as that the young model Pattie Boyd, in some promotional photographs from *A Hard Day's Night* that she had seen recently. Cynthia went on to say how beautiful she thought Pattie was and how similar they would look once she got her styled in the same way. She added that after the hairdressers they could pop into HMV in Oxford Street too and spend some time listening to some records in the listening booths.

Sandra smiled impatiently and said that sounded like a good plan. Then she told Cynthia that she was popping outside with Danny for a while because he had something to show her and soon all will be revealed.

Cynthia rolled her eyes and tutted; the times she had heard that one.

'He's got something to show you has he? I bet he bleeding has…'

'No, it's nothing like that, it's well…'

As Sandra was about to explain, Danny walked past them, nodding his chin in the direction of the door. Sandra stopped mid-flow and obediently followed.

He led her along the alley to an area at the rear of The Moka. It smelt of rotting food and stale piss and a dozen flies buzzed around an overflowing dustbin. Danny spotted two discarded old wooden chairs and positioned one beside the other. He motioned to Sandra that she should sit down. She did as she was commanded to do.

Sandra screwed up her nose, trying her best to ignore the various aromas which were now trying to get up it.

'You do bring me to such lovely places Mr Francis, you really do…so come on then, what you…'

'Shush, hold on, hold on,' interrupted Danny, placing his forefinger on Sandra's lips. He put his hand into one of his Levi's jeans pockets, but didn't remove what he had straight away; he enjoyed teasing Sandra too much.

'Come on then,' Sandra was beginning to get impatient.

Eventually, very slowly, he pulled out a piece of black cloth. At first, Sandra couldn't work out what it was, then she realised that it was a thin black tie. Danny dangled the tie in the air. It swayed from side to side like a hypnotherapist's watch and Sandra's eyes followed it. She looked a little disappointed if truth were told.

'It's…er…it's a tie. So, what's the big deal Danny?'

Danny smirked.

'What's the big deal…you ask what's the big deal? This is not just any tie love. No, this thin black tie Sandra, once belonged to a certain young man from Liverpool…and his name…his name is Ringo Starr,' Danny said, rushing the last words.

At first Sandra was excited and believed him; the thought that the tie actually belonged to Ringo thrilled her. But then, slowly, doubt crept in as she came to her senses.

'Ringo's tie, is it? Yeah right,' she said, preparing to stand up and leave.

Danny hastily grabbed her wrist.

'No, it's true Sandra and I'll prove it to you. This tie came via Norman 'Normal' Smith.'

'Piss it. Now I know you're telling me lies Danny. You want me to believe that Normal - the man who has worked in the studio on Beatles records, gave you this tie and this tie belonged to Ringo? Pull the other one mate,' she said, trying to release her arm, 'it plays the national anthem...'

'I promise you,' said Danny sternly, 'it's true, I'm telling you. Norman Smith gave the tie to my uncle Jacob. It turns out that they both served in the RAF together back in the war and both were involved in the glider planes. And my uncle saw Normal recently at some reunion.'

Sandra relaxed her struggle. She knew that Danny's uncle had served in the RAF and had worked with glider pilots, and from reading all about the Fabs as she had done, she knew that Norman Smith had done the same thing. In truth, she desperately wanted to believe what Danny was saying and now his explanation started to seem plausible.

Sandra cleared her throat and, trying not to sound too excited, said 'And what, you're going to let me hold that tie?'

Danny replied in as gentle a tone as he could muster.

'Not just touch Sandra. You can have it girl. You can have this tie.'

Sandra's eyes lit-up and her mouth dropped open.

'Have it? You will let me have Ringo's tie?' The words sounded sweet and magical as they rolled off her tongue.

'Yeah that's right Sandra. That's right...but it may be nice of you, if you did something nice for me in return.'

Sandra folded her arms and crossed her legs. 'I knew it' she thought, 'here we go. Here we go. Payment time!'

'A kiss...?' Sandra offered.

'Well yes, a kiss would be lovely Sandra, but I reckon Ringo's tie is worth a bit more than a kiss, don't you?' He was now leaning in and once again whispering something in her ear.

'Piss it,' Sandra coughed.

'Well if it's good enough for Epstein and Lennon...' Danny said.

Sandra looked confused at that remark, but decided not to press for any further information.

'Give me the tie first and I'll consider it,' she said.

Danny handed Sandra the tie. The first thing she did was hold it up to her nose, close her eyes and sniff it hard. Danny watched what was, to his eyes, strange behaviour; astonished and embarrassed on her behalf. He had to cough to get Sandra's attention back and pull her away from the heavenly experience she was obviously having. She opened her blurry eyes and looked straight into his.

'Now, Danny Francis, you had better be telling me the truth. Promise me that this is Ringo's tie and that what you have been telling me is the truth.'

'Hand on heart, would I lie to you?' he replied smiling.

'Oh, go on then,' And without another word, Sandra sat down on the chair beside Danny and shoved her hand down the front of his trousers...

Chapter 3
Good Morning Good Morning

Being cruelly awoken by the sound of a passing milk float, its glass bottles crashing into each other and rattling in their metal crates, as it trundled right underneath her bedroom window was not how Cynthia had hoped to be woken on this Saturday morning.

She scolded herself for forgetting to close the window before she went to bed the previous night. So engrossed had she been in flicking through a copy of Life Magazine that featured an article and a collection of photographs of the Fab Four's trip to America earlier in the year that she had completely forgotten about it. Her American pen pal, Patricia, had sent Cynthia the magazine a couple of days before. Patricia was a Beatles person she had connected to via the pen pals section in a copy of The Beatles Monthly. Their paths had crossed because of their joint love of The Beatles and especially George Harrison.

Cynthia had never had a pen pal before and since having 'found' Patricia, her life had become so much more exciting. Having a pen pal from the States meant she could get access to newspaper and magazine articles all about The Beatles that she would have never seen otherwise and it thrilled her to bits. Whenever the postman delivered a letter or package with the now familiar USA postal mark on it, Cynthia would stop whatever she was doing, rush up to her bedroom with her mail (so she could have complete privacy) and open it immediately. She imagined Patricia did exactly the same whenever she too received letters and packages displaying a UK postal mark. The two girls wrote to each other at least once a month; there was always so much to write about where The Beatles were concerned so it was never hard to put a letter together.

The most recent package from her American friend included the copy of Life Magazine featuring her beloveds and a letter, in which Patricia informed Cynthia of all The Beatle activity of which she was aware. Before signing off, she mentioned that she would soon be in the possession of a copy of the new album Beatles album *A Hard Day's Night* and that as soon as she had her copy she would send Cynthia a letter telling her all about it. This, of course, made Cynthia feel very jealous and somewhat cross. In her opinion it just wasn't right that the new Beatles album was going to be released in the USA two weeks earlier than it was in the UK, and she didn't care who knew it!

Cynthia continued to huff and puff to herself for five minutes after she read those words, but she tried her best to disguise any hint of jealousy as she wrote her letter of reply. Instead, Cynthia decided she would write about her excitement of going to hang out on Shaftesbury Avenue with thousands of other Beatles fans on the night of the premiere of the *A Hard Day's Night* film. She knew this would stir some emotions of jealousy in her American pen pal. It wasn't long after finishing the letter that Cynthia had fallen asleep, leaving the window and an early morning wake up by a milk float guaranteed.

The faint hum of which began to fade into the distance as Cynthia stirred in her bed. It was fair to say she wasn't an early bird and always struggled going through her habitual morning routine during the week. What made waking up early today even worse, was that today was Saturday - her day off. She had worked all week in her granddad's shop and as he had half day closing on Saturdays, she got the whole day off and that meant the weekend had finally arrived. A big smile came to her face and she began daydreaming of what she had planned that day. Before she knew it, she was curled up into an instinctive, cosy foetal position and managed to remain in that position for the next thirty minutes…

Slowly, the familiar sounds of other members of the household waking up filled the silence and, once again, she began to awake. She guessed it must now have been nearing eight o'clock, when she heard the unmistakable sounds of her father William - never Bill, always William - shuffling about. The distinctive sound of her parent's bedroom door opening, his slow, steady walk along creaking passage floorboards to the bathroom, where he would push open the squeaking bathroom door. She would then hear the splashing sound of him having a wee, though she tried to pretend she never heard that!

He would then make his way downstairs to the kitchen. A sudden rush of tap water filling a kettle, followed by the whooshing sound of a hob catching alight. Next came the tinkling sound of china crockery as he selected the drinking vessels for him and his wife Dorothy. Everyone knew her mum as Dot, which she embraced, having never liked the more formal and quite old-fashioned Dorothy.

William then slowly made his way back up the carpeted wooden stairs and return to his bedroom. On a week day, he would reappear twenty minutes later, fully dressed and ready for his day's work as an insurance officer in Parsons Green, tapping on the beige painted door of Cynthia's room as he passed, a sign to tell her it was time for her to get up too. Only today, that familiar routine was stopped as it was Saturday and, like Cynthia, he didn't have to go into work.

Cynthia now lay there, trying to ignore the overwhelming signs that she needed a wee. Finally, after a small struggle, she gave in and forced herself to get up. She slipped on her light-blue towelling dressing gown and dashed to the toilet. She too then made her way to the kitchen. The family had inherited the heavily floral patterned wallpaper that greeted her. She prepared herself a cup of tea in her favourite cup and cut a thick slice of bread, which she smothered in butter and marmalade. She plonked herself down onto one of the wooden chairs at the kitchen table and took a large bite of the bread as she rubbed her eyes and yawned mid bite, scattering a few crumbs down her dressing gown.

As Cynthia sipped her refreshingly hot tea, she planned her and Sandra's day ahead in her in mind. She glanced at the wall clock above her head to the right and noted the time: 8.45 am. Her hairdresser's appointment wasn't until eleven o'clock so she still had plenty of time to get herself ready. She had already planned her outfit for the day and as she sat there, she imagined herself getting dressed and doing her make-up whilst *With The Beatles* played loudly in the background on her red and cream Dansette. The plan was then to meet Sandra, head for the hairdressers in Parsons Green and then she and Sandra would catch the District and Central line to the West End where they could have a wander around the streets and shops all day. The prospect of what lay ahead excited her.

Just as she finished the last bit of her cup of tea, her brother John entered the kitchen looking pale and very drawn, large dark bags had taken residence under his eyes and his hair was like a messy bird's nest. He had on a white vest, his red with white trim Y Fronts and last night's socks.

Upon seeing him, his little sister, couldn't help but smile. 'Cor, you look like death warmed up,' Cynthia chuckled.

Without looking at her, John grunted something in her direction, but Cynthia had no idea what he said. He shuffled over to the kettle and lit the hob, wincing at the noise it made. Cynthia could tell that everything was an effort for him. She decided she would help him out.

'Blimey, here, sit down and I'll make you some tea. Do you want some bread cut too?'

John nodded towards the kettle and gave a thumbs up, indicating a 'yes' for the tea, but shook his head whilst looking at the breadboard. In truth, he just knew he wouldn't be able to stomach any food. He sat on the chair where Cynthia had been seated, slowly closed his eyes and put his hands over his ears. Cynthia set about making the tea with as little noise as possible.

'So,' she said as nonchalantly as she could, 'what did you and your mates do last night then?'

Cynthia already suspected that John and his friends and gone to some club in Soho. They usually did on Friday and Saturday nights. But what they got up to on those nights intrigued her.

John continued to hold his hands on his ears, but he did give his younger sister a look as if to say 'mind your own'.

This wasn't going to stop Cynthia though, she was too curious.

'So, come on then, tell all...' She felt like fishing for more information, so pressed her brother a little further.

John sighed. He realised Cynthia wasn't go to stop until he gave her something in return for the mug of tea that she slid across the Formica topped table towards him.

'Alright, alright, give me strength…! If you must know, we went to The Scene. It's a club in Ham Yard, just off Great Windmill Street, Soho way.'

Cynthia smiled, content at the success in getting information from her brother. As it happens, she had heard of The Scene. With her generally being a nosey parker and ear-wigging on some of the boys' conversations down The Moka, she had become familiar with most of the clubs that they went to: The Flamingo, The Marquee, The Whiskey and The Scene. In fact, John had more or less promised to take her to one of the clubs one day, but as yet he hadn't.

'Would I like it there John?' she asked. 'Do they have bands? Does the disc jockey play Beatles records? Does…?'

John put a hand into the air and shook his head, indicating that Cynthia cease with all the quick-round questioning. She smiled and did as she was expected to do. As she hovered by the stove, John sensed her presence and looked up. Peering at her through blood-shot squinting eyes he simply whispered 'Yeah, maybe?'

Cynthia wasn't really sure what the 'maybe?' meant if she was honest, but she had a feeling she would love it there. She sensed further questions were pointless and would go unanswered, so she retreated to her bedroom.

The room was cool, which felt nice and inviting. She stepped over a pile of clothes that she had been intending to iron since the previous weekend. It would eventually get done, but so far that week there were too many pressing matters that always seemed to get in the way. Cynthia liked her bedroom, even though her green speckled carpet had seen better days. Her wallpaper had only ever been changed once as far as she could recall, but that didn't really matter because it was now covered in Beatles photos and cuttings.

Ok, first things first. Her most important job was to put on some Beatles music. For the past year or so, not a morning went by when she didn't play a Beatles record whilst she got dressed, tended to her make-up and brushed her hair. It had been this way since she owned her very own copy of the album *Please Please Me*, which she had been given on the 1st April the previous year by her eldest brother Andrew. With the date being what it was, she thought at first it was an April Fool's wind up, but it wasn't and Andrew had let her keep the album. She couldn't really believe it. That album had set her on her way to becoming a Beatle person – the term The Beatles Monthly affectionately used to address their members in editions of The Beatles Monthly magazine - and so far, she had loved taking every step along the journey.

Please Please Me rested against her bedroom wall beside her beloved Dansette. She carefully removed the vinyl from its stiff, but now slightly dog-eared, cardboard sleeve, placed its centre hole on the record player spindle and then listened for a few clicks as the needle on the playing arm made contact with her beloved vinyl. Immediately, she was humming along to *I Saw Her Standing There* as she finished getting dressed in her pre-planned outfit.

Cynthia carefully slipped off her pale blue shift dress from its wooden clothes hanger and stepped into it, accessorising it with a white belt. She had briefly considered wearing her favourite bright yellow dress but decided against it; she was going to save that for the premiere instead. Her reason behind this was that she thought she had more chance of being spotted by her George if she wore something bright.

Cynthia sat down on the wicker chair in front of her dark wooden dressing table and studied her face in its mirror. She rhythmically brushed her long sandy coloured hair before carefully applying some make-up - all the while singing along with the Fabs.

Standing up, Cynthia held onto the back of the chair and carefully slipped her right foot into some matching blue dolly shoes, repeating the process with her left foot. There, she thought to herself, I'm ready to face the world. She stepped back a few paces and did a little turn as studied herself and her outfit in the mirror, breaking into a smile as she did so.

Turning towards the Dansette, Cynthia removed the needle from the record and switched off the machine, carefully placing her treasured record back into its sleeve and placing it by the equally loved record player.

She grabbed her navy coloured leather-look clutch bag, checked it contained her purse and the photo of Miss Boyd and quickly closed her bedroom door behind her as she made her way downstairs.

Her dad was positioned in his favourite place on a Saturday - in his favourite armchair, reading his newspaper and puffing away on his pipe in the living room. Cynthia put her head round the living room door and quickly informed her mum, who was quietly doing some sewing, what she was doing and where she was going. Her mother looked up and smiled kindly whilst saying, 'Ok, be careful love,' and nodded at the fast-moving Cynthia, who was off and running to the day in front of her.

Once outside, Cynthia breathed in the sweet air of what was a gorgeous summer's day and was quickly into her regular walk to the special spot on the edge of Wimbledon Common. Here was where Cynthia and Sandra always met and Cynthia made her way to the bench that was, for some strange reason, always empty, as if it was reserved just for them. As always, she first checked that it was dry and clean before sitting down.

The bench overlooked the common and Cynthia watched the gentle sway of the leaves on the trees and tuned into the sound of the birds singing. She noticed the grass was still a little dewy and smelt sweet. Checking her watch, she realised that she was a few minutes early and, reminding herself that Sandra was bound to be running late as usual, she closed her eyes.

The sun's warmth caressed her face, arms and knees and she thought that she could easily fall asleep. Cynthia daydreamed the image of herself with her new hair-do and felt a rush of excitement, realising she was just a few hours away from walking out of the hairdressers.

However, her moment of bliss didn't last for long and was shattered abruptly.

'Hello, err, Cynthia.'

The voice brought her pleasant thoughts to a standstill. That wasn't Sandra; it was Kenny. Cynthia opened one of her eyes and focussed on him.

'Oh! Hello Kenny.' Cynthia tried her best to disguise her disappointment.

Kenny shuffled where he stood, not sure what to do with his hands. Cynthia watched on as he tucked his hands into his trouser pocket, removed them, then put them back in. It was comical to watch, but Cynthia didn't dare laugh and embarrass him.

'What you up to then?' Cynthia enquired, deciding to help him out.

'Me? Oh, you know, bit of this, bit of that,' he replied shrugging his shoulders. 'How about you?'

'I'm just waiting for Sandra. We're going down to Parsons Green; I'm getting my hair done. I'm going to get my hair cut short like those German girls in Hamburg.'

Kenny looked genuinely horrified. It was just the effect that Cynthia intended. She started to giggle.

'Stop fretting Kenny. Not really doing that, but I am having a new style. Have you seen that model in the *A Hard Day's Night* film? She has a wonderful hair style.'

'Ha, I knew it would have something to do with The Beatles. Do you do anything that doesn't involve those flipping mop-tops?' Kenny sounded almost annoyed, which Cynthia quickly sensed.

She knew she could come across as someone with an unhealthy obsession but, by the same token, in all honesty she didn't bloody care. Besides, she knew she wasn't alone in her obsession.

'Now I come to think of it, not really Kenny. Don't s'pose I do. Anyway, you know how important the band is to me.'

41

Kenny shrugged his shoulders and nodded. He knew he was on the losing side in this particular argument. After a few seconds of awkward silence, Cynthia decided to change the subject.

'So, where did you and your mates go in the end, you know, the other night?'

Kenny perked up, delighted that Cynthia took enough interest in his social life to ask him.

'We went to Shepherds Bush to see some band. I can't remember their name but they seem to be causing a bit if a stir amongst the Mods at the moment. Your brother will know who they are; he was there. You should check them out. They have this new crazy drummer, a right nut case, proper loony. It was great stuff though, the crowd loved 'em. I hear they are playing down The Marquee again soon.'

Cynthia listened politely enough, but Kenny could tell that she wasn't really that interested. Then he noticed her glance over his shoulder and wave. He swung around to see Sandra crossing the common. He decided not to hang around any longer; he wasn't in the mood for Sandra.

'Okay I've got to be off. So, maybe I'll see you around Cynthia,' said Kenny as he started to walk away.

'Yeah, yeah okay Kenny. Look, you have a nice day, okay.'

Kenny kept his head down and didn't look around.

Sandra approached her best mate with a quizzical look on her face, 'What did *he* want then?'

Cynthia looked at the fast fading sight of Kenny and said, 'Really not sure love, y'know what Kenny is like…'

Looking at Sandra with a smile on her face, Cynthia tried to sound as sarcastic as possible whilst saying 'You alright then early bird?'

Sandra stuck her tongue out revealing it to be 'pear drop orange'.

Cynthia laughed and pushed herself up from the bench. Her left arm then linked into the right arm of Sandra and off they walked towards the tube station. The two girls began chatting rapidly, rarely taking a breath as they strolled. A group of boys gathered around the station's entrance; some wearing blue and white scarves, evidently meeting up before heading off to some football match or other.

In truth, Cynthia and Sandra paid them no attention, preferring to take in the cigarette and Cadbury's chocolate posters in the ticket hall instead. There was also a large poster advertising some theatre production that was on in the West End. Cynthia wanted to read the details and tried to slow down, but Sandra was dragging her towards the ticket booth as hard as she could.

An elderly man sat in the ticket office behind some grubby, grease-smeared glass window. He wasn't the regular ticket office man; the regular man Cynthia and Sandra knew all too well and often shared a joke with him. This elderly man before them had a reddish nose, a rather spectacular konk actually, and he had a hint of rudeness about him. Not once did he look up as he took their money and silently slid two train tickets across the counter top, just into reaching distance of the two girls.

After buying their tickets, they quickly made their way to the packed platform, people milling about everywhere. Handily, within a few minutes their train was pulling in and they quickly boarded. It was only five stops to Parsons Green and then only a five-minute walk to the hairdressers.

They were heading for Angela's Salon, which was fast becoming one of the most popular women's hairdressers on the South West side of London. Angela and her team knew and understood exactly what was 'hot' and what was 'not'. Cynthia had been going here for the last twelve months, ever since she had been earning her own money. Angela's charged a little extra than most suburban hairdressers, but those few extra shillings were well worth it as far as Cynthia was concerned.

Upon arrival, she pushed open the shop door and a bell rung. The shop was always fully staffed, so no customers were ever kept waiting. Sandra followed her mate close behind, screwing up her nose as the thick pungent odours of shampoo and hairspray filled her nostrils. The shop was narrow but stretched back a good twenty feet and the walls were tiled in black and white and looked cold. Adorning the walls were prints of exotic looking women with beautiful hair.

Cynthia and Sandra were greeted by a teenage girl with a freckled face, pointy nose and a boyish looking crew cut; she was dressed very trendily and was maybe a year younger than them. She asked for Cynthia's name and put a tick beside it in the leather-bound appointments book on the shop's main desk.

She mentioned Angela was just finishing up with another customer and would be with Cynthia shortly. The two girls looked around and selected their chairs to sit on. Also waiting were two other youngish girls; one was reading from a colourful magazine, whilst the other sat

43

straight-backed, resting her folded hands on the handbag on her lap, quietly staring into space.

There was a record player behind the counter where the young assistant stood and it was her job to play the records provided. As Cynthia and Sandra had arrived, Lulu's *Shout* had been playing. This was now ending and the assistant was preparing herself to replace it with a new record which Cynthia noted was a Parlophone disc. She hoped it was a Beatles record but it turned out to be by Cilla Black. That was okay though, she didn't mind a bit of Cilla.

Whilst Cilla warbled her way through '*Anyone Who Had a Heart*', the girl sitting next to Sandra was shown to a chair where another of Angela's assistants worked. Then Angela herself appeared, ushering a customer to the till. Saying her goodbyes to the woman and thanking her for her custom, Angela made her way over to greet Cynthia.

Angela was stunningly beautiful with her high cheekbones, big brown eyes, long dark eyelashes and she was incredibly fashionable from head to toe. Before she had opened her own shop, Angela had served her apprenticeship working in a trendy hairdressers in Soho in central London. Although Angela was still only in her twenties, it was obvious she was a modern woman of the world and every bit the businesswoman with a bright future lay out before her. Soho had certainly taught Angela a thing or two and Cynthia really admired her. She also melted at the sight of the Italian leather sandals that Angela wore.

'Hello Cynthia,' said Angela, expertly remembering her name. This made Cynthia feel special because Angela had only personally cut Cynthia's hair once before. They engaged in some small talk before Angela led the way for the magic to begin. Cynthia sat in a large black leather chair and stared at a larger mirror in front of her. Angela smiled and asked what she could do for Cynthia today. Cynthia plunged her hand into her handbag producing a photograph of Patricia Boyd and showing it to Angela, explaining that was how she wanted her hair to look too. Angela carefully studied the now slightly crumpled photograph and then nodded. 'Beautiful isn't she' said Angela admiringly.

Unbeknown to Cynthia, Angela had been doing a lot of 'Patti's' recently. Sandra, meanwhile, had been reading the latest edition of Rave magazine which the other customer had been flicking through. She soon completely lost all sense of time looking at the photos of

The Dave Clark Five, Cliff Richard, Gerry and The Pacemakers and shop favourite Cilla.

Sandra then became aware of a dark shape standing directly in front of her.

'Whadya think then Sand? Sand! SANDRA! Bloody cheek this is!'

Slowly Sandra realised it was Cynthia standing in front of her, sporting her new haircut and had paid up and was ready to leave.

'Oh, welcome back,' Cynthia said sarcastically.

'Sorry Cyn, I was away with the fairies for a bit there.'

'So, what do you think then Sand?' asked Cynthia again hesitantly.

Sandra stood up and carefully had a good look. 'Wow! That looks fab Cyn. It really suits you.'

Cynthia smiled as she took another glance of herself in a nearby mirror. There was something special about the feelings evoked after getting a great hairdo and Cynthia felt confident and great inside.

Sandra opened the salon door and they bid farewell to the staff as they headed back towards Parsons Green tube station. On the way, both of them noticed a couple of younger men study Cynthia longer than usual.

The girls looked at each other and smiled.

That haircut worked then!

Chapter 4
I've Just Seen a Face

Looking up, they noticed the next train in was theirs. They alighted at South Kensington so they could pick up the Piccadilly Line. Cynthia had cleverly suggested it was best if they took the tube to Piccadilly Circus because from there they could walk to the HMV store on Oxford Street and, at the same time, map out the route they would be taking on Monday for the night of the premiere.

Leaving Piccadilly Circus, they raced onto Shaftsbury Avenue and, filled with excitement, towards The London Pavilion. They could hardly contain themselves as they stood across from the theatre and read the giant yellow and red words hanging over the theatres Victorian façade: '*In Their First Full-Length, Hilarious, and Action-Packed Film-The Beatles-A Hard Day's Night-12 Smash Hit Songs!*'

Cynthia tugged at Sandra's arm excitedly.

'This is where we will be Monday Sand. I can picture the Fab Four now, getting out of their limousines, surrounded by photographers and bodyguards and waving directly at you and me.'

'Yep, I can picture that. Can you imagine the screaming? It's going to be wild,' Sandra exclaimed.

Both girls drifted off into their individual daydreams of waving back at John, Paul, George and Ringo, oblivious to the fact they were stood in the middle of pavement and causing considerable annoyance to the multitude of shoppers huffing, puffing and milling around them.

'Come on,' urged Cynthia urgently, 'let's see if we can go for a look inside.'

In truth, Sandra didn't have time to respond. Cynthia had grabbed her hand and pulled her across the busy traffic flying up and down Shaftesbury Avenue, somehow dodging the cars, black cabs and red buses as they went. Now directly outside the venue, Cynthia pushed hard at a large glass door but it was closed. She tried it again, harder still this time. It didn't budge. Finally accepting it was shut good and proper, she pressed her little nose up against it and peered inside instead.

'The lights are on,' she said hopefully. 'Someone's got to be in there.'

Sandra had joined her mate and she too was now also pressed up against the door. 'Well it can't be long before they open,' Sandra presumed. 'Surely there must be some matinee going on this afternoon?'

'Hmm! Yeah, you're right, there must be...' Cynthia agreed and continued peering in.

Cynthia slid along the glass doorway to the next doorway and then the next; checking each one, her nose never breaking contact with the glass. She wasn't one to give up so easily. Sandra stood back and waited on the pavement and watched her friend. Cynthia started to rap her knuckles on the glass door, cautiously at first but then getting louder and louder. So intent was she on banging on her door of choice, she failed to notice one of the big glass doors to her right fly open.

'Oi! What's your game, eh? You can pack that game in my girl.'

A gruff old voice came from an elderly gentleman, dressed in an outfit covered in yellow brocade, which looked like someone had dumped scrambled egg on him. He also wore white gloves and a top hat. His face was old, worn and tired looking. He was a man who had fired rifles in both World Wars and didn't suffer fools gladly, especially two annoying teenage girls.

'What do you want? Eh? Speak up you there,' he was now glaring at Sandra.

'We, err, we...' Sandra stuttered, somewhat taken aback at this now red-faced old man looking straight at her.

'We just wanted to have a look inside. Sorry, that was all,' Cynthia interrupted.

The old warhorse turned to look at her and then looked both the girls up and down. The girls could almost hear the cogs turning in the wheels of his tired old brain. He eventually came to his decision and cleared his throat.

'Well you can't. We ain't open. We don't open until three. And even then...'

'Oh, go on sir,' Cynthia butted in, trying to look as sweet and innocent as she could.

But the old sweat had heard it all before and was having none of it. He had had a lifetime's worth of fluttering eyelashes and smiles. Such techniques to fool and charm him hadn't worked since 1946.

47

'You can turn that game in missy. Go on, be off with you. Scarper I say. You can't come in.' And with that he hobbled back off from whence he had come.

'Silly old sod!' Cynthia yelled as she stuck two fingers up against the glass door and then immediately regretted doing that, hoping the old man, or anyone else for that matter, hadn't witnessed it.

'Oh, piss it,' said Sandra. 'Come on Cyn, let's go. No point in standing here all day. Old Father Time there ain't going to help, is he? No, fingers crossed one of the Fabs notice us on Monday and invite us in then. Can you imagine how great it would feel to walk up the red carpet, right past that old duffer, arm in arm with Ringo and George?'

They both laughed at the thought and continued to discuss that eventuality as they weaved their way back through the streets of London towards Oxford Street. Half way up Regent Street, Cynthia noticed a photo booth and she made a beeline towards it, telling Sandra that she wanted to get some photos of herself with her new haircut. She added that she intended to post one to the Beatles fan club requesting that it get passed on to George. Sandra thought this was a fantastic idea.

A sign above the curtain entrance of the booth read 'Four poses for two shillings' and informed the buyer that the photos would be ready within three minutes. Cynthia positioned herself on the stool, slotted the correct money into the slot and then closed the curtain. She waited and waited. Thinking the machine was faulty, she moved just as the first one went 'flash!'. 'Piss it,' she uttered under her breath and then sat as still as she could for the other three.

She then decided to have another go and without warning grabbed Sandra from outside and dragged her into the booth too.

'Come on Sand…say BEATLES!'

Four more flashes and three minutes later the two girls stood outside the photo booth belly laughing at the images on the photographs.

'Look at YOU there,' exclaimed Cynthia at one of the photos where Sandra had sucked in her cheekbones giving it her best Twiggy impersonation.

They were still laughing when they finally reached the HMV store on Oxford Street. They entered the store through the large open doors beneath the neon lettering of His Masters Voice. The store was busy, very busy. Countless people ambled around looking at the new television sets and record players and shuffling from one section of music to the next. The store was filled with shoppers of all ages and backgrounds.

As usual Cynthia led the way, with Sandra never far behind. They snaked through the store passing a queue of eager music lovers all with a purchase under their arm and down a spiral staircase. It was then their eyes fell upon all the advertising for the new Beatles album that was due for release in less than two weeks. The first thing Cynthia thought when she saw the poster was how lucky her pen pal Patricia in America was to already have a copy of *A Hard Day's Night*. She dismissed that very thought as quickly as it had appeared though. She hated feeling jealous.

Cynthia and Sandra now stood shoulder to shoulder in front of a large life size cardboard cut-out of the Fab Four. Cynthia gazed into Harrison's dark brown eyes and Sandra into Ringo's. The Beatles' eyes seemed to look directly back at them. Both girls swooned a bit.

'I can't wait. I'm telling you, I simply, cannot, wait...' Sandra eventually muttered slowly.

'For what Sand? What can't you wait for?' asked Cynthia dreamily, not taking her gaze off George for a second.

'To get my own copy of *A Hard Day's Night* Cyn.'

Cynthia slowly nodded, her gaze transfixed on George.

'Sand, did I tell you that my pen pal Patricia sent me a package the other day?'

'You started to tell me in The Moka but you got distracted. What was in it?'

'Oh, you know few bits and bobs,' Cynthia uttered, 'and she told me that she would be getting a copy of *A Hard Day's Night* earlier than I would because of its American release date.'

'Did she? Piss it. Cow!' Sandra hissed.

'Yeah and she is probably listening to it right now.' A wave of jealousy resurfaced in Cynthia.

Sandra went quiet and then exploded, 'WHAT A COW!'

A couple of passers-by quickly turned to look at Sandra, but she never saw them.

'Not right that, is it? WE, us, should have got that first.' Then she smiled as a pleasant thought struck her.

'Ah, but never mind though, cos we'll see the film first though, wont we? So 'RASP!' to bloody pen pal Patricia.' They both laughed at the raspberry sound Sandra had just made.

'Oh, you do make me laugh Sand. Nutcase you are,' Cynthia couldn't stop smiling.

'I try my best,' said Sandra, as she liked making her best friend smile. 'Okay then, where shall we go and see the film?'

'Probably Hammersmith,' Cynthia said quickly 'I'm going to see it every night for at least a week.'

Sandra smiled, nodding vigorously, 'Make that a fortnight and I'm with you.'

Finally, they left the hypnotising gaze of Ringo and George and spent some time flicking through rows and rows of records over the next hour. After making their selection, they scuttled off to one of the listening booths where they played the record whilst they jigged and fooled about. They repeated this at least ten times; it was one their favourite things to do. Cynthia and Sandra didn't actually buy anything - no, their savings would be spent on copies of *A Hard Day's Night* on its first day of release.

Finally, after nearly two hours, they left HMV and decided to head towards Soho to find somewhere to have a drink. They walked along Oxford Street until darting off down Poland Street, making their way through some back streets into Soho Square and then down Frith Street. At the bottom, they peered through the doorway at Bar Italia. Noticing there were no vacant stools to perch on, they continued down Frith Street and turned right into Old Compton Street. Crossing the road, they walked in the direction of the infamous '2i's' coffee bar.

'I've not been inside before,' Sandra said as they approached. 'Have you Cyn?'

'Yeah, just the once. My Andrew brought me here. He had to babysit me for the day, which basically meant that I had to trudge behind him as he went from one jazz record shop to the next, as he hunted down stuff for his collection.'

Cynthia walked confidently through the door and over to the counter. A man in his late twenties smiled at them.

'Yes girls, what can I do you for?' he asked cheekily.

They ignored his nonsense and ordered up two espressos. They sat at a nearby table with their drinks, as Sandra looked all around her.

'Bit small innit Cyn? I mean, where did the skiffle groups play then?' she asked curiously.

'Down in the cellar, you daft apeth' Cynthia replied, nodding to a doorway.

Sandra was intrigued. 'Do you think we can go and have a look?'

Cynthia shrugged her shoulders, 'Can't see why not, ask the man.'

Sandra summoned up a bit of courage and coughed ever so slightly. 'Er, excuse me. Do you mind if we take a look downstairs?'

The man didn't look up or say anything but he quietly nodded. He had been asked that a thousand times and besides, he was more concerned with reading his boxing magazine. The girls smiled and left their seats, heading for the doorway. They peered down into the darkness. Cynthia pushed Sandra ever so slightly, so she that she had to go first. The old stairs creaked as they cautiously stepped down them. At the bottom, they entered a tiny dark cellar area. There was a small stage made of wooden Coca Cola crates and two light bulbs above it that only gave off a very weak glow.

'Blimey is that it?' said Sandra finally. 'This is where Cliff Richards and Tommy Steele played then?'

'Yeah s'pose so. Got to be,' said Cynthia. 'Not much to look at, is it? Giving me the creeps as it happens. Come on, not sure I like it down here,' Cynthia replied.

Both girls returned quickly to finish off their coffees.

'Fancy heading up Carnaby Street after here then? Never know who you might see up there do ya?'

Sandra fancied a walk to nearby Carnaby Street and Cynthia, not really caring what they did, simply nodded that was fine by her.

They had been there a few times before, with both girls trying their best to keep up on the latest fashions. After all, if they were going to get to meet The Beatles on Monday they needed to be seen as 'hip young things' and not second-class tickets or, even worse, them Liverpool 'totties' who flocked to the Cavern Club. Floozies that mob, utter floozies.

They drank up and politely said thank you to the '2i's' man as they left, but once again, he didn't look up.

'Charming,' said Sandra as they left.

A short stroll soon took them to the top of Carnaby Street. The first thing they saw was a handsome looking man posing by the flashiest whitest white Rolls Royce that the girls had ever seen. The choice of car mirrored completely the elegance and poise of the man who was proudly posing by it. A crowd had gathered around the photographer, his assistant and the assistant's assistant. Cynthia and Sandra also decided to get a closer look.

'Who's that then, eh?' Sandra whispered.

Cynthia shrugged her shoulders and screwed her face up. They continued to watch the photo-shoot and strained their ears trying to pick up on some of the conversations around them. Finally, they were able to ascertain that they were looking at John Stephens, who owned the shop outside which the Rolls Royce was parked. They also reckoned he owned the Roller too.

'Look,' Cynthia said reading out the words above the shops door, 'The John Stephens Men's Shop.'

'I've heard of that,' Sandra mumbled.

'Me too,' Cynthia added. 'I've heard my John and his mates talking about this shop. I think they buy clothes from there sometimes.'

'Roller man must be doing alright then if he can sell enough trousers and shirts and that to buy a car like that.' Sandra's words left her mouth a little louder than she intended and two Mods turned their heads, looking her up and down disdainfully. Sandra blushed prettily.

Finally, with the photo-shoot now over, the snapper jumped in the Rolls along with its owner and quickly whizzed off along Carnaby Street. The colourful crowd dispersed and Cynthia casually motioned that they should go and check out one of the boutiques a few doors along from John Stephens. The women's clothes displayed in the window had caught her eye.

As they entered the shop 'Just Fade Away' by The Rolling Stones could be heard. A young man in his early twenties, wearing a white polo neck jumper under a green and light blue tweed three button jacket, was clicking his fingers in time with the beat of Charlie Watts' snare drum as he began to search through a pile of 45's deciding which one to play next.

He had sensed the girls entering the shop and looked up and smiled quickly. The shelves were stacked with a variety of clothes, in a variety of fabrics and in all sorts of colours. In the middle of the shop a seamstress who was a few years older than the customer, was measuring a beautiful-looking girl's waist. She stood quite still whilst the seamstress worked at pace. The girl's stylish looking boyfriend stood nearby holding his girlfriend's coat. He looked very cool indeed and he pointedly ignored Cynthia and Sandra's presence.

At the back of the shop another shop assistant was carefully re-folding some of the clothes. There was a collection of mannequins bedecked in the very clothes that could be bought in the shop. Cynthia and Sandra simply marvelled at what they saw; all around them demonstrated the cutting edge of what was happening in the world of Carnaby Street fashion. They just knew that within weeks, most of the young women in London would be wearing similar styled 'gear' and they intended to be amongst them.

The girls spent a further fifteen minutes in the shop just wishing they could afford the clothes. They finally began to leave the shop, feeling slightly deflated at the cost of everything. As they left the shop, they both smiled at the shop DJ who was still clicking his fingers along to the songs and maintaining his air of aloofness and disapproval of them. They couldn't help but laugh at him. Silly sod thought Sandra.

Sandra was happy to follow as Cynthia led her in and out of several more shops and boutiques along the narrow Soho Street. At one point, they lingered outside a door recognising the music coming out from it. They knew the song because Sammy had installed it recently in The Moka jukebox and it was one they both loved. As they continued on their stroll down towards The Shakespeare's Head pub, they sang the words to the song in their best silly voices...'My girl lollipop, you make my heart go giddy up,' laughing as they did so.

A few scooters were parked outside the Shakespeare, their chrome and mirrors glinting in the late afternoon sun. The girls stopped singing to marvel at one of the machines; both girls were extremely impressed. They were all far more beautiful compared to the bikes they saw buzzing around in Wimbledon.

'Wow doesn't it look smashing?' Sandra said running her finger along one of the mirrors.

'Yeah, lovely isn't it,' said Cynthia looking up at the pub sign. 'I bet the owner is inside the pub, and I reckon he must be an ace face. Come on, let's have a look.'

And with that, they found themselves propping up at the bar and being served two gin and tonics with no questions asked. They had only just started going into pubs on their own and found it hard to get served locally because they were known to the landlords and barmaids. In London, however, it was a different story as they were just another pretty face and, more often than not, they got a drink.

As they sipped their drinks they surveyed the pub - it was doing a good trade. Sitting on a large wooden table, Cynthia noticed a group of young men, all dressed in the finest of Mod tailoring and instinctively knew they were the owners of the scooters. The clues were all there: from the beautifully-cut hair to the bulky green mounds next to them, being their parkas - a choice of coat worn to protect their finer clothes when on their bikes.

Cynthia spotted a vacant table with some chairs not far from them and she tugged Sandra's arm and aimed them both at it. The table was perfectly positioned so they could listen to the Mods' conversations. The boys spoke quickly and excitedly and often over the top of each other. Cynthia heard something from one sitting at the table, who had raised some issue relating to some new bands coming out from London and how they had an edgier sound compared to the bands from the Mersey Beat stable. There appeared to be various conflicting opinions.

Suddenly, and without warning, one of the Mods leaned forward towards where Cynthia and Sandra were sat. He was very smart, dressed in a blue shimmering mohair suit, complimented with a crisp white shirt, navy and cream striped tie and his hair was 'just so'. Cynthia could also smell his cologne and he smelt lovely. She was immediately attracted to him and he had certainly noticed Cynthia.

'Hello love,' he said winking in her direction. 'Who do you like the best then eh?' he asked.

Cynthia replied somewhat startled, 'What do you mean?'

The whole group of Mods then stared at Cynthia and Sandra. Cynthia responded by sitting upright and confident. Sandra, however, sank lower into her seat.

'If you had to choose between The Beatles and The Rolling Stones who would you choose?' He then smiled the sweetest smile Cynthia had ever seen.

Now this was, of course, one subject Cynthia didn't have to dwell on for too long.

'The Beatles of course,' she said quickly.

A couple of the Mods nodded in agreement, whilst others shook their heads. Then, as quickly as her new friend had appeared, he was gone, returning to the banter within his group of friends.

Cynthia couldn't decide whether he was being rude. She was still making her mind up when two more gin and tonics were placed on their table. Both girls looked up at the two young men who now stood over them. One was tall, blonde hair and with a friendly smile; the other was the one asking the music question a little earlier. 'So,' she thought, 'you've come back then…'

'Do you mind?' asked the blonde one, glancing at the two vacant chairs positioned around their table.

Cynthia and Sandra looked at each other and, reading each other's expressions perfectly, agreed it was okay to allow them to sit down with them.

'Here,' said one producing a packet of Capstan Navy Cut cigarettes, which he then offered around. Everyone accepted. 'Blondie' struck a match and proceeded to light everyone's cigarettes. 'Ladies first, naturally,' he said confidently.

That done, he extended his hand inviting the girls to shake it.

'About time we were properly introduced, don't you think? My name is Reg and this, this is Arthur. And you are?'

Cynthia introduced herself and then Sandra and they all shook one another's hands. The girls took sips from their gin and tonics and the men gulped their light ales.

'So,' began Arthur, 'going by our chat a minute ago, you're Beatles fans I'd say?'

Cynthia and Sandra nodded in unison. Both were now feeling a little tipsy as the gin began to have an effect. In truth, they were still getting used to drinking.

'So why is that then?' continued Arthur. 'Why do you like The Beatles more than the Stones?'

'It goes without saying really. Blimey, where shall we start Sand?'

'Well, they have better-looking band members for a kick off,' said Sandra cheerfully.

'Yeah, The Beatles are better-looking for a start; they have nicer hairstyles; they smile more; they really are so handsome, especially George.' Cynthia was very confident on that point.

Sandra nodded vigorously, before tossing Ringo's name into the mix. Reg screwed up his nose.

'Yeah but it's not all about their looks, is it?' he stated.

'Well, maybe not for you, but it is for us,' said Sandra. 'I mean I wouldn't be able to take one of the Rolling Stones home to meet my parents. Blimey, they would drop dead as soon as they saw how scruffy they were dressed!'

Reg laughed. He nodded that the girls did have a point.

'Plus, The Beatles are nicer blokes; not like The Rolling Stones who seem to be a bit wild and uncontrollable really,' added Cynthia.

Reg laughed again. 'Yeah, but what about the music? What about the songs?'

'You can't compare the music; the two bands are entirely different,' said Sandra, feeling comfortable in expressing these thoughts.

'Well, I like both bands if I'm honest. I think they both play good songs,' Reg added.

'I'm more of a Rolling Stones man myself,' revealed Arthur, which upset Cynthia a bit - but only a tiny bit.

For the next ten minutes, the conversation flowed freely, with Reg and Arthur deliberately teasing the girls, saying things they knew would stir them up. The girls soon had it sussed, but were enjoying it so played along, letting the boys get the drinks in.

The pub clock chimed five o'clock and Cynthia and Sandra exchanged a knowing look. It was getting on and they knew they had better be getting home. The chaps looked disappointed and to tired persuade them to stay for 'one for the road'. After a brief chat, the girls invited them to meet for more drinks on Monday.

They had revealed earlier that they would be hanging around outside the London Pavilion then, so all agreed, they would meet for a quick one back in The Shakespeare before heading for their date with George and Ringo. With that agreement in place, Cynthia and Sandra left, both feeling a little unsteady on their feet, but feeling in a pretty good mood.

On the return journey home Sandra bought two cartons of milk from the machine at the tube station. She had decided to try to sober up before she got home, knowing her mum and dad would go spare if she walked in drunk. Before long, they were back in Wimbledon and the girls hugged each other good night and parted company.

By the time Cynthia got home, she was starving. No sooner said than done, she made some cheese on toast which was quickly consumed. She had had a good day but, in truth, she was glad to be home. She knew she was growing up fast and sometimes she felt a bit daring and drank, smoked and chatted to boys and then, at another time, all she wanted to do was be at home eating cheese on toast. She was still trying to make sense of this growing up thing.

After a quick bath, she was content to simply spend the remainder of her evening attending to her Beatles scrapbook. She had collected up a week's worth of newspaper and magazine cuttings that she needed to sort and add to her books. Keeping her scrapbook up to date was one of her most important responsibilities of the week.

Sandra, meanwhile, had chosen to buy some fish and chips from the 'Frying Tonight' chippy at the end of her road. She ate them whilst perching on some rubble that was a constant reminder to her, and the other people who lived in the area, that it could have been their home which had been bombed twenty years earlier. It was certainly a reference her father often pulled out of the bag, given any opportunity to highlight to Sandra how 'fortunate she was to have a roof over her head'.

Sandra had perfectly timed getting the chips and eating them here to the precise second, because she was able to see her parents leave their home and walk up the road in the opposite direction towards The Mitre. The Mitre was their pub of choice which they went to every Saturday night; Sandra hated that pub. Well, not so much the pub, but more her memories of getting dragged along to it when she was younger, sitting bored to tears in the family room.

There she would sit, slowly sipping a Coca-Cola through a red and white striped straw, chomping on a bag of Salt 'n' Shake whilst her mother and father spent the night with nothing to say to each other - it had never been an enjoyable experience. It wasn't until Sandra was fifteen and had left school that she had been able to make a stand and refuse to go anymore. Funnily enough, she noticed her mother and father were more than happy with that new arrangement too.

So, tonight, Sandra waited until her parents were out of sight before slowly walking towards her house, eating a couple of pear drops as she pushed open the garden gate.

The first thing that hit her as she entered her home was the overwhelming smell of kippers. Of course it was kippers - her parents always had kippers for their tea on a Saturday night. Sandra detested kippers, she had done since a kid when she had been forced to eat them. It was either eat them each Saturday or go to bed with an empty stomach, so she often went to bed hungry.

Only stopping to dip her hand into the biscuit tin and remove two Rich Tea biscuits and fill a glass with some more milk, Sandra climbed the stairs to her bedroom, which was on the floor above her parents. The distant echo of her father's angry voice saying 'get up them wooden stairs now' resounded inside her head as she walked to her room. Memories of unhappier days were never far away on this journey to bed.

Sandra's bedroom was like most other teenage girls of her generation. Thankfully it was her place to retreat to, her domain, and the only place in which she really had any control. Her parents seldom ventured up as far up as Sandra's bedroom. Her mother suffered from a bad back and her father didn't really care what his daughter had done in her bedroom.

As a result, the wall space was covered with posters of The Beatles; the majority being of her beloved Ringo. Her pride and joy was a large photograph of him, underneath which she had written one of his quotes 'some people gab all day and some people play it smogo.' She felt Ringo's words reflected a trait in her own personality.

Sandra opened her bedroom window to let in some fresh air and allow the faint sickly stench of kippers out. It was still warm out; it was a lovely July evening. She noticed a few of her neighbour's kids below, who looked like they were in the process of making some bows and arrows. A little further down the street two women stood chatting, both had cigarettes hanging from the edge of their mouths.

Sandra removed her cardigan and hung it on the back of the one chairs she had in the room. The chair stayed in front of a dressing table that had been in the family for many years. It had once belonged to her grandmother and had a large mirror. Sandra often found herself gazing in the mirror reminding herself how different her appearance was now from even just a few months earlier. She had watched herself grow up in that mirror and was also aware of getting older and things beginning to change.

As a reminder of the past, she kept a photograph of her grandmother Marge sellotaped to the mirror. The old girl had died when Sandra was twelve and now she missed her deeply. All her fondest memories of being a child included her nan, for it was her who had made time to play with Sandra and take her to the park or treat her to some sweets. Nanny Marge filled in the most important gaps that her own parents couldn't or simply wouldn't.

Though it was four years ago that the old girl had passed, to Sandra it seemed like only yesterday. Sometimes, she really felt twelve again.

'Look Grandmother,' she suddenly said as she produced from her bag several magazine clippings of Ringo. Next Sandra pulled open one of the drawers on the dresser and removed her Beatles scrapbook. She then set about trimming them with some scissors and sticking them into position. The book was bulging with all sorts of photos and pictures. She reminded herself that she would need to start a new one soon - that would be her third one.

Once her scrapbook had been sorted, she went downstairs. She had looked forward to having a relaxing bath all day and now she didn't have to rush because her parents wouldn't be home until at least ten o'clock. The bath slowly filled with hot water and Sandra sprinkled some bath salts into it. She plunged her right hand in to check the temperature. Finally, it was full enough for her to get in and, as she lay there, she reflected on her day.

Sandra had really enjoyed meeting Reg and Arthur, and felt excited that she and Cynthia would be seeing them again on Monday. But, if she was honest, she felt more excited about going to the film premiere and the prospect of catching a glimpse of her Ringo.

By far the most rewarding part of her day was that she had been able to spend it with Cynthia. Her relationship with Cynthia was one that she cherished more than anything in the world. In her world, the pecking order was her best mate at the top closely followed by Ringo and then the other three Beatles. Everything else, her family, The Moka, her job, was simply something else to fill her days with.

Sandra knew she would give her life for Cynthia if needs be and it had been like that for years. They had met on their first day of junior school and by the end of the day were already best friends and had remained so far to this day.

Cynthia was exactly the sort of person that Sandra needed around her. Cynthia had been a confident child from an early age. She was brave and she had a sense of humour that Sandra found invaluable and depended upon.

By the time the girls were going to secondary school, Cynthia was already a beautiful girl with a developing body. Sandra was always playing catch up but, kindly, Cynthia never mentioned it. Cynthia was also aware that Sandra's home life wasn't as an enjoyable experience as her own. It was just acknowledged but never mentioned.

Instead, what Cynthia did was invite Sandra over to her house to play with her. Sandra's parents didn't care as they were glad to have her out of the house really. As a result, Sandra often went back to Cynthia's after school and they would play together for hours until either one of Cynthia's older brothers or her father walked her home. In Cynthia's home Sandra felt welcomed and, sadly, she felt more loved there than she did in her own home.

Stepping from the bath and wrapping her dressing gown around her body, Sandra returned to her bedroom. It was now dark outside so she closed the window, leaving it just an inch open, and closed the curtains. In a swift movement, she allowed her dressing gown to fall to the floor and then she was under her bed sheets. She took a moment to scan her Ringo and Beatles posters and the two-football scarves - Liverpool and Everton - which dangled from her bedposts.

Content that everything was as it should be, she reached across to her transistor radio and switched it on. The familiar voice of Simon Dee on Radio Caroline announced the next song and as Sandra sunk her head deeper into her pillow, the sultry tones of Dusty Springfield singing 'Anyone Who Had A Heart' helped her drift off to sleep.

Chapter 5
In My Life

Monday morning burst into Cynthia's bedroom like the charge of the light brigade. As per usual, the alarm clock, which for some time she had considered her worst enemy, sent shudders through her nervous system as it went off full bore at 7.15am. Three times in total Cynthia slammed her fist down firmly on its button but, in the end, she had to resign herself to the fact that there was nothing else for it - she had to get up.

She lay pondering her next move listening to her father go through the motions of his morning routine, slowly but steadily making his way to the outside of her bedroom door. Eventually, he rapped his knuckles on its wood and shouted, 'Come on now madam, time to get…YAWN…time to get up…'

With a slice of white toast and a cup of tea inside her, Cynthia was soon skipping down the high street towards her granddad's shop. Her mind and body now awake, she was already getting excited about going to the premiere of *A Hard Day's Night* later. Reg and Arthur were also in her thoughts, but in truth they were a poor second to The Beatles.

As she hurried along, the wonderful blue sky above caught her attention. It was without a cloud and the sun was already bright and warm.

At just after half past eight, Cynthia opened the door to the shop, to find her granddad in the process of carrying a bag of kitchen utensils across the beaten up and splintered old wooden floorboards of the shop.

'Morning Cynthia love,' he said cheerily.

'Good morning Granddad,' Cynthia replied, holding the door wide open to make it easier for him.

'Perfect timing there girl. Go on, put the kettle on my lovely.'

'Of course!' she replied, already halfway to the back kitchen.

Cynthia's granddad, Norbert to give him his proper name, was fondly known by all who knew him as Nobby. Now 75 and born in 1889, he was in his twenties when the First World War started in 1914, which made him too old to fight when the Second World War kicked off in 1939, so he proudly joined the Home Guard instead.

Over the years he had developed a bit of a stoop and his face and hands were now heavily wrinkled. In his pomp though, he had been a handsome man, with thick black hair and known to always walk briskly with a straight back. The years of dragging bags of potatoes and what-not from one side of the shop to the other had taken their toll on his much older physique and, what hair he now had left, was grey and slicked back onto his mottled scalp.

Her granddad set about laying the kitchen utensils on a hand-made wooden shelf that he also dragged through the shop each morning and which he positioned inside by the large shop window. He was proud of the wooden shelf; it was the product of his own handy-work and must have been 40 years old now, but still up to the job.

The window itself displayed an odd assortment of goods. There were things to complete everyday DIY tasks, such as nails and screws, along with stepladders and buckets and children's toys and games too. The shop sold virtually everything including a modest collection of fresh fruit and vegetables, tea, coffee and sugar, butter and sweets. Old Nobby was proud to be able to get anything his customers asked for.

Cynthia reappeared from the kitchen holding two white enamel tin mugs full of tea which she placed on the shop's counter. Alongside the mugs sat a chipped saucer, on which rested an assortment of biscuit crumbs scattered across both it and the counter - evidence of Nobby's earlier breakfast.

Cynthia dusted some of the crumbs away and plonked herself onto a stool behind the counter. As she proceeded to sip her tea, she watched her granddad place the kitchen utensils thoughtfully on his wooden shelf. She loved to watch him making his shop ready for his customers, most of them champions of the 'chimney-gram', that sooty stream of gossip that floated from house to house carrying all the latest news. She was bound to hear plenty of the latest today, it being a Monday.

Nobby loved his shop with its shelves neatly stacked with tins of this and bags of that. The long wooden counter, with its brass edging, was where Nobby sat behind most of the day; was his domain. From the counter he read his newspaper, drank his tea, chomped his biscuits when it went quiet and it was from here also that he served his loyal regulars.

He had put down roots in Wimbledon in the early 1930's. At first, he did various jobs in warehouses and factories before seizing an opportunity and starting up his own business. This had been on his mind for many years; he was just waiting for the right opportunity.

Truthfully, he never got on with the notion of working for other people so had been saving as much money as he could whilst grafting, with the idea of eventually opening a local corner shop.

He had married local girl Isabella - Bella for short - not long after leaving the army in 1919. The 'war to end all wars' had been a terrible experience and he was ready to settle down and try to forget about the horrible things he had seen in his four years of service overseas. They were happy together and within seven years had a young family. Three children in total: Vera the oldest; Joyce was next to have been born and then Cynthia's father William, which was Nobby's middle name and the name of his own father.

Finally, after five years of scrimping and saving, Nobby took a fifty-year lease on a local shop premises and established the business which, over the years, had become part of the scenery in Wimbledon.

Sadly, Bella had died before Cynthia was born so she never got to meet her, but going by everything she had heard, she was a lovely woman and adored by everyone. Her granddad would often tell Cynthia that she had her grandmother's eyes. She loved to hear that.

He never really got over the death of his wife and threw himself into the shop, trying to forget the pain he felt in his heart. Nothing was too much trouble for his customers, he valued each and every one of them.

They in turn, loved him and his variety of skills. He was known to be a demon on the bacon and meat slicer and a wizard of the ancient scales that he used for weighing out the tea and sugar. He had a similar, smaller set of scales that he reserved only for weighing out the imperial mints and cough candy which he shook from large glass jars to be bagged up by the quarter.

In truth, he made a decent living from the place, but only as the result of very hard graft and long hours. Even during the last war, barely a day passed when he didn't open, before joining up with his local Home Guard most evenings ('Don't panic' and all that!). Sundays and half-day closing on Wednesday afternoons was the only time when the closed sign hung on the door of the shop. Otherwise it was 'open all hours'. This shop was his second home.

For as long as she could remember, Cynthia had helped out around the shop, helping to put the stock on the lower shelves and sometimes being allowed to bag up some sweets. By the time she was eight, she was allowed to walk to the shop by herself to see her granddad. Her mother would often say 'can you nip down to granddad's and get some tea please?' and Cynthia would be off as fast as she could, to watch her granddad weigh out some tea on the scales and tip it into a brown paper bag. He often gave his 'special girl' a toffee, before sending her back to her parents. Cynthia loved doing this as it made her feel all grown up.

When Cynthia was thirteen, she was working in the shop on a regular basis, popping in straight after school to give old Nobby an hour's rest before he got ready to close for the day. She also worked most Saturdays, being paid a few pence, which always came in handy. Upon leaving school, and with no real plan of what to do, she began working there full-time, which was a great help to Nobby. Now she always got Saturday off, which suited her newfound lifestyle of coffee bars, clothes shops and hairdressers. And now they had settled into a familiar and well-oiled routine.

'Come on Granddad, your tea's getting cold,' she found herself saying that most mornings, smiling at the way the old man lost himself in doing his window display.

'Alright lovey, I'm coming, I'm coming,' he replied absentmindedly, his tongue poking out of the corner of his mouth as he concentrated on the apples in their straw basket, just in the right place.

Nobby took the opportunity to have a quick five-minute sit down. He dressed each day in a white warehouse coat, over which he wore a brand-new waist-high apron. He mopped his sweaty brow with a red and white spotted hankie, which he then stuffed into the back pocket of his grey flannel trousers.

It wouldn't be long before the first rush of customers would descend upon the shop. They officially opened at nine but, more often than not, a small queue would form outside ten minutes earlier. If he was ready, Nobby would let them in and soon a trickle became a constant stream, as the bell above the door 'tinkled' constantly.

But in this rare moment of peace, the two of them could catch up and chat.

'Is it today that you got that Beatles thing on?' Nobby asked Cynthia, surprising her that he had remembered.

'Well done you. Yeah, it's the film premiere tonight of *A Hard Day's Night*. Can't wait…!'

'*A Hard…Day's…Night*,' said Nobby looking puzzled, 'what the flipping hell does that even mean?'

Cynthia then patiently explained to him how Ringo had come up with that following an especially tough filming session.

'He suddenly said 'It's been a hard day's night that was!' smiled Cynthia. 'John Lennon liked what Ringo had said so much, that he suggested it as the name for the film and then the album. Clever eh?'

Nobby slowly shook his head and looked none the wiser to be honest.

'Blimey, what sort of name is that, eh? Bleedin' Ringo? I ask ya. I must be getting old lovely, I'm lost if truth be told. I can imagine it will be busy up the West End later then. You keep an eye on your hand bag young lady and stay alert for pick-pockets; they'll be out in numbers tonight.'

'I will, don't worry,' Cynthia smiled.

Her dad had married when he was just eighteen and her older brother Andrew arrived two years later. He was considered a young father and that's why Cynthia thought he never cursed the impact The Beatles were having on her. He was on her wavelength to a certain extent.

Cynthia was about to tell Nobby what she had heard about the film, when Kenny shuffled into the shop.

'Hello Kenny son,' said Nobby, 'what can I get you today?'

Kenny had been a regular customer since he was a small boy, when it had been his errand to buy his father's tobacco.

'Hello Nobby, just some tea today, please; I'm going round to see my Nan. She's a bit poorly.'

'Right you are mate. Sorry to hear that,' said Nobby as he turned around and plunged a long wooden-handled shovel into an open sack of tea leaves just behind him. 'Make sure say hello from me won't you, and tell her that I hope she starts feeling better soon.'

'Yeah will do,' said Kenny. 'Hello Cynthia, how are ya?

'Alright Kenny, I'm good thanks. Getting very excited about tonight. It's gonna be fab. Can't wait!'

Kenny smiled; he could see she was very excited. 'What time you heading into town?' he asked.

'I'm meeting Sandra at four,' Cynthia replied.

'Oh okay. She not in town already then?' asked Kenny who was keen to keep the conversation going. 'I thought she was working in the city?'

'No not today. She has taken the afternoon off so she can spend time getting dolled up. I bet she couldn't even sleep last night.'

'And what about you? Eh? Did you sleep last night?' asked Kenny.

Cynthia laughed. 'Me? Oh yeah, as soon as my head hits the pillow I'm off. I could sleep through World War Three mate.'

'Ban the bomb eh!' said Kenny punching his fist into the air, but Cynthia couldn't see the joke.

Kenny continued, going slightly red in the face and feeling a bit of a fool. 'We're going down too. I think it will be a right laugh.'

'I know you lot,' said Cynthia cynically. 'You are only going to ogle at the birds, aren't you? Go on, own up!'

Kenny laughed nervously. 'Yeah, well you never know, I might have a look Cynthia.'

'Here you go son.' They were both interrupted as Nobby handed Kenny the bag of tea he had prepared for his Nan.

'Anything else son?'

Kenny said there wasn't and asked for the bag of tea to be added to his tab, which Cynthia duly did.

Nobby grabbed his pipe. 'Lovely, my smoke. I think I'll have a sit down for five minutes; I'm feeling a bit tired. Must be the heat.'

He stuffed the bowl of his brown-coloured pipe with loose tobacco leaves and lit it as he walked out of the shop. One of his favourite things in life was to have a puff on his pipe whilst he watched Wimbledon pass him by.

Cynthia told Kenny she would keep a look out for him in the crowd at the premiere. Secretly, that little message really cheered him up.

The rest of Cynthia's working day was pretty much the norm. The 'Monday Club' of Mrs Barnes, Mrs Wood and Mrs Lewis, each of them a war widow who always bought fresh vegetables and tins of Carnation milk on the first day of the week, often descended upon the shop at the same time.

There was also a surprise visit from Cynthia's dad, who wanted to wish his daughter good luck for the evening and tell her to be careful.

He also told her that he had paid off the instalment for their holiday in Butlin's, which was just around the corner. He appeared to be very chuffed with himself; he did love his week away in Bognor Regis.

Cynthia was keeping a beady eye on the shop clock which seemed to slow down from quarter past three. She was desperate for it to get to ten to four, so she could finally get her coat and things and be ready to leave for the day and head to the West End.

'Right, Granddad, I'm off.'

'Er, hang on lovely, not so fast,' said her granddad, calling her back in to the shop.

He opened the till and removed a few crumpled green pound notes.

'Open your hand then girl,' he demanded.

At first she refused, but her granddad told her that he had been intending to give her a bonus and today was as good a day as any to start it. Cynthia finally accepted the money, a huge smile breaking out on her face and she gave her granddad a massive hug. Hugging him always felt good. She felt like a little kid again as she did so.

She finally bid him goodbye and blew him a kiss as she left the shop, all excited as she ran to meet her best mate.

As usual, they were to meet at their usual spot on the Common at four PM, but also as usual, Sandra was late, again...!

Cynthia wagged her finger at her friend, as they retraced the same train and tube journey they had made on the previous Saturday. By the time the tube reached Piccadilly Circus station, however, they could hardly move because of the amount of young people, mainly teenage girls, who stood squeezed together like sardines in the now hot and now stuffy carriage.

The decibel levels on the tube were also getting louder and louder, but it was nothing to the sound of thousands of teenagers on the pavement, as they tumbled outside the tube station. It was simply deafening. The hustle and bustle, pushing and shoving amongst them all though, only added to the excitement.

Cynthia wrapped her hand tightly around Sandra's wrist and began pushing forward. The premiere and arrival of The Beatles was still two hours away, so the girls just had time to meet Reg and Arthur for at least one drink.

The streets leading to the Shakespeare's Head were remarkably quiet, compared to Piccadilly Circus and Shaftsbury Avenue. As they approached the pub entrance, Cynthia's attention was drawn towards the aroma of a young man wearing a hat, dark sunglasses, with the collar of his jacket turned up, as he passed close-by. The smell stopped her in her tracks, but she couldn't quite put her finger on it. She knew she knew it well, but where from?

Sandra was totally unaware and didn't notice Cynthia, her gaze intently following the young man as he walked briskly away along the unusually deserted Carnaby Street. Turning towards the pub, Cynthia had a nagging sensation that something important had just occurred. But what?

The girls noticed the table and chairs where they had sat on Saturday were empty, so they headed over towards there. No sooner had they sat down, the pub door they had come in through swung open again and Reg and Arthur strolled in. Both had cigarettes on the go and both were dressed in fine Italian style suits: Reg's being a navy suit and Arthur wearing black. Crisp white button-down shirts and thin black ties could be seen under the jackets and, to finish off the look, highly polished black leather shoes, both of a weave construction and most probably imported from Italy. As she looked them up and down, Cynthia was impressed, very impressed.

'Turned up then,' said Reg smiling.

The boys seemed upbeat and pleased, although not really surprised that their dates had turned up.

'Yeah, nothing else really going on, so we thought why not?' Cynthia smiled back at Reg and winked cheekily at Arthur.

Reg asked the girls what they were drinking and soon both the chaps had joined them. The conversation between them all was slow at first, but soon got going and touched upon how work and life had been since Saturday.

Reg revealed that he worked in the printing trade and hinted that he earned a good wage; one which allowed him to spend more money than most of his peers on clothes, records and going to dancehalls and clubs. He also mentioned he owned a Lambretta, which he made clear was his pride and joy.

Arthur laughed and told the girls he wasn't earning as much as his mate, and that he worked in a factory in the East End which made parts for washing machines.

'Bleedin' boring if truth be told, but it's steady for now and I can get a fair bit of overtime, which means I could still purchase the suits, though mostly on the never never. I like to keep up to speed with the latest styles,' explained Arthur. 'I've got a bike too - a Vespa - which is currently in the garage 'cause a bloody van backed into it and crushed it.' Arthur virtually spat the words out as he described how it had happened. 'I'm hoping Reg here will get me in the print like him, be handy that.' The girls let the boys do most of the talking, nodding and smiling at the appropriate times. In fact, truth be told, their minds were on other things. Cynthia kept looking at her watch, noticing it was getting near to 'Beatle time'.

'We really should be going, well, if we want to get a decent view,' said Cynthia almost apologising.

'Eh?' said Reg in a mocking outraged tone, 'you just got here. Go on, have another one.'

Cynthia and Sandra looked at each and smiled, Sandra mouthing the words 'shall we' to her best mate.

They both laughed and finally Cynthia said, 'Go on then, just a quick one though eh.'

'You sure you don't want a drink first?' laughed Reg as he went to the bar.

They all laughed.

'Cheeky sod,' said Sandra straight at him, thinking at the same time how much she liked him.

The pub was still quite quiet, so he was soon back with the drinks.

'There's plenty of time,' Arthur said, carefully placing the glasses on the table. 'Don't stress, we'll get you to the premiere in time.'

'*Are you going then?*' Cynthia asked, a bit taken aback. On Saturday, there had been no mention of the boys even wanting to go.

'Yeah of course. We are your escorts for the evening,' Reg laughed.

Both Cynthia and Sandra looked at each other. This wasn't part of their plan and they had no intention of going to the premiere with two boys in tow.

'But we thought you had no interest in The Beatles,' Cynthia said sounding concerned.

'Well we don't really, but we still want to see what all the fuss is about, don't we mate?' Arthur replied taking a sip from his drink.

Sandra really did like Reg and Cynthia felt the same about Arthur, but they certainly didn't want any boys to be around them on this night of all nights. They both knew it would seriously reduce their

69

chances where George and Ringo were concerned and tonight was all about, and only about, George and Ringo.

Cynthia had to think quickly. 'I really don't think you'll like it. And it's already really heaving down there. We had to push through a sea of bodies just to get off Shaftesbury Avenue. Your suits and shoes will get ruined,' Cynthia said trying to sound like she genuinely cared for the boy's threads.

'Nah, we'll be okay,' said Reg. 'Besides, if our whistles get damaged, well, we'll just get new ones made eh? Come on then, drink up girls, can't have you missing your Fabs can we?'

Sandra shrugged her shoulders at Cynthia. They both knew it was pointless arguing, the chaps had made up their minds.

They left the pub and quickly walked through some back alleyways before picking up Regent Street near by Hamleys toyshop. As they started going down towards Piccadilly Circus, the number of people, and young girls in particular, grew larger and then larger still.

Though they were still a few hundred yards away from the statue Eros, the shrill and now deafening noise of thousands of young girls was almost painful. The crowd was so dense towards the top of Shaftsbury Avenue that the girls realised there was going to be a real struggle getting anywhere near the London Pavilion. It was then, that they both secretly cursed the boys for delaying them in The Shakespeare.

Cynthia decided on one last push and began to shove her way through the crowd with Sandra clinging onto her and the boys clinging on to Sandra. Blimey, it was a struggle, but this was one determined lady and she wasn't stopping for anyone. It was simply a solid mass of bodies, being held back at the front by row upon row of uniformed coppers for as far as the eye could see.

Thousands of kids now surrounded Cynthia, Sandra, Reg and Arthur. They were all now chatting, screaming, giggling and singing all the Beatles tunes they knew. Still, Cynthia ploughed on.

Such was the noise around them that it was getting harder to think, let alone speak. It was obvious that Reg and Arthur had had enough by now. They knew it would be busy, but not this busy.

Several times they called out to Cynthia, asking her to stop. She never even turned around. On and on she went. Oh, she heard them alright, but this was her night and NOTHING was going to stop her.

Arthur was now really getting the hump. He grabbed Cynthia's arm and squeezed it hard.

It hurt her and she had to wriggle her way out. Arthur looked angry and tried to grab her again, only succeeding in digging his nails into Cynthia's shoulder blade. Sandra saw this and stamped her foot down on his shin as hard as she could. That hurt him too and he then released his grip.

The girls had made their point and ploughed on, forward, forward, even more determined to get nearer to the front of The London Pavilion, and now, finally, they had escaped their escorts. Being in this crowd wasn't enough, these two wanted to look into the whites of eyes of George and Ringo. Nothing else would do...

The crowd soon swallowed up Reg and Arthur and they decided to retreat, fighting their way out from these nutty girls who had beaten them. By this time, Sandra hoped that their suits were getting ripped to shreds.

Suddenly, the volume around the girls increased again. Above their heads hundreds of banners appeared as they were raised in the air. Messages like 'I Love John', 'I Love Paul', 'We Love the Beatles', 'John please, please, marry me' and 'Beatles Forever' flapped in the early evening sky. Some, no, the majority of the crowd were bordering on hysterical. Tears streaming down faces and before long both Cynthia and Sandra were crying too.

They found themselves being shoved in every direction. A human tidal wave was carrying them here and there. They knew they had no hope of getting any closer and the realisation made them cry even more. Cynthia held Sandra's hand tightly and looked deeply into her friend's bloodshot eyes. She felt like she had failed her best friend and what was more, from where they were positioned, there would be absolutely no way that they could see The Beatles and that meant that George and Ringo couldn't see them. Just as she digested the thought and felt her heart sinking, a tall girl standing beside her accidently stubbed her cigarette out onto Cynthia's bright yellow dress. Cynthia began to cry even louder, her first thought being, 'what would George think of her dress now?'

And then as quickly as it had come, the noise faded. And then, gradually, the crowd around the girls began to thin out. They could only guess that The Beatles, their beloved George and Ringo, had arrived and had been ushered inside the safety of The London Pavilion along with Princess Margaret, her husband Lord Snowdon and all the other 'jewellery rattlers'.

Cynthia and Sandra were still clinging to each other's arms as they stood there. They were now both knackered. Some of those around them were also so weakened by the experience they had just had, that they had to have their friends prop them up.

Everyone tuned into everyone else's conversations. It was obvious that some had caught a glimpse of their idols, but it was clear that most had been less lucky. One girl even claimed that John had smiled at her and another kept repeating that Paul had actually waved at her. Cynthia and Sandra couldn't lay claim to any of that, or of anything at all, extraordinary or otherwise. All they had experienced was pain really. The throbbing pain from their feet, ankles, knees and shoulders was all they could focus on. They didn't even spare a thought for Reg and Arthur, whom they presumed had stormed off back to the pub. Good riddance to bad rubbish, thought Cynthia.

However, suddenly, there was one conversation that Sandra had picked up on. A couple of words had brought her out of her spell of suffering long enough to hear a young bloke telling his mates he had heard that the reception after the premiere was being held in the Dorchester Hotel.

One girl was excitedly telling anyone who would listen that she had heard someone say that The Beatles would also be joining The Rolling Stones in the Ad Lib club around the corner but, to Sandra, The Dorchester was the better bet. She nudged Cynthia indicating that she needed to listen in too.

They both smiled as the conversation near them wore on and came to the same conclusion. Off to The Dorchester we go!

They had to walk quickly; there was no time to lose. They had heard the hotel was over by Hyde Park and Sandra thought she knew the way, because she had once gone swimming on The Serpentine and that was near The London Hilton, which she remembered was near The Dorchester. They quickened their pace on their already aching feet; their thinking being to get there early and get a good spot.

As they turned a corner down by Swan and Edgar on to Piccadilly, to their surprise they found themselves standing bumping into Kenny. Cynthia actually felt pleased to see him. She didn't really know why, maybe it was just seeing a familiar and friendly face, following such an exhausting ordeal. Whatever it was, she almost felt like she wanted to hug him, but instead controlled herself, convinced her emotions were in tatters and it wasn't the best thing to do.

Kenny's face was a picture however. 'Blimey, fancy seeing you two! Did you get close? Did you see them?' Kenny fired off the questions at a rapid speed.

'Piss it mate, did we hell,' Sandra hissed. 'Don't tell me you did, cos I'll kill ya!'

Kenny shook his laughing, telling them he didn't get much further than outside the tube station.

Cynthia quickly told him of the story of their night so far. Kenny listened and genuinely felt sorry for them. He knew what getting a glimpse of The Beatles would have meant to these two.

'Not all lost though; we're going to the Dorchester. We've just heard they will be there after the film, so we're going. Wanna come too?' said Cynthia smiling.

Kenny laughed and thought why not. Being close to Cynthia was good enough for him. The three of them quickly set off. On the way, he told them he had come with his two friends, Pete and Eric, but they had got separated soon after arriving at Piccadilly Circus and he had lost them. Funnily enough, all of a sudden he was smiling.

'You know, I think its fate I've just bumped into you two. I've got something for you.'

The girls were looking puzzled.

'What are you on about Kenny?' demanded Cynthia, getting slightly irritated at the slow pace of walking he had suddenly dropped to.

'Wait,' said Kenny, as he finally stopped, checking every pocket in his trousers and jacket before eventually finding what he was looking for.

'What do you mean 'wait'?' shouted Sandra, 'we ain't got time to wait!'

Kenny smiling at her anger, only made her more angry.

'Look, hold out your hands,' he said grinning. They could tell he wouldn't get going again until he had done whatever it was he needed to do. They did as they were told and held out their hands.

Kenny slowly dropped two pieces of paper into the girls' hands. They looked at each other, neither having a clue as to what they were now holding.

They slowly examined the paper shapes in their hands and saw they were now holding concert tickets for The Beatles' forthcoming show at The Hippodrome in Brighton.

'What? But...how?' Cynthia began to stutter.

'They're for you two. You can have them.'

'But how...why?' repeated Sandra, as confused as her mate.

Kenny was smiling at them both now. 'I won them in a card game at work. I won't use them, they're spares, so I want you to have 'em.'

This time Cynthia couldn't resist herself and she wrapped her arms around Kenny's waist and gave him a big warm hug. Sandra joined in and they cuddled each other, laughing in a high-pitched excited way. Kenny felt made up, he felt like he had done something good.

Neither Cynthia nor Sandra had yet to see The Beatles live. Now, they could hardly believe what had just happened. It was a dream come true and suddenly all the aches and pains were gone as they danced and skipped their way to The Dorchester, waving the concert tickets in the air as they did.

In truth, Kenny struggled to keep up with them. All the disappointments relating to the London Pavilion episode earlier had now faded away. Finally, they reached The Dorchester - well, they reached the metal barriers that had been hastily erected around it. They weren't alone; there were hundreds of kids also lurking about. So, that rumour was true then, The Dorchester was the location for the reception. It had to be, going by the numbers here. There was also plenty of police, already fighting a losing battle in keeping the Beatle people away from the hotel.

Cynthia, Sandra and Kenny hung around for a couple of long hours and were almost ready to give up and go home when a bunch of teenagers run from behind them and into the mass of bodies already at the barriers. Then a young blonde girl suddenly shouted.

'It's not going here! It's going over there!' and a tide of bodies ran in the direction of which the blonde girl was pointing. Cynthia, Sandra and Kenny simply got swept along with them. As they ran, they presumed The Beatles' cars had been spotted.

About a hundred yards from the front of the hotel, the runners in front of them suddenly put the brakes on, stopped and turned away.

'Stop! Stop! It's a detour! It's a detour! We've been conned. Go back, go back!'

Now there was total confusion. No-one seemed to know what was happening. They all ran back towards the entrance of the hotel and were informed by a smug looking copper that they were too late and The Beatles had indeed arrived and been sneaked in via a side entrance. Having broken the news, he kindly advised that there was no chance of seeing the band.

'Go on, why don't you go home? Your mothers will be worried about you,' and with that he folded his hands behind his back and smirked at them all.

Hearts collectively sank all around, as the Beatle people realised they had duped and missed their opportunity. Next, more tears began to flow; this had now turned into a very emotional night. Cynthia and Sandra wondered if they were destined to never see The Beatles up close and then remembered their Brighton concert tickets and instantly cheered up.

Cynthia finally said, 'Let's call it a night eh?'

On the train home, they couldn't stop thanking Kenny enough. He was delighted to be in their good books, especially Cynthia's and he especially liked the good night peck on the cheek that he got as they said their goodbyes.

Back at home and safely tucked up in bed, Cynthia tuned in to Radio Caroline and lay staring at the concert ticket. She couldn't remember feeling this excited at any time in her life. Her thoughts turned to the week that lay ahead. On Wednesday, she and Sandra would be going to watch *A Hard Day's Night*, the first ever Beatles film. On Saturday, they would be going to Woolworths to buy copies of the long-awaited album and then on Monday they would be going to Brighton to actually see the band. What a week that was!

What a fantastic, FAB week ahead!

As she finally settled down for the night, Cynthia's thoughts turned to her family. She simply couldn't wait to tell her mum, dad and granddad about the concert; she knew they would be thrilled for her. The bonus money her granddad had given her would now come in very handy and would be spent going to the cinema, buying the album and paying for her trip to Brighton. She finally surrendered to sleep still clutching the concert ticket, with the biggest grin on her face.

The last thing Sandra did before she turned in for the night, was to say a prayer for Ringo Starr and wish him happy birthday. She just hoped the birthday card she had lovingly made herself and sent to Anne Collingham to be passed on, had reached him in time…

It was very import…ant…(snore).

Chapter 6
A Hard Day's Night

The Moka was the natural meeting point for all those going to see *A Hard Day's Night* at The Lyric in Hammersmith that evening and, sure enough, it was rammed as departure time approached.

A line of twenty-odd impressive scooters were parked up outside; it was a great turn out. Inside, Beatles song after Beatles song burst out loudly from jukebox.

As Cynthia slowly entered, several heads turned and admired her brand-new outfit. If she was honest, she enjoyed the long, admiring gazes. She had long begged her mother, a skilled seamstress, to make her a 'Nehru' suit jacket like The Beatles wore early in their career in 1962 and she had finally relented. It was made from a light grey material and like the jacket it was based on, it had no lapels.

As ever, the loyal Sandra had followed Cynthia in, wearing her brand-new dogtooth shift dress but, sadly, she noticed she didn't get the same attention.

Kenny was already propped up at the counter. He and his friends were crowded around the pinball machine alongside a bunch of other kids. There was the usual noisy 'Moka' buzz of excitement hovering in the air, only more so tonight. Going to see the first Beatles film for the first time was a big deal. The curiosity stirred by this event had well and truly gripped the young of the nation. They had all followed stories of the making of the film in the papers for months now. Of course, there had been 'teen films' before, but they had been for those who were a few years older and had featured the likes of Elvis and Cliff Richard, but now it was this generation's idols in the spotlight. And anyway, The Beatles were *different,* there had never been anyone quite like them and now they were leading the way.

Kenny wandered over and kindly offered to buy Cynthia and Sandra a coffee.

'Ta Kenny, but you are not getting this one - this one will be on me,' said Cynthia.

Kenny smiled sheepishly as Cynthia produced a handful of coins and paid for the round. Both girls then excitedly launched into Kenny telling him they hadn't been able to sleep for the past few nights due to their excitement of the week that lay ahead for them, and that a lot of that was down to him and the tickets he had given them. Kenny struggled to hide how delighted he was to have made Cynthia so happy.

Meanwhile, still they crammed in, and soon The Moka's walls felt like they were going to burst. Sammy served drink after drink, being pulled from pillar to post. Droplets of sweat formed on his forehead, which he continually wiped away with the same coffee-stained tea towel which he used to clean his chipped cups and saucers. He had never been so busy.

Danny and his mates had just turned up and soon joined the vibrant throng. Spotting Sandra, he winked over at her as he pushed his way through the heaving crowd towards the pinball machine. His gang of mates sniggered at her, but Sandra quickly turned her head away. Kenny had noticed the exchange but Cynthia, who was too busy lighting a cigarette, hadn't seen what was going on and Sandra was happy to leave it like that.

And then, gradually, The Moka started to empty. Two-stroke filled the air as scooter engines fired up and soon bikes were speeding off down the street, all with someone riding pillion.

Cynthia invited Kenny and his mates to go with her and Sandra to the cinema by tube, but only Kenny was up for that as the others had their bikes outside.

By the time the three of them had left Hammersmith tube station, Kenny was beginning to regret that decision as his ears now throbbed. He hadn't got a word in the entire journey due Cynthia and Sandra talking about the film, shouting above the rattling, all the way. He had known they were obsessed with The Beatles, but until he had spent time with them confined in that carriage, he really hadn't understood how deep it went. Blimey!

Thankfully for Kenny's ears, the Lyric Theatre in Hammersmith was only a short walk from the tube station. As they neared it, once again the smell of two-stroke filled their nostrils. Scooter after scooter was parked up along the street outside. Kenny, Cynthia and Sandra immediately joined the ever-growing queue of those eager to get in. As show-time got closer, all around them the volume rose as the excitement built. Even Kenny started to feel himself get swept up by it all.

Then, the noise of the bolts being pulled back momentarily silenced those at the front as the realisation hit them that it was nearly time.

Then the buzz returned, only louder - much louder - and as the rest of the queue cottoned on to what was happening, there came a surge forward from those behind.

The ancient commissioners, war veterans to a man, proudly displaying the medal ribbons on their black serge jackets, were simply not prepared for what was coming their way.

They were used to a more sedate and civilised theatre goer and, even the distant memory of Teddy Boys ripping up the seats and fighting as Bill Haley rocked around the clock, was a fast fading memory. No this was different. This was full-on hysteria they were now facing.

Thankfully, they just about had enough time to step to one side as hundreds of kids rushed by them up to the box office.

Elbows were flying all over the place, but Cynthia gamely stood her ground and insisted that she pay for Sandra and Kenny's ticket with the bonus money she had recently received from her granddad.

Sandra, skint anyway, smiled, nodded and thanked her best mate for her generosity. Kenny however, tried to decline. After all, Cynthia had already bought a coffee that evening and now it was his turn. Cynthia carried on without taking any notice of him. It was obvious to anyone who was boss here.

The theatre lobby was by now full of noisy chatter which mingled in with the smell of popcorn and hotdogs that had been quickly purchased from the various kiosks. Many others had raced straight through the auditorium doors and grabbed their seats.

Cynthia too was keen to get in position so, ticket tightly clenched in her left hand, charged forward, dragging Sandra and Kenny with her with her right hand. Once past the now very flustered usherette, she nimbly pushed her way past rows of legs already in seats, towards three empty spaces that she spotted. They were only ten rows from the screen. PERFECT!

As chaos ensued all around him, Kenny, a keen admirer of the architecture of old theatres, studied the faded glamour of the ornate decoration of this 19th century building. The girls though hadn't even noticed Kenny looking, let alone what he was looking at.

Sandra, now all settled in, produced a bag of her now familiar pear drops, quickly offering the bag to Cynthia and Kenny. Having taken one each, they were soon sucking the life out of her favourite confection.

The theatre had a capacity of five hundred and fifty seats and in the space of fifteen minutes since the doors had opened, they were all quickly filled. The noise of chatter and laughter was all encompassing.

The very few adults in attendance with some of the younger Beatles fans, held their hands tightly over their ears, trying desperately to get some peace from all those around them, but it was a pointless task.

A few cheers and shouts of 'oi oi' could be heard over the general din, as what looked like the cinema manager walked onto the stage. Gradually silence broke out, such was the conditioning of those who had been brought up on Saturday Morning Pictures.

The manager casually took out a folded piece of white paper from his left jacket pocket and, taking his time, carefully unfolded it. He coughed a couple of times, playing for time and complete silence from those now in front of him.

He had evidently planned-out this speech and he took his time with it, ensuring that he delivered every word with perfection. Soon though, people fidgeted about in their seats. They had come to see the greatest group EVER and not some doddery old silly sod, who was now boring them to tears as he went on about how long this cinema had been here and named some of the famous films that had been shown here over the years.

To break the boredom that was setting in and, also trying to contain the overwhelming building excitement within her, Cynthia grabbed Sandra's hand and dug her nails into her skin.

'Piss it!' hissed Sandra as she flinched trying to ignore the pain and, breaking out into a smile at her nutty mate.

Still our man cackled on and then, from out of the darkness, someone yelled…

'Come on mister, get on with it.'

Hundreds immediately giggled and laughed out loud. The manager strained his eyes, peering hard into the crowd trying in vain to see who the culprit was, but he knew he had no chance. Determined to complete his speech though, the manager pushed on but the heckles and whistles began to get louder and more frequent.

Slowly and, quietly at first, from the back of the stalls came…

'We Want The Beatles…We Want The Beatles…!' Louder and louder it became and soon 90% of the crowd was shouting it.

Eventually, the manager surrendered. He knew it was useless to continue. Sulking, he folded up his speech. He then turned towards the massive screen which was now in front of him, raised his arms and announced the words everyone wanted to hear.

'Tonight Ladies and Gentlemen, we are delighted to have the first screening of the film you ALL want to see. So, please put your hands together for the Beatles' first motion picture A HARD DAY'S ...'

Before he had got to the word 'Nighttttt', the crowd had simply gone mad, jumping up and down and screaming at the top of their voices. The sound was simply deafening.

Kenny visibly jumped as the wave of noise hit him. He looked at Sandra and Cynthia screaming for all they were worth. The theatre manager quickly scuttled off, his index fingers jammed into his ears.

The large red velvet curtains which had been hiding the screen, slowly and dramatically parted and, within a few seconds, the theatre was filled with the strike of the single chord that announced the arrival of the film.

"CCCHHWWANNGGGGGG!!!!!"

The distinctive opening chord to the song *A Hard Day's Night* filled the auditorium and startled some of the audience who visibly trembling in their seats, really struggling to contain themselves as the opening scenes of The Beatles being chased down the street and into Marylebone train station unfolded.

Laughter then broke out at the sight of Paul wearing a beard and at some of The Fabs hiding in the telephone boxes on the station concourse. Every time the camera settled on an individual Beatle for longer than a second, certain sections of the theatre screamed and cheered louder. Whenever it was George who popped up, Cynthia dug her nails deeper into Sandra's hand, a grimacing smile on her face and a scream lodged in her throat.

The cacophony continued throughout the entire opening credits and only slowly began to quieten when the film properly started and showed The Beatles sitting in the train carriage. Only when John spoke the first words of the film, 'Eh pardon me for asking, but who's that little old man' did the audience completely shut up. Seeing their faces blown up to an enormous cinema screen size had a strange, comforting effect on the crowd. Boyfriends held their girlfriend's hands, whilst others slowly snuggled into their seats.

Nothing, apart from regular burst of laughter, stirred in the theatre until emotions were once again aroused as the first song in the film begun. *I Should Have Known Better* broke loud and clear like a thunderbolt. Everyone who knew the song heartily sang along, as onscreen The Fabs played cards in the goods van of a train, overlooked by a bunch of schoolgirls which included the model Patricia Boyd.

Cynthia suddenly felt very pleased with herself that she had gotten her hair styled in the same way just the week before. She thought Patti looked great, and secretly knew she did too.

Memorable song after memorable song, spilled from the screen - *I Wanna Be Your Man*, *Don't Bother Me* and *All My Loving* among them and then a concentrated hush occurred as new songs were heard for the first time, tunes that would soon be featured on the forthcoming album and this is the way that *If I Fell* and *Tell Me Why* gained its first exposure to the masses.

Much laughter broke out as The Beatles were seen messing about on a sports field to the tune of *Can't Buy Me Love*. This was the best part of the film so far, for a lot of the audience recognised the humour that many knew was in the band.

Cynthia leaned over and whispered in Sandra's ear.

'I can't WAIT to buy this album, I have got to have it, the minute it is available.'

Sandra gleefully nodded back at her.

This was fast turning out to be the greatest week of their lives.

Kenny recognised familiar faces from the telly among the supporting cast. Wilfrid Brambell and Norman Rossington giving sterling performances. Brambell played Paul's granddad 'The very clean old man' John McCartney, with Rossington as 'Norm', the band's manager.

Perhaps the biggest laugh of the evening though came via Ringo's response to an interviewer when she asked him 'are you a mod or a rocker?' To which Ringo replied, 'Uh, no. I'm a mocker.' That had Sandra almost rolling about on the floor and trying not to choke on her ever-present pear drop.

All too soon it was over and the closing credits rolled in. Sniffles could soon be heard as tears flowed - the majority didn't want this to end. With hundreds outside already for the next screening, the usherettes busied themselves with getting the punters to leave the cinema.

As they left, there was excited chatter as to what they had just seen. A few acted out some of the scenes they had just witnessed. Others were stunned, silenced by it, as if it had been an almost religious experience!

In the street, a crowd of Moka regulars had formed outside a café opposite the Lyric. It was Kenny who spotted them first and he, Cynthia and Sandra went over to join them. Frothy coffees flowed, as did the conversations.

Amongst the crowd, Danny was heard saying that because it was still early, why not go to a nearby bowling alley he knew? Nods all round and quickly a group of 20 had formed and were following him towards it; Cynthia, Sandra and Kenny amongst them.

Bowling wasn't a sport that Cynthia or Sandra had much experience of, but on the few occasions that they had been, they had enjoyed themselves.

Cynthia once again demanded that she pay for Kenny and Sandra's tickets and once again their protests fell on death ears. Cynthia was in a great mood and wanted to share the good times with her mates. Money was exchanged for bowling shoes, which some of the boys had already whispered wouldn't be returned at the end of the night, and they made their way to their lane where The Moka crowd had gathered.

Amongst the sound of a bowling ball hitting the wooden pins and an occasional yell of 'strike', the topic of conversation was completely about The Beatles and thoughts were already turning to go and see it again and again and again.

'Can't wait,' said Sandra. 'That film went so quick, it was like a dream.'

As potential dates were being firmed up, shouting from behind them suddenly stopped them in their tracks. They looked up and saw a gang of around a dozen rockers, dressed in their trademark black leather jackets, heavy biker boots and white silk scarves hanging from around their necks. They were surrounding Danny.

Cynthia and Sandra rushed forward, along with the rest of their group to see what was occurring. One of the rockers was a tallish young man with blonde greased-back hair and a leather jacket covered in silver metal studs and enamel pin badges with the words 'Chelsea

Bridge Boys' painted onto it. He held Danny violently by his throat, up against a wall.

The remainder of Danny's gang and the rocker's gang stood frozen, eyeballing each other, waiting for someone to make the next move. It was evident there was going to be 'a sort out'. They just needed the sight of first blood to be drawn and they'd be off.

'I know you mate,' said the rocker. 'You're the one who tricked my sister!' The rocker was roaring at the top of his voice straight into Danny's face.

By this stage, Danny's eyes were bulging and, even if he wanted to reply he couldn't, so tight was the rocker's grip. He had begun to shape words with his mouth, but they simply didn't come out. The rocker pushed Danny harder against the wall, then he turned to address the crowd that had formed around him.

'See this little tosser. He was well out of order with my young sister. Weren't ya eh? Do you know what he done to get a hand-job off her?'

His own eyes bulged as he spat out the words. It was clear that he was furious and intent on inflicting pain onto the victim he had pinned to the wall.

Cynthia looked at Danny and instantly recognised an expression of guilt across his face. The rocker wanted to let everyone know what Danny had done before he unleashed his rage onto him, feeling the need to justify his impending behaviour.

The rocker then explained that about three weeks earlier, Danny had convinced his sister that he possessed a tie which had once belonged to John Lennon, and all his sister needed to do to own the tie herself was give Danny a five knuckle shuffle. He added slowly that his sister was only fifteen. Some of the girls in Cynthia's group gasped as they heard the rocker's revelation, although the boys seemed less concerned.

Sandra felt her own blood boil.

Suddenly, and quite cleverly, Danny managed to break free from the rocker's grip and, as he did so, he swung a right-hander in his direction. This landed with some force on the nose of the greaser. For a moment, the rocker was pushed off balance, but he soon steadied himself and set about sorting out Danny. And we were off …

Within seconds, Danny's friends had steamed into the rocker and his entourage. A scene of utter violence quickly erupted, with chairs being picked up and smashed down over heads. A couple of the slower-witted blokes attempted to pick up bowling balls to use as weapons, but quickly shelved that idea as they struggled to lift them above waist height.

After loads of huffing and puffing and only a few decent blows actually being landed, the bowling staff had intervened and got between the warring factions.

Within five minutes it was all over. The rockers believed they had won, but equally so did Danny and his mob. The reality was that no one group in particular stood victorious. The only things they had in common were the messed-up hair and bloodied noses. Sadly, it was a sour end to what had been a fantastic night.

Once home and back in her bedroom, a still slightly shaken Cynthia got undressed quickly and climbed into bed. Tonight, she wasn't even in the mood for Radio Caroline. She tossed and turned for the next hour, with thoughts of the film and the fight racing through her mind. She knew this was pointless and accepting that the Sandman wasn't going to be calling upon her anytime soon, she decided to get up.

She sat on the chair in front of her bedroom mirror and shifted some objects around on the dresser until she found a pencil and some writing paper and began to write a letter…

'Hi Patricia,

I hope you are well and thank you for your recent package. Fab!

And I hope you are enjoying listening to A Hard Day's Night. I bet it's great. I can't wait to get my own copy.

This week has been a roller coaster of emotions and experiences really. Sandra and I met two boys who seemed lovely at first. We went on a date with them but they turned out to be complete drags. We will not be seeing them again. It's so hard to find a boyfriend that comes up to scratch. My mother says I am fussy, but I don't think so. I suppose I do compare the boys I meet to George, which I know is silly, but I can't help myself. Is it the same for you and American boys…?'

Cynthia stared at her bedroom mirror and drifted off into a daydream. She imagined George and her walking through a field with yellow flowers in it. They weren't holding hands, but their hands would often gently brush against each other's. In the distance there was a castle and, above the castle, a new moon was in its waxing crescent formation…

The sound of one of her brothers, which she suspected to be John making a right racket down in the kitchen, rudely interrupted Cynthia's daydream. She shrugged her shoulders and pulled her nightie tightly around her. She continued with her letter:

'Anyway, Sandra and I went to the premiere of A Hard Day's Night at the London Pavilion, but don't get too excited, we didn't even catch a glimpse of the band. There were so many screaming girls it was horrendous. I have never seen so much smudged eyeliner. We were disappointed and even went to the Dorchester Hotel on a whim that there may be a possibility of seeing them there, but we didn't. But it wasn't a failed night ... not by any means. One of the boys from The Moka gave Sandra and I tickets to go and see The Beatles in Brighton!

Patricia, I am actually going to see The Beatles. How cool is that? I'm actually still in shock.

But wait, it gets even better, because tonight I went to see the film ... and it is the greatest film ever made. I do hope you get to see it soon. There is so much that I could say about the film. It's really funny. Our boys are wonderful actors and very funny. My George will win an Oscar I'm sure.

I was actually laughing and crying throughout the majority of the film. I'm going to go and see it again and again and again. I heard some of the new songs too, which only adds to my desperation of wanting my own copy of the new L.P as soon as possible. I just know I will listen to it over and over and over again.'

Cynthia had got so involved with writing her letter that any thoughts of the fight in the bowling alley had finally left her.

She opened a drawer and found some scissors, with which she set about cutting snippets from newspapers and magazines that she had been collecting, with the intention of sending to Patricia. By the time she finished she had a reasonable pile, all glorifying the arrival of The Beatles' new film and album.

Cynthia finished off the letter by telling Patricia that she would send her another one soon and would be letting her know everything about the Brighton concert.

She then signed off.

'Love from your UK Beatle person and friend, Cynthia x'

Cynthia's postscript mentioned the newspaper cuttings and she then shoved the letter and cuttings into an envelope and put it to one side; she would write the address on it in the morning.

She yawned, the feeling of tiredness finally hitting home and she got back into her bed, pulling the bed sheets up over her head.

It had been a Hard Day's Night indeed …

Chapter 7
You Can't Do That

Cynthia woke up early, her mind racing with what she thought was, without doubt, the greatest idea that she had ever had. This was no idle boast either, because Cynthia was one who spent many a night with a thousand wild and fantastic ideas charging through her mind like the flipping Light Brigade.

But this one - this one was perfect and she just couldn't wait to tell Sandra...

As usual, her working day would be in her granddad's shop and she enjoyed regaling him with everything about the events of her past few days. Well, almost everything. She decided to leave out the bowling alley incident as she didn't want her granddad to think she mixed with the wrong crowd. She really didn't want to worry him. Cynthia remembered all too well his reaction when he read the newspaper reports on the Mods and Rockers Bank Holiday riots. He huffed and puffed all day, mumbling that a stint in the Forces would 'set them hooligans straight and do 'em the world of good.'

Nobby enjoyed hearing of a young life being lived. His 'usuals' were all of a certain age and creatures of habit. Mrs Brown buying her crusty bloomer 'just the way' she liked her bread to be. Then there was Mrs Elphick with her usual four tins of sardines. The only surprise that week had been Mrs Daniels, who had surprised them all by buying TWO tins of tomato soup, instead of her usual one.

As long as Cynthia made endless cups of tea for him, he was happy to listen to her stories of the film premieres and such like.

Then, in came Mrs Agatha Reynolds, a white-haired old woman with more wrinkles on her face than a newspaper usually wrapped around a portion of fish and chips. Whilst paying for her sugar, flour and tin of treacle, she happened to mention that her Derek's Morris Minor was currently in the garage because it needed some repairs and was going to cost her a small fortune. She was still muttering and complaining as she left the shop. However, the mention of the Morris Minor triggered a memory for Nobby.

'Morris Minors eh?' he said somewhat absentmindedly. 'Do you remember your dad getting one of those Morris Minor 1000s Cynthia?'

The new model had only been production for a few months and Cynthia had just turned eight years old.

She did indeed remember it and was fascinated by its flashing indicators. It thrilled them to watch the indicators flash on and off and keep repeating.

'Yeah, remember it well Granddad. We had that picnic not long after,' she replied.

On that day in question, William was driving with Dot sat up front beside him and Cynthia sharing the rear seat, squashed up against her granddad, Andrew and John.

They drove out as far as Kent; not far from the town of Dartford. Once in the Garden of England they drove through country lanes and journeyed on until they happened upon a field which they decided would be a perfect place to sit and have their picnic. The hamper that Cynthia's mother had lovingly crafted earlier was carried to a shaded area below an old English Oak tree. Andrew and John shot off to explore a nearby wood, but resolutely refused to take Cynthia with them when asked by their mother, '*because she was a girl*'. So, as a special treat and an act of compensation, Cynthia was given the last homemade scone, which she gobbled down whilst smiling at her brothers; much to their disappointment.

Throughout the picnic, Cynthia's mum and dad played cards whilst they sipped at their lemonades. Cynthia spent most of her time playing dominoes with her granddad when she noticed that her parents had dozed off, her mum laying with her head on her dad's chest.

Cynthia looked at her mum, sleeping peacefully and looking like a little girl, not much older than herself.

'Granddad. What was Mum's wedding day like? asked Cynthia.

Nobby smiled and was more than happy to walk his granddaughter through his fond memories of that lovely day. The ceremony was at St Mary's church in Wimbledon and he told her how beautiful the bride had been. Nobby listed all of the guests who had turned out for the occasion. He then told Cynthia about how they all went to the function room attached to the pub opposite the church and how Cynthia's parents pretended to cut the cake, which was actually hired and made of cardboard, before everyone tucked into cheese and cucumber sandwiches and fairy cakes and then danced the night away.

He added that her parents disappeared about ten o clock but, realising where that conversation was going, stopped himself and instead told Cynthia that the following morning they went on their honeymoon which was a two-day trip spent in Bournemouth.

Cynthia then noticed that Nobby was also looking sleepy, so she decided to leave him alone and let him sleep.

It had been such a gloriously sunny day, one in some ways that the entire family didn't want to end, but finally the time came to pack away the picnic things and begin the journey home. Before the trek back into Wimbledon though, Nobby had bought everyone an Orange Maid from an ice cream van he spotted near to Dartford.

As Nobby re-focused to the present day, he seemed a little sad, muttering about it being a shame they didn't do things like that anymore. Cynthia tried to cheer him up by reminding him they would all be going on their summer holiday to Butlin's soon and thankfully that seemed to do the trick.

It was now midday and time for her lunch break. Sometimes she stayed there and read a magazine, but today Cynthia decided to go home to have her favourite cheese and pickle sandwich. She didn't really know why, but she felt compelled to go home.

As she approached her house, she noticed the postman walking away from her in the distance and, as she opened her front door, immediately saw an envelope addressed to her lying on the floor. Cynthia instantly recognised the envelope and quickly grabbed at it. All thoughts of that cheese and pickle sandwich she had promised herself was quickly forgotten as Cynthia raced up to her bedroom excitedly, with the letter tightly gripped in her hand. She dived onto her bed and tore at the envelope.

Once she had discarded of the manila packaging, she was now proudly holding the July issue of The Beatles Monthly. Receiving the official Beatle's fans' magazine was one of life's highlights. She had taken out a yearly subscription, so each month a copy would be sent to her and it was something she cherished and would pore over again and again, devouring every word. She would save the copies in a special box so that they could be kept safe.

As always, its contents were a surprise. Nobody outside the inner Beatles circle ever knew what would be in each month's issue, so there was always a great deal of excitement when a new edition came out. And from her first impressions of this July issue, this one wouldn't disappoint.

Cynthia couldn't wait to make a start on it and so carefully held the thirty-page magazine in her hand and began to read each word on the cover slowly, savouring every sentence.

The Beatles Monthly book, no.12 July 1964. Price one shilling and sixpence.

The first thing to catch her eye was a photograph of John Lennon. He was sat hunched over a piano, grinning a naughty 'I'm being sarcastic' grin, as he looked directly into the camera lens. Cynthia stared directly back at John. She always felt a girlish connection to him that she supposed was unique to herself and Lennon. It was built on the fact that John had married his teenage sweetheart, Cynthia Powell, two years earlier and, although they and The Beatles' management tried to keep the marriage a secret for fear of putting off his teenage girl admirers, virtually everybody she knew was already aware of their marriage.

Cynthia could feel the anticipation rising in her as she then turned the first page. She laughed out loud as soon as she saw the photograph of Paul McCartney sitting at a table with a large chunk of cheese in front of him. The caption read 'Paul, pictured in Holland, just about to make a determined attack on one of the local cheeses.'

Still laughing Cynthia began to read the editor's page written by Johnny Dean.

'Hi!' he wrote, 'There are now Beatle people in Europe, America, Canada, Africa, Australia, New Zealand, in fact all over the world.'

Cynthia felt great pride reading those words; she loved feeling like she belonged to something so special and amazing. Johnny continued to explain how difficult it was for the band to perform in everyone's hometown. He added that in the previous month The Beatles had flown over thirty thousand miles. As he excused them, he sort of apologised and asked them to...

'Put yourself in their shoes - or rather ankle boots - and imagine that YOU are a Beatle. What would YOU do?'

Cynthia found herself nodding sympathetically. Oh, how she wished she could have travelled with them on their mammoth aeroplane trip. Johnny then began to share some of the thinking behind making the *A Hard Day's Night* film and explained it was thought that if the band couldn't make personal appearances everywhere then the film could. This made perfect sense to Cynthia and she found herself reflecting on her experiences at the night of the premiere and then actually going to see the film in Hammersmith. The pen pals column got a mention, as did the announcement of a 'big new feature' which would be starting in the next month's issue and then Johnny Dean wished Ringo Starr a happy birthday for the 7th of July.

It was then the turn of the official Beatles fan club secretaries, Bettina Rose and Anne Collingham, who wrote a column each month. As ever, it opened with:

'Dear Beatle People.'

Cynthia loved being considered as one of them, it felt like a real club.

It continued *'July 1964 will go down in Beatle history as A Hard Day's Month!'*

Cynthia loved this play on the words. She even rubbed her hands together excitedly. She read on, savouring every word about the forthcoming Beatles tour and series of Sunday concerts at seaside resorts, the twice-yearly special free gift for fan club members and how important it will be to renew subscriptions to the fan club as soon as possible, so as to not miss out on future issues. Included in the secretaries' newsletter was a picture of John Lennon aged eight and a half and sitting beside some of his cousins. Cynthia let out a long 'ahhhhh' when she saw it and her heart skipped a beat.

Turning now to page number six, once again she laughed out loud, this time at the funny face Ringo was pulling as he held a teacup in one hand and a can of Pepsi in the other. She just knew that Sandra would be thrilled when she saw that! The accompanying feature was written by Billy Shepherd and was all about the Beatles on holiday. The author said that Paul and Ringo had gone on holiday to the Virgin Islands and John and George to Honolulu.

Cynthia lapped up every word as the author gave an account of 'what the boys had gotten up to' on their holidays. He informed that Paul and Ringo had gone fishing and the feature included some words direct from the Beatles themselves. Paul said:

'I remember taking the dinghy out to do some spear fishing. I had this clumsy old spear with me – honestly, it was big enough to catch whales.'

Cynthia lay back on her bed and tried to imagine Paul and Ringo fishing in the tropical waters. Ringo went on to say:

'Trust Paul to get into trouble. He even went out walking on the beach in his bare feet. That was real stupid. There were these cactus things all over the place, so naturally he got the spikes into his feet. Just call him 'Limpy'.'

Now completely forgetting the time and the hunger she was once suffering from, Cynthia came to the part which documented George and John's holiday. She was really looking forward to reading this. First, she read George's personal account of also having gone fishing, and then diving and having fun harpooning. John chipped in by telling his story of catching an octopus. Cynthia marvelled at the very thought.

George went on to talk about the fun he and John had had whilst they made 8mm cine films and how they had shocked the natives. It all sounded wonderful until Cynthia started to read George's account of nearly dying because of an incident that occurred whilst he was out water-skiing. Cynthia read the words with her mouth wide-open. She felt so relieved when she got to the end and George had reassured everyone that although it was a near miss he was in fact okay.

On the next page of the magazine there was a new photograph of George and Ringo. It was also the page of 'This Month's Beatle Song', which included the words to *Hold Me Tight*. Cynthia was still singing the words as she turned to the centre-spread, which was a two-sided photograph of Paul McCartney holding a teacup and grinning cheekily.

Cynthia was not so much reading this as devouring it and next up was the 'Letters from Beatle People' feature that Cynthia so looked forward to each month. She had sent in several letters herself for the attention of George, naturally, but, as yet, nothing had managed to get printed.

She read the letters from Evelyn from Glasgow; Susan from Dagenham and Jennifer from Newcastle-Upon-Tyne. But it was the letter from twelve-year-old Lynda from Sheffield and John Lennon's reply that made her chuckle the most.

'Dear John, I think all the letters on the letter page of this magazine are 'made up' by you and the other Beatles. In fact, I think you made this one up too! So prove me wrong.'

John answered, *'you're quite right Lynda. I also made up the other Beatles too. There's only one of us really!'*

The 'Following The Beatles' feature told the reader all about the Beatles tour which passed through Denmark, Holland, Hong Kong, Australia and New Zealand. Cynthia read how Jimmy Nicol, the replacement drummer for Ringo whilst he was in hospital suffering from a 'bad case of tonsillitis', had actually been mistaken by some people as being the real Ringo! She knew Sandra wouldn't understand that one!

There was also mention of riots at some shows and how the Beatles took a canal boat trip in Amsterdam and some fans jumped into the canal and tried to get on the boat. It also mentioned that John Lennon had been shocked at the way the fans had been manhandled by some of the police and he felt the need to protest about the matter. A photo showed George trying on a pair of clogs, she loved that one. The piece finished off by saying that Ringo had gotten better and had been discharged from the University College Hospital on 11th June and he went on to re-join his bandmates as soon as was possible.

The remaining pages of the magazine included addresses for 'Beatle pen pals'; more photographs of The Beatles; the names of the four competition winners and their prizes of a transistor radio and a Beatles letter would be posted out to them soon; 'The Beatles News page' and a 'Beatles bits you can buy' page.

Cynthia noted that there wasn't a single glossy print of George available in this current edition so she decided that she wouldn't buy anything from it this month.

Finally, she got to the end and the back cover showed the smiling face of Ringo Starr. She had never had tonsillitis herself, but she remembered when Sandra had had it and it was a most dreadful thing. Sandra was most upset that she had been banned from eating any pear drops for a whole month. Torture!

Cynthia laid the magazine down and lay still on her bed, just for a moment to churn over all the things she just read.

Yes, yes, yes…she just loved being a Beatle person.

Then suddenly - panic! What was the time? Noticing that her hour was nearly up, she upped and dashed back to the shop. Once there, she found her granddad sitting on an old wooden stool that he had made, puffing away quite happily on his pipe. Phew…the Fabs had nearly made her late.

***

Their working day over, Cynthia and Sandra met up as usual. Cynthia saw Sandra coming towards her clutching her own copy of that month's Beatles Monthly. She was really pleased that her mate had got hers too.

As soon as Sandra was close enough, Cynthia just couldn't wait to blurt the brilliant idea that had awoken her up that very morning. In fact, she spoke so fast, that Sandra initially struggled to keep up with what she was being told, but she eventually tuned in and slowly digested Cynthia's idea.

Sandra slowly smiled. She simply loved the idea of visiting all the locations included in the *A Hard Day's Night* film.

'One of your better ones, I'll give you that,' Sandra said cheekily.

'Pleased you said that,' said Cynthia, 'cos we start right now!'

Whilst it had been quiet in the shop, Cynthia had plotted the route for the locations, using her excellent memory and her granddad's old A-Z to write down the names of places she could recall that were included in the film.

On a bit of brown wrapping paper, she had written the name of The Scala Theatre and it was there they were to begin.

Throughout the train and tube journey to the West End, they talked really quickly about their personal favourite contents in the new Beatles monthly. Sandra was especially pleased that there had been a picture of Ringo on the back cover. Ringo, George, Ringo, George so the conversation went.

Getting off at Tottenham Court Road tube, they walked into crowds of commuters trying to make their way home. London at this time of an early evening was its usual vibrant self, full of excitement and promise. In truth, Sandra was actually more familiar with this immediate area, so on this occasion she took the lead.

Sandra told Cynthia about the Peter Pan pantomimes her grandmother used to take her to every Christmas for years at The Scala. They had both loved coming to this annual event and, even now, Sandra missed going, although she wouldn't have told too many people that.

So, hand in hand, Cynthia and Sandra walked along Oxford Street, ducking down into Rathbone Place which eventually joined up with Charlotte Street, where The Scala Theatre was waiting for them at number 58.

They stood in front of it and gazed up at the Victorian façade. Little did these two know, but this theatre had been in use since the eighteenth century and had undergone several refurbishments. It carried a reputation as being cold and unfriendly, and it certainly looked like that from the outside.

Cynthia and Sandra wondered why The Beatles had chosen it as the location? They guessed it was simply due to availability. There were advertising posters pasted on some of its walls, but it seemed there were no performances due on that night.

'So, now we are here what we going to do Cyn? What's the plan?' Sandra enquired.

'Well, we're going to find a way to get inside,' Cynthia replied boldly.

'What? In there?' Sandra wasn't feeling as confident as Cynthia. The building also appeared to be securely locked up and she didn't fancy breaking in.

'It doesn't look too inviting,' said Sandra somewhat warily.

'It'll be fine. We haven't come all this way just to stand here, have we? Come on you!'

Cynthia boldly walked up to the theatre's main doors and began banging her fists hard on them. They waited and they waited. No response. Cynthia tried again, with Sandra deciding to join her mate this time. They waited again, but once more there was no response.

'Piss it!' Sandra said, 'there's no one here Cyn. Looks like we'll have to come back.'

'Not giving up that easy are ya? There must be someone in. All we want to do is have a look around and see the stage where The Beatles were filmed. There must be a way in. Besides we'll only have to come back and I want to go to that Thornbury Fields before we go to Brighton.'

'To where?' asked Sandra. But Cynthia wasn't listening; she was too busy looking around to see where else she could gain entry.

Sandra couldn't really understand what the urgency was, but decided not to press the matter. Instead, she followed Cynthia who was already walking down the side of the building and about to turn into an alleyway. This part of the area surrounding The Scala obviously never got any sunlight as it was damp and, to be honest, had quite a pungent urine odour to it. Unbeknown to our two Beatle people, it was also a spot where many a brass 'entertained' a client in the dead of the night too.

Half-way along the alley, the girls noticed a chipped and weather-beaten green wooden door. There was nothing on it to indicate where it led. The two girls looked at each other and shuffled their feet as they loitered in front of the door for a few moments, before Cynthia puffed out her cheeks and gave the door one mighty old push.

To her surprise and, if she was honest, Sandra's disappointment, the door opened.

Cynthia tentatively stuck her head inside and had a look around. There was a shaft of light coming from somewhere above, so she was able to make out a narrow passageway directly in front of her, with a small light bulb glowing away which gave off a dim light leading the way down it.

There were boxes lined up along the passageway and at the far end there was a staircase. Cynthia looked at Sandra and beckoned her to follow. Sandra really didn't want to and was about to protest but Cynthia, sensing her best friend's reluctance, grabbed her by the arm and pulled her in with her. Sandra wobbled as she went through the doorway, but soon regained her balance.

They both now walked slowly and steadily down the badly-lit passage, trying to be as quiet as possible. Sandra couldn't really remember ever feeling so scared as at that moment.

Eventually, they could go no further, other than going up the stairs now in front of them in the shadows. They hovered at the bottom of the staircase, with even Cynthia now weighing up whether they should precede any further.

'Cyn, I'm really not sure we should go any further,' Sandra whispered.

'Sshh!' Cynthia replied, 'be quiet. I thought I heard something?'

'We don't even know if we are in the right building. We could be anywhere. I don't like this. I want to go home.'

'Will you sssh!' repeated Cynthia and, as she finished the shushing sound, Sandra froze as they both heard something in the distance.

'What was that?' Sandra whispered.

'Blimey. Don't know,' said Cynthia, 'but we are about to find out. Come on.' And with that she headed up the stairs towards the 'sound'.

Sandra started to tremble but with Cynthia half way up the stairs, she felt she had no option but to follow her friend; after all she couldn't let Cynthia do this alone and she didn't fancy being left behind. Several of the stairs they stepped on creaked loudly, which didn't exactly help in trying to keep quiet. By the time they had reached the top and the last step, both girls had beads of sweat forming on their foreheads.

They found themselves in front of another door. This one was clearly marked in hand-painted white words though.

'To The Stage'

They looked at each other, smiles breaking their faces in two.

'We've done it, we've only bloody done it,' said Sandra excitedly.

Cynthia had turned the door handle and pushed at it. The door creaked as it opened to reveal the inside of The Scala Theatre. They both eased forward and now walked on the outskirts of the stage. Directly in front of them were rows and rows of empty red velvet seats which sloped downwards and towards them on the stage.

Sandra suddenly remembered the various seats that she sat in during the Peter Pan pantomimes and her eyes darted about as she tried to locate where they were. The theatre looked pretty much as she remembered; nothing much had changed since its days as a popular music hall.

A few lights that had been left on, which allowed Cynthia and Sandra to get a sense of the size of the place.

'Wow, I can't believe it we are actually here, inside The Scala. The Beatles actually performed on *this very stage we are standing on*!' Cynthia's eyes lit up as she spoke.

She looked out into the auditorium and at the wooden seats and tried to imagine how wonderful it must have been one of the girls in the audience on the day they were filming. She looked at the large pillars and curved features on either side of where she stood. She closed her eyes and could visualise the demented girls in the film waving, crying, reaching out and tearing at their hair.

Our two brave girls were now grinning at each other, excited at the thought of treading the same boards on which the Fab Four had performed. Sandra frantically walked around trying to picture in her mind where Ringo and his drum kit had been positioned, whilst Cynthia explored every inch of the stage soaking up the thought of The Beatles having actually been *here*.

Cynthia turned again to look up towards the back of the different levels of seating now stacked in front of them.

'Come on Sand, we've got up there,' Cynthia said nodding out and up.

They ran down the steps at the side of the stage that took them to other steps which they could see led up to the first level. Cynthia went left and Sandra right. They both ran excitedly, giggling all the way. Once at the first level they ran to the middle row of seats and plonked themselves down, both instantly acting out scenes from the film, not having to try too hard to be hysterical girls. They were having a great time. At that moment, they really didn't have a care in the world.

They gazed down onto the stage and with frightening accuracy visualised the final scenes of the movie which was seared into their memory. They could imagine The Beatles on stage, all dressed in matching suits and launching into the jaunty '*Tell Me Why*' with Paul and George sharing a microphone, whilst John took command of the lead vocals as he waved his Rickenbacker up and down. The next song was the gentle rocker '*If I Fell*', this time the vocals shared by both Paul and John. Cynthia really loved this song.

Then '*I Should Have Known Better*', one of the sweetest songs ever written and a real toe-tapper. Cynthia recalled the little jig performed by George, and Sandra 'saw' Ringo's infamous head shaking like crazy. The last song performed by the band was '*She Loves You.*'

In the film, this was virtually drowned out by the onslaught of screams from the audience. Then Wilfrid Brambell appeared, rising from the stage's trap door and the song ends and the four Beatles take a bow, followed by an unexpected crazy legs dance from John Lennon. Being here, here where it all happened, brought it all back into sharp relief. The girls simply couldn't wait to see the movie again.

'This is great isn't it Sand?' Cynthia said.

'Yes, it is, it's magical. And we can tick off the first location on our list. What's next, where else are we going to visit?'

'Well, as I said, I think Thornbury Fields over in Isleworth should be next, you know where they did the running about in the film and, err and I want to go to Liverpool too.' Cynthia was suddenly dreaming of a trip far from home.

'What did you say? Liverpool!' Sandra couldn't really believe what she had just heard.

'Yes! Liverpool Sandra! Why not? I want to see where George went was born and went to school and the streets that he played in.'

'Blimey. Liverpool.' Sandra thought it was yet another great idea from her friend. She wished she could come up with such imaginative ideas. She too would like to see visit places relating to Ringo's personal story. She had always wanted to visit the Cavern Club too.

'Let's go tomorrow,' Cynthia suggested.

'Go where? Liverpool?' said Sandra somewhat startled.

'No, you daft wotsit, to Thornbury Fields. Look, let's both take the day off work. *A Hard Day's Night* will be in the shops tomorrow. Both our copies should be available to be picked up from Woolies. We could take my records back to mine, play it and then we could go and visit Thornbury Fields.'

'But we're supposed to be at work Cyn,' Sandra sounded confused.

'Phone in sick. Come on, you haven't had to get a doctor's sick note for ages. And I'll ask my granddad for the day off; he won't mind, especially after I tell him why.'

Sandra was tempted but unsure. She sensed Cynthia's eyes burning into her.

How could she refuse, besides Cynthia's plan was perfect. They could pick up their albums in the morning, listen to them, then go to Thornbury Fields. It would take a while to get there but they could do it and still be home for their tea.

'You know what? I will. I'll throw a sickie. Let's do it. It's a FAB idea.'

Cynthia laughed and squeezed her friend's hands warmly. Sandra rifled into a bag in her pocket and produced two pear drops. Both girls popped one into their mouths and sunk deep into their seats and their daydreams.

Suddenly, a loud booming cockney voice woke them from their contentment.

'Oi! What the bleeding 'ell do you think you are doing? Eh?'

The girls seized up. They were literally too frightened to move. Neither could say a word or turn their head, but they could sense man moving closer towards them.

He started again as he got closer. He was towering over them, shining a torch into their now panicking faces. He was dressed in a pair of old tattered dungarees, which Cynthia thought meant he was the caretaker or something like that. Well, she hoped he was…

'Who are ya? Eh? You know you ain't supposed to be in here? How the bleedin' 'ell did you manage it?'

'We, we, we just, sorry, we just…' Cynthia tried to explain.

The man screwed up his nose and frowned. 'Stone me…I know girly, I know,' he said, 'you're here because of those bloody mop tops aren't ya? You are the flipping third lot this week.'

'We're sorry sir,' said Sandra, 'we meant no harm. We just wanted to have a look around. We did knock on the front door, honest we did. We haven't caused any damage sir.'

Cynthia then tried fluttering her eyelashes.

'Got something in your eye love?' asked the man, working out exactly what she was doing. He liked the fact that Sandra had a called him sir; bit of respect that was. Not a bad pair of kids it appeared he thought. As it happened, ever since the filming back in the spring, The Scala had been frequented daily by Beatles fans. He had got used to the odd interruption.

Suddenly there was a silence. The man could see that Sandra was on the verge of crying and that he couldn't tolerate.

'Look missy,' he said kindly, 'don't worry, you're not in trouble. I'm the caretaker for the place. Tell you what, do you want me to show you round? Only if you promise not to tell my guvnor mind?'

Both the girls grinned broadly.

'Thought as much. Would you like to see the dressing room where The Beatles changed before they went onto the stage?'

Cynthia and Sandra couldn't believe their ears. Sandra dabbed at her eyes with a tissue.

'Yes, yes we certainly would. That would be ever so kind of you,' Cynthia chirped.

'All right then, follow me. It'll cost you a pound each,' he added somewhat abruptly.

Both girls were a little shocked at first to hear him say that, but then thought they were not going to pass up the opportunity of having a look around the changing room in which The Beatles had actually taken off their clothes.

Besides, it seemed a small price to pay not to annoy the nice old man any further, so they dipped into their respective purses and each gave him a pound note. The caretaker quickly thrust the green notes into his right trouser pocket and led them back down towards the stage and through a narrow gap which led to an even narrower passageway and a doorway.

Stopping to inform the girls that the changing room was behind the door, he motioned for the girls to squeeze past him, which they did, and catching a whiff of his breath as they did so. It reeked of stale beer and cigarettes.

Sandra screwed up her face. 'Urgggh,' she said as quietly as she could.

'Right, stand there, with your backs to me,' he commanded.

They did as requested. He then suddenly came up from behind them, pushed the door in front of them open and then shoved the girls through it. Before they realised what was happening, the door slammed shut behind them and they found themselves standing back on Charlotte Street. The man had fooled them - and taken their money.

'Piss it!' Sandra screamed whilst Cynthia turned and kicked at the door she had just come through. It certainly didn't help that they could hear the man laughing from behind it.

'Rotten old basket,' hissed Sandra loudly. 'Did you hear me, you're a rotten old sod!' The caretaker just laughed louder.

The two glared at the door and, in that moment, they didn't know whether they wanted to laugh or to cry.

'Come on,' said Cynthia with a resigned look on her face, 'let's go home.'

They began a slow stroll, arm in arm, back towards Tottenham Court Road tube station. They had only walked a few yards when Cynthia got a waft of a sweet, fragrant odour that she had definitely smelled before. She slowed her pace and, as she did so, an old-looking man wearing a brown overcoat, with a flat-cap pulled down hard on his head which hid the majority of his face, ambled past them.

'Evening girls, turned out nice again,' he said in a strange 'trying to be posh' accent.

Sandra looked confused and frowned while Cynthia stopped and simply watched the man walk off into the distance. It was only when he was out of sight that Cynthia remembered what the odour was.

'Bibby and Son! That was the smell of Bibby and Son soap,' she said turning to Sandra.

Sandra shrugged her shoulders; she had no idea what her mate was going on about.

'Come on Cyn, enough's enough. My dogs are barking and that caretaker has given me the right pip. I want to get home.'

On towards the tube station they went and, although upset at the way it had turned out in the end, they both knew they had seen more of the theatre than they expected and it had been fun whilst it lasted. They also knew they could have got into a lot more trouble at The Scala than they did. One good thing though - at least they could tick off one of the *A Hard Day's Night* locations from their list.

And on top of that, Friday was around the corner. All Sandra had to do was make sure she got a doctor's certificate.

Cynthia's thoughts returned to the man and the smell of soap. She couldn't get him out of her mind for some reason.

'No,' she thought silently, 'it can't have been…can it?'

Chapter 8
When I Get Home

The next morning Cynthia woke from a night's sleep that seemed to have been filled with dream after dream after dream. She was still in the middle of the most pleasant one, which naturally featured the lovely George, when the tapping on her bedroom door interrupted it. Her dad was not so subtlety reminding her that it was time to get up.

In that strange half-awake/half-asleep moment, Cynthia tried her uttermost to hold onto to it for as long as she could. For some reason, which was not immediately clear, George was sucking a lollipop whilst riding a white horse. And then, he was gone and she was wide awake.

As her eyes opened, she was feeling warm inside and a big smile was on her face. Today, she just knew, was going to be a good day and she was ready for it. She began to map out the day as she lay there. In an hour she would be meeting Sandra, usual spot, and then precisely (and she had timed it) twenty minutes after that, they would be at the local Woolworths just as it opened, where they would descend upon the record counter and collect their *A Hard Day's Night* LPs already pre-ordered weeks earlier.

Once up, Cynthia made her way downstairs and entered the kitchen. John was sat at the table sipping at a cup of tea whilst smoking a cigarette. His suit jacket hung on the back of his chair and his black and white spotted tie was folded neatly on the table. With his shirtsleeves rolled up and grease on his hands, he didn't look in the best of moods. Cynthia glanced at the kitchen clock to double-check the time.

'You ain't half got a face on you. What you still doing home anyway?' Cynthia asked.

'Sodding scooter broke down on the way in this morning. I had to push the bleeding thing home,' John moaned.

Cynthia couldn't help but break into a small smile.

'You taking the day off then?' she asked. 'You had a day off last week as well didn't you? Dad will have a moan up you know.'

John looked at her blankly and couldn't even be bothered to reply; he simply lit another cigarette and was doing his best to ignore his irritating little sister. His current nocturnal lifestyle of pills, thrills and bellyaches was one he worked hard at keeping secret and out of the ears and potential scrutiny of his family, especially his younger sister.

'Do me a favour - fill that up will ya?' John held out his teacup, suddenly breaking his silence. Cynthia, somewhat grumpily, poured some tea into it.

Cynthia then tried a new approach.

'So, what you and your mates doing this weekend? Are you gonna go to the Palais? And maybe the fete?'

John winced at the F word.

'Out tonight, yeah, but we'll avoid the fete I think,' he said John dismissively.

'Why? It's normally a good laugh. You've never missed one before.'

'I'm going out tonight and don't expect I'll be home until late. So, I don't think I'll fancy a day hanging about Wimbledon Common tomorrow.'

Cynthia looked a little pained, which John noticed. 'I suppose you've got to go to the fete, haven't you?'

'Yeah, Sandra and me said we would help out on the white elephant stall again. St. Mary's are still trying to raise enough cash to fix their bloody roof. We've only got to do a couple of hours though. Not so bad.'

Cynthia had helped at the fete since she was a kid and always enjoyed it. But this year she felt different, like it was a bit of a nuisance and as though she had outgrown it.

She then slid onto one of the chairs around the table and took a sip of her own tea.

John looked her way. 'I suppose you'll be going to pick up the new Beatles LP wont ya? Heard it was out today.'

This brought an instant smile to her face. 'Sure am. I'm meeting Sandra in a bit.'

'What about work?' John enquired.

'I'm going to ask Granddad for the day off. He will be all right. He'll understand that I'll want to play the LP straight away.'

John laughed, 'Cheeky...' He then stubbed out his cigarette in the bevelled-edged glass ashtray that lived in the kitchen and stood up.

'Right, I've got to fix my flipping scooter. Told work I'll try to get in as soon as possible. Besides I'll need it for tonight. Ta la then kid,' he sighed as he exited the kitchen.

Cynthia buttered some bread and smothered some honey onto it and ate it quickly. Now she had woken up a bit, her thoughts were hurtling towards what lay in store for the day ahead of her.

Washed, dressed and off to meet Sandra, Cynthia stopped by her granddad's shop to ask if she could have the day off. She found Nobby pouring some loose-leaf tea from one large bag into a much smaller one.

'Morning Granddad. Lovely day isn't it? It'll be just perfect for the fete tomorrow, if it stays like this.'

'Hello Cynthia. It certainly is and it certainly will. Mind you, I can't remember the last time it rained on the day of the fete.'

Cynthia then watched her granddad search his memory of a rainy day at the fete.

'Put the kettle on then lovely?' he said as he quickly abandoned the search.

Cynthia shuffled on the spot a little.

'Ah, well, actually Granddad I haven't really got time.'

Nobby continued to handle the bags of tea and Cynthia could sense her granddad was waiting for the next part of her conversation.

'The thing is,' Cynthia continued, 'I, er, I need to go and get something from Woolworths.'

'Oh yeah? And what is so important that you have to go and get it today then?'

Cynthia could sense her granddad was teasing her slightly. Cynthia, however, didn't have time for games.

'Well, you know I told you the other day that the new Beatles LP is coming out? Well, I need to go and collect my copy from Woolworths TODAY!'

Nobby, already feeling playful, decided he wasn't going to make it easy for his granddaughter, even though he knew he'd be agreeing to allow her the time off.

'Well I should have thought it would have something to do with those Beatles lads. But can't you just go and get it on Saturday lovely?'

'NO! No, I can't Granddad, that just won't do,' said Cynthia dreading the thought.

'So, you have to go and get it today? And why is that?'

Cynthia snapped straight back and began to talk really quickly.

'Because it's the most important thing in my life. It's very, very important that I get my copy of the new LP today. It can't wait until Saturday. No, I have to have it today. I HAVE to hear the new songs.'

Nobby, his back now to Cynthia, smiled broadly. He finished handling the bags of tea and then set about stacking some tins of Carnation milk on some shelves.

'Well, it goes right over my head you know; I have never known anything like it. The way you and your friends go on about that group mystifies me, it really does.'

He then turned to face his granddaughter.

'Come on, tell me, what is it all about? Explain it to me?'

Cynthia checked the time on the clock behind the counter. She knew had to get a move on. She took a deep breath and then spoke even quicker.

'I do understand that your generation had less than us. I mean you have had wars, you've had rationing and you probably didn't have much to look forward to, but my generation is different. I mean, we have pop music. We have radio stations that play *our* music, songs from groups where the people playing the music are like us. They are teenagers, they dress like us, use the same language, dance like us. We all watch the same films and go to the same dances and we want to discover and explore and have adventure.' She took a breath and then gasped '...and I have to have my new Beatles LP today Granddad.'

Nobby smiled and then leaned in to give his granddaughter a hug and kissed her on the forehead.

'Do you really think it was so very different for me and my generation?' he asked as he gave her a knowing smile. He had no intention to refuse, he knew he couldn't. He knew how important The Beatles were to her and he wasn't going to deny her the opportunity to enjoy herself; he loved her too much for that. He sent her on her way with a few coins he fished out from his pocket, telling her she could get something nice to eat for her lunch.

Cynthia ran out of the shop, arriving at their usual bench on the Common with a few minutes to spare whilst waiting for Sandra. She took a minute to gaze around her.

Ever since she could walk, Cynthia had played on Wimbledon Common. The thousand-acre Common had been a gathering place for generations. She had fond and happy memories of spending

107

weekends running all over it, climbing trees, running around the windmill and generally just getting up to all sorts of mischief. In recent years, it had seen its fair share of punch-ups with the boys from the Putney side fighting with the boys from the Wimbledon side.

In some cases, family vendettas raged on, being passed down from brother to brother. John had taken a nasty beating when he was fifteen. It transpired that he started to date a girl from the Putney side but her older brother wasn't having any of it and beat John up in protest. The relationship, not surprisingly, ceased soon after that.

Cynthia's favourite spot, when she was a kid, was near the Beverly Brook. She liked being around water; it seemed to her to be teeming with all sorts of weird and wonderful little creatures. Cynthia enjoyed the bog area too because the flowers were always stunning and she liked to watch the boys searching for stag beetles there.

Every July, the Common hosted the Wimbledon annual fete. It was partly organised by the local St Mary's church and partly by the local council. When they were around ten years old, Sandra had asked Cynthia if she would go to the Sunday school club with her one week. Cynthia agreed because Sandra sold it to her on the basis that all the children got free biscuits. Indeed, they did receive a biscuit each, but also an invitation to help out on the white elephant stall at the forthcoming fete. They had taken the bait and now didn't feel they could refuse. That was six years ago and they were still getting the yearly invites which they felt they couldn't avoid. One last year maybe, Cynthia thought daydreaming...

'Come on then missus, Woolies will be open soon,' said Sandra excitedly.

Cynthia hadn't even noticed her friend crossing the Common because she had been so engrossed in her own reflections.

'Well you seem excited. Go alright at the doctors then?' Cynthia asked.

Sandra had already begun to wave her doctor's note in the air like she had won the pools.

'The queue was bleeding long as usual and that woman who works on the reception was her usual rude self. I had to sit in the waiting room for over half an hour with lots of others who were either coughing, choking, mumbling to themselves or groaning. I hate doctor's waiting rooms, they're full of ill people. I weren't half pleased to see the doctor. I did my dying swan act, gave him some old tosh about a stomach ache, he bought it and I got out as fast as I could.'

'Well done you. Pleased to say I didn't have any trouble getting some time off with my granddad. He even gave me a couple of bob for my dinner.'

'Of course he did. He's lovely your granddad; thinks the world of you. Right, come on then, I can't wait to get my hands on that LP.'

Cynthia smiled and was soon linking arms with Sandra and marching her off towards town. As they approached Woolworths on the high street, they saw its large glass doors already open and a dozen young girls who had been in the queue outside, bundled into the store. Cynthia and Sandra obviously hadn't been alone in pre-ordering the new album. They charged forward like the other girls but unfortunately only managed to position themselves towards the back of the slowly moving queue. Cynthia had to scold Sandra for asking if they could go via the pick 'n' mix en-route to the record counter.

The front of the queue had reached the record counter, which wasn't yet open. Cynthia and Sandra stood with their arms folded; they just wanted to collect their own copies of the LP and then race back to Cynthia's to listen to them. A new Beatles release was always an occasion for them now. Even though there were other bands that the girls liked, like Gerry and the Pacemakers for Cynthia and The Searchers for Sandra, no other group was felt about quite the same way as The Beatles. They were simply special in a way they couldn't even describe most of the time.

At last, the collection point opened and one by one the girls shuffled forward. The woman serving only had one speed, which was slow. Eventually, Cynthia and Sandra handed over their receipts and collected their own vinyl, handed to them in brown paper bags with a curt 'thank you'. In seconds, they were out of the shop and racing back to Cynthia's bedroom.

As they arrived, they found John still trying to fix his scooter. Sandra said hello as she stepped over him as he lay on the floor, his oily hands in amongst the machinery. John didn't hear her. They bolted in through the open back door and headed straight for the Dansette in Cynthia's bedroom.

Both girls crashed to the floor and hastily removed their LPs from the paper bags. They studied the front cover, slowly absorbing every detail on the faces of their idols, with Cynthia immediately being drawn to the images of George, and Sandra to Ringo.

Sandra pointed to the image of George with his back to the camera, as if searching for an answer. Cynthia simply shrugged her shoulders then slid the vinyl from its protective sleeve and carefully placed it onto the record deck. Both girls shivered with excitement.

The initial crackles and pops were soon replaced by that now familiar clang of the strident opening chord of the first song on side one - '*A Hard Day's Night*'. Both girls had heard the song many times before, but playing it from the LP was like listening to it with fresh ears. They heard the bongos and cowbell and heard George's twelve-string Rickenbacker guitar in a new light, and they loved the way the song really did seem to push itself along. Even the arpeggio guitar outro sounded different to them.

Then, both girls lit-up as the sound of John's harmonica introduced *I Should Have Known Better*, another song they remembered from the movie. Everything was perfect. George's strumming, Paul's plucky bass and Ringo's drums. What more could they want? This was another example of a Beatles feel-good song.

The third song, the ballad *If I Fell* then started and Sandra and Cynthia lay on their backs and enjoyed being carried along by Paul's sentimental love song.

'Lovely that, innit Sand?'

Cynthia's thoughts turned to one day lying in the arms of a lover, someone like her George and listening to the song and sharing a special moment.

The tempo then speeded up with the arrival of *I'm Happy Just to Dance With You*. Cynthia had been waiting for this song because she knew it was the only one on the LP where George sung the lead vocal. Soon, she melted inside. Sandra simply loved the way Ringo drove the song along.

Whilst *And I Love Her* played, Cynthia and Sandra stole some time to have a read of the words on the LP sleeve. They already knew that this was the first LP on which John and Paul had written every song and they knew it was produced by the brilliant George Martin. They also noted it had been recorded in the Abbey Road Studios; another location they had added to their list of places to visit.

The rock and roll roots of *Tell Me Why* focussed Cynthia and Sandra's attention and they couldn't stop themselves clapping along to the song. They were still clapping vigorously when the last song on side one, and the last of the songs which had been included in the movie, *Can't Buy Me Love*, began. This was another hand clapper, aggressive at times and totally breath-taking. The girls knew the song well and, not being able to control themselves, leapt up and started to dance energetically around Cynthia's bedroom.

Only on the last note did the girls collapse to the floor again, out of breath, but feeling elated. Whilst Cynthia quickly turned over the record, Sandra rummaged through a nearby pile of Beatles merchandise that Cynthia had been collecting over the past year. There was an apron, adorned with the Fabs that would never make it as far as the kitchen; a jigsaw; some miniature Ringo drums; and even an unopened packet of Beatles chewing gum. She also found the Christmas card that she had given Cynthia the previous Christmas, where she had written the words '*Cynthia have a very happy chrimble and a gear new year.*' But it was the collection of Beatles wigs and the way Sandra placed all four onto her head at the same time which created the biggest smiles.

Sandra was still wearing the wigs when *Any Time At All* opened side two of the album. This was another catchy rock and roll tune that the girls instantly fell in love with.

I'll Cry Instead and *Things We Said Today* basically brought tears to the girls' eyes. Paul's sombre lyrics on *Things We Said Today* had really stirred them up.

When I Get Home burst forward without any warning and was another song where George got to show off his skills on his new Rickenbacker and Cynthia adored the way he played his 'jangly' guitar.

It was perfect and led nicely into *You Can't Do That*. Cynthia and Sandra pretended to play along; Cynthia on the cowbell and Sandra on the bongos. There was certainly something about the way the groove of the song seemed to drag along. And then it was time for the final song - *I'll Be Back*. Of this, both Cynthia and Sandra were certain they would be; they couldn't imagine their worlds without The Beatles in it.

The last song hadn't even faded completely before Cynthia picked it off the Dansette and had spun it over once again. They listened to both sides of the LP in its entirety twice more and hardly spoke to each other as they did so. There was the occasional outburst of head shaking and pretend playing of various instruments, but mainly their concentration focussed on John and Paul's singing and the lyrics. They knew it wouldn't be long until they memorised every word of every song, knowing them inside and out.

They could of course spend the rest of the day playing *A Hard Day's Night* over and over again, and, for a minute or two they did consider it as an option, but Sandra managed to persuade Cynthia that they should stick to their original plan and go and visit Thornbury Fields. Cynthia played *Can't Buy Me Love* one last time before they headed out though.

They travelled by train at first and then by bus and the journey to Isleworth seemed to drag, even though the talk about *A Hard Day's Night* for most of the way helped to pass the time. Sandra was glad that she had stocked up on pear drops.

Richmond was about as far West as Sandra had ever ventured, so being this far out added to her sense of adventure. Cynthia had a relative who lived in Hounslow and knew that wasn't too far from Isleworth. However, she hadn't visited the relative in years and wasn't even sure if they were still alive.

It was Sandra who spotted the bus stop where they needed to get off. They were the only passengers to alight here and hummed *Can't Buy Me Love* as they head off in the direction of the Thornbury Fields which was plainly in sight.

They strolled down a street which appeared to run parallel to where they wanted to be. It was Cynthia who noticed an alleyway that suggested it might lead to the fields. They took the chance but eventually found themselves standing in front of a tall metal fence. Through the gaps in the fence they could see the concrete square area that had featured in the movie.

'Piss it, where's the bleeding entrance?' Sandra cried. It hadn't occurred to them that the part of Thornbury Fields they wanted might be private property.

'Bleeding typical! We'll we haven't come all this way to have to turn back,' Cynthia replied, already formulating a plan.

Sandra could see her friend going through the motions and it worried her, especially after their recent Scala Theatre incident.

'Come on,' Cynthia said pushing past Sandra and following the fence alongside the field. Eventually Cynthia found what she had been looking for - a section of the fence that had been damaged. She had remembered that all fences have sections that have been trodden down or ripped open by kids.

Sure enough, the gap they found was just big enough for her to get through, but Sandra being a little bit bigger, had a real struggle to create a bigger gap to eventually crawl through.

Once they were both through, large grins formed on their faces and then they both ran off in the direction of the concrete area. As they reached it, they both went through the motions of mimicking what they had seen The Beatles do in the film. They jumped and leapt around like mad people; Sandra even copied Ringo's comical little jumps. Cynthia then lay on the floor and Sandra pretended to 'put the boot in'. It was all great fun.

Sandra spotted the running lanes and they raced towards them, each choosing a lane and then charging down it, just like they had seen the Fabs do. They hardly got half way down, when they completely stopped from laughing so much.

Returning to the concrete area, Sandra fell to the floor pretending to be dead like Ringo had done. An equally exhausted Cynthia collapsed beside her and they lay on their backs with the crowns of their heads touching each other. They gazed up into the beautiful clear blue sky above them; the sun's warmth on their tired faces felt wonderful.

They lay in silence simply daydreaming about The Beatles until Cynthia pushed herself up onto one arm and peered down at Sandra. Sandra, shielding her eyes from the sunlight, saw 'that' look in her friend's face; she could almost see the cogs in Cynthia's brain formulating a brand-new idea.

'I've had an idea and it's the best yet!' Cynthia announced looking extremely pleased with herself.

Sandra had heard that before. 'Here we go again,' she sighed. 'Okay, and what is it?'

Cynthia said, 'Let's make it our mission to get our copies of *A Hard Day's Night* autographed by all The Beatles?'

Sandra pushed herself up so she rested onto her elbows.

'Yeah right…and just how we gonna do that?'

'Well, we'll take our albums with us to Brighton and we'll try to get them to sign them there and if not then, well, we will go to the Blackpool concert, and then we'll go to Liverpool. You know how much you want to go Liverpool and see the places where Ringo was born and went to school and then there's The Cavern. We will take our LPs there and we will track the Fabs down. They don't go to Stockholm until the 28th July so they might go back to Liverpool to see their families. It's worth a try. Oh, come on Sand, let's do it. Let's agree to make it our mission. I want my LP autographed by George, Paul, John and Ringo…don't you?'

'Nice idea Cyn and wonderful if it could be done, but I think it's nearly impossible. Besides, I can't afford all of that travelling.' Sandra was sad to have to sound like a killjoy.

'Excuses, excuses, don't worry about that. I'll pay for the travel expenses and B&Bs with the bonus money that my granddad gave me and I'm sure he'll let me have a few days off work if I ask him nicely. We can go to Liverpool soon after Brighton.'

Cynthia wasn't in the mood to take no for an answer.

'But I have to go to work Cyn,' Sandra said seriously.

'Oh come on, you are due some holiday time from that agency aren't you?'

Sandra looked concerned but, yes, she was due some time off. Besides, she could see she wasn't going to win this one with Cyn and she truly did like the idea. Blimey, it would be her prized possession to have her copy of *A Hard Day's Night* autographed by all of The Beatles.

She thought for a few seconds more and then declared, 'I'll do it!'

As the words left her mouth, they heard a man shout at them very authoritatively.

'I suppose you realise this is private property!'

***

Cynthia arrived home just as a forlorn-looking John was pushing his scooter into the garden shed. He had a face like thunder and hands like a bad mechanic; full of cuts and abrasions and smothered in black shiny oil. Cynthia stepped over the tools he had yet to clear away and walked into the kitchen; she knew it was best to avoid him. Her mother was just serving up plates of fish and chips - it was their Friday tradition. Cynthia's dad joined them at the kitchen table, closely followed by John, who had wiped his hands a little cleaner before using them to shovel his tea into his mouth, making him instantly feel better.

Cynthia dominated the mealtime chat by the telling them all of the events of her day from the moment she collected her copy of *A Hard Day's Night*. Both of Cynthia's parents gave her their full attention.

John was less interested in truth. Cynthia wasn't sure how her parents would react to her idea, or even if they would be okay with the notion, but she was building up the courage to ask. She waited until the homemade rice pudding was being served up and then approached the subject.

'Mum…Dad…Do you think I'm quite grown-up for my age?' she started.

William and Dot didn't look up from their rice puddings. John, however, lifted his gaze, winking in Cynthia's direction.

'It's just that I have made some plans that I would like you to agree to.'

Still nothing!

'Would it be okay if Sandra and me went to Liverpool for a few days? Well, actually, Liverpool and one or two other places. We really want to get our LPs autographed and we believe that if we go to Liverpool we have a decent enough chance. I have some money saved up and Granddad gave me a little bonus the other day.'

Cynthia's father finally looked up and turned to his wife, before returning to his rice pudding. Cynthia glanced at her mother, who seemed to take her time chewing the last mouthful of rice pudding.

Finally, she spoke. 'And this plan, does it include anyone else? Are you sure it's only to be you and Sandra?'

'Yes of course, no one else,' Cynthia replied, taking a while to understand what her mother was suggesting.

John stifled a giggle.

'Just me and Sandra,' Cynthia huffed, as the penny dropped.

'Well, it depends what your father thinks,' said Dot, quickly passing the buck. She really didn't have any concerns about her daughter's intentions. In fact, she quite liked that Cynthia had an adventurous spirit; just like she had had when she was fifteen.

Cynthia put down her spoon and stared hard at her father. He could feel her eyes boring into his forehead. He had already made up his mind; he had no concerns for the safety of his daughter. He knew he could trust her and had decided years before that he would encourage her adventurous spirit. He finished his mouthful of rice pudding, looked up and smiled.

'Course you can go girl. Just be careful.'

And that was that. Cynthia grinned back at her father and then her mum, thanked them both and then stuck her tongue out at John. She offered to do the washing up, which she did quickly, before racing to the telephone and ringing Sandra to tell her the good news.

Cynthia felt like she was really growing up. She was also pleased that they considered her sensible and responsible enough to even embark on such an adventure, and still a few months from her next birthday.

It was John who heard the Ready Steady Go theme tune playing from the telly which had been left on in the front room. Hastily, he gobbled up the last mouthfuls of his dinner before rushing into the living room and leaping onto the sofa. Bang on 6pm, show time!

Before the sound of Manfred Mann singing '54321' had finished and Ready Steady Go's slogan 'the weekend starts here' had faded, Cynthia had also joined her brother on the sofa. She had only recently started to watch the show on a regular basis, but John wouldn't miss a single Friday. Week after week he lapped up the music which the bands performed and scrutinised what the folk in the audience were wearing and how they danced. Cynthia was now finding that she too was starting to take a new level of interest.

This Friday's episode was of special importance to Cynthia, however, because the guest for this week's show was former Beatle, Pete Best. Cynthia had been keeping a keen eye on Best's career since he had left The Beatles and started his own group - The Pete Best Combo. She hoped he would still make it in the music business.

She loved the dancing too and marvelled at the moves performed by resident dancers, Patrick Kerr and Sandy Sarjeant. Kerr was a handsome man, dark hair, slim and he always seemed to smile whilst he danced. He also had had a great hip moving technique. Sarjeant, with her delicious long dark hair, pretty face and her strikingly high cheekbones, was simply meant to be a dancer; she was a natural mover. Both had been responsible for introducing and then teaching many of the nation's youths new dances, such as the Hitchhiker or the Block, over previous weeks on the show.

Both presenters, the elegant Cathy McGowan and the formal Keith Fordyce were also becoming TV stars in their own right. They were an unlikely pairing, with McGowan beautiful and young with her shoulder length dark hair and fashionable clothes. She had been given

116

the job after answering an advert asking for 'a typical teenager', even though at the time of making her first appearance on Ready Steady Go she had turned twenty-one. She was hip, stylish and didn't shy away from being called the Queen of the Mods. Fordyce, on the other hand, was much older than McGowan and he had been a familiar face on TV since compering Come Dancing and hosting the extremely popular family favourite Thank Your Lucky Stars.

Cynthia and John sat through the entire show which included performances from Manfred Mann, The Searchers and The Four Pennies. But it was Dusty Springfield's performance of I Just Don't Know What to do With Myself that really launched the show into outer space for them both. Cynthia and John had been transfixed by Dusty and even their parents had entered the room just to hear Dusty sing too. Words couldn't describe how wonderful she sounded.

The audience was jam-packed with Mods dressed to the nines in their latest suits and outfits as always. Cynthia kept one eye on her brother, as he took mental notes of the size of jacket lapels or rolls on the collars of the shirts. Cynthia found herself scrutinising the girls' shoes and studying how they danced. They all looked so hip and so cool and she wanted to be just like them. She wanted to know what it would feel like to be one of them.

After the show, John retreated to the bathroom saying he needed to scrub off more of the oil and grease and get himself 'suited and booted' and ready for his night 'on the town'. Cynthia enquired where he would be going, but he didn't let on; he just gave her another cheeky wink.

Cynthia sank into the sofa and crossed her arms. Then an idea flashed through her head and before she knew it she had charged up the stairs and was standing at John's bedroom door. She paused for a moment then sucked in a deep breath and entered John's bedroom, being careful to not make a sound.

She couldn't remember the last time she had been inside her brother's bedroom. It smelled of stale clothing because of his habit of allowing his dirty washing to gather up before he handed them on to his mother to be sorted out. To the outside world, John was a Mod - sharp, clean and tidy. In truth, his bedroom didn't reflect this at all. But then his late nights and amphetamine-fuelled lifestyle probably had a lot to do with that.

The other dominant smell in John's bedroom, above all others, was Old Spice aftershave. There were several suits hanging from anything that would hold their weight, in an assortment of colours and fabrics. Cynthia knew her brother spent quite a bit of his wages on getting new suits made, but she had no idea how many he actually had.

Scattered across the bedroom floor were dozens of seven-inch records on labels such as Decca, Brunswick, Chess, Motown and Atlantic. There were piles of dirty socks, shirts and discarded ties too. Cynthia carefully stepped over the dirty piles, aiming for her brother's wardrobe which she thought was as good a place as any to start looking.

She searched frantically through jackets, coats and trouser pockets, but nothing. She opened drawer after drawer on his dressing table but still, nothing. Whilst she searched, she kept an ear open for her brother and her parents. As far as she could work out, he was still in the bathroom and they were downstairs talking over a cup of tea in the kitchen.

So far, so safe, but Cynthia knew she didn't have long; her brother wasn't one for having long relaxing baths.

She was just about to give up, but decided to have one good last look round. Then she spotted a pork pie hat almost hidden on top of the wardrobe. She had to stretch to reach it, but managed to get a grip of it. A collection of handkerchiefs were stuffed inside. Cynthia slowly removed them and finally found what she was looking for.

Carefully, she reached into her brother's hat and pulled out a clear polythene bag containing a few dozen coloured pills. These were the French Blues that she had overheard many of the boys down The Moka talking about. These and others such as Purple Hearts and Black Bombers, often called 'Leapers' on the streets.

It sounded like all the boys in the café and a few of the girls were on these. It simply seemed the trendy Mod thing to do.

Cynthia opened the bag and removed a few pills, being careful to take just enough so that her brother wouldn't miss them. She shoved them into her dress pocket, smartly replaced the bag into the hat and carefully repositioned the hankies before expertly exiting her brother's bedroom as quickly as possible.

Cynthia darted off to her own bedroom on her tip-toes, her heart bursting out of her dress with the exhilaration of what she had just done.

She immediately hid the pills amongst her Beatles merchandise, then sat on the edge of her bed and began to bite her nails as she pondered on what she had done.

She even considered returning them, but after battling with her conscience decided she would keep them. She planned to take the pills to the dance down the Wimbledon Palais the following night.

Her main concern was how she was going to tell Sandra…

Chapter 9
A Day In The Life

'Cynthia! Phone!' Cynthia bounded down the stairs from her bedroom to the hallway, responding to the call from her father. She found a very excited Sandra saying something about meeting Kenny, but her best mate was talking so fast, she was having trouble following her.

'Sand! Slow down, will ya,' said Cynthia with a laugh in her voice.

'Sorry Cyn,' gasped Sandra taking a deep breath.

Once breathing properly again, she began to tell the tale of how she had bumped into Kenny on her way home and he had told her that he had somehow managed to get hold of more tickets for The Beatles concert in Brighton in two days' time. He explained how one of his friends had won the tickets in a card game, but didn't even like The Beatles and, because he owed Kenny a favour, he had offered them to him instead as 'payment'.

'Wow!' said a now equally excited Cynthia, 'he's done it again. That's amazing!'

'I know! But hang on though, cos I'm not finished. Kenny is also going to drive us down there and back, so transport is organised too!'

'Blimey, good old Kenny eh?' Cynthia was beginning to think more and more fondly of Kenny although, in her heart, she was afraid that she still didn't fancy him.

'Yeah, we can now go down there and get back without paying for a B&B, very handy that, eh Cyn…Cyn, you there?'

Cynthia was 'there' but her mind was already daydreaming about her 'Brighton outfit'. She'd decided to save her 'Beatles suit' for the trip up North, so instead she selected a yellow polka dot shift dress, which was another recent purchase. Her look would be topped off with a matching yellow Alice-band, bag and granny shoes.

'Eh? Sorry Sand, drifted off there. Listen that's enough excitement for one night. I'm going to turn in. Got a long day and night tomorrow, what with the fete and then off to The Palais after. I mean, a girl has got to get her beauty sleep hasn't she.'

Sandra reluctantly agreed to end the call, although how she was going to go sleep after the Brighton news was hard to imagine. As for the beauty sleep, she was beginning to realise that it might be a little bit late for it to start working in her case…

With clothes on her mind as she settled down in her bed, Cynthia began to think of what to wear at The Palais.

She knew the venue would get busy, so it would soon be hot and sweaty in there. After some careful consideration, she opted for a pale blue dress with a white belt and white high-heeled shoes. She thought she might even pull her hair back into a ponytail for the occasion. Once that outfit had been mentally sorted, her mind began to drift into a half sleep and it wasn't long before The Fabs entered the equation.

Her thoughts turned to the day The Beatles had played at The Wimbledon Palais before last Christmas on 14th December. The band had recently played a gig for their Northern area fan club members and so it was organised that they would play a similar one for their Southern area fans. Three thousand tickets were made available for the show, but neither her nor Sandra could get one. In fact, only a couple of the usual Moka crowd managed to get tickets. Cue a lot of sad faces around the coffee bar that weekend.

No-one was more upset than Cynthia and Sandra though. The thought that they couldn't get tickets to see 'their' band in 'their' own backyard was hard to take. In fact, it was unbelievable. They still decided to hang about outside The Palais on Merton High Street on the day, as at least they would be close to John, Paul, Ringo and George.

As was now the norm, wherever the Fabs appeared in concert, there were hundreds of fans outside the building when the girls arrived. Cynthia and Sandra pleaded and begged with the already harassed police to be allowed in, as did hundreds of others. Of course, the boys in blue were having none of it and tried to disperse the now baying crowd. Those with tickets then entered.

It was simply torture for Cynthia and Sandra, sat on the pavement with their feet in the gutter, as they watched the smiling faces before them. They held each other and cried, as they both strained to hear the faint sounds of The Beatles performing inside above their sobs.

Both girls agreed that this night had been the worst night of their lives and it would even dampen their Christmas to some extent, such was their disappointment.

Of course, it didn't help when they heard some of the fortunate ones in The Moka a week or two later, bragging about how amazing the show was. Cynthia and Sandra tried their best to look unconcerned as they heard account after account of the show, the fanatical audience and the metal cage that had been installed at the front of the stage as protection for the band. The girls had read in the music papers that John Lennon had commented, '*if they pressed any harder, they'll come through as chips*'.

Both Cynthia and Sandra had been to the Wimbledon Palais several times since that terrible December night because they held regular dance and band events there. Cynthia really liked the venue, especially its wooden dancefloor. It was starting to gain a bit of a reputation as being a place where the hip Mod kids hung out.

Well, John and his mates went sometimes, so it must have been true. Cynthia now found herself looking forward to her night out. She thought of the French blues she had stolen from her brother and then she drifted off to sleep.

***

A rap on her bedroom door stirred Cynthia from her slumber. It was early and it was the day of the fete. One of the first things Cynthia found herself thinking of was the pills she had stolen. The feeling of guilt was now one which was beginning to overwhelm her, and it was one she tried to shake off as she walked to the Common on her way to the annual fete half an hour later.

The annual Wimbledon fete always attracted many hundreds of people from all over the neighbouring areas. However, in recent years, there had been bad blood and trouble flare up between the local boys and those visiting from another manor, who were seen as outsiders and rivals. This usually happened at the end of the day, when most of the locals who knew it was coming were on their way home. Cynthia certainly had no wish to see any fighting today.

Although it was still early, only eight thirty, the usually peaceful acreage spread before her was already one in a state of chaos and confusion. It certainly wasn't like this most Saturdays.

Cynthia spied Sandra already at the white elephant stall, where she was already busy building some kind of display from all the donations.

'Hiya,' said Sandra cheerily as she saw Cynthia get near to her, 'you alright? You look like something's up.'

Cynthia quickly shook her head, worried though that her sense of guilt was that obvious.

'Me? No, I'm fine. What we doing then?'

'Well, Mrs Arnold has given me instructions. She asked that we display all the donations in themed sections, so the ceramic bits over there, books over here, toys go there and then anything else we're to place on this table, here.'

'Where is Mrs Arnold?' Cynthia asked.

'Over there, giving instructions to old Mr Bailey on the bat and rat stall.'

Cynthia glanced over to see Mrs Arnold barking out orders and wagging her finger at no-one in particular. Mr Bailey certainly wasn't taking any notice; in fact, no-one ever took any notice of Mrs Arnold. She took it upon herself to get busy and be the 'general' on this day, but the other stallholders mostly dismissed her, knowing she loved the sound of her voice.

Mrs Arnold was a familiar face around the area of Wimbledon. She was tall and lanky with particularly long arms, and it was those very arms that she waved around more than she needed to.

Her reputation as being a bit of a busybody and a nosy parker went before her, and both Sandra and Cynthia usually tried their utmost to avoid her. Her life revolved around organising the fete and attending church, where she prided herself on her ability to organise the quarterly jumble sale that Cynthia and Sandra steadfastly avoided.

But the fete was different, so Cynthia started to help Sandra finish the display on their stall. To be honest, what they had on it was the usual tat and rubbish which got donated each year and Cynthia was sure she recognised some un-sold bits from the previous year's fete.

All the stalls were up just before 10am, as was the refreshment tent, and the first wave of fun-loving fete goers were beginning to arrive. As the second hand on her watch ticked to 10am precisely, Mrs Arnold nodded to Mr Hewitt, who was on duty as the disc jockey on the information stall, signalling for him to start playing his records. The Bachelors opened proceedings, followed by Andy Williams and then Jet Harris and Tony Meehan.

He was under strict instructions not to play anything too 'rock and roll' until later. Gradually, as the morning wore on, he began to slip in The Beatles, Cliff Richards and Buddy Holly, which changed the 'safe' atmosphere to one with a slightly more adventurous feel.

By 11am, the Common was awash with the inviting smells of hot dogs, tea, candy floss and vanilla ice cream as the food and drink stalls did a roaring trade. Sandra even took a day off from eating her beloved pear drops, instead opting to try a toffee apple.

Sales on the white elephant stall, along with the bat and rat and coconut shy stalls, were also booming. Everyone seemed in good spirits and the weather was glorious, with the sun beaming down from a cloudless blue sky.

On a small reserved area just in front of their stall, Cynthia and Sandra had to suffer three appalling appearances from the always baffling Morris dancers and then several activities such as the sack race and the tug o' war.

Mainly to cheer themselves up, the girls teased the old men standing by the stall, crying out, 'Give us a kiss' and 'Who's that little old man? Very clean isn't he.' An in-joke that they knew only Beatles fans who had seen *A Hard Day's Night* would have understood. Their friend Violet was rumoured to have seen the film ten times already; they didn't doubt it either.

Women huddled together on woolly tartan blankets, chatting away whilst their children ran in and around the crowds and their husbands sneaked off to the refreshment tent to *sample* the beer on offer.

Now and then, Mrs Arnold would pop up like a jack in the box to give out her instructions and then just as quickly disappear again. She assured Cynthia and Sandra that they were doing a sterling job and would be relieved of their duties as soon as replacements were found.

As it happened, those replacements didn't materialise until 3pm, by which time Cynthia and Sandra were starving. They quickly bought some hot dogs and bottles of Pepsi and took a wander around the rest of the fete. Most of the people had been there all day and were now looking tired and, in some cases with the men, plain drunk. A lot of the kids had sunburnt skin and grubby faces.

Whilst they watched some old man be sick by the homemade cake stall, Kenny sidled up to them. He hadn't long arrived; his face looking clean and freshly shaved and his hair was tidy and lacquered.

'Your hair looks smart Kenny. Have you been to the barbers?' asked Sandra.

Starting to shuffle on the spot, he quickly replied, 'Yes, I er, went lunchtime. It needed doing badly.'

'We know why don't we. You want to look your best for tonight,' Cynthia remarked smiling at him.

'And for Brighton on Sunday, don't forget that,' Sandra added.

Kenny couldn't deny it; he was excited about both events.

'Are you looking forward to tonight then?' he asked. 'You know it goes on until midnight, which is fine by me, though it'll make it a long day tomorrow.'

'Yeah, that is all fine by me Kenny. I can do both, don't worry,' replied Cynthia. 'By the way, thanks for the invite to get a lift to Brighton. Sandra phoned me last night. That will be fab.'

Cynthia was genuinely grateful, continuing, 'and its fab the way you managed to get hold of the tickets; Sandra told me the whole story.'

Kenny felt his face start to blush. He tried hard to stop it happening, but he couldn't.

'No problem, honestly. I'm just pleased you'll get a chance to see your boys. I'm thinking we might leave at, say, nine in the morning; we could spend some of the day hanging about in Brighton - have a wander round and that? We also want to give ourselves plenty of time because you just know we'll end up getting stuck behind a few caravans on the way.' He gave out a small laugh, 'that work for you two?'

Cynthia smiled and looked at Sandra, and Sandra nodded.

'Yeah that'll be fab. It sounds like a good plan.' Cynthia took a big swig of her Pepsi then continued, 'did Sandra tell you about our mission?'

Kenny looked at Sandra and shook his head.

'Mission? No, what mission is that then?'

'Well,' began Sandra slowly, spitting out small bits of hot dog as she talked, 'we are going to get our copies of *A Hard Day's Night* autographed by the Fab Four. We are going to take them to Brighton with us and, if we can't get them signed by the band during the day, we'll have to take them into the concert with us.'

Kenny thought they were both mad but didn't comment; he didn't really know what to say. He knew it would be almost impossible to get the signatures, but also knew it would be equally impossible to stop these two trying!

He then bid his farewells and made arrangements to see them both later. Once he had left, Cynthia and Sandra found a quiet spot and chatted about their impending trip up North and then talked about some of the boys who would likely show up at the Palais at some point later that evening. Both girls lost track of the time, but realised it was getting late into the afternoon and they still needed to hand over the takings from the stall to Mrs Arnold.

They eventually found her collapsed in a deck chair beside the coconut shy. She looked exhausted and flushed as her long arms dangled on the grass. She also looked very upset.

'Hello Mrs Arnold, er, is there something the matter?' Cynthia asked, 'you do look cross.' She instantly regretted those words as they left her mouth.

Mrs Arnold had been waiting for someone to ask her.

'Boys! Irresponsible, rowdy, boys! As usual…' Mrs Arnold shook her head as she spoke.

Cynthia and Sandra looked at each other mystified, but Mrs Arnold didn't delay in launching into the story of how local boys, some of whom she recognised, had had a punch up - this year earlier than ever.

'Girls! As is becoming the norm, it was the girls,' she continued, getting very flustered.

From what Cynthia and Sandra could piece together, one of the local girls had flirted with one of the boys from another area, who then took the bait. This led to the local boys taking offence, making a big deal of it and this in turn developed into some brawl beside the hot dog stall; and all in front of an audience of drunken old men, gossiping old woman, laughing children and the local vicar - and of course Mrs Arnold who had taken the fisticuffs all very personally.

Cynthia and Sandra listened to Mrs Arnold rant on for a minute or two longer, realising they had to make a run for it otherwise they'd be there all night. They said they were sorry to hear the news, before carefully dropping the money from the stall into her lap and quickly made their exit. Old Mother Arnold just carried on talking to no-one in particular, and they could still hear her as they hurriedly made their way from the crowds and the Common.

It was nearly 6pm when Cynthia finally got home. This meant she only had an hour to have a bath, a quick scoff of some tea and then get ready for her night out. The plan was that she would meet Sandra at their usual spot at seven, then go to The Moka for a brief coffee before heading off to The Palais.

As she passed John's bedroom on her way out, she could hear him playing some of his American R&B records as he too got ready to hit the dance. She silently prayed he wouldn't notice that his bag of blues was a few pills lighter.

126

She scuttled along the landing and down the flight of stairs very quickly. She was off!

For the first time for as long as they could both remember, Cynthia was late and Sandra was sitting on their bench. Cynthia hated being late; it was possibly the thing that irked her the most. She hated it when others were late but it destroyed her when she was running late herself. She apologised profusely to Sandra, but Sandra just smiled and couldn't have cared less in all honesty. Cynthia commented on Sandra's pretty pale green and purple candy striped shift dress, telling her best friend that she thought she looked amazing. Sandra kindly lapped up the compliment, before heading for The Moka both dressed to the nines and feeling fantastic.

The coffee bar was as loud and smoky as ever as they entered. It was also packed, like it was most Saturday nights. It was *the* gathering place for all the 'with it' kids before they headed off on their adventures.

The Gaggia machine hissed constantly as it churned out its mouthwatering exotic coffee, giving off a delicious aroma. Sammy rushed from table to table, delivering customer's orders with sweat pouring off him. Danny and his mates huddled around the pinball machine as usual and Kenny and his mates leaned against the jukebox. The Moka was simply buzzing with excitement and anticipation.

As politely as she could, Cynthia pushed through the crowd to the counter with Sandra close behind. Sammy noticed them and silently mouthed, 'I'll be there in a minute.' The girls nodded and sparked up a fag whilst they waited.

Finally, he was ready for them.

'Girls, girls,' he begun, 'you look beautiful...beautiful. Let me see,' he said looking them up and down. 'I reckon you are off to The Palais? Going with this rowdy bunch, are you?'

The girls looked around them, smiled and nodded, 'Some of them yeah,' replied Cynthia who smiled sweetly at him.

'OK, so what can I get you?' Sammy asked leaning forward on the counter.

'Two espressos please Sammy. By the way, do you like my shoes?' Cynthia asked, lifting up one of her legs.

'Nice those Cynthia, very nice. And the shoes ain't bad either,' said Sammy. 'Italian or French?' he enquired.

Cynthia giggled, 'Ravels.'

Sammy turned away to get the espressos, while Cynthia stubbed out her cigarette and immediately popped another into her mouth. Sandra frowned.

'You alright Cyn, you seem a bit quiet?' asked Sandra.

'Me? I'm alright, fine really.'

'I don't know, you've been a bit strange all day. I mean, you were late tonight and now you seem a touch nervous. Not like you at all.'

'No, I'm fine, just excited I guess. Some big days coming up eh?' Cynthia replied.

Sandra didn't reply at first. After a few seconds she tutted and said, 'Yeah I know that, but it's more than that; I know you too well. Come on, tell me! Something's up. I know something is bothering you!'

'Sand, will you leave it. I'm okay, really I am. I've never done anything like this before, that's all,' Cynthia lied.

Finally, that seemed to satisfy Sandra.

'Ooh, to be honest, I'm a bit nervous too. It's going to be fun isn't it? I'm really looking forward to it. We really should make a list of all the places that we want to visit. We could do that whilst we are on the train. What do you think?'

'Yeah that's a fab idea. I honestly can't wait. But tomorrow and Brighton first eh? We…you and me…are actually going to go and see actual Beatles! It's going to be so amazing. And if we get our LPs signed too…well!'

'I know!' said Sandra, shrieking so loudly that it caused heads in The Moka to turn their way, looking to see what all the fuss was.

'Reckon we'll need some luck to get those autographs though,' continued Sandra. 'Oh, I do hope we get our LPs signed tomorrow Cyn.'

Cynthia nodded, imagining herself standing shoulder to shoulder with other Beatles fans, all as fanatical as she was. She pictured herself also crying, screaming and waving her handkerchief in the air whilst trying to get George's attention. Then she imagined George coming over towards her and him actually looking her in the eyes. She felt herself shudder.

She also told herself it *was* possible…

Chapter 10
I'm Happy Just to Dance With You

As the 'Craven A' clock hit the stroke of half past seven, The Moka emptied out as the majority made their way to the Wimbledon Palais. Cynthia and Sandra quickly fell into step behind a group of about twenty Mods as they bowled along towards the venue. Their nostrils were filled with the heady concoction of Old Spice and Brut, mixed with the fumes from the multitude of Lambrettas and Vespas that also zipped up and down the high street. It was certainly an impressive turnout of South West London's finest.

The stylish parade slowed to a halt outside The Palais. Cynthia and Sandra were excited just to be in the queue outside and, by the look of it, they were two of the youngest there. The throng of the sharply-dressed moved quickly forward, so it didn't take them long to get to the ticket office, which was manned by a miserable looking, middle-aged grey haired woman sitting inside a wooden cubicle. The fag she was chewing seemed to be a heavy habit going by the yellowish nicotine streak that infiltrated her silver hair at the front.

The girls paid their admission fee of two bob and then handed over their coats to the cloakroom attendant, a bloke going on sixty who looked even more miserable than '40 a day' in the ticket office. Strong rumour had it that they were actually married. Mr and Mrs Jolly indeed. Cynthia and Sandra carefully put their reclaim tickets in their respective purses, then followed a large group heading towards two huge wooden doors. Behind these chunks of brass-handled oak, pulsating music was being played. The excitement was rising in them and about to go into overdrive.

With the doors opened, Cynthia and Sandra found themselves in a large dimly-lit room. Their eyes fell on the stage at the far end of the room and they pictured The Beatles playing on it, protected by the now infamous metal cage.

The disc jockey for the night stood behind his equipment which had been set up to the far right hand side of the stage. A single spotlight hovered above him, picking him out in the gloom.

Cynthia and Sandra had been amongst some of the earliest to arrive, so the place was only a third full, though they knew the crowd would thicken as the night progressed. They stood and marvelled at the sight before them. There was a balanced mixture of boys and girls in front of them, with a blend of mop tops and French lines, beehives and bobs. Most of the boys wore suits with ties and the majority of the girls wore short dresses which clung tightly to their figures - all finished off with an assortment of shoes, mostly Beatle boots and high-heels. It was a wonderful display of cutting-edge fashion.

Everywhere, groups of fresh-faced young people gathered together, chatting, smoking, heads nodding like crazy. The dancefloor was already filling up nicely and Cynthia studied everything about the people around her. She scrutinised the way they held themselves, leaned against walls, clutched their bags, held their cigarettes and tucked their hands in their pockets. Sandra, on the other hand, was only interested in one thing - boys.

The music boomed across the dancefloor. As one record finished some members of the crowd clapped. Cynthia then spotted one boy dancing and she simply couldn't take her eyes off him. He danced in a way that she had only ever seen on 'Ready Steady Go'. Cynthia continued to watch him as he shook his hips through *Tic-Tac-Toe* by Booker T and the MG's, *Soulville* by Aretha Franklin and *Run Run Run* from The Supremes.

'Come on, I'm thirsty,' Sandra said tapping Cynthia's arm, which broke her concentration.

Her gaze broken, Cynthia nodded and they made their way to the bar. The queue was already two deep and it wasn't even like there was any alcohol on sale.

'Look,' Sandra said, tapping Cynthia's arm once again, 'it's your brother John. Did you know he was coming tonight? You didn't mention it.'

Cynthia searched through the crowd until she spotted her brother. He was holding court with a bunch of stunning looking girls, all with Dusty Springfield hair and panda eyes to match. Cynthia could also see John's friends standing behind him. They all looked extremely cool and aloof.

'Shall we go and say hello?' Sandra asked.

Cynthia shook her head, 'No fear. Little point Sand, he won't talk to us. Besides we'll lose our place in this queue.'

Sandra sighed, but knew Cynthia was right; John rarely spoke to her. Sandra's mind immediately went back to a day when she 'felt' something for John and it was a feeling that she hadn't been able to shake off since. It started last summer when she and Cynthia had just started to go to The Moka on a regular basis. Their age group was just starting to get serious about music, fashion and hanging out in coffee-bars, but John and his crowd had been doing it for a couple of years already. As the younger ones started to infiltrate '*their*' scene, John and his crew moved on to other haunts. It was the natural order of things.

However, just before John and his friends moved on, they all met in The Moka one night. John was in good spirits and Sandra remembered that he wore a pork pie hat and dark glasses. John noticed their arrival and beckoned them over to where he and his group of mates were sitting. Both Cynthia and Sandra expected that John would tease them over their recent conversion to the church of rock and roll, but instead he welcomed them and introduced them to his friends. He actually seemed proud of his sister and her best friend. Sandra liked the way John treated her as a young woman that night and, ever since then, she had tried anything to get his attention. A year later, sadly she was still trying.

So, deciding to quench their thirst rather than pursue John, they edged their way to the bar. They ordered two bottles of Pepsi and were about to hand over the money, when a hand appeared and paid for their drinks. Sandra turned around and found her cheek was only a few inches from John's.

'You two staying out mischief I hope?' John said parting the crowd, allowing the girls to ease their way through.

'Us? Course we are,' Cynthia replied.

'The question is, are you John?' Sandra could barely believe those words had left her mouth.

John looked surprised as he turned to face Sandra. 'Piss it,' thought Sandra, 'surely John will blank me now.' Instead he smiled.

'You having a dance later then Sandra?' he asked.

'Er, maybe, I dunno. There are some really cool dancers out there, not sure I'm in their league,' Sandra replied.

'Certainly are. Some 'Ace Faces' are in tonight from the East too. You wait until they start dancing, they'll blow the shirts off the backs of most of that lot.'

Neither Cynthia nor Sandra really had a clue what John was on about, but they didn't let on. As it happened, John knew they didn't understand, but didn't pull them up on it. Instead he just pushed some more chewing gum into his mouth.

John hung around talking with Cynthia and Sandra for the next five minutes. He even told them the names of the artists behind a couple of the records being played; he appeared thrilled to hear them. John also asked about their intended trip to the north and asked if they were excited about going to see The Beatles in concert?

He seemed to enjoy telling them that he considered The Rolling Stones to be the better band.

He told them that he had been following them since they had played at The Crawdaddy Club in Richmond and he tried his best to explain that the Stones were sexier and raunchier and their music had more edge and attack about it.

Both Cynthia and Sandra just laughed.

Eventually though, he got dragged away by his friends. Sandra watched him disappear into the darkness, her heart now thumping in time to the music, which also seemed to have got louder. The venue was now near full and every table and chair around the dancefloor was occupied. Sandra had quickly finished her drink and now wanted another.

Cynthia suggested that Sandra should queue up for the drinks whilst she quickly nip to the toilets. Sandra immediately thought this was a bit odd as they always went to the toilet together, but Cynthia persuaded her that it was the best idea, seeing how busy the bar was. Cynthia said it was likely that Sandra would still be in the queue by the time she returned and Sandra reluctantly accepted the logic and watched her best mate wander off to the toilets.

Once inside one of the cubicles, Cynthia fished into the bottom of her bag, producing the French blues she had stolen from John. She had six in all, not knowing how many she was supposed to take, but she had heard the boys down The Moka brag about taking dozens over the course of a night. She stared at the small blue pills lying in the palm of her right hand for what seemed like an hour, but in reality was only a couple of minutes. Finally, she muttered 'here goes' and popped three in her mouth, one by one. As she gulped them down, she wrapped the rest in some toilet paper and tucked them away in her pocket. Taking a deep breath, Cynthia patted herself down, popped a cigarette into her mouth and exited the cubicle, trying to look as cool as she could despite her hands now shaking like a leaf on a tree.

As she emerged, Cynthia was confronted by the sight of several girls carefully grooming themselves in front of the mirrors by the washbasins. Make-up and hair was being checked forensically. A further group of three girls stood chatting whilst they waited their turn to get near a mirror. One of these girls had the tallest beehive hairstyle that Cynthia had ever seen; jet black and matching the mascara painted around her eyes, her eyelashes black and long. She wore a dogtooth pattern shift dress and bright white high-heel shoes. She caught Cynthia looking and returned the gaze, now looking Cynthia up and down.

Cynthia stood back, hovering by the cubicle door and finally lit her cigarette, watching the girls who were grooming themselves as she blew a plume of greyish blue smoke into the air. The girl immediately in front of her was leaning as close to the mirror as she could, applying even more eyeliner on top of the eyeliner already in place. Cynthia could see she had sparkling emerald green eyes that complimented her outfit. Her striking ginger hair seemed only to enhance her eyes and outfit. To her left, another girl brushed her long brunette hair, brushing it so vigorously Cynthia thought if she brushed any harder, surely it would start to come out. The last girl in the row stood as still as a post, with only her hand moving as it slowly applied more white lipstick to her pouting lips. The colour matched her boots. None of these girls appeared to be in any rush, despite the crowd forming behind them. Cynthia took another drag of her cigarette and couldn't help herself tuning into the conversation between the girl with the tall beehive and one of her skinny friends.

'Well I told him that I wasn't interested didn't I,' the beehive girl was saying, 'he must have been a bit deaf cos I had to tell him at least three times.'

'So what did he do then?' asked one of the others.

'Well, he told me to piss off and stormed off didn't he.'

'No! He never did,' the skinny friend replied. 'Blimey, what will your brother say?'

'Oh, leave off, I haven't told him yet have I. As it happens, I'm not sure that I will. Besides, I wanna see if Pete comes crawling back with his tail between his legs.'

Cynthia noted Beehive's friends all nodding in agreement. Cynthia was intrigued. She wished she knew what Peter had or hadn't done. The beehive girl was about to continue with her story when suddenly the toilet door opened and two more girls walked in. Their eyes met the eyes of the beehive girl and Cynthia could more or less taste the venom. Beehive immediately stopped what she was saying, a deathly silence filling the atmosphere. Fortunately, the girl who had been applying her white lipstick finished what she was doing and left the toilet. Cynthia seized the opportunity and slipped into the vacant space, quickly combing her hair and checking her outfit. She wasn't too sure what was about to happen in there, but it felt the right move to get out of the way sharpish, before it all kicked off.

Once back outside, Cynthia looked over at the bar and could see Sandra was still waiting in the queue. Cynthia pushed her way through the crowd and, just as she reached Sandra, she felt the first rush as the speed started to surge through her blood stream. The sensation was unlike anything Cynthia had ever felt before. Suddenly she felt lighter, the skin on her hands, arms and face began to tingle and then her legs felt weird. Her whole body felt like it was being forced to wake up. She felt her mouth dry up, which instantly triggered a need to grind her teeth and Cynthia wasn't sure whether she liked what was happening to her body. She tried to reassure herself that everything was okay. Besides, she reminded herself forcibly, it was too late to turn back now.

Steadying herself, Cynthia tapped Sandra on the shoulder. By now, she had a huge grin on her face and her eyes were as wide as tea-saucers.

'Alright!' she said.

'Eh? Yeah, I'm okay,' replied a somewhat startled Sandra. 'This bleeding queue doesn't seem to be getting any closer to the bar.'

Cynthia craned her neck to get an idea of how many more people stood between them and the bar. She was now gasping for a drink.

'Sand, you got any chewing gum?' Cynthia asked.

'No sorry. Anyway, what do you want chewing gum for? You bloody hate chewing gum,' Sandra replied, a puzzled look on her face.

Cynthia tried desperately to disguise that her teeth were on the verge of grinding themselves to little more than dust particles. Nor had she realised that she had been tapping Sandra's shoulder furiously in time with the rhythm of the song that was playing. Sandra finally shrugged her shoulder alerting Cynthia to it and Cynthia stopped and apologised. Then a hand appeared out of the darkness, dangling a piece of chewing gum.

'Here you go. It looks like you need this.' A young man dressed very stylishly in a tonic suit and crisp white shirt appeared from nowhere. He gave Cynthia *that* knowing look.

'Thanks,' Cynthia replied, accepting the chewing gum and dropping it straight into her mouth. She gave the man a weak smile whilst Sandra observed the exchange with a curious expression.

Cynthia then became more agitated and eager to get to the bar. She was in desperate need of a drink and she kept telling Sandra so. Eventually, Cynthia spotted a gap in the crowd and darted into it. Sandra couldn't follow because the gap was too small and she was still sandwiched between two taller boys. Through some cunning moves, Cynthia managed to navigate her way to the bar, purchase two bottles of Pepsi and push her way back out of the crowd, grabbing Sandra en route.

Virtually leaping into a spot that had opened up on the edge of the dancefloor, Cynthia spoke quickly as she pointed to various dancers and then gave Sandra her review of what they were doing.

By now the pills had really taken hold of the whole of Cynthia's being and she felt alive. Her body felt alert and every nerve and muscle buzzed from head to toe. She loved this wonderful feeling and wanted more of it. Taking the toilet tissue from her pocket and pretending to sneeze into it, Cynthia managed to pop the remaining pills into her mouth without Sandra even noticing. Within ten minutes she felt a second almighty whoosh as the pills dissolved into her blood stream.

Cynthia's eyes darted in each and every direction as she scanned the room, lapping up the sights of cool people dancing and enjoying themselves. She felt very connected to them. She could feel the wooden dancefloor pulling her towards it and knew it wouldn't be long before she would surrender and allow herself to fall under its spell. The music sounded great too; it wasn't her first choice of music but she definitely recognised some of the songs, having heard John play a lot of it in his bedroom.

She then found her attention drawn towards a certain young man who danced like no other. A lot of the crowd had also noticed him, and a small circle formed around him. This allowed him to swing his arms and twist and turn in complete, pinpoint accuracy with the beat of the record playing in the background. As well as being a great mover, he looked great too, dressed in a dark pin-stripe suit and shiny pointed black leather shoes. He appeared to glide effortlessly across the wooden dancefloor and Cynthia was in awe. As she was about to take the plunge and step onto the dancefloor, Kenny appeared, stopping her dead in her tracks.

'Alright Kenny,' she heard Sandra shout.

'Hello you two, alright? It's great, isn't it?' Kenny said nodding his chin towards the dancefloor.

'It's brilliant,' Cynthia replied glancing at Kenny, the piercing look in her eyes almost knocking him off balance.

'Er…are you alright Cynthia?' asked Kenny, concerned and sensing all was not right.

'Me? Yeah, of course, fab. I'm having a great time. Look at the dancers will you. Look at their gear. It's… fab.'

Kenny and Sandra looked at each other and shrugged their shoulders.

'She looks like she's totally blocked,' Kenny whispered to Sandra. 'Guessing she must be really excited about going to Brighton tomorrow.'

Sandra nodded and agreed, but at the same time she felt there was more behind her friend's behaviour than just their trip to Brighton. She had seen Cynthia excited and even hysterical on numerous occasions, but not like this; this was different. Sandra hadn't seen Cynthia as confident and lively before.

Suddenly, Cynthia walked onto the dancefloor. Sandra and Kenny's mouths dropped to the floor as they watched their friend launch herself into the next song, picking up and joining in with the rhythm perfectly. She had a huge grin on her face as she shuffled from side to side. The pace of the song was quite quick and the bodies of the dancers surrounding Cynthia jerked from side to side and up and down. Cynthia was a fast learner, she always had been, and was copying the movements of the other dancers with ease. By the end of the record she had perfected some tricky dance moves.

Cynthia joined in with the clapping as the song faded, then the crowd quickly erupted back to life as the disc jockey played the popular track from back in '63 by The Jaynetts *Sally Go Round The Roses*. The dancefloor swelled with even more bodies and Kenny and Sandra had to retreat a few steps to make way for the gyrating figures coming their way.

Cynthia had her eyes closed. She simply loved the feeling of dancing and had done since she was a toddler. Her parents weren't big music fans, but her older brother Andrew certainly was. He loved jazz, with London's Jazz Couriers being a particular favourite. He would often play records to the family on a Sunday afternoon after that day's roast had been consumed and Cynthia just couldn't help herself and would get up and dance to them. A couple of years on, John had started to buy rock and roll records and he took over the Sunday afternoon slot and Cynthia would dance energetically along to Little Richard and early Cliff Richard records. And now? Now, not a day went by when she didn't have a little jig about in her bedroom to a Beatles song. Dancing made her feel alive and connected her to her inner-self, a place she looked forward to visiting.

Cynthia remained glued to the dancefloor for the next five records. Sometimes she waved at Sandra and Kenny as she whizzed near them and then launched into some dance moves that mimicked Ringo's dancing from the *A Hard Day's Night* film. She danced like she was picking wild berries from a bush or plucking apples from a tree. She would then jump up and down on the spot and wiggle her head at the same time. It looked ridiculous and she got some funny looks from some of the more serious dancers who were stood nearby, but Cynthia didn't notice, so she just carried on.

Finally, suddenly feeling hot - very hot - and in need of another Pepsi, Cynthia walked off the dancefloor and bounced over to Sandra and Kenny. She pointed to Sandra's almost empty bottle of Pepsi.

'Come on let's go and get another drink. Kenny, do you want one?'

'I'm okay thanks Cynthia. I had better go and find my mate.'

'Okay,' Cynthia said, still panting. 'Sandra?'

'Yeah, come on then. You'll need a drink or else you might faint,' Sandra replied sarcastically.

They walked towards the bar and joined the queue once again. Cynthia talked and talked and talked, until Sandra could bear it no longer.

'Cyn! What is the matter with you? You're not yourself at all. I know when you're just over excited, but I've not seen you like this before, you're being...too strange.'

Sandra stared hard into Cynthia's eyes. Cynthia stared back, hard.

'Sand,' she slowly replied, 'I've swallowed some French blues.'

Sandra just couldn't believe what she was hearing and at first, thought she'd misheard her friend.

'You've done what? Where did you get French Blues from? Did one of those Mods out there give you some?'

'No, no. I...I, pinched some from John.'

'You what! Pinched! But how? Why?' Sandra was really confused now.

Cynthia attempted to explain. She spoke very quickly as she told Sandra how she had been watching Ready Steady Go and how she had been so impressed by the hip people on the show who danced really cool and wore 'fab gear'. She added that she wanted to feel a part of their 'scene' and she thought taking some French blues would help. Sandra listened quietly at first, but could feel anger stirring up inside of her. Finally, she couldn't resist telling her friend what she thought.

'Oh, piss it! You silly cow. What were you thinking? Flipping hell, you ain't half let yourself down. I mean, what about your mum and dad and your granddad? What do you think your granddad would say if he found out?'

Cynthia suddenly felt quite hurt. A cloud of confusion darkened what had been an upbeat mood. She didn't expect the reaction she got from Sandra. She felt judged and foolish.

'Oh, leave it out Sand, I mean what's the big deal?' Cynthia yelled, which only ignited an exchange of even louder yelling from Sandra.

'Big deal! Big deal! You are flaming joking, aren't you?'

Cynthia looked around her, feeling a little embarrassed at the scene developing between them. She quickly noted, however, that no-one else standing around them was taking a blind bit of notice. They simply couldn't hear them, with the music being so loud.

The screaming match between them continued. Words, harsh words, were exchanged, resulting in Sandra storming off. Cynthia watched her disappear in to the crowd and saw her best mate make a beeline for the exit.

Once outside, Sandra sat on a wooden bench and quickly popped a cigarette into her mouth, shakily grappling with the box of matches. She felt angry and disappointed with Cynthia. Whilst she sat there she thought back to the last time she and Cynthia had argued. In truth, it was a rarity as they didn't argue much. They had the occasional disagreement over the years they had known each other and had fallen out a few times, but those times had been brief, as neither held onto any 'beefs' for too long. They valued their friendship too much.

In fact, the last time, they had argued, it was over The Beatles. Of course it was! The Beatles had gone through a style change, with Sandra saying she preferred the leather jacket and trousers look, which the band wore back in their Star Club days and Cynthia had said she preferred the band's current look, saying it was smarter. They shouted at each other for a while, but then realised it was a pointless argument really and both made friends again like nothing had happened.

But now, Sandra angrily blew the cigarette smoke through her nostrils, something she only did when she was cross about something. She thought about the French blues, accepting she didn't know too much about them. Sure, she had overheard the boys in The Moka talking about them and how they enhanced their mood and made them feel more alert and alive but, most importantly of all, how they helped them dance all night without feeling tired.

She had also overheard her dad telling her mum a story over breakfast the other morning. He had just read about 'The Drug Menace of The Mods' in his Sunday newspaper and relayed stories of how soldiers were using pills such as French blues and Purple Hearts in the last war because it helped them stay awake and vigilant.

Sandra had also heard about some of her friends' parents taking them, some as slimming pills and some to help them get them through their shifts at work. She knew of at least two friends whose fathers were postman who used them.

But Sandra had also seen some of the damage and harmful side-effects the pills were having on people. She had watched some of the Mods go from handsome and healthy young men, full of life and natural energy to being reduced to stick thin, gaunt individuals, with eyes sunken deep into their heads and generally looking older than their years.

Sandra knew one thing for certain - she didn't want her best friend end up looking like that. Okay, she was probably blowing things out of proportion, but at that precise moment she felt way too angry with her friend. Feeling sad, she stood up, stubbed out her fag on the pavement and made her way home.

Back inside The Palais, Cynthia continued to queue up for a Pepsi. She tried to shake off her argument with Sandra, telling herself that her friend was being irrational and stupid. After all, it was only a few pills and she suspected half the people on the dancefloor were also buzzing from them. However, a tiny part of her did feel some pangs of guilt and she was disappointed that she had argued with Sandra.

Cynthia finally purchased her Pepsi and returned to mingle with the crowd. She scanned the room trying to spot Sandra, but suspected she had stormed off home in a huff and wouldn't be seen again tonight. She knew her best mate was prone to such drama.

She asked a boy standing next to her what the time was. He told her it was gone eleven bells. Cynthia smiled and decided she would stay a little longer but promised herself she would be home by midnight. She knew she would need to be up early the next day as Brighton awaited.

Her brother John came back into view. Standing next to her, he casually asked her where Sandra was after noticing her absence. Cynthia said that Sandra had gone home because she felt tired and that she wanted to go early because of their Brighton trip. John listened whilst he chewed gum frantically. He then caught a familiar look in his baby sister's eyes.

'Cyn. Look at ME,' he said sharply.

Cynthia did as she was asked and John's suspicions were instantly confirmed.

'Jesus! Go on then, how many did you swallow?'

John didn't sound angry or judgemental and Cynthia also knew there was no point in denying it; she suspected her large pupils and the ferocious gum chewing gave it away.

'About six,' she replied.

John puffed out his cheeks. He then smiled as he told her he thought his stash felt a little lighter. Cynthia apologised, but John didn't make a big deal of it. They quietly stood side by side for the next twenty minutes, with Cynthia resting her head on the upper arm of her brother as they watched the dancers and listened to the music.

John then turned to look at his younger sister, 'Come on you, let's get you home.'

On their way out, it took John the best part of ten minutes to leave The Palais because he had to say goodnight to so many people. Cynthia liked that her brother was popular.

They didn't speak much on the short walk back home. It was a pleasant enough walk, although they walked at a pace because the pills were still very much alive in their system. Once they got home,

John took Cynthia into the kitchen, making a 'shushing' noise as he held a finger to his lips, keen not to wake their mum and dad.

'Cuppa tea sis?' he whispered.

Cynthia nodded. She hoped the tea might help calm her down because she certainly didn't feel ready for her bed, even though she did feel a little sleepy. She could sense a real battle going on inside of her, where part of her wanted to go to bed and the other part wanted to put some records on and dance.

John filled the kettle with water and lit the hob, then used the same match to light his and Cynthia's cigarettes. He asked Cynthia if she wanted a slice of bread, but he already knew the answer. As he spooned some tea leaves into the teapot and collected two cups and some milk, Cynthia sat at the table watching her brother's every move. Her ears were ringing with white noise and her head buzzed like a beehive.

John filled the teapot with the now boiling water and sat down at the table opposite Cynthia. He looked at her and found himself now looking at a young woman; he hadn't really noticed her in that way before.

Sure enough, they saw each other every day and, apart from the occasional teasing and mickey taking, they both got on pretty well, they always had. He had always felt he had more in common with Cynthia rather than Andrew. For one thing, John was closer in age to his sister than their elder brother. Cynthia was nearer to his generation and what his generation liked. Andrew was almost of a different era, one that, although they were into jazz and wearing 'Modern' clothes, were still in some ways carrying some of the more traditional attitudes like those of their parents.

John actually admired Cynthia. She was intelligent, fun to be around and loyal, deeply loyal. He couldn't find it in him to scold her for stealing his pills and then popping them. He knew he probably should have, but he also accepted she was an adventurous person and one who needed to explore and experiment with things. She always had been and was a bit of a tomboy really.

Even as a kid she was always constructing things out of bits and bobs and, in her own way, she was very creative. She had never been frightened to climb trees or walls and she was in her element playing on the bombsites that had been destroyed in the Second World War.

141

As he poured the tea into the cups he felt pleased that he had a sister like Cynthia.

'You're not going to say anything to anyone are you John?' asked Cynthia sheepishly, 'I mean, I've got enough grief with Sandra knowing.'

She hoped she already knew the answer, then John shook his head and gave her a look which confirmed what Cynthia was hoping.

'Why do you take those pills John?' she asked quietly.

John took a long sip of his tea and lit another cigarette. He offered one to Cynthia but she shook her head.

'Blimey,' John said looking serious for a second whilst giving the question some thought. Puffing out his cheeks, John continued, well, I suppose it goes with who I am. I'm a Mod ain't I?'

'Yeah, but what does that mean?' Cynthia pressed.

'Look, I'm eighteen and in my prime, or so I'm told. I have money in my pocket and a good job, but if I don't like the job anymore, I can throw in the towel and by the afternoon know I'll have another one. I give mum a little bit of housekeeping money and the rest I can do what I like with. And what I like to do is get my suits and shirts made. I get to choose what I wear and there's no better feeling than walking into a club wearing a brand-new whistle that you know nobody else will have. It's about feeling like an individual. It's about feeling like your unique, and the clothes and the scooters do that for my mates and me.

And then there's the music. I feel like I've been born at just the right time really. I mean I like a bit of that jazz stuff that Andrew plays, but it's mostly old-fashioned now ain't it? I mean, I remember the first time I went to The Crawdaddy Club, it was a couple of days before my sixteenth birthday and I went down on the back of a scooter with some of the older boys from The Moka.

Jesus Cyn, everything changed that night. The Yardbirds were playing and the place was packed to the rafters with the coolest looking people I had ever seen. There was a real buzz in the air, with the fellas looking smart and the girls looking lovely. Even I could sense that something was really starting to happen. And the music! I had never heard such sounds. That just hit me in the chest BAM!

I asked around as to who these records were by and was told names you couldn't find in Woolworths. I finally found out you had to import them from America. This was a serious business and I began to get my hands on records unlike anything I had ever heard before; they totally blew away all that Tommy Steele and Billy Fury stuff I used to play. Then, as much as the music, clothes started to become really, really important and then the haircuts and the scooters too. My scooter is a big part of me. You getting it Cyn? It's a lifestyle, it's all a big part of being a Mod.'

Cynthia could feel John's passion for what being a Mod was all about. She took a large gulp of her tea while he continued.

'And then more clubs started to open. The DJs at these places were playing music I just couldn't find. Places like The Scene just off Great Windmill Street is a really special place to go. You go there to be seen, and being seen is a big part of it, but you got to wear the right gear and have the latest haircut to get noticed and get any respect and I like that feeling. Then the music starts and then the dancing, and then the girls watch yer.

Now I've worked hard all week and sometimes feel a little tired, so I began to be offered some pills. As you have found out tonight, they liven you right up and so they become a big part of your scene too. You know you love being in THOSE places, with THOSE people, listening to THOSE special tunes...and THOSE little pills help prolong that experience.

I mean when the music is right and you're in the moment, dressed in your latest and finest and the coolest girls are watching you, you want that feeling to continue, you don't want it to stop. We all do it. Being a Mod is like being a part of the future. We are clearing the old rubbish away and paving the way for the future. Living for the day! Going to Brighton and Southend, the scooters, the suits, the music, the dancing, the clubs and the people is what being a Mod is all about.

It's me. It's who I am and that's how I like it.'

Cynthia smiled and simply sat there with her thoughts, feeling pleased she had a brother like John. She knew he would look after her.

He gulped the last of his tea and stubbed out his cigarette. 'Right, I'm going to turn in. Word of warning missy, you might struggle to get to sleep straightaway after what you have taken tonight. Think of it as a small price to pay for having such a good time.'

With that he planted a kiss on her forehead and left her sitting there. Cynthia smiled and finished off her now lukewarm tea.

He was right she thought, I really did have good time!

Chapter 11
Day Tripper

John had been right. Cynthia just couldn't get to sleep.

She had tossed and turned the entire night and was now all wrapped up amongst her bed sheets as her thoughts raced from one thing to another, all with the soundtrack of *Can't Buy Me Love* repeating over and over again in her mind.

Finally, after what seemed like hours of non-sleep, the Sandman embraced her and she slipped away. For what felt like a few blissful minutes she was asleep, only for her alarm to wake her once again.

Only, it didn't sound like her alarm, it sounded more like an old air raid siren she had heard on the old war films at the pictures. It startled her and reignited some of the speed still flowing through her bloodstream. Cynthia sat bolt upright and tentatively opened her sore aching eyes. As she did so, an overwhelming feeling of nausea hit home and her head throbbed as hard as her beloved Ringo pounding his pagan drums.

Willing herself to get up, Cynthia slid out of her bed. Staggering slightly, she remained upright and sluggishly made her way to the bathroom. Every movement was a challenge; even turning on the tap seemed to be hard work. Halving the amount of time of her normal ablutions, a five-year-old would have done a better job of brushing their teeth. At best, she had managed a quick 'wash and brush up'. Glancing in the mirror, Cynthia looked like one of Count Dracula's concubines. She had to look away, then quickly spun around just in time for the spume of vomit to reach the toilet pan rather than the floor.

Cynthia emptied the contents of her stomach, steadied herself then returned to her bedroom. Somehow, she had to get ready, so slowly slipped into the outfit she had chosen for Brighton. Finishing the packing her holdall for the day ahead, finally she was done. Feeling anything but 'fab', she carefully made her way down to the kitchen.

To her surprise, John was already up, drinking tea and smashing his way into a boiled egg. As she almost fell onto one of the vacant chairs, John winked at her.

'Alright sis?' he said all too chirpily.

Cynthia stuck her green coloured tongue out at him. As she did so, her mother charged into the kitchen.

'Next door's flipping cat has shat in our garden again. I'm going to have to have words...oh, morning Cynthia, enjoy yourself last night?'

It was all too loud for Cynthia's delicate condition, but she tried not to reveal it, weakly nodding at her red-faced mother.

'Good. Would you like a boiled egg love?' her mum asked, already placing two eggs into a saucepan, 'or you can have them scrambled?'

'Boiled...will...be fab...thanks Mum,' Cynthia replied slowly. The thought of food made her feel unwell again and not really sure she was even capable of stomaching any breakfast. But, most of all, she knew she needed to keep up this pretence and present her normal Sunday self.

'Ooh, bet you're excited about your day today Cynthia?' asked her mum. 'I must say though, you don't seem very excited. In fact, you look a little bit peaky.'

'Yeah, I am a bit,' said Cynthia, smiling her best false smile, 'I just didn't sleep very well.'

'Probably the noise of that bloody woman's cats fighting and crapping in the garden,' snorted her mum. 'Did you hear it John?'

John grunted something unintelligible that was ignored anyway. Once the eggs were ready, Cynthia's mother placed them on the table, along with a fresh pot of tea, and continued mumbling on about the cats.

Cynthia picked slowly at the food in front of her. Both she and John nodded from time to time, but generally tried to disconnect themselves from the conversation of what cat shat where.

Eventually, Cynthia could stand it no longer and forced down the last of her breakfast, washing it down with a slurp of tea. Making her excuses with a mouthful of food, she grabbed her coat and bag from the bannister. The bag contained her copy of *A Hard Day's Night*, a change of clothes for the concert and a few other items she'd need for the trip. Cynthia quickly made her exit, mentioning she needed to go and meet Sandra, which was true, and shouting 'BYE!' as she shut the front door behind her.

As she walked along, Cynthia contemplated what mood Sandra would be in, virtually collapsing once she reached '*their*' bench on the Common. She felt dreadful as she sat there and was unable to compare how she felt now to anything she had experienced before. She couldn't work out how John survived if he felt this way weekend after weekend.

It was the sound of coughing that woke Cynthia up; she hadn't even realised she had nodded off. Her blurry eyes looked up at to see Sandra staring down at her.

In truth, she didn't look impressed as she stood there towering over Cynthia with folded arms. Cynthia could sense Sandra wanted to say something, however, she didn't get the opportunity because a green Mini Minor pulled up beside them and honked its horn, instantly attracting the attention from both girls. Kenny wound down his window and waved them over.

'Come on then, if you're coming,' said Sandra snottily.

Kenny quickly jumped out, allowing the girls to climb into the back seats. They both noticed the car had a smell of oil and petrol fumes. Cynthia instantly wondered if she would be able make it to Brighton with that smell in her nostrils, as the queasy feeling in her stomach just wasn't relaxing its grip on her.

The bloke in the driver's seat was about Kenny's age with neatly combed hair, complete with side parting. He wore a white shirt on which he'd rolled up the sleeves and casually leant one arm out of the window. He turned and smiled at the girls.

Kenny made the necessary introductions, 'Girls, this is Rod. Rod, meet Cynthia and Sandra.'

'Alright girls,' said Rod cheerily.

The girls meekly smiled back, nodding their heads. Cynthia hardly paid him any attention, however Sandra immediately noticed his pointy nose, pointy chin and even pointier ears. She thought to herself he'd make a terrific character in a Walt Disney film.

After the pleasantries, they were soon speeding off in the direction of the South coast and Brighton. Kenny appeared especially excited about the day ahead; Rod was somewhat calmer. Sandra and Cynthia, however, stared directly in front of themselves and didn't say a single word to each other.

Getting out of London on a Sunday was the easy part, but once they hit the 'A' roads heading to Brighton they were forced to slow down, mainly due to the many cars in towing caravans. Kenny valiantly tried to prompt conversations with the girls, but he only got one word answers in reply. He sensed, correctly, all was not well between them.

About five miles outside of Brighton they hit yet another traffic jam and, by now, the sun was at its hottest. All the windows in the car were fully opened, which Cynthia welcomed as she had felt sick again for the past twenty miles. There had been a couple times when she was close to demanding Rod pull over just so she could throw up again, but somehow she managed to avoid having to do so. She felt terrible though.

She quietly gazed out of the window at the other vehicles, all creeping along in the never-ending traffic jam. Most were Morris Minors and Vauxhall Victors and her attention was drawn to one car in particular, with three kids looking bored in the back seats, whilst their father puffed merrily on his pipe and their mother read a knitting magazine.

She fell into some kind of daydream, in which she suddenly felt a lot better, but was sharply brought back to reality by the sound of an Alfa Romeo Giula grinding to a halt beside them. Painted in an unusual creamy white, Cynthia recognised it as being the same vehicle which had roared passed them ten miles back.

Kenny, Rod and Sandra were suitably impressed, although Cynthia was indifferent; she didn't care much for cars, scooters, or motorbikes for that matter.

She would often say to Sandra 'cars, scooters and bikes are not cool Sandra, it's only the people who drive or ride them that are...'

Sandra did see her best friend's point of view and did her best to try and remember that but, on this particular occasion, the Alfa Romeo won hands down.

Cynthia then noticed a large coach pull up alongside them. It was packed full of young people, mostly girls, and attached on the inside of the back window was what looked like an old bed sheet with 'Yalding Village Hall Beatles Trip' painted on it in black letters of varying sizes.

Cynthia read the words and broke into a smile. This released a feeling of some excitement, which jolted her back to her normal self. 'Good,' she thought, 'I'm starting to feel like my old self again.' Glancing sneakily to her right, Cynthia caught a glimpse of a glum-looking Sandra. She had had enough of the atmosphere between them.

'What time did you get home then?' Cynthia asked quietly.

Sandra made a sniffing sound and took her time to answer, 'About eleven.'

'Did you go straight to bed then?'

'No...not straight away. I still had to sort my outfit out for today and I also started a letter to Anne Collingham.'

'Oh yeah,' said Cynthia perking up slightly, 'what's that's about?' She genuinely wanted to know more.

Sandra was now beginning to soften too. 'Well, I just want her to pass on some questions to Ringo for me,' she replied.

Kenny blew out his cheeks and winked at Rod.

'Lovely,' Kenny sighed quietly. 'Anyone want a mint Imperial?' he asked as he waved a white paper bag in the air. Both Cynthia and Sandra took one and popped them into their mouths. The heavy atmosphere in the car had finally, thankfully, started to lift.

'Sorry Sand. I...er...I was...' But before she could finish her apology, Sandra touched Cynthia's hand with hers.

'It's alright Cyn...honest, you silly cow,' and they both smiled at each other.

Sandra reached into her handbag and offered her bag of pear drops around. Gradually, the flow of traffic increased and they were soon travelling at a decent speed. The bag of pear drops was almost empty by the time they reached Brighton.

'I can see the sea!' Sandra yelled, screaming the traditional announcement.

Seeing the large expanse of blue-grey sea before them lifted everyone's spirits immediately and, thankfully, Cynthia's nausea had all but disappeared. With the first wafts of fresh sea air reaching her nostrils., she began to breathe in deeply, filling her lungs with the stuff. Blimey, it felt good.

They soon found themselves in central Brighton and the excitement in the car was beginning to reach fever pitch. Luckily, Rod managed to find a parking space near the Palace Pier and they each jumped out and stretched. The journey had taken them an hour longer than they had hoped, but they were now in Brighton and it felt good. Lunchtime was fast approaching and even Cynthia now felt peckish.

'Shall we go and get some food then?' suggested Cynthia. Sandra nodded her head with eager agreement.

'Yeah, why not. I could do with a cuppa and a bite to eat,' Rod added.

'There'll be loads of cafes round here,' Kenny said waving in several directions.

'Over there…there's one,' Cynthia said pointing to a café on a street corner.

They set off along the promenade in the direction of the café. To their left, the pebble beach eventually gave way to the sea. Frothy white waves crashed in, kissed the pebbles and departed again, leaving behind a distinctive and evocative rattling sound, as stone bounced off stone. It was one of Cynthia's favourite noises and she instantly smiled as she heard it.

The four day trippers were now filled with the smell of the fresh sea salt, enlivening their senses. At long last, Cynthia felt completely back to her normal self and she imagined the waves carrying away her guilty feelings from the previous night. She was glad Sandra hadn't raised the issue of the pills and hoped all was forgotten. Cynthia brushed her arm against Sandra, to which Sandra replied with a smile. They looked into each other's eyes and instinctively knew that all was okay between them again. Today they were in Brighton and they were going to see The Beatles. What more could a girl want in life!

They carefully crossed the busy road and entered the café, being greeted by the aroma of fish and chips, malt vinegar and strong coffee. They managed to grab the last remaining table and quickly ordered some food and drinks with the middle-aged waitress who had cheerily welcomed them.

The café door was propped open by a large grey stone, so the sea breeze continued to waft through and remind them where they were. Cynthia felt wonderful to be in Brighton and once again drew in deep breaths as though her life depended on it. 'You don't get this back home,' she thought.

'Are you going to the concert?' Cynthia's love affair with the ozone was briefly interrupted and her ears pricked up. She looked around in the direction from where the question came and saw it was a young girl sitting with a friend, who had asked a boy at a nearby table.

'Aye, we all have tickets,' he replied, looking towards his three friends as he answered in an accent that Cynthia couldn't quite determine, but suspected may have been Geordie.

'Ah great. There's going to be such a buzz, especially as this is their first concert in the UK since they returned from Australia and New Zealand,' the girl continued.

Her eyes were bright and her complexion glowing. Cynthia wondered if she would see her again at the concert and whether she would be one of the girls screaming and crying her head off. Of course she will be, Cynthia told herself and, what's more, so will I!

The Fabs had spent most of June on a World Tour. Kicking off in Copenhagen, passing through Denmark and The Netherlands before being flown out to Hong Kong, onto Australia and New Zealand, then returning to the UK from Brisbane for this Brighton concert. Cynthia imagined her George must be very exhausted, but also very tanned too!

A silence fell over their table as the four of them sipped their teas and chomped on bacon sandwiches smothered in either red or brown sauce, all the while gazing out of the café window towards the sea and promenade.

There was only a light wind blowing, so the children outside didn't have to grapple too hard with their balloons. Couples casually strolling hand in hand, mingled with dog walkers and the obvious Beatles fans, many of who were wearing Beatles wigs much to the amusement of the more elderly passers-by.

Kenny, finishing up his food, was the first one to break the silence.

'Rod and me are thinking of having a walk towards Hove, have a drink and that. Do you fancy coming girls?' Kenny asked.

Cynthia and Sandra shook their heads in unison.

'No thanks Kenny,' said Cynthia, 'We're going to just hang around the pier for a bit and then head up to The Hippodrome for a while until it's time to get spruced up. We'll find a ladies toilet somewhere to do that, eh Sand?' Sandra nodded smiling.

'Why go and hang around the Hippodrome?' Rod suddenly enquired. Sandra explained their mission to get their LPs autographed.

Rod laughed out loud, he just couldn't help it. 'You'd have more chance of getting an audience with the Pope or a birthday card off the Queen.'

Sandra and Cynthia certainly didn't laugh out loud, choosing to ignore Rod's comment.

'Ain't listening to you Rod, so there. Whatever you say, we're going to try,' said Sandra. 'We'll just hang around The Hippodrome and see what happens.'

Poor old Kenny felt an overwhelming disappointment; he had been looking forward to spending the day with Cynthia. He had had it all planned out, but now he was trying not to let his disappointment show. Instead, gamely, he suggested they all meet up back at the same café at 6pm. That would still give them plenty of time to get to The Hippodrome and hopefully be near the front of the queue.

Just as they were about to leave the café, they overheard some Beatles fans discussing a rumour that George Harrison had had a car accident earlier that morning and had damaged his new E Type Jag on his way through Fulham.

Cynthia desperately hoped it was just a nasty rumour but, if it turned out to be true, then she just hoped George was okay. She also, selfishly, hoped the concert would still be going ahead.

Once outside the café, the boys turned right and the girls turned left.

Cynthia suggested they go straight to The Hippodrome, for no other reason than to see if they could find out more about the car accident. As they turned around, sure enough, they caught Kenny looking back. They quickly waved and then set off, virtually skipping as they went.

"Poor old Kenny,' said Sandra kindly.

Cynthia just smiled then shouted, 'Come on then,' as she quickened her pace.

Turning into Middle Street on their left, they immediately noticed a large crowd of Beatles fans hanging around outside the venue already. Two white-helmeted policemen were doing their best to usher any fans towards a wall so they didn't block the road and pavement, but they were severely outnumbered and it was a thankless task.

Cynthia, recognising the distinctive headwear, thought it was odd that the London Metropolitan Police Force had been called in to help control proceedings. She chuckled to herself thinking that the last time they would have been in Brighton, they were probably chasing her brother John and his mates across the beach.

As Cynthia and Sandra got near to the crowd of fans, they too were suddenly ushered against a brick wall. They hadn't even noticed the local coppers who had grabbed them were standing behind them. Cynthia tried to protest but the policeman ignored her. She found herself pushed up against a rather large girl clutching a flag, on which someone had scribbled 'Love The Beatles'.

''Ere. Have you heard about George?' the girl said in a thick as syrup Northern Irish accent.

'Yeah, yeah we did. It's just a rumour though isn't it?' Cynthia asked.

'No, tis true. George is okay, thank god, and he should be getting into Brighton very soon.'

Cynthia thought for a moment. If George were driving alone, where would he park his car? But it was if her new Irish mate had read her thoughts.

'Ha-ha,' she laughed, 'no that doesn't mean that George's Jaguar will roar up Middle Street any minute now. No, he will have a meeting point with the rest of the band somewhere secret.'

Cynthia smiled and nodded. Of course, that made perfect sense.

'What's in yer bag?' the girl asked nosily.

'We have brought our copies of *A Hard Day's Night*,' said Cynthia, nodding towards Sandra. 'We want to get them autographed.'

'It's possible,' replied the girl sounding optimistic. 'I got my Cavern membership club autographed by Ringo a while back,' she announced, virtually patting herself on the back and sticking out her rather large breasts.

'Fab, how did you manage that?' Sandra butted in.

'I waited outside the Cavern for three hours one afternoon. It was on the 4th February last year. I have it framed and hanging from my bedpost. I kiss it every night before I pray and go to sleep.'

Sandra was in awe of the Irish girl's prized possession. It made her feel even more determined to get her LP autographed.

'When we get our LPs autographed Cyn, I'm going to frame it too. I'm going to buy another copy anyway and that other copy will be the one I play, the other I'll keep in pristine condition,' Sandra said.

'Yeah and me,' Cynthia agreed nodding, but her attention had been drawn towards an incident that was unfolding in front of her. A handful of girls had slipped away from the crowd and had dived into a half-open window at the front of the theatre. The police had seen them and were now busy pulling at some girl's legs which were now dangling from the window. The event was generating some commotion which inevitably attracted the attention of passers-by.

'Go on girl,' yelled one man, egging on the youngsters. 'Let her be,' barked another. There was a lot of squealing going on and it was now getting louder and more frenzied. Some pushing and shoving between the mass of young girls and the handful of police ensued, which neither Cynthia or Sandra liked the look of.

The Irish girl, however, smelled blood and suddenly charged towards the mayhem. Seeing an opportunity to escape, Cynthia took Sandra's hand and ran away from the crowd. They kept running without looking back until they reached the end of Middle Street. The crowd behind them was clearly at risk of getting out of control and looked like it had swelled in numbers in the last half hour or so. More Metropolitan Police officers had also appeared, having leapt out of a couple of nearby police vans.

The girls stood and watched for a while, curious as to what may happen next. There seemed to be a lot of shouting and screaming and they could see their Irish friend standing in front of one policeman, her fiery and flushed red face only an inch from his as she shouted into his deadpan face.

Cynthia and Sandra felt pleased they had made their exit; they knew it was a good move. As they continued walking, they considered their options. They could hang around the smaller streets near The Hippodrome on the off chance they might be lucky enough to catch a Beatle, or they could try and find a way into the Hippodrome. Sandra was less keen on the last idea, recalling their ordeal at The Scala theatre. The last thing she wanted to do was get caught breaking into the venue, getting thrown out and not being allowed back in.

No, it was becoming obvious that the most favourable option, and the one they finally agreed upon, was to simply enjoy the day by spending it exploring Brighton. Sandra said she really wanted to visit the Royal Pavilion, whilst Cynthia said she just wanted to have a go on some rides at the end of the pier. They agreed they had time to do both, so set off in the direction of the Pavilion.

As they walked, Cynthia asked Sandra why she wanted to go to there. Sandra revealed she had a relative who had worked in the Pavilion in the days before it had been turned into a hospital for injured soldiers from the Imperial Indian Army during the Great War. She said that her grandmother had often mentioned the relative who Sandra, in her romantic fantasising, suspected was actually a lover of her grandmother's, albeit she couldn't recall why she thought that.

Many times over, Sandra's fantasy had taken her on a romantic journey and she always imagined the same scene. She pictured her grandmother as a younger woman, beautiful and elegantly dressed in a long, flowing satin dress. She was at a party and a handsome young man, with an impressive moustache and in his army medic's uniform, holds out his hand and invites her grandmother to dance. She accepts and the two young people dance. The image of everyone else in the room fades away, leaving just the two dancers who swirl and twirl and gaze into one another's eyes. That was where the fantasy ended. It went nowhere else, but it was enough for her to enjoy the suggestion of where it might have ended up.

Before long, Cynthia and Sandra entered the grounds via its beautiful gardens. The scent of summer flowers filled the air as they followed the path which led nearer to the main building. Neither girl had ever seen anything like it in real life. Parts of the building looked like pictures they had seen in the National Geographic magazine of palaces in India. They paused at a sign which explained some of the history relating to the building, reading it had been built in the 18th Century and was used as a seaside retreat for George, the Prince of Wales.

Apparently Queen Victoria never stayed here because she thought the Pavilion was not private enough for her. There was also a photograph of sick Indian soldiers being cared for by doctors and nurses. Sandra read every word carefully, but Cynthia just wanted to look around the building as quickly as she could; impatient to have fun on the rides at the end of the pier.

As it transpired, it didn't take long to walk around the outside of the Royal Pavilion and, in the end, Cynthia was pleased they had done so. It really was very impressive and Sandra actually appeared to be quite overwhelmed by it all.

'To the pier!' shouted Cynthia at the top of her voice, making her best mate giggle loudly as she did so.

Just seeing its wooden boards was a magical and thrilling experience for Cynthia. She loved them and had been fortunate enough to visit many in her short life, the one at Hastings holding especially fond memories for her. She had only been seven years old the first time her granddad had taken her to Hastings pier and it too had been a warm summer's day.

The sea had been rougher then than it was today in Brighton and the waves had crashed against the pier's supports. Cynthia could recall how her granddad had held her up so she could see the waves.

There had even been a few swimmers battling against the waves below them and some tiny fishing boats returning from their early morning out at sea.

Cynthia's granddad had treated her to everything that day - candyfloss, fish and chips, ice creams and even a ride on a donkey called Nora. Cynthia could still remember the big beaming smile on her granddad's face as he watched her have so much fun. She even remembered his famous donkey joke.

'Cynthia,' he said, 'what do donkeys on this beach get for lunch?'

Cynthia thought for a second and then quietly spoke, 'I don't know Granddad.'

'An hour,' he said and then laughed loudly at his own joke. Cynthia smiled but didn't really understand it at the time. She had heard it so many times since then and now it made her smile when she thought of it.

At the end of that fantastic day, she had been totally tired out and had to be carried half asleep to his car. It really had been wonderful and now it all seemed like such a long time ago.

It was only with Sandra tugging at her arm, that Cynthia slowly came around from those cherished memories. Sandra had spotted a doughnut stall and she wanted to buy one.

'DOUGHNUTS!' Sandra shouted, 'c'mon Cyn, they've only got flipping doughnuts!' She excitedly stuffed her bag of pear drops back in her handbag.

Sandra managed to claim a spot in the queue for the doughnut stall just in front of a large family. The family's smaller children ran around their parent's feet. They had so much energy to burn, the prospect of a warm sugary doughnut was simply too much for them and they just couldn't stand still.

As Cynthia and Sandra queued, their senses were filled with the smells from this particular bit of the seaside. Candyfloss and toffee apples mixed with fish and chips, burgers and hot dogs, all mingling with alcoholic fumes and cigarette smoke. The seaside with all its delights was truly a wonderful place.

Finally, they were served and happily strolled away with Sandra clutching a small, brown paper bag containing four doughnuts in total - two each. Cynthia noticed two vacant deck chairs and quickened her pace towards them. Sandra followed, one eye on the chair and the other on the feast in the bag that awaited them.

155

As Cynthia nestled into her seat, the suns heat washed over her face. The soft, warm sea breeze felt wonderful too. Sandra sat beside her, dipping her hand into the bag and pulling out a sugary brown delight. She dangled it in front of Cynthia before finally letting it drop into Cynthia's hands. Sandra managed to take a large bite of her doughnut before Cynthia had even sat up.

The first bite, as always, was the best. Both girls spent a few moments sitting in silence as they savoured their warm treat. Sandra kept her eyes tightly closed as she slowly chewed her doughnut. Cynthia, watching the spectacle of her friend, mustered as much self-control as she could so she didn't burst out laughing at her.

Sandra, sensing something was happening, opened one eye and caught Cynthia looking at her, her face bright red and tears of laughter welling up in her eyes and preparing to be unleashed.

'What?' Sandra mumbled, spraying sugary doughnut crumbs all over herself and her friend.

That was it, that was all it took. Cynthia was unable to contain her laughter any longer and out it burst like a busted dam. So loud was the joyful, squealing, happy noise she created, that it caused several passers-by to turn their heads towards them to see what was occurring.

'Bloody hell Cyn!' Sandra tried to say, starting to shake with laughter herself, so infectious was Cynthia's laugh. 'WHAT?!' Sandra tried to demand, but caved in and was soon crying so hard with laughter, that sugary tears mingled in with a snotty nose.

After twenty seconds or so, when neither could actually speak, Cynthia calmed down and began wiping the tears from her eyes and cheeks as she sunk back into her deck chair. Her belly hurt from her outburst and she simply couldn't eat any more of her doughnut. She handed what was left to Sandra, who now was calming down and who also didn't turn down the extra helping.

Cynthia suddenly leapt up, her face a mixture of wonder and surprise which startled Sandra. Cynthia grabbed her friend's hand and dragged her up.

'What?' asked Sandra, trying to find out what was going on. 'What is it? What you seen?'

Cynthia didn't reveal what had caught her attention but, with her right hand tightly wrapped around Sandra's left wrist, she yanked her through the crowd, carefully avoiding seasiders and the low-flying seagulls as she did so, until she finally came to a stop upon reaching their destination.

Cynthia grinned at Sandra, who then smiled back. Cynthia rapped her knuckles on the door of the stationary gypsy wagon. There was complete silence and no apparent sign of life inside the caravan. Cynthia knocked again.

'Perhaps she's popped out?' suggested Sandra.

'How do you know she is a she? There are male clairvoyants too you know.'

'What? I've never seen any,' Sandra replied whilst reading the beautifully painted colourful letters on the caravan door. It read, 'Come in and meet Gypsy Queenie Rose'.

'There you go, it's a woman. Queenie, says so there'.

The door also displayed the others arts that were on offer, such as palmistry, phrenology, reading tea leaves and tarot readings.

'You having a go then?' asked Cynthia as she prepared to bang again on the door, but Sandra didn't have time to reply. Instead the caravan door eased open, creaking as it did so, and a bony hand lifted some of the beads which hung across the door. Both Cynthia and Sandra peered into the dark caravan but they couldn't see much apart for a lone candle with its flame dancing about merrily from the breeze. There was a moments silence where neither girls nor the owner of the bony hand said anything. Sandra thought it was all a little scary and very mysterious and Cynthia wasn't sure what to think.

'Step inside girls, please step inside,' spoke the owner of the bony hand whilst retreating deeper into the dimly-lit caravan.

Cynthia tried to push Sandra forward but she wasn't having any of that. After a small scuffle on the steps, Cynthia found herself leading the way and pulling aside the beads. They both stepped inside and closed the door behind them, shutting off the noisy world outside. The inside of the caravan was bigger than the girls expected it to be, but even so, they still had to crouch a little as they climbed across strange objects to reach the stools which the woman dressed in brightly coloured clothing directed them towards.

There was a strong smell of incense and the smoke from it hung in the air like a dawn mist. Both girls positioned themselves on the stools and sat with their backs as straight as they could, whilst resting their hands flat on their laps.

'What will it be then?' asked Queenie Rose, 'palmistry?'

'Err, yes, I guess so,' Cynthia replied speaking softly.

'I'm impressed already. I mean, how did she know?' Sandra whispered, nudging Cynthia and winking.

Cynthia tried her best to ignore Sandra's joke and stretched her hand out so that it could be inspected. The gypsy's right hand held Cynthia's, whilst motioning towards a white ceramic bowl containing a few coins with her left hand. Cynthia understood and added some more coins to the collection.

Cynthia hadn't picked up on it immediately, but as the clairvoyant spoke she realised she was Scottish. This struck Cynthia as odd, but she didn't know why exactly.

'Ahh…this is your head line,' the clairvoyant began, running the tip of her finger along one of the creases on Cynthia's palm. Cynthia leaned in to get a closer look and Sandra shuffled forward too. This was, after all, a new experience for both girls. The closest Sandra had ever got to anything similar was a distant memory of spending an afternoon with an old auntie who, apparently, could read the tea leaves.

The clairvoyant continued to run her long bony finger along Cynthia's head line. Her breathing appeared to get louder as she did and Sandra wanted to laugh, considering it to be a little too dramatic and, well, silly.

However, Cynthia sat as still as she could and followed the clairvoyant's finger.

Suddenly the clairvoyant sat forward, her head veil swaying about, which caused the candle flame to wake from its peaceful slumber and dance about frantically. Both Cynthia and Sandra jumped.

'You think a great deal about a singular thing, far too much than is healthy for you girl. Your head line is intense. There are other parts that are stifled because of your pre-occupation with that one, singular thing.'

Queenie Rose then raised her head and through her veil Cynthia could see two small bright green eyes peering at her. Cynthia nodded slowly, although she wasn't really sure why she was nodding at all.

The clairvoyant lowered her head and continued, stroking each of Cynthia's fingers and prodding parts of her palm, which tickled. There was an unnerving silence in the room and even the sounds of the people outside and the arcades appeared distant. Queenie Rose was now examining another part of Cynthia's hand.

'This is your heart line. This is where…' the clairvoyant paused. Cynthia turned to Sandra and frowned. Was the clairvoyant's pause for effect? Because, if so, the girls weren't convinced if they liked the theatrics of it all or not.

'Your heart line is like your headline. It is concerned with a singular thing. It appears to be a boy. But there are four shadows. Four distinct shadows…'

Sandra now tapped Cynthia's knee trying to get her attention, but Cynthia was too busy watching the clairvoyant who had held up Cynthia's hand close to her eyes and was studying the lines.

'You are going on an adventure soon and all the shadows will reveal themselves, but be observant because the shadows come and they go…and have already done so.'

And with that, Queenie Rose quickly released Cynthia's hand and allowed it to drop gently onto the table. Next, the clairvoyant's hand slid across the table and she placed her bony fingers on a pack of dog-eared tarot cards. She nudged them forward towards Sandra, however Sandra was far too spooked to get involved in any of this.

She made her excuses and then shoved Cynthia off her stool towards the door. Cynthia tried to say thank you to Queenie Rose, but Sandra was rushing to get out of the clairvoyant's den. The 'whoosh' they created in the air around them blew out the candle in the room and threw everything into darkness. They somehow tumbled out the caravan door and down the small flight of wooden steps in front of it. To tell the truth, they both now felt relieved to be out in the bright sunshine.

Sandra and Cynthia sucked in the clean sea air and then heard a 'whack!' as Queenie Rose's bony hand slammed the caravan door behind them.

Both girls shrugged their shoulders and giggled as they strolled arm in arm further along the pier. Cynthia tried to make light of the experience but Sandra felt uneasy to say the very least. Matters of anything religious, spiritual or occult had no place in her life; she didn't feel the need for invisible friends. Even at school she hated the idea of having to pray at the end of assembly, so instead of saying 'Amen' she would mumble 'fat men' and this always made Cynthia chuckle.

'That was weird, wasn't it? I wonder what she meant, especially about the shadows,' queried Cynthia, 'I mean, I don't even like Hank Marvin.'

'Oooh you are silly. I wonder if she is actually a clairvoyant at all Cyn. She's probably just another charlatan.'

'I dunno Sand, I think she was right you know. I mean, I suppose I do think about one 'singular' thing a lot,' said Cynthia, now pondering upon what she had just heard.

'What you mean The Beatles?' Sandra said, 'your George an' that?'

Cynthia nodded, 'Well, as it happens, yeah.'

Sandra wasn't having any of that. 'Oh, come on Cyn, what sixteen year old girl isn't thinking about The Beatles right now eh? Even I could have told you that without having to sit in a caravan, burn incense and wear a veil.'

Cynthia shrugged her shoulders. 'I guess you're right. And it cost me flipping six pence that did…anyway, there were some other things that don't make much sense. I wonder what she meant by…'

However, Sandra was no longer listening; she had spotted four clowns being mobbed by a steadily increasing group of children. What was more, she could see the clowns were handing out candyfloss and balloons? She decided she would try her luck and approached them; she'd always had a soft spot for a balloon.

Cynthia, on the other hand, had never been a great fan of clowns. They were, well, creepy in her opinion and she did what she could to avoid them. So instead of following Sandra, she hovered by a Coca Cola vending machine and lit a cigarette.

Sandra hustled her way through the group of noisy and excitable children, the tallest of them not even reaching her shoulders. A couple of little ones were trying to climb onto the back of one of the clowns. That particular clown wore a bright red and white outfit and his large nose was also painted a bright red. It amused Sandra that the clown's nose was exactly the same shape as Ringo's.

Noticing that one of their colleagues was at risk of being pulled to the ground, two of the other clowns intervened. Both wore large curly wigs and large rimmed glasses, which still didn't hide their bushy eyebrows. Sandra caught the attention of one of the clowns and they briefly looked into each other's eyes. Sandra felt there was something very familiar about the eyes she looked into.

The fourth clown, the tallest of them all, was too busy handing out sticks of candyfloss and balloons to get involved in saving his mate. Sandra made a beeline for him; she loved candyfloss. Seconds later Sandra excused herself from the maddening scene clutching a stick of candyfloss in one hand and a large red balloon in the other.

'Here you go,' Sandra said handing Cynthia the balloon.

Cynthia smiled as she held it, but then her attention was also drawn to the clowns. There was something about the way the clowns moved and interacted with one another. Sure enough, they appeared to having a great time and fully enjoying what they were doing, but there was something more going on, only Cynthia couldn't quite work out what.

The candyfloss was of course sweet and delicious and didn't disappoint. Sandra was too busy biting off large mouthfuls, which stuck to her lips, cheek and her hair as she did, to pay any more attention to the clowns. But one of them in particular - the one who had been handing out the candyfloss and balloons - was of special interest to Cynthia. There really was something about his composure and cheeky grin that was still shining through, even underneath all his make-up.

Cynthia continued to watch them as they slowly moved away from her, struggling against the tide of yet more children jumping all over them. For a brief moment a gap opened up and, although Cynthia couldn't be certain, she thought she caught a glimpse of the clown's footwear. They were wearing Cuban heeled Beatle boots rather than big floppy clown shoes.

That's odd she thought. Very odd indeed!

Cynthia saw one of them take off his white cotton glove from his right hand and wipe his sweaty brow with it. As he did so, she was momentarily blinded by the shaft of bright sunshine that glinted off a ring, or maybe two, which adorned the clown's hand. Quickly, he put the glove back on.

'Strange,' Cynthia said quietly to herself.

'What is?' Sandra asked, scraping candyfloss from her left cheek.

Cynthia slowly shook her head.

'You know, if I didn't know better...no, couldn't be, could it? No...come on. Let's go right to the end of the pier, before we have to leave and meet the boys.'

To get there, they had to navigate their way through the penny slot arcades and collection of fairground rides. The sound of coins rattling into the machines, the excited screams of those on the rides and that of the pop music blasting out from the various tannoy speakers, blended in with the sights and sounds of macho boyfriends trying to impress their girlfriends as they threw balls at coconuts and fired air rifles at tin cans.

Through all of this, Cynthia could think of only one thing - the clown in the Cuban heels...

***

In truth, the day trip to Brighton was beginning to become all too much for Cynthia. She was glad when she eventually leaned against the railings at the end of the pier. The previous night with the dancing, the pills and now the belly full of food, was catching up with Cynthia. She felt like she needed to rest.

'Sand, I'm going to have to take a breather.'

'Lightweight,' Sandra smiled at her mate and popped a pear drop in her gob.

Cynthia leant her elbows on the railings and gazed out to sea. The sun's rays bounced off the waves, she could see how such a scene would inspire some of the world's leading marine artists, greats such as Claude Monet and J.M.W. Turner, who she had learnt about at school.

Art was the one subject Cynthia had ever really enjoyed. Grabbing some pencils or paints and drawing or sketching had been Cynthia's favourite pastime when she was younger. She could lose herself for hours doing that and, by the age of ten, all she wanted to do was draw. She was a creative person and it took many forms.

The dolls she owned when younger had been put away when art had taken over, but when her mum taught her how to knit and sew, she combined her love of drawing with designing and making outfits for the dolls. By the time she was thirteen, she was even making some of her own clothes and developing a keen interest in the world of fashion.

For a couple of years, she dreamed of going to art school to study fashion and design. Cynthia's final two years at school were meant guide her towards her dream, but then she started to work in her granddad's shop and, as the months went by, she spent more time helping him rather than studying.

Gradually, her dreams of art school faded and she got used to having money in her pocket, discovering that she liked having money to spend. Money opened up a whole new world for her and with her own money came freedom. Freedom to buy clothes, shoes, handbags and records - and Cynthia liked to buy records. She had become accustomed to earning a certain wage and knew there was no way she could have amassed all the Beatles memorabilia that she had without it, and that was the most important thing in the whole world to her. Cynthia had come to accept that her art dreams had suffered as a result of the love she had for The Beatles and, for that, she had no regrets.

'Come on Cyn, I'm getting bored here,' Sandra interrupted her mate's thoughts.

'Let's go and get some food with the boys, have that wash and brush up and then, hmm, let me see…LETS GO AND SEE THE BEATLES!'

Cynthia smiled and seemed to get a second wind. Arm in arm, the pair of them strolled off the pier. There were fewer people around now as it was nearly teatime. Cynthia popped another fag in her mouth; it was only her second of the day, so busy was she talking and eating.

'Blimey, that's handy. Hang on Cyn.'

Cynthia watched on as her friend dashed towards a kiosk selling sticks of rock and other confectionary. Sandra purchased a large bag of pear drops and quickly sampled a couple before stuffing the remainder of the bag into her handbag.

Cynthia suggested they get cleaned up before finding the boys and then go for some tea, so they headed in the direction of Madeira Drive. They passed several packed cafés, all of which were full of day-trippers, Mods and assorted Beatles fans. Collections of scooters were parked in amongst the arches, their chrome panels reflecting the fading sunlight into people's eyes as they passed by. Several posters had been pasted on the walls of the arches and a brightly coloured yellow one especially caught their eye:

All Nite Mod Rave
Florida Rooms (Aquarium)
11.00 pm -7.00am
Top DJs

Licensed Bar
Admission 2 Shillings

Cynthia and Sandra liked the sound of that. It would be a nice way to round off the day following The Beatles concert, but they suspected the boys would want to return straight home so didn't dwell on it too much.

Nestled between a café and a fish and chip shop, they finally found some public toilets. The girls quickly dived inside. Of the three cubicles, two were in a disgusting state, so they took it in turns using the one remaining cubicle as their changing room. Cynthia went first and Sandra waited, guarding the door.

Sandra lit a cigarette and giggled whilst listening to Cynthia struggling to get changed. A few minutes later, Cynthia emerged looking stunning in a tartan dress with a white belt and matching tartan patterned granny shoes. Sandra went in next, which caused an equal amount of laughter from Cynthia as she heard her friend huffing and puffing. Taking much longer than Cynthia, Sandra eventually appeared also looking fabulous in her new purchase of a red shift dress with a black belt and red suede shoes. Both girls spent a few more minutes applying some make-up, mostly around their eyes and a little bit of white lipstick which gave their lips a ghostly effect. Outfits complete, they were ready to leave the toilets feeling freshened-up and ready for some food.

'Come on, I've had enough of this stinking place, let's get some fresh air,' said Cynthia as she headed for the exit.

Briskly, they walked back in the direction of the café they had used earlier and could soon see the two boys waiting outside. Cynthia waved and caught Kenny's attention, who waved back smiling.

'Hello you two,' said Kenny, 'you look great. Had a good day, have we?'

Sandra smiled at him, 'Thanks Kenny, we don't scrub up too bad do we? It's been a great day, but now I'm starving. Let's get some food down us eh?'

Like all the others, this café was also very busy, but after a short wait for a table to become clear, they were all seated and scanning the menu.

'What you having?' Kenny asked Cynthia.

Cynthia took her time scanning the menu, 'Hmm, not sure.'

164

'How about you Sandra - what do you fancy? I find the sea air always stokes up an appetite.'

'Piss it! Steak and chips Kenny…always steak and chips,' Sandra replied. To be honest, she hadn't even bothered to read the menu.

'Oh yeah and why is that then?' asked Rod, 'Hold on don't tell me…has it got some Beatles connection?'

Sandra smiled, 'Ha-ha, you've got me sussed Rod. It's Ringo's favourite meal, he loves steak and chips. What he doesn't like is anything spicy. He is also a big fan of beans on toast too…but then, who isn't I s'pose.'

The waitress arrived, a short dumpy woman with pinkish hair and a big hairy mole on her chin. She was already into a six-hour shift and the gloomy expression on her face and sweat on her forehead gave it away. Cynthia was still trying to decide what she wanted to eat. Sandra ordered and the waitress hovered, waiting for Cynthia to place her order. Eventually, like Kenny and Rod, Cynthia went for fish and chips.

'Well, when in Rome,' she muttered.

While they waited for the food, the girls regaled the boys with the story of their day, including the old gypsy Queenie Rose and the dodgy looking clowns. The boys mentioned they had spent most of the day in and out of various pubs and amusement arcades and looking in the various clothes shops.

Within ten minutes, the waitress was back with their food. In between mouthfuls of fish, steak, mushy peas and chips, the talk focused on The Beatles and the impending concert. Even cynical old Rod now seemed to be getting excited.

'I just hope we have good seats,' said Cynthia.

'Yeah, close to the stage, close enough to see the whites of The Beatles' eyes,' said Kenny.

'The bags under their eyes you mean!' joked Rod.

The girls were not amused.

'What do you think they'll be wearing Cyn? Do you think it'll be the same outfits they took on their last tour?'

Before she could answer, Rod piped up. 'They get their suits made from Dougie Millings and Sons you know,' he said, catching the girls' attention.

'Who?' they both asked in unison.

Rod had polished off his tea in record time and slowly pushed his now empty plate away from him as he sparked up a cigarette.

'Dougie Millings and Sons; they have a shop down Old Compton Street. I heard they kitted The Beatles for their first American tour. Loads of stars go there - Cliff Richard, Adam Faith and Tommy Steele.'

Cynthia was especially impressed with Rod's knowledge. She realised she had noted the shop in Old Compton Street during her recent visit to town with Sandra when they popped into the 2i's. If only she had known the Beatles' connection, she would have definitely stepped inside the shop just for a nose around. That'll be on my list of things to do for next time she decided.

The rest of them quickly gobbled down their meals and washed it down with cups of tea. Kenny looked at his watch and said it was time to go, so they paid up and hit the pavement.

The streets leading towards The Hippodrome were packed, and getting busier by the second the nearer they got to the venue. The sense of anticipation and excitement hung like a thick winter's fog in the air; it affected anyone that passed through it. Groups of excited girls walked arm in arm, whilst others waved their Beatles flags with messages to the Fab Four painted on them in lipstick, powder and paint.

Even though the police tried their best to organise the chaos in Middle Street, there was still a great deal of confusion. It was Kenny who eventually worked out where the end of the queue was - and it was much longer than they had hoped.

Such was the noise of chatter that it was hard to hear what the person nearest to you was saying. Cynthia was in her element though, she just loved the buzz of the crowd. With each step forward towards The Hippodrome door, her heart skipped to a quicker beat. She could hardly believe that the moment when she would actually get to see her idols…for real…on stage…in concert, was almost upon her.

Finally, The Hippodrome doors swung open and the expectant crowd surged forward. Cynthia grabbed Sandra's arm and both girls clung tightly to their bags containing their copies of *A Hard Day's Night*, having left all their other belongings in the boot of Rod's car.

They knew they must protect those records at all costs and, once through the doors, they moved quickly towards the auditorium.

It was lovely inside and Kenny took in the full flamboyant decoration noting the Rococo embellishments. The stage had been trodden on by some of the most famous and respected artists from the last fifty years. Not that any Beatles fans cared much for any of the architecture or, for that matter, Harry Houdini, Buster Keaton and Laurel and Hardy, all of whom had performed there. But a lot of tonight's audience knew that The Beatles had performed here once before, back in June 1963 with Roy Orbinson on the same bill.

Cynthia, elbows raised slightly, pushed her way through a host of bodies until she found their seats. They were great - lower stalls and about 10 rows from the front; Kenny had done well winning these. She plonked herself down into her chair and pulled Sandra down beside her. The boys sat either side of the girls, with Kenny sat next to Cynthia and Rod beside Sandra. Four young people lost amongst four thousand overly excited others.

Before too long, the concert was under way and a couple of support acts hit the stage. The audience showed their appreciation for The Fourmost, another band from Liverpool and also managed by Brian Epstein, but it was Jimmy Nicol, the drummer with The Shubdubs who got the biggest applause on the night so far. Jimmy had toured with The Beatles on their Australasian venture a few months earlier, replacing Ringo who was sick in hospital after having his tonsils attended to.

The noise the audience made for The Fourmost and Jimmy Nicol and The Shubdubs was certainly impressive and certainly set the tone. But now, the crowd knew the moment they were waiting for was almost upon them. The sense of anticipation in the auditorium was tangible.

And then…

Bang!

There they were! Thousands of voices screamed like they had never screamed before.

For Cynthia though, it was all unfolding in complete silence, so intense was her concentration on seeing those four figures walk out in front of her. Everything moved in slow motion for a few moments as she watched the Fab Four, including her beloved George, take their familiar positions on stage.

She daren't blink and she didn't breathe; she could hardly believe what she was seeing. Finally, as the enormity of what was in front of her became real, she tried to shout and scream, but nothing came out.

Everyone around her had channelled every ounce of energy towards the stage. Cynthia thought she had known what to expect but nothing could have prepared her for the reality of the situation.

She saw Ringo start beating his drums, then the silence lifted and she could hear him and the rest of the band playing. *She Loves You*, a tune she knew inside out and back to front came alive, and finally her voice came back and she let out the loudest scream she could muster.

Cynthia was swept along with the screeching and high-pitched squealing, plus the crying all around her. It was simply overwhelming and it penetrated Cynthia's inner core. There was nothing she could do other than join in. Then came the next wave of the assault as thousands of jellybeans were tossed towards the stage. Cynthia thought it was a shocking and yet marvellous sight. She glanced momentarily at Sandra, who was now weeping uncontrollably beside her, and burst into tears of laughter as she watched Sandra throw a handful of her precious pear drops at The Beatles.

Kenny and Rod sat there looking stunned, with their hands up to their ears trying in vain to protect them, actual pain etched on their faces.

The Beatles were definitely up there performing, but nobody could actually hear the music, such was the noise produced by this hysterical crowd.

Not being able to hear the music didn't matter to anyone - this was The Beatles for god's sake. The band looked out into a sea of girls who screamed and yelled their names at them, stuffed their fists or handkerchiefs into their mouths and jerked and trembled as they sat in their seats. And yet the band still played as hard as they ever could.

The assault of noise showed no sign of letting up and all The Beatles could do was to continue to play their instruments, even though they knew they had lost this battle.

At one point, someone threw a toilet roll onto the stage, much to the amusement of John and George who took the opportunity to have a little kick-about with it. The audience cheered and roared at the spectacle.

The Beatles performed a few more songs and it seemed no sooner had they appeared that they disappeared, leaving behind them an empty stage littered with sweets, pieces of screwed up paper inscribed with personal messages and uncoiled toilet rolls.

Cynthia had no idea how long The Beatles had been on the stage, but it had only felt like seconds. Whatever it was, it really hadn't been long enough for her and she wasn't prepared for the overhead lights being switched on. Cynthia felt a combination of being elated, drained and exhausted and, as she looked at Sandra, she could see that she was in the same condition.

Cynthia glanced around at the other girls. Virtually every face was flushed and their cheeks covered in smudged mascara. Many had a dazed look in their eyes; it was as if they had witnessed the second coming of Christ and, for some, the experience had been a truly religious affair.

It was Kenny's hand on Cynthia's shoulder which brought her back to some sense of reality. Kenny could feel that Cynthia's dress was soaking wet and she was still trembling, so he pointed towards the exit sign and gently pushed Cynthia towards it. As they walked, the boys tried their best to avoid the smell and puddles of urine left by some of the most emotional girls. Kenny certainly hadn't expected that from the sugar and spices.

Rod turned to Sandra and asked, 'Why do you scream like that?'

Sandra looked at him like he was mad. 'The question is Rod, why weren't you?'

As the crowd spilled out into Middle Street, the mixture of stunned silence from some and hysterical chatter from others continued.

Cynthia and Sandra quietly walked back to Rod's car in a dazed silence, each trying to digest what they had just witnessed. They were spent, done in. All thoughts of that 'All Nite' Mod event and getting their albums signed were long, long forgotten. They pretty much remained in that state for the entire journey back to London.

This was simply, mission accomplished...

Chapter 12
Tell Me What You See

'Cynthia…you awake?'

'Cyn–thia…'

'CYNTHIA!'

Cynthia simply hadn't heard the first two gentle shouts from her father, but she certainly heard the third one, accompanied by his robust banging on her door.

As usual, she was in a Beatle induced sleep. She turned, slowly, and tried to focus on her alarm clock. Gradually the numbers focused enough for her to recognise it was seven thirty. She let out a small groan at the very thought…

'You awake then girl?' It was her dad again.

'Sort of…whaddyawant - yawn - Dad?'

'Me? I don't want anything missy. It's your little mate Sandra on the phone, though God knows why this early…'

His voice trailed off as he made his way down the stairs to continue his usual morning routine.

On opening her eyes more fully, Cynthia realised she was smiling. Despite its abrupt ending, that was what you call a happy sleep. She climbed out of bed and, although weary, she felt fantastic.

She crept downstairs to the shelf where the telephone lived and found its receiver resting on a dog-eared Yellow Pages.

'Hello…Sand…you there?'

This was pretty much the extent of her part in the conversation as Sandra began talking, not taking a breath for what felt like ten minutes as she babbled on about the trip to Brighton and the concert from the previous night. Cynthia noticed the wall clock in the hallway was approaching 7.45am by the time the conversation began to slow down. Sandra must also have been conscious of the time because she kept saying 'quick, before I go' but then continued to talk, never bringing it all to an end.

Finally, Cynthia knew she had to stop her best mate.

'Sand…Sand…we both need to get ready to go to work. Stop now eh mate?'

Sandra did as she was told, but not before quickly agreeing to meet at *their* bench after their respective teas and go to The Moka to continue the catch up. In truth, Cynthia spent the rest of the day in some kind of a strange daze. The cumulative effects of a very busy weekend were now very much in evidence.

At the shop, Nobby tried several times to ask Cynthia how her day in Brighton had been, but it was as if his granddaughter was on a different planet as he couldn't get any sense out of her. She mumbled something about needing to go and update her scrapbook and diary. He could sense how eager she was to do that and appreciated that she had been filling it with Beatles stuff since she had first discovered The Beatles back in '62.

'Tell you what girl,' said an exasperated but understanding looking Nobby, 'you're about as much use to me as a chocolate teapot. Why don't you go off home early; I actually think I'll get more done with you not here today.'

Cynthia smiled and within seconds had put on her coat. She kissed her granddad on the cheek and swiftly ran home.

On arriving home, Cynthia quickly made herself a cup of tea and grabbed a bright red apple from the white and brown ceramic fruit bowl. Finding some cheese in the fridge, she helped herself to a slice and carried it all carefully in her hands as she darted off to her bedroom. Quickly wolfing down the slice of cheddar and taking several large bites of the crunchy apple, Cynthia had a large swig of tea before virtually collapsing onto her bed. After a few minutes, she turned and grabbed the scrapbook and notepad from her bedside cabinet and, with pencil poised, she was ready.

Cynthia held her Beatles concert ticket in her hand and closed her eyes as she soaked up the memories from the previous night. She then kissed the piece of paper and pasted it into the scrapbook. This was a special moment in the life of her book, as she had long dreamed of being able to stick a real ticket into it.

She proudly stuck the ticket into the centre of one of the empty pages and in her best handwriting wrote the date underneath. Cynthia thought it looked brilliant and was undoubtedly her most prized Beatles possession to date. She had another slurp of tea as she once again marvelled at her new trophy.

Next up, Cynthia positioned her writing pad on her lap. Sitting straight legged on her bed and with pencil in hand, she began to write...

'Dear Patricia,

Yesterday was without any doubt the best day of my life. In fact, yesterday was the most moving experience of my life. Words can hardly express what I felt actually going to see THE BEATLES IN CONCERT! My best friend Sandra and I got a lift in a car with two boys to a popular seaside resort called Brighton. The Beatles were performing at the Brighton Hippodrome, but you probably already knew that. The Hippodrome is a lovely venue that was built in the Victorian times.

We actually waited outside earlier in the day, hoping to get a glimpse of The Beatles, but sadly they didn't appear. There was a rumour going around that George had a car accident on the way to Brighton, but I don't know if that's true or not.

We also carried our copies of A Hard Day's Night around Brighton all day and even took them to the concert. We so hoped that we would manage to get them autographed. That is our mission and we still intend to fulfil this dream. We are soon going on an adventure that will take us to both Liverpool and Blackpool, with the intention of tracking down the Fab Four and getting our LPs autographed. I truly believe we can do this. I'm not convinced Sandra thinks so, but I will prove her wrong and she, like me, will then be delighted to actually have The Beatles' signatures.

It's really hard to describe how incredible and how amazing the concert was. I loved every second of it and was so sad when it ended, but I understand the boys have to go and perform elsewhere. They must be exhausted after all the travelling they have done recently. In fact, John did look a little tired.

I wish I could tell you how great the songs sounded live but, in all honesty, I cannot because, from the moment they walked onto the stage, everyone started screaming and calling out their names and that drowned them out. The noise was almost painful at times and my ears are still ringing even now - and it's now Monday afternoon.

I just know that I will carry the memory of the concert with me forever and suspect not a day will pass when I don't think about it at least ten times a day. I can't wait to tell my children about it one day.

After my tea this evening I am going to meet Sandra and go to The Moka. Apart from the two boys we went with (and I must add here they're not our boyfriends), I don't know any others who went to the concert, so I think I'll be busy telling everyone about it this evening.

So many of my friends are going to be so jealous, but I won't rub it in, well, maybe a bit ha-ha.

Hope all is well with you and you are having a fab time and I will write you another letter after my adventures and family holiday at Butlin's.

Lots of love, your UK pen pal
Cynthia'

Once finished, she began to read it back to herself but felt her eyes getting heavy half way through and, by the last paragraph, she had dropped the letter on the floor and was fast asleep.

The weekend ended here…

The shrill ringing in her ears, plus a new sound of rattling plates, pots and pans coming from her family kitchen slowly woke Cynthia a couple of hours later. Checking her alarm clock, she saw it was nearly 6pm so family teatime was about to start. She made her way down to the kitchen, where she found her whole family present. This was a rare occurrence nowadays and it had seemed like weeks since Andrew had joined them for a meal.

For most of the next half hour, in between mouthfuls of sausage and mash topped with onion gravy, Cynthia regaled them all with her tales of Brighton. She talked on, although the rest of the family were patently bored with the whole escapade five minutes in. Meals were finished ahead of time and John and Andrew even offered to take over Cynthia's turn to do the washing up, just so they could get rid of her.

Cynthia certainly didn't complain at that and smiled as she plucked her cardigan from the hook on the back of the kitchen door and took off to meet Sandra. As she approached their usual meeting point, Cynthia had to pinch herself and do a double take because Sandra was already waiting for her on *their* bench. Cynthia was in the process of forming the words 'early again' but Sandra beat her to the punch, jumping straight in to continue their conversation from the exact point where they had left it earlier that morning.

Sandra continued to do most of the talking as they strolled to The Moka. In truth, Cynthia didn't mind as she was pleased that Sandra was so happy. If it was possible, their spirits were lifted even higher as they entered The Moka and were met by the sounds of The Beatles playing *Ask Me Why* on the Jukebox. It was the B-side to *Please Please Me* and had become one of The Moka crowd's most regular plays.

173

Disappointingly, however, the place was virtually empty, which took some of the wind out of the girl's sails because they wanted to tell the whole place about the fabulous Sunday they had had.

Two couples, who Cynthia vaguely knew, sat around one of the tables and two young men, who Cynthia didn't recognise at all, stood near the Juke box. And that was that. Sammy was sat on his stool behind the counter, reading a newspaper.

'Where is everyone Sammy?' Cynthia enquired.

'Hello Cynthia. I don't know really. I did hear there's some film on that the kids were talking about going to see. Maybe they've all gone tonight?'

Sammy tried to sound like he had been abandoned by his loyal customers, but Cynthia suspected he was happy to have a quiet night. Cynthia turned to Sandra and shrugged her shoulders; neither girl could think what new movie was being shown. They had been so caught up in their Brighton trip they hadn't been paying much attention to what else was going on in the coming week.

So, not wanting to waste a good story, Cynthia and Sandra set about 'chewing' Sammy's ear off. He tried his utmost to look disinterested but soon realised resistance was futile, so folded his paper, popped a cigarette into his mouth and sat and listened, a resigned look on his face as he realised he was in for a long night. It was gone ten before the girls decided to leave him alone and go home to bed.

***

'Good morning Granddad,' said Cynthia cheerily as she entered the shop on this bright and sunny morning.

'Morning Cynthia, my love,' he replied pulling a heavy sack of potatoes through the door; a task which seemed to knock the wind out of him. He gave out a few coughs as Cynthia brushed by him, however she decided not to dwell on it and set about making a pot of tea.

Once he was finished displaying the spuds, old Nobby sat next to Cynthia at the counter and began sipping his tea. Cynthia studied his face and couldn't help but notice the beads of sweat forming on his forehead. She also noticed he had loosened his shirt collar a little and didn't think he looked his normal self at all.

'Are you okay Granddad?' she asked kindly.

'Me? I'm fine. It's a hot one out there this morning my girl, that's all,' replied Nobby in a clipped tone which suggested he didn't want his granddaughter to pursue the matter any further.

As Cynthia sat looking out through the main shop window, she didn't think it was an especially hot day. She glanced back her granddad, examining him once again. He looked a little out of sorts and she was just about to ask him again how he was feeling when Mrs Arnold walked into the shop. She was a Tuesday regular who lived just around the corner and, as a result, rarely ventured further than the shop.

Cynthia often wondered what Mrs Arnold did with her days. She guessed she was a lonely woman as she had lost her husband in the war and then tragically lost her two sons in a motorcar accident in the late fifties. It was soon after the loss of her sons that Mrs Arnold became a virtual recluse.

Cynthia often thought that the Tuesday shopping trip must be the highlight of Mrs Arnold's week. Her order was nearly always the same: an assortment of tinned meats from Spam to corned beef, tea and sugar and, on the last week of each month, a bag of barley sugars. Cynthia's granddad once told her that Mrs Arnold had a reasonable sized garden and grew her own vegetables, so that was why veg was never on her shopping list.

Cynthia was also told on a regular basis about the garden by Miss Ford, who was another shop regular who lived five doors down from Mrs Arnold. Miss Ford kept Cynthia and everyone informed of her neighbour's daily gardening habits. By all accounts, Mrs Arnold's runner beans were something to behold.

'Good morning Mrs Arnold,' Cynthia said politely.

'Morning Irene,' said Nobby with a hint of familiarity.

Mrs Arnold returned the greetings with a polite smile, 'Morning Cynthia, morning Nobby.'

She placed a scrap of paper which served as the shopping list on the counter. As Cynthia took the paper to check the order, Mrs Arnold spoke to Cynthia's granddad.

'Oooh, you alright there Nobby? You don't look in the pink if truth were told. Not feeling very well today then?'

'Don't you start an' all. Nothing the matter with me,' barked Nobby in her general direction. 'It's the infernal heat. That's all.'

With that he ambled off into the back room. Both Cynthia and Mrs Arnold looked at each other, raising their eyebrows as they heard him cough a few times. Cynthia shrugged her shoulders, a weak smile playing on her lips, and set about fulfilling Mrs Arnold's order.

Nobby didn't return to the shop front for about half hour after. When he finally reappeared, he told Cynthia that if it was alright by her, he needed some time to sort out the paperwork so could she look after the shop.

Cynthia nodded and back he went. She saw to all the customers' needs as they came and went over the next few hours. On the whole, business was good for a Tuesday morning and there were plenty of conversations about the weather and even more gossip about who had done what in the past week. Cynthia loved a bit of gossip, but all she really wanted to talk about was The Beatles concert in Brighton, but most of her elderly customers just didn't seem interested. Strange lot, she thought…

A little before noon, Nobby emerged from the back room. Cynthia really didn't think he looked at all well, so suggested he go and sit down whilst she close the shop for dinner-time and make them both a nice cup of tea and a cheese and cucumber sandwich. This time, the old man didn't put up a fight and seemed more than happy to retreat to his armchair, which confirmed Cynthia's suspicions even further.

She couldn't help but notice the dark rings which had formed under his eyes and, if anything, he seemed a little worse than he did earlier. Cynthia gently tried to press him for more info on how he was feeling, but being the old soldier he was, he didn't want any fuss made of what he considered to be nothing more than a little cough.

'Stop fussing round now Cynthia, I'm ok girl,' said Nobby.

Cynthia took the hint and decided to change tack by talking about their forthcoming holiday to Butlin's. She knew how much he looked forward to the family holiday to Butlin's and hoped the thought of that time away might make him feel better in himself. As they drank their tea and chewed their sandwiches, they recalled some of their fond memories from previous Butlin's holidays. There was plenty to discuss too as Cynthia had been going to Butlin's holiday camps since she was a toddler. Some of her earliest memories were from holidaying at one of the camps, but for the last few years the family had decided on Bognor Regis as their favourite destination.

Although Cynthia was looking forward to the holiday with her family, it had needed careful planning. In the end, the dates had worked out okay and meant Cynthia could still catch The Beatles' planned London Palladium appearance on Thursday 23rd July because the family wasn't leaving for Butlin's until the day after, the Friday.

This made Cynthia very happy as she was determined to have her *A Hard Day's Night* album autographed by all four of The Fabs before the holiday, which would mean she would have something to brag about to the other teenagers and the Redcoats at the camp.

The remainder of the shop day was quiet compared to the morning and Cynthia did most of the work, letting her granddad have a rest. By the time he locked up dead on five o' clock, he really didn't look well at all and this bothered Cynthia a great deal.

Before they parted, she kissed him tenderly on his forehead and in her best school teacher voice told him to go straight home, do himself some sardines on toast for his tea and then get an early night. He nodded obediently, mumbled some reply and set off towards the comfort of his favourite armchair in his own front room.

Around the dinner table that evening Cynthia told her parents that granddad hadn't been looking very well during the day.

'Really Cynthia? I'll give him a call in a minute,' said her mum, 'see what's up with him. I just hope whatever it is, it's cleared up by the time we go to Butlin's as I honestly can't wait.'

Any more talk of bugs and Butlin's was soon forgotten, as Cynthia's mum produced a steaming hot homemade apple crumble from the oven and placed it on the kitchen table, followed by a jug of steaming hot custard, saying to all, 'Get that down you.' The whole lot disappeared in minutes.

Cynthia didn't go to The Moka that evening as Sandra had some family commitment so couldn't go. Opting for a night in instead, Cynthia decamped to her bedroom, playing Beatles records back to back before tuning into Radio Caroline and attending to her scrapbook. She was also getting excited mulling over the idea of the next planned Beatles adventure.

The thought of it had only occurred in the car on the way back from Brighton, but as soon as it had she immediately screamed at Sandra, 'We need to go to the Abbey Road Studios!'

Sandra agreed instantly and it was decided there and then that they would do just that on Wednesday, when the shop shut for half day closing. As a result, Cynthia would be free and Sandra said she would simply take the afternoon off to join her.

The next morning before leaving for work, Dot told Cynthia she had spoken to her granddad last night and he had told her in no uncertain terms that he was alright, that it was nothing and that her daughter was a flipping fusspot!

'Umm, not sure about that,' said Cynthia smiling, 'he wasn't great yesterday.'

'I know, I know,' replied her mum. 'I could hear him coughing down the phone. Do me a favour Cynthia - if he gets worse, will you let me know?'

Cynthia nodded, gave her mum a goodbye hug and set off for the shop.

The morning passed quickly which suited Cynthia.

However, she was now genuinely concerned at the condition of her granddad's health. He had spent most of the morning coughing and complaining to no-one in particular about a few aches and pains, which was very unlike him. It was now nearly closing time and it was clear he was getting no better. She thought about what her mum had said earlier and weighed up whether to call her.

'Shall I call mum, let her know you're not well?' Cynthia asked kindly but loaded with concern.

'Oh, will you stop fussing girl, I'm alright. Don't tell her as she'll only worry and drive me mad. Anyway, I'm alright. Go on, off with you if you are going.'

Cynthia looked at him and smiled. She repeated what she had told him the day before: to go straight home to bed and try to get some rest.

'Love you Granddad,' she said. He smiled.

But she suspected he wouldn't go straight home and would find somewhere else to go first, be it the pub, the dogs or maybe just sit on the Common for a while. He was never one for being told what to do.

Just for a change, Cynthia decided to walk a different route on her way to meet Sandra. She had a bit of time to kill and, anticipating that Sandra would be late as she always was, found herself taking a cut-through beside the local allotments. Cynthia ambled along the dusty path; the sun beamed a blistering heat and she wanted avoid building up a sweat. She gently swung her bag which always contained her copy of *A Hard Day's Night*, whilst humming *Can't Buy Me Love*.

Despite Cynthia's concern for her granddad's health, she felt in a pleasant summery mood, checking out the various allotments as she passed. The first thing that caught her eye was a collection of bamboo canes with strings of runner beans clinging to them. For Cynthia, summer wasn't complete without the sight of runner beans. A few feet from them an elderly man sat crouched on an up-turned tin bucket. He had a white-knotted handkerchief on his head that provided him with some degree of protection from the sun's powerful rays.

He puffed away contentedly on his pipe and Cynthia got a whiff of the pipe smoke and it made her tingle. There was something about the smell of pipe tobacco which the old men smoked that she had liked since she was a child. The old man appeared not to notice Cynthia. Instead he just puffed on his pipe and studied an area of soil beside him that he had clearly been tending to.

The allotment stretched a good few hundred feet into the distance. Cynthia looked hard and could just about see where it ended, that being where it reached a long red brick wall. Behind the wall was a coal merchants, the very same one which had delivered coal to her own home when she was growing up. In fact, her first boyfriend, Carl, had worked there on Saturday mornings. The relationship hadn't lasted long, but Cynthia was only twelve, with Carl being thirteen. She noticed quite quickly that he always had dirt under his fingernails and it wasn't long before this began to put Cynthia off, but she smiled at the memory just the same.

Seeing the red brick also reminded her of something which, at the time, was quite an event. At the end of the wall and in one of the corners where it joined the allotment, there were the sheds which belonged to residents. These were hand-built from an assortment of discarded pieces of wood and not much bigger than an outdoors toilet. They had been painted a dark green colour that seemed to be everywhere and Cynthia had often wondered why so many of the sheds were painted the same colour. Someone must have got a job lot of paint somehow she thought...

She and Carl had only recently become 'officially' boyfriend and girlfriend and they hung out with a gang who called themselves The Wild Wimbledon Commoners. It was made up of six boys and seven girls who were all of a similar age, give or take a year here and there. The eldest boy, Sid, was thirteen and, being exactly two months older than Carl, he assumed the position of gang leader. The youngest was a skinny frail girl called Laura, who was ten, and who pretty much just followed the rest of the gang around like a lost puppy.

Before the summer holidays had begun that year, the gang had spent their time clambering over the remains of a bombsite, which was a gift to Wimbledon courtesy of Hitler's Luftwaffe. This particular site had once housed three families, but in 1942 their homes and lives had been destroyed by one enormous bomb. Tragically, every family member from each of the three families lost their lives.

The memories of the horrific event had further served as a source of entertainment for Cynthia's gang in the form of ghost stories. 'Snotty nose Nigel' was the gang's best storyteller and it was his sole responsibility to create and deliver the ghostly tales as the rest of the gang sat cross-legged around him.

It was a week before the summer holidays commenced that builders stepped in to spoil the gang's fun by fencing off the bombsite and putting up a notice about trespassing and the building of some new homes. The gang complained to anyone who would listen and felt hard done by, especially as the bombsite had been left unattended for almost two decades. But of course, no one listened.

Once the holidays had begun, the gang would meet up most days just after ten in the morning, near the sheds by the allotments which Cynthia had seen and vividly remembered earlier. There were never any adults around because this area was still to be allocated by the council, which resulted in land they could muck about on to their heart's content.

After a few days, one of the corner sheds had become Gang Head Quarters and they would sit in there for hours, particularly if it started to rain.

Gang leader, Sid, had laid down some rules, among them, 'no pissing on any vegetable patches, no pulling up any vegetables and no stealing any garden tools from sheds.' Pretty much anything else was allowed...encouraged even!

But if they found anything around the grounds, then that was considered 'finders keepers' and as a result, the wooden shelves of HQ were now lined with bits of old tools, broken pottery, and assorted bird feathers.

As she walked, Cynthia was recalled one particular day with some fondness. The gang had been out in full force and spirits were high.

Sid had impressed everyone with his story of beating up an older boy on Wimbledon Common earlier that day. Cynthia listened intently along with everybody else, but felt that she wasn't being told the full story. However, she kept quiet for fear of upsetting the leader and went along with what she heard.

Somehow, the topic of conversation went from the leader's victory over the older boy, to meeting a girl and copping a feel of one of her breasts. This diversion certainly caught the gang's attention, apart from little Laura, who seemed content playing with a hammer and some nails she had found.

The 'copping a feel' of a girl's breast provided the opportunity for several excited conversations to erupt. The boys could hardly contain themselves, telling all who would listen that they too had done this, only for the girls to roll their eyes in an 'of course you have' gesture. It was obvious after five minutes of shouting that this topic wasn't going to extinguish itself easily. Instead it developed into much more and had in fact triggered an idea in Sid's head.

He suddenly asked everyone to leave the shed and then, with the exception of Laura, he lined up all the girls outside and got the boys to do the same in a separate line facing them. He told the gang that each boy would take turns to step inside the shed and then they would pick a girl who they wanted to go in with them. Once inside the shed, each person would participate in a 'you show me yours and I'll show you mine' session.

He added that 'copping a feel' would be acceptable if the other person gave their permission. Everyone in the gang began giggling excitedly and agreed it was a fun idea. If anyone felt otherwise, they didn't let on and instead opted to go along with their leader's idea for fear of embarrassing themselves in front of the rest of the gang.

Sure enough, Sid went first and called for Sandra to enter the shed. This she did, looking a little nervous, but obviously not wanting to chicken out in front of everyone. The shed door was abruptly slammed shut and the remaining gang members hid their smiling faces and giggles behind their hands as they stood patiently in the queue.

One boy and one girl after another followed suit, entering the shed for a couple of minutes before reappearing - both usually giggling and blushing at the same.

Carl was the last boy to go in and it was obvious he was happy that Cynthia was the only girl left because, over the past few weeks, he had begun to fancy her something rotten. And as luck would have it, Cynthia felt the same about Carl.

Once inside the shed, Cynthia closed the door behind her. The thing they both noticed immediately was that it was very dark in there; only thin beams of light got through the gaps and slivers in the wood panels. Cynthia was now stood in front of Carl, neither of them said anything but Cynthia felt that she wanted to giggle. She knew she felt nervous and was about to take part in a completely new experience.

She smiled to herself as the memory of sharing a bath with her brother John and seeing his 'willy' suddenly struck her. Back then, as small children, it had been a totally normal thing. In fact, she thought as she stood there now, that was the last time she could remember seeing one.

Carl, his hands shaking ever so slightly, started to undo the zipper on his Tesco Bomber jeans and suddenly Cynthia felt quite awkward and now a little bit scared. But Cynthia also felt a new sensation, a tingle and an excitement, and it was this which drove her on and, before she knew it, she was gawping at the Carl's quite small willy.

He had scooped it out and allowed it to dangle from the slit in his Y fronts. Cynthia found at first that she couldn't look away. Maybe ten seconds passed before she couldn't contain herself any longer and burst out laughing. She quickly covered her mouth with her hands to try and stifle the noise, but the laughter made Carl quickly push his penis back into his pants and somewhat carefully zip up his fly.

Of course, now it was Cynthia's turn. After what she had just seen, she now didn't really have a choice in the matter. Carl looked at the buttons on her blouse and nodded in their direction. Cynthia's hand trembled as she slowly undid her buttons. She let the blouse fall open, exposing the white lacy trainer bra she had begun to wear earlier that year. She took a deep breath as she slowly pulled down the right cup to reveal her tiny, still growing breast. She knew she wasn't exactly the most formed girl in their gang; Sandra was much more developed than herself and they all knew now that Sid had certainly noticed that!

Cynthia stood in the darkness feeling very conscious that one of her breasts was on display and being stared at by a boy. Carl reached out his hand but Cynthia took a step back. Carl immediately retracted his arm.

'Can I?' he asked quietly and respectfully. Cynthia considered his question for a few seconds. She wondered how many of the other girls had allowed him to touch them and understood the consequences of possibly being the odd one out. She looked him directly in the eyes, took another deep breath and then slowly nodded.

Carl once again reached out his hand and gently caressed the rounded edges and small nipple. He then withdrew his hand and tucked it into his jeans pocket.

Both Cynthia and Carl stood in silence, still looking into each other's eyes. Cynthia wasn't sure what she was supposed to do next.

'You can touch too…if you want to,' Carl eventually said. The thought hadn't even crossed Cynthia's mind and for a moment she didn't know how to reply. In fact she didn't, she just simply shook her head. She decided that she had seen and certainly revealed enough for one day. They both smiled at each other and held hands as they left the shed.

And that was the first time, but certainly not the last, that she noticed Carl's dirty fingernails…

Chapter 13
Come Together

'It's the 15th July Cyn!' Sandra cried in amongst their greetings.

Cynthia first heard and then saw her best mate as she headed towards their meeting point. She was already smiling at the thought of showing hers to Carl and the dirty fingernails, and that smile grew broader as she now saw her nutty little mate.

'I know Sand, you loon, Julia's day,' Cynthia was now frantically trying to tuck the bag containing her LP under her arm so she could reach for her packet of cigarettes from her pocket.

'Just think, it was six years ago that Julia died. Six years Cyn! If only she knew what that five pounds and ten shillings she spent on buying John his first guitar would lead to eh?'

'Just shows you, a mother's love,' Cynthia mused.

With thoughts of John Lennon's long lost mum mulling over in their minds, the girls skipped down towards the tube station. It was a fair trek to reach St John's Wood station, but the girls hardly noticed the distance as they gassed all the way there.

As they exited into the leafy surroundings, Sandra quizzed Cynthia as to the intended plan for the day. Cynthia, shrugging her shoulders, informed Sandra that she didn't really have one.

'I just thought we'd get over here and see what happens. Fingers crossed, you never know Sand, one of the Beatles will be visiting the studios and we can say hello.'

Sandra pulled a 'can't see that happening' face.

'Oi you,' said Cynthia giggling, 'a girl can dream, can't she?'

It was just after half past one now and the roads around the EMI Studios were busy with lunchtime traffic. The girls waited at the nearby zebra crossing, but several cars and even a London bus refused to give way. Eventually, two nuns complete with habits, joined them at the zebra crossing and the next car stopped, allowing them all to cross safely. Cynthia wondered if the nuns could still be seen on the crossing and it made her smile.

As they approached the studios, both Cynthia and Sandra spotted a group of four girls lurking by the white wall which stood in front of the entrance to the front door of the Georgian townhouse. Just being at this location it was obvious they were Beatles fans too.

The girls noticed Cynthia and Sandra looking at them and gave them an approving glance and a smile. Cynthia and Sandra nodded at them and returned the smile, whilst pressing themselves up against the black iron railings to survey the building and car park now in front of them. A uniformed commissionaire stood resolute by the large wooden front doors. He tried to appear disinterested in the group of girls gathering on Abbey Road; after all, it was a scene he had seen daily over the last two years.

One of the girls from the other group bounced over to Cynthia and Sandra, almost startling them. She was a tall, lanky girl with long mousy coloured hair that she kept twiddling in the fingers of her right hand as she spoke to them. She looked to be in her early teens, her face blotchy and spotty.

'I haven't seen you here before, is this your first time?' she asked in a well-spoken voice.

Cynthia and Sandra looked at each other and then at the girl. The girl twiddled her hair faster as she waited for their reply.

'Yes, actually,' Cynthia replied hesitantly, feeling like she had said the wrong thing. 'I'm Cynthia and this is my friend Sandra.'

'Guessed you were new. My name's Catherine and my friends and I come here at least twice a week and I knew I hadn't seen you before,' she said, still twiddling with her hair. 'We're regulars here and we sometimes go to other places where the boys might be. You know, where they might be living or clubs like the Scotch of St James. It's always such a thrill to see one of them and I've lost count how many times I have seen Paul. He's my Beatle.'

Sandra shyly smiled at Catherine, 'I love Ringo and Cyn loves George.'

Catherine turned in the direction of her friends, coughing dramatically to get their attention and called out, 'Girls, wave to our recruits...' Her three friends did as they were commanded to do.

Catherine continued, 'See the girl in the duffle coat, and God knows why she has to wear it in the middle of summer, her name is Clare and Ringo is her Beatle. The pretty girl in the white cardigan beside her is Amanda and she will probably end up marrying John.'

'Eh?' said Sandra looking puzzled.

'Well, he has winked at her,' Catherine replied sternly; a comment Cynthia had to try very hard not to laugh at.

'And that's Marjorie with the jet-black hair. She is by far the biggest George fan in the world. Ask her any question about George and she will tell you the right answer. It was Marjorie's idea for us to frequent this spot and others as much as we do. We love it here.'

Cynthia found herself staring intently at her 'George rival' and nearly threw down a challenge, but decided to join Sandra in waving back at them instead.

'Piss it Catherine, how do you find the time to get down here?' enquired Sandra.

Catherine frowned at Sandra and, sounding every inch like a headmistress, she growled, 'Please don't swear! We have to make sure that we don't cause any problems. They only let us hang about here if we don't cause any bother or annoy the passers-by and swearing of any kind is simply not tolerated. You see him at the door? He knows our names and just leaves us alone...'

'Oh, I am sorry,' Sandra mumbled sarcastically, which made Cynthia grin once again.

Catherine was obviously in her element and the leader of this particular pack of Beatles fans.

'You'd be amazed how many girls come here and from all over. I've spoken to girls from America, Australia and even Japan. When they come and visit England they just have to come and look at the place where The Beatles record their songs; it's simply a mecca for Beatles fans. But anyway, you know that already, otherwise you wouldn't be standing there.'

'Where...' Cynthia began to ask a question, but having taken a short breath Catherine fired off again.

'Well, it's just gone two and we always go the café down the end of the road for a pot of tea at around this time. We won't be long, so we can chat some more when I get back, okay. See you soon girls, see you soon.'

With that Catherine turned, gathered up her little friends and marched them off down Abbey Road.

'Phew!' Sandra said quietly, 'please don't rush back on our behalf...'

'Blimey...she was hard work weren't she,' said Cynthia as she puffed out her cheeks. 'Ere' Sand, you got a pen?'

Sandra, busy digging through her pockets trying to find her much-needed pear drops, shook her head.

'No why?' she asked.

'Well, I was going to scribble my name on the wall here.'

'Err, I don't think that would go down too well with Catherine now would it!' replied Sandra in the headmistress-like tone of Catherine. Cynthia giggled at her friend.

'Blimey, as it happens I wish I had a pen now,' laughed Sandra.

Cynthia continued, 'Ooh I think it's a smashing idea. We could even start a trend whereby every Beatle fan that comes to visit the studios has to write their name or leave a message for the Fabs on the white wall. It would look fantastic.'

'Wow, that would look fantastic. Shall we go and ask the captain at the door?'

'It would wouldn't it,' smiled Cynthia. 'Yeah, c'mon, let's go and ask him. It'll be a laugh.'

So, trying to stifle their laughter and linking arms, Cynthia and Sandra marched through the black iron gates and approached the stone steps that led to the front door and the commissionaire.

The ever-vigilant guard had noticed them as they made their way towards him and was now glaring at them. He was already preparing to give them his usual spiel of, 'You're wasting your time, there are no Beatles here today and no, you can't come inside to have a look around.'

How he wished he had a pound for every time he said that during his long day on duty.

Cynthia and Sandra halted at the bottom of the steps and looked up towards the guard who had now positioned himself directly in the middle of the doorway. He crossed his arms and waited for the girls' questions.

It threw him somewhat when only a pen was requested. He even found himself checking his pockets automatically, before abandoning that idea.

'What d'ya want a pen for?' he asked suspiciously.

Thinking quickly on her feet Cynthia replied, 'Err, I have to write down my friend's phone number.'

'Are you good friends?' he asked.

Cynthia and Sandra nodded their heads in unison.

'Then why don't you have her phone number?'

Cynthia thought quickly and was about to reply when the door behind the guard suddenly swung open. Appearing in the doorway was a tall middle-aged man with a narrow face, his light-coloured hair brushed back onto his scalp, and wearing a short sleeved white shirt with a black knitted tie. He was carrying a large pile of paper, held in his long slender fingers, and appeared to be struggling to see where he was going.

At first, he didn't notice the guard and as he brushed past him, lost his balance and slipped on the top step.

Cynthia watched the incident unfold as if in slow motion. The man's legs gave way beneath him and his arms soared into the air as the pile of papers he was carrying flew upwards, scattering themselves in every direction. Slowly and gently they fluttered down to the ground. As they did so, the man bounced down the rest of the steps, landing with a sickening thud.

Cynthia, Sandra and the guard rushed to the man's aid. They helped him to his feet and then sat him down on the lowest step. He looked shocked and it took him a few moments to compose himself. Once it was evident the man was okay and no serious harm had occurred, the guard went inside to fetch the man a cup of tea. Cynthia sat by his side whilst Sandra set about gathering up the pieces of paper from all around her.

'A nice cup of tea will help,' said Cynthia gently, 'that's what my granddad always says when someone has fallen over. Sometimes the customers trip over the bags of spuds on their way out of the shop. I've seen that happen a few times and sometimes it's hard not to laugh.'

The man stopped brushing the dust off of him and turned to face Cynthia. She wasn't sure what the expression on his face meant, but she stopped talking about customers tripping up. If anything, she thought the man looked embarrassed.

'Thank you,' he said in a soft, kind voice.

Whilst Cynthia asked him how he felt and if anything hurt, Sandra joined them on the step and placed the pile of papers beside the man.

'Sorry, I didn't know what order the papers should have been collected,' said Sandra apologetically.

This amused the man and he started to laugh, which in turn triggered the two girls to laugh along with him. They were all still laughing when the guard returned carrying a white china cup containing the tea with two rich tea biscuits placed carefully in the saucer. For some reason this caused them to laugh even louder. The guard looked confused.

'Thank you Alf, but I think these two young ladies deserve a cup of tea too don't you?' The man nodded towards his pile of paper, 'It's the least we can do, after all.'

'Yes of course,' replied Alf and, taking the cup of tea and biscuits with him, disappeared back inside the building.

'Girls, would you mind helping me up please and then let's go inside. By the way my name is Eric. Eric Perkins.'

It took Cynthia and Sandra a moment for the man's name to sink in, but once it had both their mouths dropped wide open. They looked at each other and their eyes grew wider and wider. It was a name they had grown familiar with by reading their Beatles Monthly. Old Eric here, well he seemed old to them, was the head engineer at Abbey Road and had worked on the Fabs' recordings so far in their career. They couldn't believe their luck!

The girls did as they were asked and helped Eric up the steps with his pile of papers. He pushed open the door, holding it ajar for the girls to follow him in. He placed his pile of papers on a wooden desk situated just inside the door, beside a hat and coat stand and told the girls to follow him.

The girls did just that. Eric led them through a hallway and down a passageway. Both girls were looking this way and that, their heads swivelling off their necks trying to take it all in. They marvelled at the décor and paintings on the wall and could hardly believe they were inside the EMI studios and in the presence of the great Eric Perkins.

As they walked, Cynthia remained quiet and content just to soak up the atmosphere, but Sandra fired question after question about The Beatles at Eric: 'When did you first meet them?'...'Do you have a favourite one?'...'Does your wife like The Beatles?'

He tried his best to answer Sandra's questions but eventually gave up and put his finger to his smiling lips. He then asked Sandra what the girls had in their bags. In fact, he had already spotted their LPs so knew the answer.

Sandra informed Eric about their mission to get the LPs signed. Cynthia secretly hoped he might volunteer some help with their mission but, as she was about to ask, she noticed they had arrived at a doorway, above which a sign read 'Studio Two'.

The girls had often read about this very studio, also in their copies of The Beatles Monthly, and knew that it was here that Eric had assisted Mister Martin to produce all The Beatles' records to date. They could hardly contain their excitement as they followed him into the room. In fact Sandra didn't and, no matter how hard she tried - and my, she did try hard - she let out a tiny scream of joy which simply made Eric laugh again.

Cynthia looked around her and was simply in awe. She had no idea what to expect and, in truth, this was all a little overwhelming; she was in the Beatles' playroom and couldn't stop smiling.

She shot a look at Eric that said 'may I?' and he nodded kindly. With permission granted she began to explore the studio, walking slowly around the edge of the room, taking note of the parquet flooring. She studied the size of the room and all its nooks and crannies and weaved her way in and around the Vox amplifiers, microphone stands and carefully stepped over the black electric cables that lay scattered across large patterned rug on the floor. There were no guitars on show, but there was a dismantled drum kit piled up on the floor beside one of the fire exits and a couple of bongo drums. Cynthia guessed these were probably the very ones that had been used by Norman 'Normal' Smith on *A Hard Day's Night*. She looked at Eric, who had been following her movements, and he nodded knowingly.

Sandra had also seen the drums and now raced towards Ringo's kit. She slowly stroked the skin on the snare drum and ran her index finger over the hi-hat cymbals. Just to be able to touch one of Ringo's drums was an absolutely electrifying experience for her.

Cynthia then found herself being drawn towards a beautiful Steinway grand piano which was positioned in the centre of the room. Going over to it, she too ran her fingers across the instrument, gently caressing the highly-polished wood. Noticing her reflection in it, she smiled. She felt like she was in an almost dreamlike state, which was further enhanced when she noticed three LPs lying on the piano stool: *Please Please Me*; *With The Beatles* and *A Hard Day's Night*.

This was all simply too surreal.

Eric allowed the girls to explore at will and although he didn't feel the need to rush them, he did want to treat them to something special so finally broke their current trance-like state.

'This way girls,' he said, beckoning them to follow him.

Eric walked towards a flight of stairs tucked up against a wall and calmly walked up them with the girls following behind, still completely overwhelmed at what they were now doing.

In a matter of seconds, they were all in the control booth of Studio Two. Sandra noticed a couple of dirty ashtrays and a discarded coat hung on the back of one of the chairs as she entered, but soon found the room dominated by the large desk which was full of knobs and lights. There was also a reel-to-reel tape machine in one corner.

Eric invited the girls to sit in one of the vacant chairs while he positioned himself in another beside the desk, a task he had done countless times over the past few years. With a flick of a few switches, the four-track recording desk lit up and sparked into life.

Cynthia and Sandra, now perched on their edge of the chair they were sharing, followed Eric's every move as he turned, flicked, poked and prodded buttons and slid dials up and down. Once he appeared to be satisfied that everything was in the right position, he swung around in his chair and looked at the girls. At first he said nothing and only stared, but then he smiled and the girls sensed something special was about to happen.

'Ok, have a listen to this; I think it will be familiar to you,' said Eric. 'It's truly hard, even for me, to comprehend that in just a matter of a few hours on 16th April this year, we produced this.' Eric proceeded to press a button with now a huge smile on his face.

The familiar opening chord to *A Hard Day's Night* played over and over. The mouths of both Cynthia and Sandra dropped wide open as Eric kept pressing the button over and over again.

'We knew it would open the film and in fact the soundtrack LP, so we wanted a particularly strong and effective beginning. This strident guitar chord proved to be the perfect launch.'

Sandra leaned forward and asked, 'What chord is it anyway?' She surprised even herself with that question and wasn't even sure why she had asked.

'Good question!' replied George smiling, 'It's an F with a G on top. That's what George told me anyway, but there's also a piano in there too. His twelve-string Rickenbacker sounds fabulous, doesn't it? It's just perfect.'

Both Cynthia and Sandra nodded vigorously in agreement. Then with another flick of a button, the sound of John Lennon's voice suddenly filled the recording booth, making both the girls jump.

Eric continued to slide the desk faders up and down which, as the song progressed, resulted in him isolating and separating different parts of the song. He allowed Lennon's vocals to continue for a bit longer before replacing it with the sound of Paul McCartney singing his high harmonies. Eric then added Lennon's low harmonies and switched between adding parts of George's guitar and his guitar solo and Ringo's drums. He even isolated some of George Martin's piano playing.

Throughout the remainder of the song, Eric continued to introduce and exit various parts until he finally allowed Harrison's arpeggio to fade out by operating a slide button manually; it was just like he had done during that wonderful recording session back in April. Eric then sunk deep into his chair and stretched his long arms, rightly proud of his achievements.

Both girls sat speechless, unable to form any words. Cynthia and Sandra couldn't believe what they had just heard and doubted anyone would believe they were sitting where they were. And one thing was certain - NO-ONE back at The Moka would believe a word of this. They knew they had been privy to something normally only available for the very important and select few.

Eric eventually broke the silence, 'Well girls, I hope you enjoyed that?'

Both girls nodded, virtually in tears. Eric grinned at them then, glancing at his watch, informed the girls that he had to be getting off because he was on his way to a meeting at the London Palladium. As he led them back the way they had come and towards the front door, he finally asked them why they were carrying their copies of *A Hard Day's Night*. Cynthia explained their mission to which Eric listened, nodding politely.

'So where do you go next?' he asked as they reached the front door being held open by Alf, the commissionaire.

'Well, we're off to Liverpool to have a look around and then we are going to Blackpool for the concert,' Cynthia replied.

'I see. You do know that show is being broadcast on the television? You do have tickets I take it?' Eric asked the questions as if he already knew the answer.

The girls shook their heads in the negative, quickly explaining their plan would be to try and get them somehow on the day of the performance. Eric smiled an 'I thought so' smile, telling the girls to wait where they were whilst nodding to Alf as if to say, 'they are with me, leave them where they are.' He dashed back into an adjoining office, leaving the girls standing as still as statues as they had been asked. Moments later Eric re-appeared waving two passes for the Blackpool ABC Theatre performance in the air. He stuffed the tickets into Cynthia's hand.

'Use these when you get up there. Go to the box office and they'll let you in with them, I promise. OK?'

Cynthia was stunned, but somehow muttered a very quiet 'thank you'.

'And thank you too,' said Eric, 'It has been a real pleasure to meet two delightful Beatle people.'

'Bloody...pissing...hell,' mouthed Sandra.

Eric threw his head back and laughed out loud as he led them towards the front door and out into the car park. Getting into his car, he wished them good luck with getting their LPs autographed and drove off.

Cynthia and Sandra, still somewhat shell-shocked from what had been a surreal forty-five minutes, walked slowly back onto Abbey Road. It was then the girls noticed snotty Catherine and her mates gawping at them, not one of whom could believe their eyes.

Sandra and Cynthia looked at each other, smiled and then sarcastically waved at the group, bidding them a fond farewell before skipping off back towards St Johns Wood, laughing at the top of their voices!

Chapter 14
When I'm Sixty-Four

William's routine on a weekday morning was on rails. Nothing ever changed: his alarm went off promptly at 6.45am and he moaned, groaned, cursed silently and then yawned, careful all the while not to wake his wife any further, seeing as she didn't need to rise until half an hour after him.

He carefully threw back the bed covers and slid to his right hand side. Even though he had yet to focus his eyes, his feet automatically searched for his slippers in the very location he left them when getting into bed the night before.

As he made his way to the bathroom he would always tap on Cynthia's door, wait a second or two and then hear some noise coming from his young daughter, which would tell him he had broken her sleep. After taking his time to ensure he was extra careful with his aim and having washed his hands, the thought occurred to him that this morning he hadn't heard Cynthia moan and groan like she normally did. In fact, there hadn't been any noise at all.

So, instead of heading directly down the stairs to his destination of cornflakes and tea, he returned to Cynthia's bedroom door and knocked again. Still nothing. Without raising his voice too much, in a hushed whisper he called out, 'Cynthia…Cynthia, it's time to get up for work.'

He waited a few seconds and began to feel a little concerned if truth were told. Nothing - he could hear nothing. Placing his hand on the door handle, William slowly and cautiously opened the door. He peered inside only to find the curtains drawn and an empty bed. Then the doubts came.

What the hell was going on? Don't tell me she's been out all night?

He scratched his head and then began to mutter, 'I'll bloody kill her if she's been out all night, I will, I'll…' The sound of the kettle beginning to whistle downstairs stopped him in his tracks.

William could count the times on one hand when his teenage daughter was up before him in the morning and the confusion showed on his face as he entered the kitchen a few seconds later. He was also still a little concerned, but once he caught sight of the grin Cynthia had on her face, he visibly relaxed.

'Blimey, someone's in a good mood. Up early too. What's caused that then?' he asked.

'Actually, I'm in a great mood. I just feel FAB!' Cynthia replied with a smile as wide as she could manage.

She placed a freshly brewed pot of tea on the kitchen table beside a small blue and white edged plate, upon which two thick slices of toast took pride of place. Next to that, Cynthia carefully placed two boiled eggs, one in a blue and white striped egg cup and the other on the top slice of toast.

'There you are,' Cynthia said handing her dad a teaspoon.

'Eh? Oh, okay, err, thank you,' William sounded both surprised and somewhat suspicious.

'Right,' said Cynthia, 'I can't stand here all day. I'm off to Granddad's to see how he is and then walk with him to the shop. It's been a long time since I have done that.'

Cynthia grabbed her cardigan from the back of the kitchen chair and her bag which was hanging from a metal hook on the back of the kitchen door. She then left her still bewildered father slicing off the top of one of his boiled eggs.

It was a brisk ten-minute stroll to Nobby's house. He lived in a two-up two-down with a small, but tidy and well-tended front garden. Cynthia couldn't help but notice the garden gate was open as she approached it. This was unusual because her granddad usually made sure the gate was shut when he was at home. Cynthia decided not to dwell on it however, thinking that maybe someone else had been to see him.

Making her way up the narrow garden path to the front door, Cynthia placed her hand on the door handle expecting it to open but, to her surprise, found it was locked. Strange, she thought, his door was never locked at this time of the morning. Cynthia was fully aware that her granddad's morning routine began with him unlocking the door and opening the curtains.

The curtains!

Cynthia stepped back to check if the curtains were open. They weren't and

she frowned. Stepping back further so she could look up to her granddad's bedroom window, Cynthia could see those curtains were closed too.   Concerned, she went back to the door where she proceeded to bang hard with her clenched fist.

Cynthia repeated this action several times; her anxiety increasing with each blow, but there was no noise coming from inside. She lifted the flap on the letterbox and peered through. All was quiet.

'No sign of, er…life,' she heard herself whisper.

She now felt she couldn't wait any longer, so stepped back into the front garden.

'Spare key? Spare key…' she muttered.

Cynthia knew there was one and was now frantically trying to recall where it was. She had never had to use it, but knew her mum had once when she had to urgently get some pills from the house. After a couple of false moves, Cynthia finally found the right terracotta flower pot. The key was wrapped in an old tobacco pouch stuffed in an even older 'Nutty Cut' pipe tobacco tin, just under the surface of the dry and crunchy soil.

A sudden wave of relief came over Cynthia as she rushed to the front door, clutching the key very tightly in her right hand. Fumbling at first, she eventually heard the locks click and within a few seconds was standing in the hallway. It was dark so Cynthia flicked on the light switch to her left. To her right was the small front room, the least used room in her granddad's home. She pushed open the door and peered inside; the room felt very still and smelled musky. Poking her head around the door, Cynthia had a good look scanning for any sign of Nobby.

Apart from the curtains still being drawn, everything seemed to be in order and just like it always was. There wasn't much furniture in the room, just an old armchair and a wooden table with a few old black and white family photographs hanging from the walls.

Cynthia pulled open the curtains, letting in a brilliant shaft of early morning light and disturbing the dust. She made her way back to the small and narrow hallway. It was very bare apart from a fairly worn carpet rug, it not being wide enough to accommodate any furniture. At the end of the hallway was another door leading to the front room. Cynthia was about to turn the doorknob when she heard the sound of her granddad coughing. She immediately sighed with relief and looked up to the top of stairs on her left.

Nobby stood at the top of the stairs, his normally neatly-combed hair sticking up all over the place. Wearing a white vest, on which a few burn holes and splashes of tea could be noticed, he coupled this with a pair of checked woollen slippers and grey trousers held up by grey and red stripy braces. Nobby was frantically trying to get the brace over his left shoulder with one hand, whilst he rubbed sleep from his eye with the other hand.

Coughing aggressively, he finally cleared his throat and focussed on the shape at the bottom of his stairs.

'Cynthia? Is…is that you girl?' he croaked.

'Yes, yes, it's me Granddad. Are you feeling okay? You had me worried there,' she replied, failing miserably to disguise the worry she was feeling in her voice.

'What time is it? How did you get in?' Nobby was sounding very confused.

'It's about 7.30 in the morning Granddad. I used the spare key to get in. I came to walk to the shop with you, but I was worried when I saw the curtains were still drawn and the front door was locked, so…' Cynthia's answer then tailed off.

'Worried? Worried? What about? There's nothing to be worried about girl, it's just a bit of a bug that's all. Go and put the kettle on and I'll be down in a minute,' Nobby said trying his best to reassure her. '7.30, in the MORNING…cheeky scamp, I KNOW it's the morning girl…'

Cynthia could hear her granddad continue to mutter as he went back to his bedroom and waved in Cynthia's general direction, motioning for her to get his kettle boiling, before he disappeared out of sight.

Cynthia loitered at the bottom of the stairs for a second or two longer though, listening to his footsteps as he shuffled back to his bedroom. He was still coughing in between muttering as he did so, louder now and it sounded much worse than it had the day before.

Cynthia sighed and made her way to the front room. Making a beeline for the drawn curtains and pulling them open, she then pulled back the catch on the window frame and pushed up the bottom part of the window, allowing the warm, sweet-smelling summer fresh air to waft in.

The sight of some dirty and tattered masking tape still stuck to the inside of the windowpanes always made her smile. It had originally been stuck on during the last war to help prevent the glass from shattering if caught up in the effect of any stray bombs.

Cynthia had asked her granddad many times why he hadn't removed all the tape, but he had never given her a straight answer, certainly not one that had truly satisfied her. She was left to presume it was something he had done to act as some sort of reminder that he and his home had survived Hitler's bombing raids, but she didn't know this for sure.

Cynthia walked through to the small kitchen, where she proceeded to fill the kettle and lit the hob with a red topped Swan Vesta from a matchbox she found on a nearby shelf. Having to remove various dirty plates from the sink so she could fill the kettle, Cynthia thought this was also out of character for her granddad. Cynthia then knew that the cough and the subsequent illness were affecting him much more than he was letting on.

With the kettle now cheerfully boiling away on the hob, Cynthia returned to the front room with the intention of seeing what else needed tidying up. She was stopped in her tracks, however, as beside her granddad's favourite armchair were various items, now sorted into neat sections.

Feeling curious, Cynthia plonked herself down on the chair and examined the various artefacts, including a pile of letters which looked very official. She carefully moved a couple and could see they were documents relating to her granddad's house and his shop. She wondered to herself what he was doing with them.

Beside them was a collection of old, fading post cards. She knew that collecting postcards was his hobby and had been since he was a small boy. Cynthia estimated that there must be nearly five hundred postcards in the collection here on the floor, with some dating back as far 1901. Many of them had been sent to England from other countries around Europe and she knew her granddad even had a few sent from Australia and Canada too. Cynthia couldn't help but wonder what kind of value may be attached to them.

An old Peek Frean & Co. biscuit tin box caught her eye. Cynthia recognised it instantly from her childhood, but she hadn't seen it for years. She picked it up and prised open the lid. All the objects inside were individually wrapped in handkerchiefs.

It was exactly how Cynthia remembered as a small child and she reached in to remove one of the small bundles. Returning the tin to where she had found it on the floor, she placed the still wrapped handkerchief on her lap and started to unfold it. As the last flap of the

198

handkerchief fell to one side, the contents were revealed and she gazed at a collection of shiny war medals. It really had been years since Cynthia had last seen these.

She instantly recalled that there were ten medals in total. The medals had been awarded to members of the family in some of the British Empire's most victorious achievements. Cynthia glanced at the tin box on the floor thinking how it housed a wonderful piece of her family's history. She knew her granddad was very proud of his medals, as was she and the rest of the family.

Her thoughts were interrupted by an eruption of coughing coming from upstairs, which caused Cynthia to jump. The front room had been so silent and still and so lost was she in her thoughts, she was now startled. The high-pitched sound of a boiled kettle filled her ears and she sensed that her granddad would be joining her soon, so she hastily re-wrapped the medals and placed them back gently into the tin box. Taking one last look at the various objects lying on the floor and still wondering what her granddad was doing with them, Cynthia got up and went back into the kitchen to attend to the now fully boiled water.

By the time Cynthia had made a pot of tea and prepared the cups, her granddad had joined her in the kitchen. Cynthia leaned against the oven whilst her granddad slumped into one of the chairs beside the very small table. He had now combed his hair and looked a bit tidier, but something wasn't right. Cynthia studied his face: he looked pale, tired and somehow thinner. She had never seen her granddad looking like this.

She asked if he wanted any breakfast, but he just shook his head. Accepting his decision, she poured his tea for him instead and spooned in two large heaps of sugar. She stirred the pale brown liquid, finishing off by tapping the teaspoon on the rim of the cup.

Cynthia let her granddad take a few sips of the hot brew before plucking up the courage to ask him what he had been doing with all his prized possessions and legal documents.

'Eh? Them? Oh, I'm just having a sort out of a few things, that's all girly,' he said, 'Nothing to concern yourself with my love.'

She sensed that her granddad wasn't in a mood to elaborate so she decided to leave any further questioning. Asking if he wanted a top up of tea, Nobby shook his head firmly, triggering off the coughing again. Cynthia could see he was struggling as she glanced at the clock on the wall. Her granddad would normally be opening his shop by now.

'Granddad, listen...'

Cynthia was about to suggest that she go and open the shop and he come down a bit later in the morning when he felt up to it. But she was interrupted...

'Tell you what girl, would you mind opening up the shop today please Cynthia? I'll come down in an hour or so. I think I should rest a little longer, just get my bearings and that.'

Hearing him say that came as a total surprise and Cynthia knew then that her granddad was very unwell. In all the time she had worked with him, blimey, even as far back as her memory would go, Cynthia couldn't recall a single day that he had had off due to sickness. The only time he closed was to attend a funeral or because he was legally obliged to do so. Cynthia had never opened up the shop on her own before.

'Of course I will Granddad. Funnily enough, I was just about to suggest that. Great minds eh?' she said, which brought a small smile to his grey and lined old face. 'Yeah, you see how you feel in a bit and come in later. If you don't feel up to it, just stay at home - I can manage and I'll come and see you after work. And I'll ring mum?'

Nobby was mid sip of his still warm tea and that last statement made him spit a little bit on to the kitchen table.

'Now Cynthia,' he said, wiping his chin with the back of his right hand, 'You leave your mum out of it, you hear me? I'm alright girly, I just need a bit of kip is all.'

Cynthia shook her head, tears welling up in her eyes as she told her granddad that she couldn't agree to this.

'I got to tell Mum, Granddad, she'll go mad if she finds you like this and I've not said something.'

He sat there quietly as she said she would be ringing her mum as soon as she got to the shop and that he should expect a visit from both her and the family doctor. He knew his granddaughter was right, and the stubbornness in him was slowly letting go.

'Come on, give me the keys. Let's get that shop open and you get back into bed and we'll check up on you in a couple of hours or so.'

Nobby reluctantly nodded his head as he removed the bunch keys from his trouser pocket. He handed them to Cynthia and carefully gave her instructions as to what she needed to do when opening the shop. She nodded caringly and then she kissed him on the forehead, noting it felt hot and clammy. She assured him that she could run the shop okay and he had nothing to worry about.

Her granddad's health preoccupied Cynthia's thoughts as she walked to the shop and she decided that she would call her mum upon her arrival. First though, on went the kettle and then she went through the daily routine of opening the cupboard doors, followed by dragging the bags of fruit and vegetables across the shop floor which had been dropped off by Nobby's mate, old Ted, on his way home from Covent Garden. Cynthia would put these on display later.

It was now dead on nine o'clock, as Cynthia perched herself on the seat at the counter and took a big gulp of the tea she had just made. No sooner had she done so, when the first customer of the day entered the shop.

'Good morning Mrs Winslow, how are you today? Hang on, Thursday - we don't normally see you on a Thursday?' Cynthia tried to sound upbeat and cheerful.

'Good morning Cynthia dear. I know, but I just need to pick up a few things today because I am going to spend the weekend with my son in Whitstable and I'm going down tomorrow morning. I need to get some of that honey that he likes,' came the reply as Mrs Winslow pointed to the jars of honey on a shelf just to the right of Cynthia's ear.

'Old Nobby not about?

Cynthia turned and fetched down one of the jars, placing it onto the counter top.

'Er, no he's having the morning off, attending to some business or other with the accountant. Just the one jar will it be?' asked Cynthia trying to quickly change the subject.

'Right. Yes, just the one jar dear. I'll get him another one later, for his birthday treat.'

Just as Mrs Winslow was settling up for the honey, they were joined by Mrs Turner.

'Good morning Mrs Turner,' Cynthia called out as cheerfully as she could.

'And good morning Cynthia. Hello Edith, you all right dear?' replied Mrs Turner nodding in the general direction of Mrs Winslow.

Mrs Winslow returned the greeting, 'Hello Rene, as well as could be expected. Off to my Michael's today for a bit of a break.'

'Oooh that is nice, good boy you've got there.'

These two women had been neighbours for decades and knew each other's lives inside out. They had gone to the same schools, had been guests at each other's weddings, had witnessed each other's children be born, grow up and start families of their own. They had even attended the funerals of one another's husbands.

The two women had seen every aspect of life as it unfolded around the streets of Wimbledon Common. Between them, they certainly had a few tales to tell and Cynthia had heard most of them! But, she liked both women; she admired the way they seem content with their lives, but then Cynthia saw this trait in most of the locals who passed through her granddad's shop.

In truth, Cynthia felt very at home in her community and she knew that women like Mrs Winslow and Mrs Turner had contributed to making it what it was. These were the women who remained behind holding the fort, propping it up while their husbands were away fighting in the two World Wars. It was women like Edith and Rene who had protected their children during the air raids and still got up early the morning after to sweep the streets and wash away the broken glass, dust and damage from their doorsteps. It was these women who waited patiently and loyally, maintaining their homes until their husbands returned from wars or, later, from their day's work.

It was women like this who took care of *their* community. It wasn't the local bobby or the local council. It wasn't even *their* men. It was the women who knew what was going on and who was up to what - good and bad. It was the women who kept the order and the peace. It was them who gave the local tearaways a clip around the earhole and threatened to tell their dads if they didn't 'pull their socks up' - and for a cocky tearaway to be dragged up before his father BY A WOMAN was the most feared punishment of all.

Simply put, women like Edith and Rene commanded respect and in Cynthia's eyes they deserved every ounce that they got.

'Right, can't stand here all day gassing, got to get a shake on, things to do.'

Mrs Winslow bid them both a cheery goodbye as she left the shop.

Cynthia then tended to Mrs Turner's shopping list. Pouring a few extra grams of tea into the bag, she added it to the shopping basket. Mrs Turner didn't actually notice and that's how Cynthia liked it.

Before she left, Mrs Turner also enquired after Cynthia's granddad. Cynthia felt bad at the little white lie she had told Mrs Winslow, so instead explained that he was a little under the weather and was having a lay in and a morning off.

Mrs Turner shrugged her shoulders. 'Blimey, he must be poorly - never known him do that before. None of us getting any younger Cynthia, but don't worry though love, he's as tough as old boots and made of sterner stuff than a lot of them going about today. Give him my best won't cha ducks.'

Cynthia smiled and waved off Mrs Turner.

After a few more customers popped in and she had tidied up and put new stock away, it was fast approaching lunchtime, but still seen no sign of her granddad.

She decided to shut the shop for dinner and to go and check on him, taking with her some fresh fruit from the shop. She knew he would complain, but she didn't care - the Vitamin C would help him she assured herself.

Cynthia found her granddad asleep in the front garden. He looked very uncomfortable, slouched in a beaten up old wooden chair that had had certainly seen better days, but she didn't want to wake him. Instead, she sat on the grass in front of him, deciding to just sit and wait and bathe in the sun for a while. Ten minutes passed before Nobby finally stirred.

'Oh, hello. What time is it?' he asked, sounding confused as he opened his eyes and looked at Cynthia.

'It's dinnertime Granddad. I've just popped back to see how you are.'

'You mean check on me,' he groaned.

'Yes, okay, to check on you,' she said smiling, 'How are you feeling now?'

'A little better, but tired, very tired. I didn't realise I had fallen asleep for so long. Is everything okay in the shop? Have all the orders been fulfilled?'

'Yes Granddad, don't you worry, everything is fine. I'm handling everything OK,' Cynthia assured him.

'Good girl,' he said as he exploding into another coughing fit. 'I knew...cough...COUGH...you...cough...would be fine.'

Cynthia sat with him for a further twenty minutes, all the while trying to persuade him to go indoors and get into bed him. In the end, she told him she could manage the shop today and old Nobby didn't put up a fight, which by now she was expecting.

She made a pot of tea and a cheese and pickle sandwich and Nobby promised he would have a lay down after finishing them both. She tried to make his old wooden chair a bit more comfortable before she left and said she would return after work to drop the keys off and 'check' on him. He managed to crack a smile at that, which lifted Cynthia's spirits and made her afternoon more tolerable.

The remainder of the afternoon went quickly. Customers came and went and all the regulars noted the absence of Cynthia's granddad and asked her to pass on their well-wishes. It pleased her to know that he was so well thought of and respected.

At five o' clock, her day was done, so she locked up the shop for the night and made her way back to Nobby's house. She found him in the front room, where he explained he had slept for an hour or two and had then moved in here to listen to the Test match on the radio.

Cynthia cooked him some tea using some spam she had brought with her from the shop, while she told her granddad what the day had been like, who had been in and what the day's takings were. It was agreed that Cynthia would return in the morning to pick up the shop keys and would run the shop again if her granddad still wasn't feeling well enough, although he tried to assure Cynthia that he would be fighting fit by the morning.

Cynthia couldn't help but notice that Nobby had hardly touched his food, saying he just felt too tired to finish it. Cynthia took the plate and proceeded to scrape the leftovers into the kitchen dustbin before quickly washing up the crockery and cutlery he had used. She kissed him on his forehead and wished him good night and set off home.

On the way there, she suddenly remembered she hadn't called her mum to let her know how her dad was.

'Piss it,' she blurted out as she headed up the garden path to the family front door.

Once in, she quickly updated her parents as to her granddad's health.

'You should have called me Cynthia,' moaned Dot.

'Oh mum, I intended to, but as soon as I opened the shop it all got very busy and well, I just forgot.'

Dot tutted and reluctantly nodded her head, 'Well, I'll go around in the morning and get him up the doctors if he's no better. I mean, it's not like him to not go to work. You know he's not well when that happens and we've got to get him right and 'in the pink' for Butlin's, haven't we, eh?'

Cynthia said sorry again, as she could see the worry in her mum's face. She wolfed down the boiled potatoes and kippers that her mother had made and, once finished, she went to her bedroom to begin packing for her and Sandra's forthcoming trip.

With all that was going on, Cynthia wanted to get her packing out of the way because she guessed she wouldn't have much time to do it the following day, especially as they were intending to catch the train to Liverpool straight after work. Also, Cynthia had arranged to meet Sandra and go to The Moka later, so she had to use her time tonight wisely.

Cynthia discovered the bag she intended to take on her trip had a broken zip.

'Piss it! Forgot about that,' she said.

She went and knocked on John's bedroom door. He opened the door wearing a shirt Cynthia hadn't seen before.

'Alright squirt,' he said smiling as he stood there.

Cynthia poked her tongue out at him in a joking way. 'Ooh, is that a new shirt?' she asked.

'Ah ha, well spotted. I'm just trying it on. Picked it up today; lovely isn't it. 'Ere feel the weight of the cotton, I had it ordered from Italy,' said John, purring with delight over his new purchase.

'Hmm very nice!' Cynthia replied.

'What you after?' John said turning his back and heading over to his record player. He was playing his favourite Yardbirds' album, which was coming to an end. John bent down to his collection of records and flicked through his beloved vinyl.

'I need a bag for my trip.'

'Oh yeah...and where are you going?' John asked, nodding his chin in the direction of a brown leather holdall that Cynthia could see was stuffed under a chair.

Cynthia grabbed the bag, 'Ta. Liverpool and Blackpool...Phew...Blimey!' she suddenly exclaimed.

'What's up with you?' John asked slightly alarmed.

Cynthia cautiously put her hand into the bag and pulled out some Y fronts and a pair of black socks, which she dangled in the air, holding them aloft and turning her face away to make the point.

'YUK!'

John chuckled.

'Oh, I forgot about them. I haven't used that bag since Brighton.'

Cynthia flicked her wrist and sent the pants and socks flying through the air in John's direction. He headed them away and then punched his fist into the air, mouthing the words 'goal' which made Cynthia giggle.

Cynthia decided to search the rest of the bag as she walked back to her bedroom. She certainly wasn't too keen on finding any more surprises and, by the time she reached her bedroom, was satisfied the bag had nothing more untoward lurking within it.

She sprayed a small blast of her favourite scent into the holdall to freshen it up and then placed her carefully-chosen outfits into it, along with her toothbrush and toothpaste. Cynthia paused, sensing she had forgotten something. Scanning the room in the hope of seeing something to nudge her memory, Cynthia spotted Ringo on one of her Beatles posters - which did the trick.

'Ah Sandra,' she muttered and plucked some cotton wool from another bag. Cynthia remembered that Sandra could be a right 'window rattler' and seeing that they would be sharing a room for a couple of nights, Cynthia didn't want to run the risk of spending half the night kicking and prodding Sandra to stop her snoring.

Satisfied that the bag was filled with everything that she needed, Cynthia zipped it up and placed it by the front door. It could sit and wait there until the morning when she would take it to work. The plan was to knock off early and catch the 16.35 train to Liverpool.

Her final job before leaving her bedroom was to place the bag containing her *A Hard Day's Night* LP on top of the travel bag. One last glance at the LP and reminding herself to stay optimistic that she could get it autographed was enough for Cynthia.

She smiled as she said, 'Hello John, Paul, Ringo and especially you George. See you all very soon.'

She then closed her bedroom door behind her.

Chapter 15
Act Naturally

Sandra was on a battlefield. Well, that was what it felt like.

Elbows out, she pushed, barged and edged through the rush hour crowds as she tried to make her way home. She already had the hump and having to deal with inconsiderate commuters wasn't helping her feel any better. It had been a truly awful day for a variety of reasons, all of which left Sandra longing for the clock to tick round to 5pm, so it would be another day closer to Friday and for her trip up north to begin.

Funnily enough, her day had actually started okay. She had woke feeling refreshed and had got to work on time, which was always a result and somewhat of a minor miracle when you take into consideration her notoriously bad time-keeping.

But things soured just before lunchtime and it was all down to a certain Mr Green; Sandra simply couldn't stomach the man.

Douglas Green was in his early forties, tall and thin in body - and in hair (it was receding quite rapidly and something he tried his hardest to conceal). He arrived each morning with a combed over bird's nest on his head, which of course highlighted he was going bald, thus completely defeating the object. He had been working in Sandra's office for five years and had what he considered to be 'many important responsibilities' on a daily basis.

It was true he held a certain degree of power, but he made sure all the office girls knew it. He was also a total letch, bordering on being a pervert. By the end of her very first day, he had pinched Sandra's buttocks. She had wanted to complain, but knew old Douglas would have her out of there so fast, it wouldn't be worth it. So she suffered it, as did the rest of the girls there. Sandra detested 'Dirty Douglas', that being the name given to him by 95% of the staff, both male and female; they all knew what he got up to.

At sixteen, Sandra thought anyone over the age of twenty-one was old, so him being the age he was, and being from an entirely different generation, meant they had absolutely nothing in common. If being a sex pest wasn't enough, he also dismissed The Beatles, calling them a bunch of 'scruffs' and 'long-haired nancy boys'.

He took a wicked delight in continually reprimanding her for replying to his requests with 'fab'. But as she did so deliberately rather than out of habit, they were forever at loggerheads.

As revenge for her cheek, 'Dirty Douglas' hovered over Sandra when he talked to her and he never looked her in the eye. Instead he focussed his gaze on her breasts, leaving Sandra feeling incredibly uncomfortable.

Today, she had been required to spend the majority of her '9 to 5' in his office and was therefore constantly being leered at. By home time, she was honestly ready and indeed willing to scratch his eyes out. But, thinking that she needed the job and its wages, she just hurriedly grabbed her handbag and swiftly made her exit. By the time Douglas had looked up, she was already half way out of the office.

Eventually, after battling through the commuter crowds, Sandra reached Wimbledon and felt a lot better for it. She checked her watch and smiled. Good, she still had time to call in on Rosie Andrews. Sandra had visited the old lady at least once a week for many years now.

Old Rosie had been in Sandra's life as far back as she could remember and felt a special connection to her and believed Rosie felt the same way. Sandra called her 'auntie' although she wasn't a real aunt in the biological sense.

Rosie lived four doors along from Sandra and was now well into her seventies, but despite her age and now being quite frail, she still possessed all her wit and a mental sharpness that Sandra had always known. Standing at only five feet and two inches, she seemed shorter due to her severely stooped back, brought on by the onset of osteoporosis.

She had been a widow all of Sandra's life as her husband, a childhood sweetheart, had been killed within the first few weeks of World War One and Rosie had suffered the remainder of the war alone. She watched thousands of other young men sign up and march off to the same war, however many of those once cheery faces that returned, never looked as cheery ever again.

When she was younger, Sandra's parents would let her stay at Rosie's home while they went to the pub and, on occasion, when they went away for long weekends. Not that Sandra cared she might be missing out, she was more than happy to spend her time in the old lady's company.

There were hours of fun to be had at Rosie's when Sandra was younger. For a start, there was Bill the tortoise who Sandra loved feeding lettuce leaves to. Rosie also taught Sandra how to make perfume from flower petals picked from her garden and spent hours teaching her how to knit. And not forgetting the card games such as snap and rummy. They were wonderful times.

But Sandra's favourite thing of all was to spend an afternoon making toffee and other delicious sweets. As a result, she often wondered if the root of her addiction to pear drops lay in those afternoons spent in Rosie's kitchen?

'It's only me, just popping in,' Sandra called out quite loudly, as she always did when entering the back door of Rosie's garden.

She found the old lady sitting in the living room in her favourite chair, with her favourite pink cardigan around her shoulders, trying to complete a jigsaw puzzle of a Constable landscape scenery. The kitchen door and living room window were wide open, which meant only one thing - Rosie hadn't made it to the toilet in time again.

'I'll put the kettle on,' Sandra said cheerily, not giving Rosie the slightest hint that she could still smell the fresh urine.

'Hello Sandra love. That'll be lovely dear and can you fetch those crumpets too,' Rosie smiled.

Sandra opened the bread bin and removed two relatively new crumpets. She couldn't help but notice the stale bread in there too, but chose to ignore that. It wasn't mouldy yet so she figured Rosie still had time to at least make toast with it.

Sandra made a pot of tea and poured some into old-fashioned china teacups for Rosie and herself. Walking from the kitchen to the living room, Sandra placed a cup near her dear old friend.

'Here's your rosy, Rosie,' said Sandra not for the first time, but hearing that always made the old lady smile. Sandra reached towards the open fire, then handed Rosie a poker to hold tightly whilst Sandra pierced a crumpet on the other end.

Sandra then did the same with the poker she was holding. They both leaned closer to the fire and enjoyed the ritual of toasting their crumpets. With the fire well established, the crumpets didn't take long to toast up with the heat and it wasn't too much longer before Sandra was buttering both the crumpets. Buttering was a task Rosie's shaking, arthritic-riddled hands could no longer cope with; it was painful enough watching her trying to drink her tea.

'Ooh, that does taste nice dear. So, how has your day been?' Rosie enquired kindly.

'So-so I suppose. I had to spend the day working in that Mr Green's office all day.' Sandra made a 'yuk' type face just by saying his name.

'Oh, you poor thing! That is a shame.'

Sandra had told Rosie many times about the office 'creep'.

'Listen to me my girl, that ghastly man will get what's coming to him don't you worry about that, they always do...just remember Sandra, never give him the satisfaction of knowing he has got under your skin. The world is full of self-important men who think they have power over us women. You just keep spraying on your perfume and wearing those pretty clothes and make sure he can smell and see you. It will hurt him more than you know, him knowing he will never be able have you.'

Sandra had heard these words of advice before, but they still made her blush. Not that Rosie seemed to notice; she was too busy nibbling away on her crumpet with what teeth she had left in her head and wiping the butter off her whiskery old chin. But Sandra suspected that Rosie was fully aware of the effect her words had had on her.

'Is it tomorrow when you go to Liverpool then dear?' Rosie said, knowing her point had been made and changing the direction of the conversation.

'Yes, that's right Rosie, we are heading up straight after work. We want to be in Liverpool before its dark you see. Cynthia thinks we should arrive about eight o'clock.'

Rosie nodded, then spent the next fifteen minutes telling Sandra her own stories about the one and only time she had visited Liverpool.

'We travelled up by train in 1897,' she said, pausing to sigh before telling Sandra that it felt like such a long time ago - which was of course true. Rosie had only been a small girl and Queen Victoria was still sitting on the throne.

'I don't remember too many details of the place itself; it seemed so big and industrial. But I remember the docks and of course that magnificent and wondrous train ride.'

She fell silent for a few minutes as the memories flooded back. Sandra studied Rosie's smiling face for a minute or two, trying to read her mind. Then, glancing at her watch, she knew she had to make a move.

'Right, well I've got a full day tomorrow, so I had better get home to get ready.'

After a quick clear up of the cups and plates and after making sure the old lady had everything she needed, Sandra bade her farewell and headed home.

Her own house was empty upon arrival, which Sandra was pleased about. She ran herself a bath, which she only dipped in and out of quickly, then set about packing her things to take on the trip. The last thing she stuffed into her tartan canvas holdall was her copy of John Lennon's book 'In His Own Write', which she knew would make an excellent travelling companion to indulge in when Cynthia was dozing. As soon as she was packed, Sandra left her still empty home and headed off to meet Cynthia.

Cynthia was perched on the edge of 'their' bench, her eyes closed and face turned towards the dying sun. Sandra plonked herself down beside her and, keeping her eyes closed, Cynthia quietly said hello. Sandra copied Cynthia and closed her eyes. The feel of the sun's warmth on her face was just what she needed.

'How has your day been then?' Cynthia asked.

'Yuk, don't ask...Dirty Douglas!' replied Sandra.

Cynthia opened her eyes to find Sandra making a horrible face and she laughed.

'Come on then, I know what you need,' Cynthia said a few moments later, 'The Moka!'

There were a few scooters parked outside as they arrived, a couple of which Cynthia recognised but the others were new to her. She spotted the new faces grouped around one of the tables just inside. They all turned and clocked Cynthia and Sandra as they strolled in. Sammy, who was drying some mugs with a red and white cloth that was, in truth, in need of a clean itself, also noticed his regulars.

'Alright ladies, what can I do you for?' he asked smiling, puffing away on the cigarette firmly wedged between his lips.

'Hello Sammy. Two Pepsi's please,' Cynthia answered cheerily.

Sammy slung the cloth he was holding over his left shoulder and went off to collect the drinks. Cynthia searched her bag for some cigarettes while Sandra snarled in the direction of Danny the king mixer. He pretended that he hadn't seen her.

'Here,' Cynthia said handing Sandra a smoke.

Sandra accepted and in return produced a flash looking lighter.

'That's nice. Where did you get that?' Cynthia asked admiring it.

'I nicked it off Dirty Douglas. He has been such a tosser today and wound me up so much, that I nicked it when he was busy staring at my tits.'

'Haha, that'll teach him,' Cynthia laughed.

'I doubt it. He can't help himself, the dirty sod. But at least he'll have to buy himself a new lighter which will hurt him because he is as tight as a camel's arse in a sandstorm.'

'Oi oi! Less of that language please! This is a respectable café and, besides, young girls like you shouldn't be using language like that,' Sammy said half-jokingly.

'Sorry Sammy,' Sandra replied, fluttering her eye lashes theatrically which made Cynthia laugh.

'Ere, it's the first time your mate Danny has shown his face in here for a while isn't it,' Cynthia said, now also looking his way.

Sandra nodded trying to look unconcerned, which in truth she was. Although she still hadn't shaken off the feeling of being fooled by him over the 'tie of Ringo' palaver.

'Cobblers to him…'

She diverted the conversation towards their trip up north.

'You all packed then?' Sandra asked.

'Yes, all done and you?' replied Cynthia excitedly

Sandra nodded and said she was. They then discussed the plan for the following day. Cynthia said that she would go and see her granddad in the morning and then go to the shop. She added that she was going to eat a big dinner too because she didn't know if the food on the train would be up to much.

'Good idea there, think I'll do the same.'

Cynthia suggested they meet on their bench at 3.30pm and then go from there to catch the train. The plan appeared like a good one, except Sandra suddenly remembered she had forgotten to ask old Douglas if it would be okay to knock off early. She kicked herself for forgetting, but didn't mention her failure to Cynthia. Instead she just popped a pear drop into her mouth; that always helped her think.

Cynthia and Sandra were still discussing their trip and what they were most excited about when Kenny arrived. They hadn't noticed him come in but, seeing he was alone, invited him to sit with them. Kenny looked hot and sweaty and in desperate need of a cold drink so Cynthia ordered him a cool Pepsi.

'Ahhh!' said Kenny enjoying a long sip, 'Did I need that.'

'Busy day Kenny?' Cynthia asked, offering him a cigarette.

'Ta. Yeah you could say that. My mate Brian, you know, the one who lives in Clapham? His bloody scooter broke down in Brixton and I had to help him get it back home.'

'What was the matter with it?' Sandra enquired.

Kenny shrugged his shoulders. 'I haven't got a clue and I'm not sure Brian has either. That Vespa he has is always breaking down. It spends more time in his dad's bleeding garage than it does being ridden around South London.'

'My John is forever mending something on his scooter. His mates are the same. It's a good job they look the part, cos they seem bloody useless eh?' Cynthia interrupted.

Sandra nodded, sucking some more Pepsi up the straw at the same time.

'Anyway, how are you two? Is it tomorrow that you continue with your 'mission'?'

'Oh yeah,' Cynthia replied, 'And it's going to be fab.'

'What are you gonna do when you're there?'

'Use our tickets that Eric Perkins gave us to go and see The Beatles at Blackpool.' Sandra raised her voice, just to make sure that the new gang of Mods sitting nearby heard her. It worked and they looked over, although not seemingly that impressed.

'What, the engineer Eric Perkins? Really? How did that happen?' Kenny asked excitedly.

Cynthia and Sandra didn't hesitate in telling Kenny all about them visiting Abbey Road studios, helping Eric and then getting the tour of studio two and him being generous enough to give them the concert tickets. Kenny was a bit sceptical about the story to start, but could see by the way they were talking that this was genuine. He was really pleased for them and told them so.

'All being well, we should get to Liverpool by eight and then we'll go and find a B&B. Once we're settled we intend to go to The Cavern. We just hope there's a decent group on - there should be anyway. Then, on Saturday we have a full list of places to visit,' Cynthia informed.

'I take it The Beatles' old homes are on that list?' Kenny quizzed.

Both Cynthia and Sandra nodded in unison, smiling broadly.

'It sounds like you're going to have a really fab time. Anyway, I hope you do. If you get time, take a ferry trip across the Mersey; it's a really fab thing to do.'

'Oooh, not thought of that Kenny,' Cynthia said, 'I'll add that add to my list.'

'And then on Sunday, it's the performance!' Sandra added excitedly.

'Yeah fantastic! Wow, two Beatles concerts in one month. That takes some beating,' Kenny exclaimed.

Both girls clapped their hands excitedly. They had lost count how many times they had reminded themselves that by the end of July they would have seen The Beatles in concert twice. They still couldn't believe it.

Kenny bought another round of Pepsi's and wished them every success with their mission of getting their LPs autographed. Not long after, Cynthia and Sandra looked at their watches and both decided an early night was in order.

As Sandra hoovered up the last drops of her Pepsi she nodded at Kenny.

'Cheers then Kenny, catch up soon. Tell you all about it when we get back,' and then they were gone.

The regular knock on the bedroom door from William seemed to arrive soon, too soon, after she had gone to bed. Cynthia had returned home with the best intentions to be in bed and fast asleep before ten o'clock. Instead, she sat around the kitchen table talking to John for the best part of an hour, then spent another hour quietly playing *A Hard Day's Night* and updating her diary and scrapbook.

So, it was in fact just after midnight when Cynthia finally climbed into bed. She struggled to sink into a slumber and was still tossing and turning gone 3am; the day ahead filling her mind and stopping her from dropping off. Now laying there having been woken up, Cynthia estimated that she eventually fell asleep at four, so her father's habitual wake-up call wasn't exactly welcomed.

She crawled out of bed and went through her morning rituals.

'Dad, I'm gonna check in on Granddad, so tell Mum not to worry this morning and I'll call her later, before leaving London.'

'Aright girl, mum will pop in on him later. You be safe, you hear?'

Her dad then kissed her gently on her forehead, telling her she was a good 'un.

Somehow within the hour, she found herself walking up her granddad's garden path. The milkman had left two bottles of red top on the doorstep, so Cynthia picked them up and let herself into her granddad's house. It was quiet and felt still and undisturbed.

It was evident her granddad was still in bed, so Cynthia decided she would give him a few more minutes and rush around the house opening the curtains and prepare a pot of tea. She noticed the legal papers and box of medals had been returned to their rightful place in the chest of drawers, out of sight, but certainly not out of mind.

Cynthia reached the kettle just as it began to whistle, so spooned some loose tea into the teapot and poured in the boiling water. Collecting her granddad's favourite cup, she placed it on a tray beside some sugar and a small jug of milk. She considered making him some toast but decided to check if he could stomach any food.

As she approached her granddad's bedroom she could hear him snoring; the sound causing her to sigh with relief. Gently pushing open her granddad's bedroom door and ignoring the smell, Cynthia carefully placed the tray on a table beside her granddad's bed. In no rush to wake him up, she walked over to the window and slowly opened the curtains, however, the sound of a creaking floorboard caused Cynthia's granddad to stir.

She sat on the edge of the bed and waited for her granddad to unfold from his slumber in his own time. Cynthia studied his face, with its deeply etched wrinkles that told a thousand stories, and noticed that he hadn't shaved for a few days going by the growth on his face. She couldn't recall ever seeing her granddad with stubble before. Nobby slowly opened his misty pale blue eyes and, taking a moment to focus, he strained to smile at her whilst struggling to pull himself up. Cynthia adjusted his pillows behind his back and neck to make him feel more comfortable.

'Hello,' she said softly, 'how are you feeling today granddad?'

'Hello girly. Me? Oh, better…much, much better. It's just a bit of flu or something.'

In truth, they both suspected there was more to it.

'I was going to make you some toast - do you want some now? I could make it before I go and open the shop.'

Nobby shook his head as he reached for his tea. Cynthia pushed the tray closer to him and it saddened her to see him so weak and frail; it's not how she knew her granddad.

'What day is it?' Nobby asked suddenly.

'It's Friday Granddad.'

'Is it? There will be a delivery from the Kings today then, I...I...'

'You're not going anywhere. I remembered that and I can handle it,' Cynthia assured her granddad quietly, but firmly.

Nobby nodded and smiled, which told Cynthia her granddad knew his shop was in safe hands.

'Do you want me to wait for you to get up or are you going to stay in bed today?' Cynthia was hoping he would agree to stay in bed and rest.

'I think I'll stay here a bit longer girly, maybe until nine-ish.'

He glanced at the old clock on the wall the facing him; Cynthia looked at it too. That clock had been in the same position as far back as she could remember and must have been a well-made clock too because not once, to her knowledge, had it stopped working.

She then recalled the story of how her granddad had purchased it from Petticoat Lane market in the 1930's as her dad had told her it one day a few years ago. Her granddad and grandmother had an argument and, in the process, her granddad had knocked over and broken the only clock in their home. What was more, it had been a wedding present. Apparently, Emma, Cynthia's grandmother, had been devastated and, being a very superstitious person, had read all sorts of things into the 'breaking' of their wedding clock.

Nobby tried to assure his wife that the breaking of the clock was only an accident and certainly didn't mean that their time as husband and wife was coming to an end, however Emma couldn't stop crying. Feeling there was only one way he could help is wife, Nobby skipped going to football for the afternoon and caught the bus down to Petticoat Lane instead, where he spent his football ticket and beer money on the clock which now hung in the bedroom. Cynthia loved that story.

'I had better be off Granddad,' said Cynthia. 'Dad mentioned that mum would pop in this morning.'

Nobby started to make a face of disapproval, but Cynthia cut him short. Instead, he smiled a weak smile, nodded and then reminded her once again about the Kings delivery. Cynthia assured him again that everything was going to be alright and told him she would see him when she came back from her trip. She stroked his hand and kissed him softly before leaving.

Cynthia felt a mixture of feelings as she strolled to her granddad's shop. She was excited about her and Sandra's trip and was optimistic they could get their LPs autographed, but all the positive stuff had a negative shadow hanging over it because of her granddad's state of health. She knew he wasn't getting any better and struggled to dump such thoughts out of her mind.

However, by the time she got to the shop she was in a better frame of mind. She knew he was in good hands and her mum would look after him in her absence. Soon, she'd be counting down the hours to shutting the shop, meeting Sandra and catching their train to Liverpool.

In the meantime, every customer who came into the shop had to endure stories about Cynthia's pending weekend. In all honesty, it didn't surprise Cynthia that even the most elderly of her customers had heard of The Beatles. By the summer of 1964, it seemed to her that the whole world had!

It was just after 11am and Cynthia's latest pot of tea had just begun to brew when the 'King and Sons of Putney Bridge' delivery van ground to a squealing halt outside the shop. Suddenly the shop went dark as the van blocked out the sunlight. Cynthia looked up and abandoned finishing off the tea to attend to the delivery.

The Kings had been delivering goods to Nobby's shop every other Friday for over two decades. Albie King, the grandfather, had originally set up the business and his son Arnie had helped him build it up and expand it in the 50's. In the last few years, Arnie's son Alfie had also come on board.

Cynthia liked the Kings chaps and it seemed they had always been in her life. She loved the way that granddad King always carried toffees with him, which he would hand out to select people that he liked. Cynthia always got a toffee.

Cynthia also liked Alfie. He was more John's age, always cheerful and seemed to take pride in his work and feel proud to be working for the family business. Now that granddad King was older, it was mostly only Arnie and Alfie who made the deliveries. They always arrived dead on time, which was why Cynthia was making this particular brew as they always stopped for a cuppa.

By the time Cynthia reached the van out front, the Kings were already fumbling around in the back of it, sorting out the goods that had been ordered by Nobby. She stood in front of the open doors at the back, only to be faced by the top of two bums peering out from behind brown work coats. She felt herself blushing, but was also conscious that one of the behinds was quite attractive. Hoping that the one she admired was Alfie's, Cynthia coughed to let the Kings know she was present.

Arnie King turned around first and greeted Cynthia with a large smile. He was always smiling and why wouldn't he be, Cynthia often told herself, he was part of a successful business and had a wonderful, supportive family around him. Cynthia was pleased for him and even forgave him for not dishing out toffees like his father.

Arnie stepped down two small steps from the van carrying a large box and Cynthia hastily got out of his way as he huffed and puffed his way into the shop. Cynthia was expecting to see Alfie close at his father's heels, but instead a younger boy, whom she hadn't seen before, jumped down from the van. He had jet-black hair, just like all the males in the King family, only his was styled in a very Beatles fashion. The boy also possessed the Kings nose, which wasn't dissimilar to Ringo's, a fact that always amused Cynthia.

'Alright,' the boy said as he flung a sack over his shoulder and marched off into the shop.

Cynthia followed close behind, but far enough away so that she could continue to admire his behind. Arnie and Cynthia had a brief exchange, where he informed her what was on his delivery list, saying he was sorry, but he couldn't stop for a cup of tea because he had to drop into Mr Patterson's who lived a few along from the shop.

Before he made his exit though, he introduced Cynthia to James, who turned out to be his youngest son. He told the boy to finish off unloading the van and then have a cup of tea and wait for him.

Cynthia finished off making the tea whilst James did as he was told. She sneakily kept one eye on him as he carried boxes and sacks back and forth the van and had known there was a younger brother in the Kings clan but she had never met him. She figured he was of a similar age to her, if not a year younger, and was also aware that she actually felt quite attracted to him, which surprised her because she pretty much evaded any feelings of attraction to any boy because she was saving herself for George Harrison.

Once James had finished his task, he hung around the van instead of going back into the shop so Cynthia filled a cup with some tea and carried it out to him. He was just about to light a cigarette so Cynthia waited and then removed a cigarette from the box that he now held out to her. James leaned his back against the van, took a drag of his cigarette and a sip of his tea. There was an awkward silence between them that Cynthia decided to do something about.

'So, how come your name doesn't start with an A?' she asked.

James smiled and then let out a little laugh, followed by a plume of greyish smoke.

'Noticed that eh? Dad said mum put her foot down when I turned up, cos she always liked the name James and that was that. The end of the 'A' line...'

Cynthia smiled and considered the 'ice' broken.

'I reckon you're a Beatles fan then rather than the Rolling Stones. Am I right?'

James continued smiling, 'Beatles all day long, yeah that's right. As it happens, I can't stand the Rolling Stones, they're too scruffy for my liking.'

'Yeah I can always tell you know. It's actually quite obvious if a boy is into The Beatles or not,' Cynthia added.

James looked intrigued, 'Oh yeah, how?'

'I don't know really, I just can,' she replied, a small pink blush blooming upon her cheeks.

James had noticed it and smiled even more as he looked towards the pavement. 'Are you alone today?' James asked, 'Only dad was saying you work with your granddad?'

Cynthia explained that her granddad was sick and that she'd been taking care of the shop for the past few days. James said he hoped he would get well soon, adding that he had heard a great deal about Nobby and was aware that her granddad and his granddad went back a long time.

Their conversation started to flow and come naturally, something both the teenagers felt. They talked more about the difference between The Beatles and The Stones and then the *A Hard Day's Night* LP, something James was very much in awe of too. He then lit the end of a fresh cigarette using the end of previous one to fire it up.

'You got a steady boy then?' he asked Cynthia somewhat abruptly.

She was caught off guard, this one wasn't messing about. 'Err, no, not really. Why?' she asked.

'Well, I just wondered if you fancied going out tomorrow...pictures...something like that?'

'Hmm I'd like that, but I can't,' Cynthia replied feeling quite stunned. She hadn't been expecting the offer.

'Oh okay. I'm not a skinflint you know, I can take you somewhere nice,' James said looking embarrassed.

Cynthia could see and feel his disappointment and then she did something that she didn't expect to do.

'No, no, it's not that, it's just that I have plans for tomorrow. But, you can, er, take me out next week, if you like?'

Cynthia wasn't sure whether she regretted the words leaving her mouth. She felt like she was in completely new territory - and that was before the feeling of betraying George Harrison had struck her.

'Really!' James virtually squeaked. 'Err, I mean, that would be, er, great.'

'Yeah, ok then, it's a date. I'm actually going on a trip this weekend.'

'Oh yeah. Where are you going?' James asked sounding genuinely interested.

Cynthia told James about her plans, schemes, dreams and mission that the next few days held in store for her. He said it sounded like a wonderful weekend and wished her well with her 'mission' in particular.

Cynthia was still raving on about her trip when father King returned. He sensed he had walked into something occurring between the two teenagers and grinned. As he closed the van's rear doors, he asked Cynthia to pass on his best wishes to Nobby and said he'd be back in a fortnight and hoped he'd back in the shop by then. He then jumped into the driver's seat side of the van.

James and Cynthia said their goodbyes and it was left that James would visit Cynthia at the shop after this weekend. Cynthia told him that the Tuesday or Wednesday would be better because Thursday she and Sandra would be going down to join the throng of Beatle people outside the London Palladium. James nodded, said a sort of awkward goodbye and then jumped in the van, which quickly disappeared down the road with him waving out his van door window as it did so.

Cynthia suddenly felt wonderful. All warm inside and she simply couldn't wait to tell Sandra. Then George Harrison entered her mind and she felt a trifle confused; he was the love of her life, but she also liked James now too. It took Cynthia the rest of the afternoon up until she finally locked the shop's door, to shake off - or at least keep at bay - the feeling of confusion she was now experiencing.

She fired in a call to her mum and they talked about Nobby, then her mum said for her to be careful and 'keep her hand on her 'appenny' whatever that meant?

Now it action stations and, slinging her bag over her shoulder with one hand and clutching her *A Hard Day's Night* LP in the other, Cynthia charged off to meet Sandra.

As she approached her best mate at 'the bench', she was delighted to see her best mate was already there and grinning like a Cheshire cat. Before Cynthia could say a word about her being there, or James, Sandra was off and running...

'I've done it Cyn. I've done it, ha ha,' Sandra barked.

'Done what? What you done?' Cynthia, now beginning to laugh, linked arms with Sandra and they headed for the tube station.

'I've told old Dirty Douglas to stuff his job sideways and walked out.'

'You did what!' Cynthia exclaimed.

'I told him to shove it. Yeah piss it Cyn. I had forgotten to ask for a quick get-away today, so I mentioned it this morning. First of all, he said no way. When I complained and tried to explain, he told me that, well, there was one way he might reconsider and then he pinched my bum! I was left in no doubt what he meant and what he was after, so I swung for him!'

Cynthia put her hands to her face and laughed even louder.

'Don't Cyn,' said Sandra, now beginning to laugh too, 'I actually missed his big hooter, God knows how, but I came flipping close! Then he started yelling at me, so I started screaming back. It was a right commotion. And then I told him what he could do with his job, grabbed my coat and bag and walked out.'

'Blimey Sand. What will the agency say?'

Sandra shrugged her shoulders like she didn't care. In truth she did, but she just hadn't allowed herself to think about it. Anyway, if they threaten to sack her, she'd tell them all about him, so there.

The two continued their walk to the tube station arm in arm. Once Sandra had calmed down, Cynthia casually told her all about meeting James and agreeing on going on a date.

'But Cyn, what about your George?' Sandra yelped. 'He'll be devastated!'

Chapter 16
Love Me Do

'The train now standing at platform four is the 15.50 train to Liverpool – James Street Station, calling at…'

The sound of the platform announcer brought broad smiles to the faces of the two intrepid explorers.

There had only been a short queue at Euston Station so, tickets in hands, they excitedly skipped towards their transport north. They found an empty carriage, which had a smell of stale smoke from its previous occupants.

Sandra threw her suitcase onto the overhead metal shelf and after taking her seat, grabbed her travelling companion - Lennon's book - and was ready to dip into it once they were underway.

Cynthia clutched a copy of Mersey Beat, given to her by wrinkly old Doris who had come into the shop to buy some Carnation milk. She knew Cynthia was intending a trip to Liverpool and that she loved The Beatles, so she kindly bought a copy of the paper and gave it to her.

'Anything of interest in that issue?' Sandra asked nosily.

'Not really Sand. I had a quick flick through last night to see if there was any mention of what groups might be playing in the Cavern tonight, but I couldn't see anything. Bound to be some groups though, cos I read somewhere that there are over five hundred groups in Liverpool now, all playing similar music at various venues around the town. As it happens though, there are some articles on The Big Three and Ringo's old band Rory Storm and the Hurricanes. You can have a read after me if you want?'

Sandra screwed up her nose and shook her head. She wasn't particularly interested in Ringo's old band, only his current one. The train suddenly began to hum, then jerked forward as it started to depart from the station, gradually picking up speed. They were told at the ticket office that the journey to Liverpool would take four hours, less if all went to plan, so both girls knew they had plenty of time to natter and still have a read. Sandra thought to herself that she might even have a doze. As it happened, within the hour both girls were fast asleep and neither had read a word.

Cynthia's mum had packed her some sandwiches for the trip and put them in her holdall that morning, even though Cynthia protested she was *'too old for a packed lunch'* and was a little embarrassed to be carrying them. However, after only a couple of hours into the journey, Cynthia was feeling very peckish and the sarnies were now calling her to eat them. She handed Sandra a cheese one and they both devoured them in seconds. Cynthia said a silent 'thank you' to her mum and smiled to herself.

After a little sleep and then a chat about 'where, there and how', the four hours shot by and the train was pulling into its final destination. The girls excitedly stretched and, now feeling rested, they were raring to go. Once the engine had finally ground to a halt, the girls grabbed their belongings and marched their way past the ticket guard and onto the streets of the city of which they had often dreamed.

Thankfully, it was still relatively light and both girls took a moment to survey what was around them. In truth, Liverpool didn't look that much different to London and this came as a surprise to Cynthia. She didn't know why but she anticipated Liverpool, the home of the fab four, would somehow appear different. However, now she could see it was just another dirty city, seemingly overcrowded with people, cars and buses, albeit the buses were a different colour to what she was familiar with.

A green double decker displaying the number 86 and the words Penny Lane passed by. Cynthia pointed it out to Sandra, mentioning she liked the sound of the place name. As they now she strolled down the street, she wondered to herself if any of the Beatles had any connection to Penny Lane?

While Cynthia was pointing to yet another number 86 bus, she accidently nudged Sandra's book out of her hand. Before either had chance to pick it up, a small hand had swooped in and beat them to it. A young boy of about eleven and with a mucky face now dangled the book in the air by his fingertips. He was wearing khaki coloured shorts and a white, well now grey-ish, t-shirt and naturally had one sock rolled up and one down. His leather shoes were battered and worn and he could have been easily mistaken for an orphan from thirty years earlier.

'Here's your boook luv,' he said in a broad Scouse accent as thick as treacle as he handed the tome back to her.

'Thank you,' Sandra replied somewhat startled, but still remembering her manners as she looked the boy up and down. The girls turned and started to walk away.

'Eh, go 'ed. Giz a look at your boook then? Eh…will ya missus?' he was now calling after them.

Sandra slowly turned back and, not wanting to be rude to the boy, held her book up so that he could see it.

'I've actually never heard of dat,' he said as he sniffed before wiping a copious amount of slimy snot onto the back of his grubby hand.

Sandra smiled a kind smile, shrugged her shoulders and began to walk away a second time.

'I might never heard of it, butttt I know the man who wrote it. He's me cousin.'

Sandra and Cynthia stopped dead in their tracks and turned to look at the boy who had followed them along the street. Cynthia placed one hand on her hip.

'Yeah right, course he is,' she said, sounding like she didn't believe a word of it. 'Do you really expect us to believe that you're related to John Lennon?' Cynthia said smiling.

'Oh aye, dat's right. He's me cousin 'onest. Cross me heart. Now, if you give me some money I'll even introduce ya to him. Call it a fiver eh? That's fur enough innit?'

Cynthia looked at Sandra and laughed. 'Cheeky little fella ain't he?'

She certainly wasn't going to be fooled by the boy's story and hand over any money. 'Come on Sand, let's go,' said Cynthia, grabbing Sandra's arm and leading her away.

'Okay…okay, make it two pound den. C'mon that's a good deal that is,' the boy persisted but the girls were now ignoring him.

They continued to walk along the street and away from the station, now aware of the boy following close behind them. They reached the corner of the street and tried to work out where they were. They had been told that there were lots of B&Bs in the area between the train station and Mathew Street. The only problem was, they had no idea where Mathew Street was?

Cynthia turned to the boy, 'Right you. Make yourself useful and you can have this if you tell us the way to Mathew Street.' She was holding a five-shilling coin in her hand and waving it at him.

The boy quickly realised this was the best he was going to get from these two, so quickly agreed. He approached the girls and explained the fastest route, which didn't actually appear to be that far away.

'How do we know you've told us the right way?' Cynthia quizzed, scrutinising the boy for his response.

'Would I lie to you love? Come 'ed, giv us der money,' he said, a cheeky grin slowly breaking out on his face.

'Would you lie to us? Yes, you flipping would!' laughed Sandra. 'Not five minutes ago, you were telling us you were the cousin of our favourite singer!' This time however, the girls both suspected he was on the level.

'Go on then,' said Cynthia as she dropped the coin into the boy's grubby hand, watching his face light up.

'Ta love. Err listen, are you hungry too missus?' he quickly asked.

Cynthia and Sandra now did their best to ignore him; he was becoming a right pain in the wotsit.

'Only, me mam is the best coook in Liverpool. She makes the best Scouse yous will ever taste. Gis us another shilling and I'll take you to our 'ouse.'

But Cynthia was already dragging Sandra away from him, in search of finding a B&B and marching off in the direction of Mathew Street. This time, the small boy didn't follow them; he knew he had exhausted his patter. Instead, he turned away and made his way back to the train station to try and find someone else who might fall for his stories and hand over some money – three pounds often graced his small palm as he used his charm, wit and convincing spiel to tell people his cousin happened to be a member of the most famous band in the world and, for that very sum of money, he could organise an audience with him.

In the past twelve months, many a naïve and vulnerable teenage girl had become a victim of his scam. Once the three pounds was handed over, the boy would march them off in the direction of the busy city centre then, within a few swift moves, would disappear into the crowds and shadows, never to be seen again.

As Cynthia and Sandra strolled on, they were happy that had lost their little mate. They now began taking in the sights of Liverpool. Cynthia remembered her granddad telling her how the city had suffered during the war. He told her to look out for the massive slum clearance that had begun too.

Sandra however was busy contemplating something else that was bothering her.

''Ere Cyn, what's Scouse?' she asked.

Her best mate smiled. 'Oh Sandra, you do make me smile sometimes. Well, 'Scouse' is a sort of cheap meat dish. Traditionally the poor people eat it; I guess it's like a stew. From what I remember being told by my granddad, the people of Liverpool got it from the sailors who got off the ships which docked here centuries ago. We don't seem to eat it down south, don't know why.'

As Cynthia finished explaining the meal, they both noticed a red flickering neon 'Vacancies' sign hanging in the window of what looked like a B&B. The two girls studied the pale blue painted house in front of them. The walls had evidently been recently painted as spots of the pale blue paint were splashed on the pavement. They both quickly agreed that if it looked clean on the outside there'd be a good chance it would clean on the inside too. Cynthia took a deep breath and walked up to the door and knocked.

Both girls waited patiently on the pavement until the door slowly opened. A woman in her sixties stood before them, wearing a blue and green headscarf, which just about covered her black dyed bouffant, and a brown sauce-stained pinny. A cigarette with an inch of ash at its tip was hanging from the corner of her mouth, performing an unlikely balancing act and which completed her look.

Cynthia sized up the woman, quickly looking her up down before explaining that they were looking for a cheap room for two nights.

'I'm Vera' she replied, 'how d'ya do?' She then informed them that yes, she did have one room left, but it only had a double sized bed. Cynthia smiled and said it didn't matter, adding 'We're good mates.'

The woman blew out smoke through her nostrils and told the girls it was a fiver for the room per night, with a breakfast thrown in, all payable in advance.

'You don't look like you'd eat too much,' she said with a frosty smile.

Cynthia looked at Sandra, who quickly nodded, agreeing that the price was very reasonable. The woman didn't really care if the two girls from London thought the price was good or not and flicked what was left of her cigarette into the street, telling the girls to follow her inside.

Only once inside and with the door shut behind them, did Cynthia give Sandra a look that said 'you should never judge a book by its cover'. The inside was dead grotty and it smelled horrible. The woman led Cynthia and Sandra up two flights of stairs until they reached a scruffy looking door with grey paint peeling from it. She fished in the pocket of her pinny for a bunch of keys and opened the door, escorting the girls inside. The room had a smell like there was a dead mouse or three under the floorboards…and plenty of live ones above them.

The woman rapidly rattled off the house rules to the girls. The front door would be locked and bolted at 11.15pm sharp, breakfast was served from 7am until 9.30am and she then pointed to where the shared bathroom was. She added that the lock on that door was currently broken so advised guests to push a chair up against it whilst they bathed.

Then she asked for her money. Cynthia produced a fiver from her purse, which Sandra then matched and Vera stuffed both down the V neck of her purple sweater and into the edges of her white lacey bra, all while lighting up another fag and handing over the room key to Cynthia.

She then left the girls alone in the room, coughing on the smoke plume she had left behind.

'Well then, she's a right card isn't she?' Sandra whispered after a few silent seconds.

Cynthia was less amused however, as she examined the tired looking room with its filthy net curtains and threadbare floral carpet. She daren't think about how many sailors had been 'entertained' in the bed she was now testing for springy-ness. At least the sheets looked fairly clean she thought. Cynthia then went over to the window and looked out to see what the view offered. Oh, it was a cracker - before her, in all its glory, was the B&B's neglected garden containing an old rusting cooker and a nylon washing line, from which a few wooden pegs awaited the next day's washing.

'Oh, piss it,' Cynthia replied employing Sandra's favourite line and then both girls fell onto the bed laughing.

Sandra glanced at her watch - it was now 8.30 pm. Within 10 minutes, both girls had unpacked and hung their creased clothes onto the wire hangers provided in the wardrobe, which they then noticed had no actual door.

They quickly agreed it would be a good idea to have a 'cats lick' to freshen up before they went out to visit the most famous live music club in the world. They decided to work the bathroom in shifts and, thankfully, because it was still relatively early in the evening, there didn't seem to be anyone else in the B&B.

Still, they wouldn't be taking any chances. With no time for a proper bath, Cynthia filled the hand basin and washed herself down, drying herself on the grubby towel hanging on a hook on the back of the door whilst Sandra sat on a stool outside acting as guard.

Thankfully the water was reasonably hot and, once Cynthia had finished, she returned the favour. They quickly retreated back to their room, slapped on some make-up, put on their glad rags and then tucked their *A Hard Day's Night* LPs under their arms and headed out into the Liverpool night. It was just before 9pm and getting a little gloomy.

As Sandra said she was feeling hungry, they decided to head in the direction of the docks, thinking that was the perfect place to find a fish and chip shop.

They found themselves following groups of people who seemed to be going the same way and thankfully it didn't take them long to reach the River Mersey. As hoped, they spotted a fish and chip shop and made a beeline for it. Once their meal was purchased, they scouted around for a quiet spot overlooking the murky old river and where they could sit and eat in relative peace.

It was Sandra who spotted the vacant bench and both girls plonked themselves down and unwrapped their newspapers, revealing steaming hot chunks of cod and piles of golden chips. As Cynthia popped a hot salt and vinegar soaked piece of fried potato into her mouth, she noticed the headline on her wrapping: '*Donald Campbell Reaches 400 Miles in Blue Bird*'. This immediately brought her granddad to mind, who was a big admirer of the Campbell family and she wondered if he had seen that news.

She winced when a splash of the malty vinegar disturbed a mouth ulcer she had been nursing for a few days, as she continued to gaze out across the Mersey. The view thrilled her. There were several boats and ships of all sizes moored along the river's banks and there was still plenty of activity as sailors pushed wheelbarrows and carts back and forth. Groups of rugged-looking men in flat caps and shirts with their sleeves rolled up stood around chatting and smoking, but none of them paid any attention to the two young girls enjoying their suppers.

'Look,' said Sandra nodding her chin into the air and towards the direction of the Royal Liver Building. Cynthia looked up at the tall clock tower. What was left of the sun was positioned exactly behind the Liver bird and the Liverpool city symbol looked amazing with a now golden and red backdrop. The expanded wings on the statue made it appear truly majestic and the sight held both Cynthia and Sandra's gaze for the duration of the time it took them to eat their fish and chips. Noticing the time on the Liver Building clock, twenty past nine to be exact, Cynthia squashed up her now empty chip wrapper and got to her feet.

'C'mon missus,' Cynthia said, 'it's time to go to THE CAVERN!'

Cynthia led the way, even though she had no idea where she was going. She somehow knew instinctively in what direction to go and by chance, they found themselves walking through Lord Street into North John Street before finally joining Mathew Street. As they turned into it, they could suddenly see the lights outside The Cavern. There was still quite a lot of activity going on around it, with what looked like dockers gathered outside a pub enjoying a refreshing pint.

Cynthia and Sandra linked arms as they got nearer to their destination; hanging onto each other and now a team more than ever. Excitement rising, they could see the famous Mersey beat club just a few feet in front of from them. They watched their footing as they walked, avoiding any squashed pieces of fruit left over from the market which had been in full flow a few hours earlier. With her eyes to the ground, a piece of pink card caught Cynthia's eye.

She leaned forward and picked it up. It was a little soggy but was what she suspected, having recognised it from previous issues of The Beatles Monthly. Cynthia had never seen a real Cavern Club membership card and placed the card in the palm of her hand so they could both study it. It was a junior membership card for girls and Cynthia was in awe of it; she felt like she had found some long-lost treasure. Only to her, the membership card was a greater find than some old treasure - this membership card made her feel like she was touching a piece of The Beatles' history.

After all, George, Paul, Ringo and John had first performed in the Cavern as The Beatles in 1961, but even before that John and Paul had stood shoulder to shoulder on stage here as the Quarry Men. Cynthia felt all tingly inside as she carefully placed the membership card into her purse and then clipped it shut.

After a few more steps, Cynthia and Sandra now stood outside No. 10 Mathew Street. Even though it was 9.30ish, it was still early by Liverpool's Friday night standards. They joined the end of the queue of people looking to get into the club. Thankfully, it moved fairly quick and within 5 minutes, Cynthia and Sandra, arms still linked, were walking down some stone steps, with the general noise and hubbub of inside getting louder with their every step. Just the thought of walking down the same steps that the Fab Four had done countless times before, simply thrilled the girls.

Reaching the bottom, they passed through some doors and they were in! It was The Cavern Club and it was everything that they hoped it would be. It really was a cavernous place and both girls stood like statues and surveyed the club around them, soaking up its atmosphere and making mental notes of all its features: the archways, the brick walls, the sturdy brick pillars, the benches and the large banner that said simply said CAVERN. They recognised so much of the venue because of the hours they had spent studying photographs of The Beatles playing on the very stage that was now in front of them.

Cynthia simply stared at it and imagined the Fab Four performing upon it. She pictured them huddled together, surrounded by their amplifiers and clutching their guitars, dressed in their white shirts and black waistcoats. She looked at Sandra who also stood gawping at the stage and suspected she was imaging Ringo behind his drums, shaking his head and grinning away like he didn't have a care in the world.

'I read The Beatles played here something like 292 times,' said Cynthia.

'It's incredible innit?' said Sandra. 'How I wish I could have come and seen them here just once...I would have loved that. Can you imagine joining one of those massive queues at lunch time, being one of the Beatle people in this crowded place and seeing the band play...actually play and being able to hear them?'

'And then coming back in the afternoon and then again in the evening,' Cynthia interrupted laughing.

Sandra nodded. 'Not half,' she said and then suggested they explore the nooks and crannies of the place. And they did just that, leaving nothing out. They even had to experience the toilets and the infamous cloakroom where Cilla Black had once worked. Exploration over, they both bought a bottle of Coca Cola from the bar.

Their thirst quenching was interrupted by the crackling noise of a guitar being plugged into an amplifier, filling the club with a buzzing sound. Cynthia and Sandra hadn't noticed just how busy the club had become and, by the time they had, a few dozen youngsters had gathered in front of the stage.

'Come on,' Cynthia said, grabbing Sandra's arm and leading her towards the same area. So wrapped up were they by simply being there, they hadn't taken any notice of the posters outside the club, so had no idea what groups were about to start playing.

A four-piece group had positioned themselves on the stage. They were evidently Beatle people because they wore the style of suits that the Fabs wore. All young and fairly good-looking, except for the drummer, and both guitarists were clutching Rickenbackers.

The group's opening song was a cover of *Twist And Shout*, a song which The Beatles had also covered and it wasn't a bad effort at all and thrilled the crowd. The next song up was a Billy J Kramer hit *Bad To Me*, followed by *I'm Telling You Now*, which was a popular number performed by Freddie and the Dreamers. It was obvious their whole set was going to be covers.

Cynthia and Sandra didn't mind at all - in fact they were delighted as it gave them the chance to sing along. The next two groups on stage also covered a lot of Beatles songs, which delighted the girls as they had the chance to hear their songs in this place of worship.

All the groups had played short sets of 25 minutes, which meant the evening went quickly and it was just after eleven when Cynthia and Sandra finally left the Cavern Club. They were now hot and sweaty, just like everyone else, and the club had been filled to capacity by the time they left. On their way out, they got to say hello to the club's resident DJ, Bob Wooler, which especially pleased Sandra.

By doing that, she had now actually shaken the hand of someone who had shaken the hand of Ringo. The only disappointment the girls felt when walking back to the B&B, was that they hadn't bumped into any of The Beatles or got their albums autographed. But deep down they knew it had always been a long, long shot.

They worked out they had about ten minutes to get back to the B&B before the bolts went on. However, to their despair and despite managing to find their way back quite easily, they were still too late and they found the front door was bolted. They had a key to their room, but they found out that didn't work on the main front door.

'Piss it!' shrieked Sandra, 'I mean, what sort of silly time is 11.15 to lock a door anyway, eh?'

'It's mean really. Looks like old Vera gives the men staying here just enough time to drink up their beer in a local pub and then they have to scuttle back here.'

The B&B was in total darkness inside. It was also evident that the landlady was either out herself or in bed.

'Piss it,' Sandra cursed again, stroking her chin. 'What the flipping hell we going to do?' she asked.

Cynthia knocked on the door several times, getting bolder and louder each time, but nothing stirred inside the house.

'Oh, this is useless. Well...nothing else for it...follow me,' stated Cynthia.

Sandra looked puzzled as she did as she was instructed, following Cynthia along the street and into a dark alley that ran alongside the B&B.

'What we doing Cyn? CYN?' Sandra whispered.

'Will you ssshh!' Cynthia demanded, concerned about waking up any of the neighbours and not needing any extra complication to this present situation.

'Look, we're going to have to find a way to get in, right? Well, I'm wondering if this alley will lead us to the B&B's garden. If it does, the back door might be open or a window, so come on...'

It was pitch-black in the alley and both girls stuck close together. The ground beneath their feet felt soft and uneven and they suspected they were walking on grass and soil - at least that's what they hoped it was...

Cynthia paused at a wooden gate which she thought was the rear garden gate to the B&B, but she really couldn't be sure. Feeling nervous and a little frightened, she slowly pushed it open. As she did so, a cat squealed and dashed past her, making them both jump. Cynthia placed one hand over her heart and the other over her mouth. Sandra already had both of her hands over her mouth and was shaking her head.

'I don't like this Cyn. I'm telling you, I don't like this...one...little...bit.'

'Come on silly. Just tread carefully,' Cynthia whispered.

The garden they now found themselves in was long and narrow and had a stone path leading to some steps, at the top of which was the back door.

Cynthia tried the door handle. It too was locked.

'Oh, double piss it!' she hissed, wanting to stamp her feet angrily but somehow controlling herself.

'What we going to do now?' Sandra asked desperately.

Cynthia shrugged her shoulders, then took a step back to get a good look at the outside of the building. She searched for their bedroom window.

'That's our room I think,' Cynthia pointed.

'Are you sure?' Sandra replied in a whisper, not feeling convinced.

'Yeah. Look, you jump on my back and see if you can reach that bit of drain pipe half way up because, if you can, I reckon you could get onto that window ledge and then pull yourself up above it and then see if our bedroom window is open.'

'Piss it Cyn. No, I can't do that. You do it!' came Sandra's reply.

'Come on Sand. I'm a rubbish climber, you know that. You were always the better climber than me. You were always the first to climb on top of the sheds down the allotment.'

'But, that was when I was ten!' Sandra tried to protest, knowing it was in vain, as in her heart she knew Cynthia was right and she knew the task was going to be hers. Cynthia leaned over and braced herself for Sandra climbing onto her back.

'Hold on, what are you doing? Take your shoes off first,' Cynthia demanded.

Sandra tutted but did as she was told. She then climbed unsteadily onto Cynthia's back and reached for the first wooden window ledge. It actually wasn't that hard and in a jiffy she had managed to grab both hands onto it. She pulled herself up and was just about to scramble onto the next window ledge when a light shone in her face and a man's voice shouted.

'Stop there you. I can see ya's. What are you doing?'

Such was the surprise, Sandra lost her grip and fell, landing on top of Cynthia; both girls lying in a heap on the floor. They looked up to see who was shouting at them and then realised a large policeman was shining his torch into their faces.

'Come on then. What's going on here?' he asked somewhat impatiently.

The girls shakily got to their feet.

'Hello Sir. We, we are staying here, but...but got locked out by the landlady,' Cynthia explained.

'Can you prove it?' he asked, noticing the girl's accent didn't place her from around his beat. 'What's it like inside the B&B?'

For a split second, Sandra was tempted to say 'flipping horrible', but thought better of it.

Cynthia described the B&B and its owner perfectly, which seemed to satisfy the PC. He told them to follow him back out into the street, adding that if they tried anything silly like trying to scarper, he would catch them and they would have him to answer to. The girls assured him that they wouldn't be that foolish.

The policeman led them to the B&B's front door, where he banged on it extremely hard several times. Almost instantly, a light went on in one of the rooms to the right of the street door. Within seconds, the front door opened and there stood the B&B's owner, dressed in a heavy cotton nightie and curlers hanging from her hair.

'Alright Vera love. Are these two staying with you?' the policeman asked.

The B&B owner looked at the girls, frowned and nodded with a disgusted look on her face.

'They are. Where did you find them?'

'Now come on now, don't be too hard on them. I found them round the back door, trying to get in. You know what it's like, you were young once yourself girl.'

'You'd need to have a good memory to remember that,' thought Sandra.

The policeman turned to the girls and began telling them off for being so stupid, but winked when he had finished berating them. He then bid goodnight to the lovely Vera and walked off into the darkness.

Vera stepped to one side and told Cynthia and Sandra to go in. She didn't need to say anything else, the expression on her wrinkly and now makeup-free face said it all. The two girls offered their apologies as they scuttled off to their room feeling like two naughty schoolgirls.

They were certainly happy to lock the door behind them and jump into bed. Within minutes they felt warm and cosy and began drifting off to sleep. The only thing stopping that happening was the thought of Vera's face scowling at them over breakfast in the morning. They certainly weren't looking forward to facing her at breakfast time.

Chapter 17
Magical Mystery Tour

After a surprisingly decent night's sleep, the girls decided it was best to avoid the wrath of the scary Vera after all, so they got up and dressed in record time and sneaked out very quietly, both firmly clutching their copies of *A Hard Day's Night* LP and their overnight bags. They could hear Vera in her kitchen, rattling those pots and pans and cursing, but she never noticed them creeping down the stairs, open the B&B's front door and make their escape. Once outside, they ran as fast as their legs could carry them away from the little house of horrors. They were heading for a café they had noticed at the end of Mathew Street and decided they would get some breakfast there.

Mathew Street was already a hive of activity when they got there. Market stalls were already out and doing decent business and the café they now walked into was full of builders and dockers and had the lovely smell of eggs, sausages and bacon cooking in fat.

Cynthia and Sandra opted for the full English which included black pudding and tomatoes. Silence enveloped them as they ate quickly, washing it all down with sweet, milky tea.

Cynthia then relayed the details of the full day she had planned, including what buses went to the various Beatles-related locations. She had written down general street directions using her granddad's UK map book as a reference.

The first task on the list was to find a bus top which would take them to their first destination. Using the bus stop just off North John Street, it was only a fifteen-minute bus ride and a short walk to 10 Admiral Grove. This was where Ringo had once lived as a child.

Cynthia definitely wanted to start their Liverpool Beatles tour at one of Ringo's childhood homes as she knew this would mean a lot to her best friend. And it did. Sandra visibly shook as she passed St Silas Primary School, where Ringo had been a pupil, and The Empress pub where Ringo's mother, Elsie, had worked as a barmaid.

But as Sandra now stood in front of the modest terraced house, she couldn't prevent herself from crying. Cynthia put her arm around Sandra's shoulder to comfort her and even though Ringo was Sandra's Beatle, Cynthia also felt like she wanted to weep. A couple of elderly women walked past the two emotional girls and shook their heads. It wasn't the first time they had seen Beatle people standing on the doorstep of 10.

'They nicknamed him Lazarus you know,' Sandra blurted out during a gap in her sobbing.

Cynthia wiped the tears from her eyes. 'Who Sand?' she gulped.

'Ringo. The other kids at St Silas used to call him Lazarus. It was because he was so sick when he was smalllll ah ah…' Sandra couldn't stop herself from sobbing again and Cynthia held her friend tight.

There was still plenty to do on their list and they had a full day ahead of them, but even though Cynthia was eager to get to George's childhood home, she didn't want to rush Sandra. The two girls remained embraced in each other's arms for what felt to Cynthia like a good ten minutes, but in reality was much less. As they stood there, several more people passed them and mumbled their disgust - 'Bleedin' dozy divvies' being one of the kinder ones they heard…

'Oi, you soppy pair of mares.' They looked up to see a coal lorry and the driver shouting at them as he went by, 'You've just missed 'im. Go 'ed, he's in the barbers getting his hair cut.'

Neither girl thought that was funny.

'Come on Sand, pull yourself together. We're attracting too much attention now,' said Cynthia finally. Nodding her chin in the direction of the number 10 and smiling, she asked, 'We've come all this way, are we going to knock then?'

Sandra nodded firmly and then made an effort to compose herself. Flattening the creases on her dress and running her fingers through her hair, she plucked up the courage and approached the door. Cynthia stood close behind her.

Sandra knocked twice and waited. Nothing. She knocked again. Both girls held their *A Hard Day's Night* LPs out in front of them like they were trays. They thought the LPs would do the talking for them, should someone actually open the door.

Cynthia joined in with the knocking until it was obvious that nobody was home. Eventually Cynthia had to break the bad news to Sandra that it was time to move on and, reluctantly, Sandra agreed and pulled herself away from Ringo's old home. Feeling Sandra's disappointment and seeing an opportunity to try and lift her friend's spirits, Cynthia pulled a face and in an old woman's voice croaked, 'Now it's, I, me mine's turn.' It worked as Sandra immediately broke out in to smile.

They did the short walk to George Harrison's former home in Arnold Grove within a few minutes and found the cul-de-sac with no problems. Now it was Cynthia's turn to get all emotional as the nearer she got to number twelve, the more her legs felt like jelly. She wasn't anticipating such a reaction and although Cynthia didn't know how she would react, this surprised her.

The size of the Harrison's home wasn't much different to the Starkey's; it was just another small terraced house. Cynthia removed her *A Hard Day's Night* LP from her bag and, wasting no time, walked swiftly and boldly up to the front door and knocked on it. Sandra hovered a few feet back, checking the windows and trying to spot any movement inside.

Cynthia and Sandra waited patiently a few moments longer before getting the same sinking feeling they felt at Ringo's old house.

Cynthia tried one more time. Nothing.

They had to surrender to the fact that nobody was home. Devastated, both girls dropped to the pavement and perched themselves on the edge of the kerb. Now Cynthia knew how Sandra had felt. They knew all along it was going to be a long shot to be lucky enough to find one of the Fab Four visiting their old homes, but somehow they had convinced themselves, it might just happen.

As they sat in silence pondering their next move, Sandra suddenly perked up telling Cynthia that she was busting for a wee. Cynthia held out her arms as if to say 'what can I do?'

'Cyn! I really need to GO!'

Cynthia smiled a devilish grin, saying 'Come on then,' and helped Sandra to her feet.

'Where are we going?' Sandra asked.

Cynthia didn't say a word, but instead led Sandra down the narrow alleyway that she suspected would take them to the rear of the terraces in Arnold Grove. And it did. Both girls were impressed how clean and tidy the alleyway was kept, with several dustbins lined up like soldiers against the rear gardens of Arnold Grove.

Guessing that they were outside the Harrison's, Cynthia nodded to Sandra.

'In you go. Go on then.'

'Go on then what?' Sandra replied all confused.

'You said you was busting. Well, there's a toilet,' Cynthia said nodding in the direction of the outdoor toilet.

'What you mean...no, I can't...I can't...can I?'

Cynthia crossed her arms, smiled and slowly nodded as if to say 'dare you'.

Sandra was now so badly in need of a wee that she was getting desperate and, mixed with a sense of excitement and nerves, it was proving to be a dangerous cocktail. She decided there was nothing else for it, so handed Cynthia her bag, looked up and down the alley, took a deep breath and cautiously pushed open the garden gate.

The outside toilet, her target, was only a few feet away. She quickly scanned the rear of the house and then that of the neighbours and, feeling satisfied nobody was around, rushed towards the toilet. Within seconds she was safely inside and it was only then it occurred to her that her bum was sharing the same toilet seat as George Harrison. She found it quite overwhelming and such was the experience that, by the time she returned to Cynthia, she once again had tears in her eyes.

As Sandra tearfully approached Cynthia, Cynthia just rushed past her laughing.

'My turn! Ha ha!'

They were still giggling at their exploits minutes later whilst sitting on the top deck of one of the green buses they had noticed on the day they had arrived.

They were pleased to have a brief sit down and take in the sights of the Liverpool streets that their idols would have walked as teenagers. En route, they passed a sign saying 'Strawberry Field Salvation Army Children's Home', to which both girls smiled at the name.

They jumped off at the stop in Menlove Avenue and walked arm in arm to the next location on their tour. Both girls had seen photographs of John Lennon's aunt Mimi's house at 251 and now they stopped at the end of its path, each mouthing the word 'Mendips'.

Unfortunately, they soon found that John Lennon's old home and the next address on their list, Paul McCartney's old family home at 20 Forthlin Road, presented exactly the same result as Ringo and George with nobody being home.

If life is all about timing, theirs was very poor today.

Deflated, Cynthia and Sandra retreated back to the city centre with their Beatles LPs still unsigned. This task of theirs was proving to be a lot harder than they expected, impossible even. As they sipped their mugs of teas back in the café at the end of Mathew Street, both girls felt like crying. It had been an emotional day on several levels and it was beginning to take its toll on them.

But, revived by several cups of sweet tea and a welcome bacon sandwich, they ploughed on with their plans and took a bus ride out to the location of the Casbah Club which was owned by Mona Best, mother of one time Beatle drummer Pete, in Hayman's Green, West Derby. After that, a visit to the NEMS record store in Whitechapel, where Brian Epstein once worked to help build up the family's empire.

The remainder of the afternoon was simply spent exploring the streets of Liverpool. They constantly dived in and out of clothes and record shops, keeping an eye out for any Beatles posters and memorabilia. By the time they sneaked back into their room at the B&B, both had managed to collect a few items to add to their personal collections, with Sandra picking up 'authentic' Beatles talcum powder and Cynthia a collection of Fab Four pin badges and a Beatles thermos flask.

They just had enough time to each have a bath, and an even briefer time to apply make-up, before they were back out on the town. First stop, to find a pub where they would get served and then drink away the disappointment of not managing to find a Beatle and get their LPs autographed.

Thankfully, it didn't take them long to find a pub near the docks, where they were also bought quite a few gin and tonics by willing and obviously randy sailors trying their luck.

Both girls were aware they couldn't stay here much longer and managed to skip out while the men of the sea were taking a leak. They knew when to call an end to an adventurous day before it got TOO adventurous.

Back in their room, as predicted, Sandra rattled the windows most of the night, despite on occasion being pinched and kicked by Cynthia. Although, somehow through all that, both girls awoke refreshed and ready for their trip to Blackpool and the highlight of the trip - their Beatles concert.

***

The Blackpool of the 1960's was noisy, colourful, and bustling with holiday makers and energy.

On leaving the train station, the girls strolled cheerfully in the direction of the town's most recognised feature, The Blackpool Tower. The streets surrounding it were busy with families soaking up the unique atmosphere of this famous seaside resort, on what was a nice sunny day.

Children licked ice creams and carried bucket and spades, while their parents led the way to the beach carrying bags packed full of towels to sit on and cheese and cucumber sandwiches to get gritty sand all over later.

Between them, Cynthia and Sandra had visited many seaside resorts but none of them had offered quite the amount of choice of hotels and B&Bs that Blackpool now laid in front of them.

Street after street was packed with them, so much so that it seemed unusual to stumble across a corner shop or a hairdresser's, although pubs ran a close second in number. But which B&B should they choose? After the dreadful experience with Vera for two nights, they were in no hurry to make a hasty decision.

It was fast approaching dinner time so, as the girls got their bearings, Cynthia suggested that they find a café to have something to eat before embarking on their search to find a suitable B&B.

Sandra didn't argue. She was famished as, once again, they had sneaked out of their B&B in Liverpool without having any breakfast. Neither girl could face the Liverpool landlady from hell.

Sandra heartily scoffed her sausage, beans and chips, quickly making up for the lack of breakfast. Cynthia got stuck into a shepherd's pie and chips and that too went down very nicely.

It became obvious the girls were sharing the café with several other Beatle people who were in town for the performance that evening. Exchanging small talk about the band and tonight's concert with those around them, simply ramped up the excitement levels the girls were beginning to feel. They checked their watches over and over; the concert just couldn't come around quick enough.

They finally settled on a modest B&B nestled in between many others. Cynthia liked the way the terraced house stood out because it had been painted a bright yellow, and was the same colour of her new favourite dress which she had been saving to wear to the concert. Sandra didn't much care what B&B was chosen, just as long as it was cleaner than the Liverpool one and had a lock on the bathroom door.

They walked inside and found themselves in the reception area. It even had a small bar with shelves at the back and upon which sat several competition dancing trophies. An elderly man was sat fast asleep in the armchair behind a small desk. He was snoring, which caused the Sandra to chuckle.

'No idea why you're laughing, he sounds like you,' said Cynthia, abruptly bringing Sandra's laughter to a halt.

The girls were soon joined by a woman in her late-forties entering the room, carrying a tray of cups and saucers which were on their way to be washed up. The girls instantly noticed the lady's natural beauty, drop-dead figure and the obvious likeness to Audrey Hepburn. They were most impressed.

'Hello,' said the woman kindly, 'how may I help you?'

'Hello,' Cynthia replied, 'do you have a room that my friend and I could share please?'

Smiling, the woman placed the tray onto a coffee table pushed up against a wall at the end of the bar. She searched for a book which was hidden amongst some magazines. Cynthia watched the woman's long slender fingers with their beautifully painted nails as she thumbed her way through several pages.

'I have two rooms available that would suit you, but I'll put you in the one at the back of the house. It's a bit quieter at night time so you shouldn't get any broken sleep. Would six pounds be agreeable?'

Cynthia and Sandra nodded at the fee and thanked the woman for her thoughtfulness whilst handing over the fee for the room. The woman was friendly and the complete opposite to the old witch in Liverpool. The girls sensed she was pleased to have two youngsters staying at her B&B.

'Now, don't tell me, but I think I know what brings you two to Blackpool,' she said.

'The Beatles!' Sandra replied.

Cynthia smiled, 'She said don't tell her Sand.'

'Oh yeah. Sorry,' said Sandra.

'Tsk, tsk, don't be silly dear. I simply love their new song.'

The landlady then broke into a hum of *Can't Buy Me Love*, which caused the old snorer to stir a little. Cynthia, Sandra and the woman all giggled his way.

'Lovely looking boys too. Tell you what, do you girls fancy a cuppa before I show you to your room?' she added.

The girls nodded and were invited to pull out two of the bar stools whilst she disappeared into a room behind the bar.

'You've done well here Cyn. She's nice, isn't she?' Sandra said.

'Lovely - and she's stunning for her age,' Cynthia replied.

'By the way, my name's Audrey,' the landlady announced, returning with a pot of tea and some cups and saucers. Cynthia gave Sandra a look, which said surely she must have been joking. They told her their names and Audrey entered those in the register.

She then served the tea and perched on her stool positioned behind the bar.

'Have you been to Blackpool before? Audrey asked.

Cynthia and Sandra told her about their experiences of Blackpool, which wasn't much at all, just a couple of weekends in caravans.

'Have you been in Blackpool long?' Cynthia asked.

'Me? Yes, over twenty years now and I've had this B&B for fifteen of them.'

'You don't have a Lancashire accent though. Are you from somewhere else?' Sandra butted in.

'You're right. Well spotted. I'm actually from Cambridge, but I left there when I was about the age you are now.'

'How did you come to be in Blackpool then and get this B&B?' Cynthia asked, genuinely intrigued by the woman.

Audrey took a long sip of her tea and produced a box of cigarettes, which she offered to her guests. Cynthia even thought she held her cigarette like Audrey Hepburn.

'A man,' Audrey began.

Cynthia sat bolt upright. She had a feeling she was going to like Audrey's story.

'His name was Henry and he was an American soldier, a marine. He was stationed just outside Liverpool. When he had R&R, Henry would come to Blackpool and enjoy himself. It so happened that we met one night while I was also in Blackpool, as I had a summer job here working in a clothes shop. We were both at a dance in the Blackpool Tower ballroom and we spotted each other while we queued for drinks and instantly fell in love. Love at first sight truly does exist girls, I'm telling you - and it really didn't matter that he was obviously several years older than me.

I can still picture him casually walking over to me and inviting me to dance. He was very handsome. He didn't even introduce himself until we were dancing together, and then we danced and danced all that night.

Soon, Henry returned to see me in Blackpool every opportunity he got and, after the war, he stayed in England and ballroom dancing became our life. We got married and we danced four or five times a week. We got really good too and won several competitions, as you can see from our trophies.' Audrey turned and looked up at the shelves where they sat.

'Fab!' Sandra said.

'Henry and I danced for years. It was our thing and what we did best. But sadly, Henry got sick and he couldn't dance anymore. By this time, we were living in Blackpool and had fallen in love with the town. We wanted to stay close to the Blackpool Tower, so we purchased this B&B and on Sunday afternoons we would go and watch the dancers in the ballroom. We missed dancing ourselves, but we were happy to watch others enjoy themselves, sort of second best I guess.'

'That's a lovely story. Do you mind if I ask how long it's been since your husband died?' Sandra asked sympathetically.

Audrey almost choked on her tea before breaking into a roar of laughter.

'Henry!' she suddenly shouted, 'Henry!' And the elderly man who had been snoring in the armchair woke up immediately.

'Yes dear,' he spluttered.

***

The girls spent the remainder of the day roaming the streets of Blackpool, taking in the sights and smells of the world-famous resort. They sat on the crowded sandy beach for a couple of hours after they had wolfed down yet another bag of fish and chips mid-afternoon. It was a most pleasant afternoon watching the attractions on the beach: a muscle man competition and a beauty contest.

The winners of both got an impressive twenty pounds. Actually, Cynthia kicked herself for not entering the beauty contest as she thought she was better looking than the winner; Sandra wasn't so sure though.

They returned to the B&B around 4pm and spent another hour chatting with Audrey before heading up to their room to get ready for their big Blackpool night out.

In the room, Cynthia sat on a stool whilst she applied the last touches of makeup to her face, hogging the only mirror in the room as she did so. Sandra was perched on the edge of the same stool trying to find a gap to finish off her makeup.

'Do you think we will actually be on the television Cyn?' Sandra asked.

'We will if I have anything to do with it,' Cynthia replied quickly, leaping up from the stool.

She grabbed her yellow dress and slipped it on. She just knew she looked fantastic in it and pushed Sandra out of the way of the mirror so she could admire her figure. Cynthia decided something was missing and if she was going to grab the attention of Eric and the cameraman, she needed to *really* stand out. Diving into her bag, she pulled out two pairs of spare knickers which she stuffed into her bra. Sandra watched on, bewildered by her friend's behaviour.

'There, that should do it,' Cynthia said poking, squeezing and adjusting her new breasts. Sandra just rolled her eyes and laughed.

Church Street, where the ABC Theatre was located, was only a short walk from the B&B and by the time they reached the theatre, crowds of Beatle people were already gathering in the street and surrounding area.

Naturally, The Beatles were the main attraction of the Blackpool Night Out show being hosted by Mike and Bernie Winters, but there were also to be appearances from Chita Rivera, Frank Berry, Jimmy Edwards and Lionel Blair. The show was scheduled to be broadcast between 8.25pm and 9.25pm.

The queue was already stretching the length of the newly refurbished theatre by the time Cynthia and Sandra joined it. They could sense the excitement and anticipation in the air. The girls held their bags carrying their copies of *A Hard Day's Night* LP close to their bodies for fear of them getting crushed as the queue slowly inched forward. Their eyes shone brightly as the realisation hit that they were soon going to see The Beatles live in concert again.

The process of entering the theatre, handing over the tickets that Eric had generously given to them and being ushered to their seats, was seamless. The girls felt special and they were indeed good seats.

Cynthia and Sandra now sat on the edge of them, their LPs lay flat on their laps as they watched the theatre fill up with people of all ages. Thankfully, the immediate area where Cynthia and Sandra had been seated was packed full with other young teenage girls. Eric Perkins must have known.

Two-and-half-thousand excited people had soon filled the theatre. Although much of it was now new, it still retained a strong sense of the history of the artists who had performed there over the years. It had been a favourite venue for popular summer shows, hosting the likes of Morecombe and Wise, Tommy Steele, Frank Ifield and Cliff Richard and his Shadows

And then finally, tonight's show began and young girls were soon competing with each other to try and catch the attention of the performers and the cameraman. Once all the other acts had finished their routines, the excitement built as Beatle time approached. As usual, as they hit the stage, the noise was simply deafening.

They performed five songs in total, *A Hard Day's Night; Things We Said Today; You Can't Do That; If I Fell*, which had a false start much to the amusement of John and Paul; and *Long Tall Sally*. During the concert, some girls threw jellybeans and hair rollers and Cynthia thrust her new boobs up higher and higher, trying her best to be spotted.

Before the show finished, The Beatles were also included in comedy sketches where they dressed up as dustmen and medical surgeons. Neither Cynthia nor Sandra had expected this and belly-laughed throughout each second of the Fabs' performance.

After the show, Cynthia and Sandra were ushered out of the building and, without really realising it, found themselves standing on the pavement amongst hundreds of teenage girls, all with mascara stains smudged over their faces. Cynthia struggled to think of a way Sandra and she may be able to finally get their LPs signed. Cynthia pushed Sandra through the crowd until they were free of it and walked to the end of Church Street.

'There has to be a stage entrance. We have to find it before a thousand other girls do,' Cynthia said.

Sandra nodded, still looking dazed from having watched the performance. They ran along the street searching for some sign or indication to where the stage entrance may be. And then they found it - but unfortunately so had a few hundred or so other girls.

'Oh, piss it,' Sandra spat, suddenly returning to the real world.

Cynthia and Sandra were not going to give up that easily and started to push their way through the throng of other bobby dazzlers intent on getting as close as they possibly could to the stage door. They knew it wasn't going to be an easy task, but they also knew if they had any hope of getting their LPs autographed, they had to grab a Beatle.

The two of them were squashed at the front of a now heaving mob, being held back by a mixture of policemen and theatre commissionaires. Over an hour passed with no sign of any of the show's performers leaving and the crowd which had gathered around the stage door had thinned a little, together with the number of security, but most seemed committed to their cause.

It was almost midnight before the stage doors finally flung open and The Beatles appeared. Cynthia and Sandra cried out at the top of their voices, along with plenty of others. They found themselves caught up in the crowd that surged forward, but the security defended the assault well and within seconds The Beatles were pushed into black, gleaming, limousines and driven off at speed into the darkness.

Within seconds, the screams and squeals had died down and hundreds of girls now stood around crying into the shoulders of their companions, realising another opportunity to meet a Beatle had gone.

Cynthia and Sandra were still crying as they slowly ambled off into the night. They didn't want to admit defeat, but in their hearts they knew their chance of getting their LPs autographed was now virtually non-existent.

Cynthia was beginning to think that maybe it wasn't meant to be after all. Things were changing fast for them both and they were changing too, physically and mentally. To her, this was beginning to feel like one last summer of fun before reality would kick in and they would be expected to 'grow up'.

The signing of the album by The Fabs would perhaps signify the signing off of their childhood. She felt it simply had to be done and then they could both move on.

Chapter 18
Another Girl

It had been a somewhat sombre return journey back to London on the Monday. Cynthia seemed deeply affected by her failure to get their LPs autographed and hardly spoke throughout the entire train journey. Sandra did her best to cheer her friend up even though she too felt the same disappointment. They had believed *so much* in their mission to get their LPs signed by The Beatles that, now it hadn't happened, this had cast an awkward shadow over their adventures of the last few weeks.

Once back home, it still took Cynthia a while to properly shake off her feeling of disappointment. She had even told Sandra that she wasn't going to hang about outside the London Palladium on the Thursday for the 'Night of the 100 Stars' charity event, but Sandra suspected that by then her best mate would have had a change of heart, after all she wasn't one to let herself feel down for too long. Sandra also thought that if Cynthia saw her granddad well again and running the shop, that would also make her feel a whole lot better, and she also had her date with that James to look forward to.

As predicted, Cynthia woke up on the Tuesday morning feeling back on top form and raring to go. Deep down, however, she did feel pangs of guilt about abandoning her granddad's shop for a few days, and she was now in two minds whether to persist with the autograph mission. It was, well, beginning to feel a bit silly. She decided she needed more time to chew that one over.

A quick, gulped down breakfast was followed by Cynthia paying a visit to see her granddad and a plan to walk to the shop with him. Her mum had mentioned at the breakfast table that he was still off work, but that he was determined to get back as soon as possible, so Cynthia cheerfully headed in the direction of his house.

Sadly, instead, she found him in bed, just like she had done before going on her trip. It seemed her mum couldn't bring herself to tell Cynthia the true facts regarding his illness.

Even though he was poorly, the now increasingly frail Nobby was delighted to see her and wanted to hear all about her adventures. She could see that he was genuinely interested but also that he was very weak; too weak, in truth, to stomach her reflections.

Cynthia did her best to be upbeat though, and enjoyed telling him about both of the B&B owners, going to the Cavern, visiting the Fabs' homes, eating fish and chips down by the docks and then all about the ABC Theatre show. She avoided mentioning the incident of getting locked out of the B&B in Liverpool and having a wee in the Harrison's outdoor toilet, thinking that was probably too much information there.

'And well, did you get your album signed by the lads then love?' asked Nobby cheerily.

She shook her head as she told him she hadn't, but did her best not to show him her disappointment. She didn't want him using up any of his valuable energy feeling sorry for her.

Before leaving him for the shop, she told Nobby she would be back to see him after closing. Cynthia spent much of day worrying deeply about him and the day seemed to drag on forever. Her mind really wasn't on pounds of spuds or packets of washing powder.

It was also one of the hottest days of the month and that certainly didn't help. Most of the usual Tuesday customers came into the shop and all commented on Cynthia's granddad still not being at work. Cynthia smiled as best she could, but felt like she didn't need much reminding of that fact. She spent what would have been her normal lunch hour restocking shelves and tidying up, thereby relieving some of the guilt she had stored up from leaving he shop closed for a couple of days.

She was very glad indeed when she was eventually able to change the shop sign to 'closed' and lock the door behind her. What a day...

When Cynthia arrived at Nobby's, she found she wasn't alone. Her mum and the family GP, Doctor Jessup, were there. He didn't appear to have been particularly impressed with her granddad's rate of recovery and didn't say much to Cynthia directly, but spoke quietly to her mum in the corner of the front room. This worried Cynthia and she tried to get some information from her mum on the journey home, but was told to stop worrying as there had been nothing concrete said by Dr Jessup.

When they got home, Cynthia's dad mentioned some boy called James had telephoned.

'James eh?' said her mum, looking her way, 'tell us more then?'

'Mum!' Cynthia could feel her face blushing and she was frantically trying to pretend it wasn't.

'Ha-ha,' laughed William, 'look at her face…'

'Oh, stop it will ya,' Cynthia said, now smiling herself. 'He's just some boy. Nothing special.'

She made her way to the passage where the phone lived. 'Can I get some privacy please?' she muttered as she picked up its red receiver and searched her small pocket diary for James's number.

Her mum smiled at her and walked into the kitchen, doing as she was told.

Cynthia dialled the number, her hands shaking ever so slightly and a nervous feeling in her tummy had come to visit, which was horrible and lovely at the same time.

After a few rings, finally she heard a voice that made her smile.

James had rung to check she was still on for their date. Perhaps he had sensed something because Cynthia was in two minds whether she did or didn't when she had returned from Blackpool. Nothing was really making sense that day. There was her granddad ill and, instead of being near him, she was off chasing the Fabs around the UK to get their autographs. That didn't seem right somehow, when once it had all made perfect sense. Over the weekend, she had sort of become, well, grown up. She was all confused, if she was honest. And now here was James being added to an already confusing mix.

It was during a lengthy telephone conversation with Sandra on Monday evening, reflecting on the highs and lows of their weekend, that Cynthia noticed she got a special tingle when James got mentioned. That had surprised her. Sandra suggested Cynthia had nothing to lose by just going on a date and she added that it might help take her mind off her granddad's health too.

Cynthia finally told James yes, that she was still on for the date and suggested he meet her on Wimbledon Common near the windmill at seven o' clock tomorrow, the Wednesday.

He quickly agreed. 'Blimey,' she heard herself say. The date was on!

All the next day at work, no matter whether she was measuring out a pound of loose-leaf tea, or a quarter of black jacks, every time James and the date came to mind, she couldn't help but smile. Blimey she thought, I've never felt like this before.

A quick bath once home and Cynthia was soon in her special yellow 'Beatles' dress and ready for her meeting with James.

'Oh, stop it will ya. Grow up.' Cynthia was doing her best to ignore her brothers' wolf whistles once they saw her on her way out. She was smiling as she left the house, although already fashionably late.

James, feeling very nervous, had got there half-hour too early, so Cynthia now being ten minutes late, had left him very, very jangly.

He lived in Putney so had walked across the Common from that direction. He was dressed smart, but in a casual way, wearing a recently purchased olive green Harrington jacket, teamed with a nice Oxford blue button down shirt and tan coloured StaPrest trousers which a cousin had sent him from the States. A nice pair of sand coloured desert boots finished off the look nicely.

Cynthia shyly smiled as she got near him and after saying hello, told him that she liked his clothes and that they suited him. James returned the compliment noting Cynthia's yellow suede shoes. The nerves they both felt slowly began to fade as the date got off to a good start.

'So, where d'ya fancy going then Cynthia?'

Cynthia told James that she fancied a strawberry milkshake and then led the way, suggesting one of the cafés near the tube station. James nodded and put up no argument.

The sun was still working its magic, so it was a warm pleasant evening as they walked slowly to the café, chatting all the way and trying to find out a little bit more about each other, without being too nosey. Cynthia mentioned they had had the doctor home to Nobby and James told her he was genuinely sorry to hear that.

As she walked in to 'Mario's', she had a quick look around and thankfully didn't recognise anyone in there. She chose a stool in one of the corners which looked out onto the street. James went to the counter and returned with two large strawberry milkshakes.

Cynthia got stuck in immediately. 'Ooh, that's lovely,' she said licking her lips. 'I can't remember the last time I had a strawberry milkshake.'

'No, me neither. Just what the doctor ordered,' James added, noticing Cynthia's expression alter as soon as she heard the word doctor. James felt like banging his head against the wall.

'Blimey, hark at me, so sorry Cynthia. I just wasn't thinking.'

'It's okay. It's just been one of those weeks. Every customer asked after my granddad, which of course is nice to know he is being thought about, but it was just a bit too much today.'

'How is he though?' James enquired.

'In all honesty, he looks terrible,' Cynthia replied sadly. 'Until recently, I had never seen my granddad poorly and I thought Doctor Jessup seemed concerned last night. The problem was he didn't say too much to me, only my mum and she won't say what's what. All of which has just made me worry even more.'

Cynthia continued to talk about Nobby and their close relationship for another ten minutes, and then she paused for a moment as she looked properly looked into James' eyes. She hadn't noticed them before; they were dark brown and friendly. She liked the way he sat quietly and listened to her. She couldn't remember feeling that comfortable with a boy before.

'Sorry,' Cynthia said, realising she was now just staring at him, 'I'm doing all the talking.'

James simply smiled. 'So, what about your *A Hard Day's Night* LPs, did you get them autographed like you hoped?'

'No,' Cynthia replied, forcing a smile. 'We might have to give up on that idea soon. It's all getting a bit silly really, although Sandra remains hopeful.' She then launched into a detailed moment-by-moment account of her and Sandra's trip up north.

Again, James listened patiently until Cynthia had exhausted her story.

'You know what, don't give up Cynthia. You can make it happen. I do believe that if you want something hard enough, you will find a way to get it. Besides, your friend Sandra sounds like she is depending on you to come up with a new plan.'

Cynthia liked hearing James' encouraging words and he was right, Sandra did need her to not give up. She then mentioned to James that her and Sandra were off to the London Palladium on Thursday, where The Beatles would be appearing at a charity event and, once again, to try and get their LPs signed.

'Well, there you go,' he said kindly, 'you can have one last go I suppose.'

Cynthia and James spent another hour in the café talking about their lives so far and their dreams for the future, whilst also trying another couple of flavoured milkshakes on the menu.

252

Now feeling a little bloated, James walked Cynthia back towards her home. At the end of Cynthia's road, they talked for a further fifteen minutes, telling each other they had had a great time and both agreeing to do it again soon. James eventually plucked up the courage to kiss Cynthia.

It felt awkward, as any first kiss is, but they went home having both felt that special warm glow inside.

**

'Oh, ferchrisakes, come on Sand. Flipping hell!' Cynthia was shouting at the top of her voice.

As per, Sandra was running late and they badly needed to get into central London as soon as possible to try and beat the inevitable crowds near to the London Palladium. On top of all that, Cynthia had a new plan she couldn't wait to try out.

Once under way, the inside of the tube was now especially busy and Cynthia found her nose pushed up against one of the train's filthy windows. It was jam-packed with Beatle people versus another army, that of the 9-5 city worker. The air around them was a pungent mixture of cheap perfume and sweat. As the tube slowed down approaching their stop, Cynthia grabbed Sandra's wrist and they squeezed their way off as soon as the doors slid open. Cynthia gasped for air but found none.

Oxford Circus tube station was absolutely heaving with hordes of excitable young girls. The station's platform was dangerously overcrowded and it took twenty minutes before Cynthia and Sandra stepped onto Oxford Street itself. They both gulped down a lungful of what 'fresh' air they could find.

It was then a short shove and a push into Argyll Street, which was only a brief distance away from their final destination and from where Cynthia and Sandra wanted to be. Unfortunately for them, so did a few thousand other Beatles fans. With a great deal of struggling and heaving, Cynthia and Sandra eventually found a spot where they could at least see the entrance to the London Palladium. Once there though, they found several barriers and security guards blocking their way.

'Piss it Cyn. What we going to do now?' Sandra moaned, crunching furiously on a pear drop or two.

'Sssh, I have a plan Sand, but we need to get up to the barriers,' Cynthia answered.

'A plan!' Sandra said, spitting brittle bits of her pear drop in the general direction of her mate, 'what plan?'

'Flipping hell Sandra, will you keep your voice down. I'll let you know soon, don't worry,' Cynthia whispered.

Cynthia then surveyed the crowd between her and her destination, looking for any gaps. She grabbed Sandra's wrist again and, with a determined effort, she pushed and shoved and ducked and dived her way through the now heaving mass until she finally reached a spot beside one of the barriers.

A security guard frowned at her as hard as he could, with a look that said, 'where did you pop up from?'

'Blimey Cyn, I nearly dropped my LP there, and the cover is becoming more and more tatty and dog-eared.' Sandra then had a quick look at where they had finished up. 'This is a good spot though isn't it,' she said panting.

As the evening gradually grew darker, The London Palladium looked brilliant with its hundreds of bright lights beaming across the surrounding area. The atmosphere in Argyll Street was simply electric and buzzed with a sound like a million bees swarming around a giant Orange Maid. The 'Night of a Hundred Stars' was in aid of The Combined Theatrical Charities Appeals Council. The Beatles had been invited to share the stage with the likes of Judy Garland, Sir Lawrence Olivier and Wilfrid Bramble and Harry H Corbett in the guise of their alter egos 'Steptoe and Son'.

Cynthia and Sandra observed the scene unfold before them: dozens upon dozens of expensive cars pulled up outside the London Palladium and a whole host of wealthy-looking people stepped out from them. Each time a new car arrived and their passengers strolled along the red carpet, Argyll Street lit up even more because of the flashlights coming from the cameras of the press photographers.

After every new arrival, the crowds behind Cynthia and Sandra surged forward trying to get a better glimpse of who had just arrived. And each time a new car pulled up outside the London Palladium the crowd roared - it was a deafening.

'Do you think The Beatles have arrived yet Cyn? Perhaps we're already too late,' Sandra yelled.

'No, you're not too late. They will be here soon. I've been here for nearly four hours and they haven't arrived yet,' said a freckle-faced young girl standing beside them and clutching a flag that she was getting ready to wave in the air as soon as The Fabs arrived. 'I'm busting for a wee...'

Sandra smiled and thanked the girl. She was about to ask Cynthia again what her plan was as she simply hadn't given any clue as to what she was conjuring up and this worried Sandra. But then an almighty cheer filled the air as all around them realised the car now pulling up was carrying the four individuals they had been waiting for.

Cynthia and Sandra screamed and yelled and bounced up and down just like everyone surrounding them. Sandra waved her copy of *A Hard Day's Night* in the air. Where they stood now was the closest they had ever got to The Beatles. Surely now, today, they would be spotted.

The girls saw one of the security guards walk forward and open a rear car door; one foot wearing a black leather boot with a Cuban heel dangled out. The sight of the boot caused the crowd to erupt like a volcano. Cynthia shouted something at Sandra, but Sandra couldn't hear over the volume of the screams. Realising that Sandra couldn't hear her, she pushed her own copy of *A Hard Day's Night* into Sandra's body and mouthed as clearly as she could, 'Hold onto that.'

Cynthia shouted, 'Oh no, help me, I don't feel at all well...' then rolled her eyes and collapsed onto the floor. Sandra, startled, screamed a loud piercing scream which alerted the crowd standing near her to start pushing and heaving against one another to try and create some space around Cynthia. Sandra's scream had also got the attention of the nearest security guard and he was now alerting his colleagues that some incident was occurring.

Within moments, several security guards were forcefully clearing some space around Cynthia and a St John's Ambulance man was checking her pulse. He nodded to a police sergeant and they decided to get her out of the crowd.

As they did this, they ignored all the pleas from Sandra, desperately trying to tell them that the girl who had fainted was her friend. All she could do was watch as the medical people pulled Cynthia out of the crowd and lay her now limp body in a cleared area. Such was her panic, Sandra didn't even notice the four Beatles get out of their car and rush into the Palladium.

Cynthia, however, had seen it all and in close-up too. She had been watching everything through squinted eyes, however her plan to get the attention from one of the Fabs hadn't worked. She hoped that George, seeing what had happened, would take pity on her and ask how she was. Instead, The Beatles rushed straight inside, without a second look back, let alone greeting their fans.

As soon as she realised her plan had failed, Cynthia rose to her feet and brushed herself down. The police constable nearest to her quickly got the measure of her attempt to get the attention of The Beatles. Without a word, he and a colleague picked up Cynthia and pretty much threw her back into the crowd, where she landed near to Sandra. Sandra too had sussed what had gone on and was, by now, extremely upset. She shoved Cynthia's LP straight at her.

'Oh, don't be like that. I thought it might work.' Cynthia was now beginning to feel a little foolish.

Sandra quickly turned on her heels and began shoving her way back through the crowds to the tube station.

'Sand, where ya going? Wait…. SANDRA!' Cynthia was shouting after, just about keeping her friend within viewing distance.

As they finally walked down the stairs and onto the platform, a train was pulling in. They both plonked down wearily onto their seats.

Cynthia could see Sandra was in no mood to be friends. 'I'm sorry Sandra.'

'Piss it Cyn! That was a really stupid idea. You could have been crushed. I could have been crushed! You should have told me your plan,' Sandra huffed.

'But, I couldn't tell you my plan, could I? I needed you to be as shocked as everyone else. I tried to time it just right so that I would fake a faint as The Beatles arrived. I was hoping they would see me and rush over to help, or see if I was okay or something. I thought you'd be by my side,' Cynthia explained.

'Oh, this is getting silly. That really frightened me Cyn and, what's more, because I was so busy being concerned about you, I missed the flipping Beatles altogether! All I got to see was one poxy Beatle boot. What a bleedin' waste of time that was. Piss it Cyn, really, piss it…you went too far this time.'

Sandra was genuinely angry with Cynthia, and Cynthia certainly felt it. She was also starting to feel sorry for herself too. Her plan had seemed a good one but now she realised it wasn't at all. They sat in silence all the way back to Wimbledon station. Once there, Cynthia gently reminded Sandra that she was going on holiday to Butlin's that coming Saturday and she wouldn't see her for a whole week. She hoped they could at least part on good terms.

Instead, Sandra said a very cold 'good night' and walked off.

Back in her bedroom, Cynthia looked at the empty suitcase and thought she should start thinking about doing some packing. She then tried to update her diary and her Beatles scrap book, and even thought about starting to write a letter to her pen pal Patricia, but she couldn't find the enthusiasm for any of it.

Instead, she crawled into bed and cried herself to sleep. The realisation of her earlier stupidity and making Sandra angry had hit home and she felt foolish. She was also cross that she had clocked up another failed attempt at trying to get their *A Hard Day's Night* LPs autographed.

This was all becoming a bit too much.

***

Bang!

Bang! BANG!

BANG! BANG! BANG!

'Come on Cynthia! This is the third time I have banged on your door. It's time to get up girl. We're leaving in thirty minutes.'

'Ok...OK!' Cynthia shouted back at her dad.

Cynthia was in no mood for getting up or going on holiday. Her night's sleep had ranked as one of the worst in her life - almost as bad as the night after swallowing those French blues she had stolen from John. Somehow though she got up, threw some cold water on her face, threw a pile of clothes untidily into her suitcase and made her way downstairs.

'Good, finally you're up,' said her mum as Cynthia entered the kitchen and put two slices of bread into the toaster.

'Now, Mrs Goddard is going to keep an eye on Granddad for us and Dr Jessup says he'll pop in each day as well. It's not ideal I know, but I'm sure he'll be fine. Okay? Right. Eat that toast quickly then. Dad will take care of the suitcase.'

It wasn't too long before the luggage was packed into and on top of the car and Cynthia and her mum and dad were soon on their way.

They dropped by Nobby's first to see how he was and say their goodbyes, all the while being careful not to rub it in they were going to Butlin's without him.

Cynthia's dad had told him that they were prepared to cancel their holiday, but Nobby would have none of that and insisted they go. Cynthia really didn't like leaving her granddad behind at all and it bothered her constantly throughout the entire journey from London to Bognor Regis. She was being made to feel like a little kid and she didn't feel like that anymore - well, most of the time. She was growing up fast and that was bringing a truckload of confusion with it. She really wanted to see James too before they left, but there simply hadn't been time.

The Butlin's camp in Bognor had been their holiday destination for a few years now. They had tried other camps but Nobby had always preferred the Bognor site, so they went there to please him. When they first started going, it had been as the whole family, but Andrew hadn't been for a few years now and John hadn't been for the last three. Cynthia suspected that this year would be her last too, which made leaving her granddad behind even more painful.

Earlier in the year, Sandra had suggested to Cynthia that when they were seventeen, they should start going on holiday together. Sandra dreamed of visiting exotic places like Paris, Rome and Madrid, but somehow Cynthia suspected they would end up spending their holiday on a campsite in Great Yarmouth. One thing was for certain, she certainly had no intention of returning to Blackpool ever again.

Cynthia had liked the idea of going on holiday with her best friend and was now missing her badly. She hadn't heard anything from Sandra since The Palladium and, hoping she would forgive her at some point, promised herself that she would keep an eye out for an extra special gift for her best mate.

Every year Cynthia went on holiday, she always got Sandra a gift. The previous year, Cynthia had asked the sweet shop bloke if they made giant pear drops because, if they did, that would be the perfect present for her best friend. The man looked at her like she was mad, so she hastily bought Sandra a giant stick of rock instead.

It was a gruelling, hot and sticky journey to Bognor that required sitting in several traffic jams and driving very slowly behind countless cars towing caravans; it was the same every year.

Finally, after five hours, Cynthia's dad drove through the holiday camp's entrance and under its big sign saying 'You'll Have a Wonderful Time at Butlin's By the Sea'. She was doubly delighted to see that, as she was in desperate need of the toilet and to stretch her legs.

Whilst Cynthia and her mum skipped to the nearest convenience, her dad went into the site office to collect the keys to their chalet. When he returned, Cynthia and her mum were waiting in the car., so they drove to the car park nearest their chalet and unloaded their luggage. They had been allocated a chalet in an area they were familiar with, only this time they were placed on the top floor rather than the ground, which gave Cynthia's mother something to moan about.

Once inside, Cynthia sat herself down at the dining table. Seeing her sitting there lost in her own thoughts, her dad came over and asked her to hold out her hand. She did as he asked and he dropped a 'Butlin's 1964' pin badge into it. In previous years, Cynthia would have put it straight on. This year, however, she just stared down at it.

The pin badge was red and yellow with an image of air balloon and a lantern embossed on it. Cynthia quietly tucked it into her coat pocket; she certainly had no intention of wearing it. It was yet another step further away from her childhood, as she marched into joining the ranks of young adulthood. Cynthia felt the largest steps seemed to have occurred over the last few weeks. Reflecting on this thought, she came to the conclusion that July had been a hard day's month indeed. She sighed and then laughed as she thought back on all that had happened that summer so far.

The inside of the chalet had that unique smell that only holiday chalets in the UK possess. The rooms had been cleaned earlier that morning, but somehow still managed to smell neglected. Every year, the first task was the same: Cynthia and her mother would clean the chalet from top to bottom whilst her dad whisked himself away to enjoy a refreshing light and bitter. It was his special treat and a signal to himself that he had arrived at Butlin's and was now on holiday. Usually, Nobby would have joined him and they wouldn't return until tea time and, by which time, they would be a little worse for wear.

Once the cleaning was done, Cynthia's mother took charge of stacking the kitchen shelves with bags of tea, sugar and coffee and an assortment of tins containing various foods that would make up their meals throughout the week.

Cynthia went to her room and unpacked her luggage, consisting of a decent supply of clothes, her beloved Dansette and selected Beatles LPs. She then decided to get away for an hour and went for a walk, taking a copy of the Butlin's 1964 programme with her. She intended to find a peaceful spot to sit down and read it, this being a ritual that she had enjoyed doing the past couple of years.

The holiday camp had a cheery feel to it. Typically, British holidaymakers were determined to enjoy their well-earned breaks and nothing was going to stop them having fun and relaxing, whatever the weather had in store for them. Cynthia smiled as she ambled around the campsite. As much as she was missing her granddad, her best friend and now James too, she knew there was little she could do about it, so she decided to enjoy herself the best she could.

She passed the outdoor swimming pool, now full of children splashing around and screaming excitedly. Cynthia smiled as she fondly remembered when they first started coming to Butlin's. Andrew, being older, would pretty much disappear for most of the day, only returning at tea time for a sandwich and a glass of milk before disappearing again. Cynthia and John, however, would be paired off and the responsibility of having to look after his younger sister would rest uneasily on John's shoulders.

Having to spend the week under the wing of John was something Cynthia particularly liked, but she suspected he never liked her being his shadow. When they were young, the days typically began with their mother cooking the family a breakfast of eggs, bacon and toast, then being kicked out of the chalet and being told not to return until lunchtime.

The intervening hours between breakfast and dinner and dinner and tea were spent either larking about in the swimming pool, getting involved with some of the activities organised by the Redcoats, or generally trying to get up to as much mischief as possible without getting told off. John was highly-skilled at getting into mischief.

Every year he would find at least one other boy, usually older, to have a fight with. Many was the time Cynthia stood watching John getting other boys into headlocks and what have you, whilst the other children stood around chanting 'fight...fight...fight'. Happy days indeed...

On one of the sunbathing lawns, Cynthia found a vacant red and white striped deckchair positioned under a large red, white, yellow and blue umbrella. It was the furthest lawn from the swimming pool, so mostly out of earshot of any annoying children.

Sliding into the deck chair and shuffling her bottom to make herself comfortable, Cynthia opened up the Butlin's programme. Page one had a photograph of Mr W. E. Butlin MBE and, written in big letters beside his image, were the words 'WELCOME TO BUTLIN'S'. It amused Cynthia that immediately beneath Mr Butlin was an advert for Skol lager. She instantly thought of her dad sitting at one of the holiday camp's bars enjoying a pint of Skolt or similar.

The next page outlined the various competitions and tournaments which the Redcoats would be running that week. Cynthia made a note of the ones she thought she might enjoy, such as the 'Miss She Contest' where contestants had 'to show off your dress sense and deportment' and 'The Holiday Princess of the Year', which had a grand prize of one thousand pounds to the winner.

Cynthia wasn't fussed about the Glamorous Grandmother contest and thought she'd make herself scarce for that one. There was also a snooker tournament with a prize of twenty-five pounds and a trophy. Cynthia's dad entered that competition every year, and every year he got knocked out in the first round, always blaming the 'wonky' cue he had been given to play with.

The campsite's cinema showed fairly recently-released films each afternoon and, in the evening, the Regency ballroom boasted entertainment from 'Al Fried and the Butlin's Theatre Orchestra' along with 'Derek Ashton and his Hammond Organ'.

Cynthia had quite enjoyed the previous year's evening entertainment, but now she had The Beatles in her life and that was the only music she now wanted to hear - and she doubted Derek did a few Beatles songs.

Instead, she suspected she'd spend most evenings sitting in her bedroom in the chalet playing her Beatles records, whilst her parents went out to 'unwind'. She was actually quite looking forward to that...

On page eight, she surprisingly found something that would make the perfect gift for Sandra. It was a full-page article dedicated to Ringo Starr! There was a beautiful picture of him sporting a beard and playing drums in his previous band with Rory Storm. Cynthia

261

hungrily read through the article as it explained how Ringo had played with Rory at the Butlin's camp in Skegness back in 1962.

'Ooh!' she said to herself, 'perfect. Sand will love that.'

Chapter 19
You Say Hello and I Say Goodbye

With the full day of travelling and general excitement of the day, Cynthia's mum and dad only had a quick evening drink at the main bar before turning in for an early night. Cynthia had stayed in with a bottle of coke or two and spent the rest of the evening with The Beatles and her Dansette.

Later that night, Cynthia could hear rapping on the front door of the chalet. She tried her best to ignore it at first, hoping one of her parents would go and answer it. She lay there speculating that it would be one of the Redcoats returning some belongings to her mother, who had developed the irritating habit of leaving her handbag behind whenever she had a Babycham or three.

She heard her dad coughing as he made his way out of their bedroom to see who it was.

Cynthia didn't hear the content of the exchange that had just taken place, but she most certainly heard her dad bang on her door.

'Cyn, you awake? Come on love, emergency.'

Cynthia could hear the urgency in his voice and could sense that something was very wrong.

An hour later the family car was re-packed with the entire luggage and they were speeding their way back to London.

Other than Cynthia's dad explaining why they had to return to London, he didn't say another word throughout the whole journey; it was evident that he was deeply worried. The visitor at the chalet door was indeed a Redcoat. Only it wasn't her mum's handbag he was delivering, it was a telegram from Dr Jessup informing Cynthia's mum and dad that Nobby had taken a turn for the worse and it was recommended the family return home to be with him at once.

Total numbness was all that Cynthia could feel. She wished she had wings so she could fly back to her granddad's and hated the thought of not knowing what was happening. All she knew was that she needed to be by his side.

Fortunately, because it was approaching the early hours, the roads were very clear and Cynthia's dad was parking up the car outside her granddad's much sooner than they had anticipated. Cynthia and her parents frantically piled out of the car and Dr Jessup met them on the doorstep. He quickly, but sensitively, explained that Nobby was now struggling to survive. He led Cynthia and her parents to Nobby's room.

The curtains were still shut tight and the only light in the room was where it had pushed itself in through the hallway. Doctor Jessup stood to one side allowing Cynthia and her parents to enter the room. Cynthia stood frozen, just staring at her granddad. His illness had certainly taken a hold of him in the last twenty-four hours. The frail figure that was now lying in that bed hardly resembled Nobby at all.

Cynthia listened to her dad as he spoke softly and kindly to the man who had been a constant for most of his life. No matter how hard she tried, she couldn't prevent the tears welling up in her eyes and rolling down her face. Cynthia could almost feel the life force of her granddad departing its earthly shell. Doctor Jessup leaned nearer to Cynthia and suggested she might want to go and speak to her granddad. He spoke kindly, adding that he was sure her granddad would want to see her face and she should say a few words to him.

Cynthia's dad beckoned Cynthia to step nearer. He shifted himself out of the way, making room for her to sit beside the old man. She slowly perched herself on the edge of the bed. Her granddad had his eyes closed and was breathing slowly and heavily. She wanted to do something to help. She wanted to cast some magic spell or chant some healing words that would make her granddad well again.

Instead, Cynthia carefully placed her hand onto her granddad's hand. His hand felt cool; she wasn't expecting it to be so cool. Cynthia turned to her dad and said more blankets were needed because her granddad was cold. Her dad placed his hand on her shoulder and gently shook his head. Cynthia glanced at her mother; she too had tears rolling down her cheek.

Suddenly Cynthia's granddad coughed and he opened his eyes. He used what strength he had to turn and look at his only granddaughter whom he had known and loved deeply all her life. Somehow, he managed to produce a smile and Cynthia smiled back.

'Hello,' she said with a voice full of sorrow.

'Hello girly. How was Butlin's?' he said almost in a whisper.

'It was fun Granddad. Just like last year,' Cynthia lied.

'Did your dad win the snooker tournament?'

'Not this year, dodgy cue again. Maybe next year eh?' Cynthia sniffed as she spoke.

Nobby smiled and almost managed a laugh.

'How about those boys of yours? They signed that record of yours yet?'

This change in topic came as a surprise. It was only then she realised how often she had probably updated her granddad on the progress, or lack of it, in getting her and Sandra's copy of *A Hard Day's Night* signed.

'No, not yet Granddad, but we are still trying.'

Nobby looked at her with a kindness in his face.

'Don't give up Cynthia love. Whatever you do, never give up.'

At that precise moment, Cynthia's granddad glanced at his cherished clock on the bedroom wall as it struck on the hour.

The sound of the clock's chime prompted Cynthia to do the same. By the time Cynthia next looked at her granddad he had gone - and was gone forever.

***

Nobby's funeral was set for Saturday 1st August.

Out of respect, his shop would remain closed for a short period. Cynthia virtually lived in a daze for a week, but thankfully she had Sandra and her Beatles records to comfort her. It was lovey to have her mate back in her life.

She hardly ventured out her bedroom and, when she did, it was only to go for a walk across the Common. Cynthia spent most evenings sitting in the front room with her parents. She didn't fancy The Moka; it wasn't the time for that place.

She did, however, meet James for a milkshake one night and this helped. She could talk to him easily, despite suffering from an overwhelming feeling of grief. Cynthia had never known death before. Family bereavements were what other families had to deal with. She heard about it from time to time whilst working in the shop, but it never occurred to her that one day she too would have to face it.

Suddenly, on the Friday, the day before her granddad's funeral, Cynthia had the mad idea that she wanted to open her granddad's shop for business. It was something she felt she needed to do, maybe to give his customers a chance to pay their respects to the old place.

In reality, she actually dreaded the thought of spending another day in the shop. How could she still work there without her granddad?

Her dad gave her permission to open the shop, but only after asking if she was up really up to it.

She was, she told him, adding that old customers would pop in and say goodbye before his funeral. She couldn't really explain it; it was something she needed to do. Cynthia also knew that once she had closed up and locked the shop door that night, she would never be returning. She had made up her mind to go and get a job working in the West End. That's where she needed to be and she knew her granddad would approve and understand.

On the morning, however, Cynthia realised that she didn't actually have the key to open up the shop. She checked with her parents, only to learn they didn't either. Cynthia had no other choice but to go to Nobby's house and find the keys.

Cynthia hadn't been back there since he had passed away. Her parents had gone most days to sort out a few things, but she had stayed away. As Cynthia walked up her granddad's garden path she couldn't help notice the several rubbish bags piled up in the garden. She tried not to look at them, knowing full well they contained items that once belonged to her granddad.

Cynthia fought to hold back the tears as she turned the key in her granddad's front door and pushed it open. The sense of something missing was overwhelming and Cynthia even thought about abandoning her idea of opening the shop altogether and going back home to lock herself away in her bedroom for the rest of the day, or possibly for the week. But she knew she couldn't. Her dad had already left a note on her granddad's shop door, informing folk that the shop would be open for half day on Friday for customers wanting to pay their respects.

The hallway floor was stacked with boxes with her mother's handwritten notes pinned to them saying 'to be sorted'. Peering into the room on the right, Cynthia could see that that too was also full of boxes. It was a very sorry sight and one that turned Cynthia's stomach. A lifetime of memories now stacked in boxes.

Cynthia didn't enter that room; instead she swerved away and headed for the living room. She didn't really need to go in there, but felt compelled. Most of the furniture had been stacked into one corner of the room, but for some reason her granddad's armchair remained in the same position it always had done. It was now a solid, if a little eerie, reminder of him.

Cynthia chose not to loiter too long in there, so crept slowly upstairs and followed the passageway along to her granddad's old bedroom. The first thing Cynthia noticed when she entered the room was the bed where she had felt her granddad slip away. Only the bed frame remained; the sheets and mattress had been removed. It was a horrible sight and one that felt almost disrespectful. Cynthia felt like she wanted to run back to her own home and scold her parents for being so cold, but calmed herself down, telling herself that they knew what was best. She reminded herself that it couldn't have been easy for them either. Cynthia then turned her head and noticed her granddad's cherished clock had also been removed. She quickly scanned the room to see if it had been stuffed into one of the three boxes that were stacked under the window, but she couldn't see it; the clock wasn't there. She knew it had to be somewhere. Both her parents understood the value of the clock so surely they wouldn't have left it in rubbish bags in the garden for the dustmen to collect, would they? Cynthia decided she would ring her parents as soon as she got to the shop.

Tears suddenly welled in her eyes and, as though a dam had broken, water flooded over her eyelashes. She sat there and wept, then sobbed and cried some more.

After dabbing her eyes with a pocket tissue she found in her jacket pocket, Cynthia collected her thoughts as she walked across the room to her open her granddad's old wardrobe. She sighed with relief when she saw her granddad's old jackets and coats still hanging up, and then she remembered her parents saying that they hadn't yet got around to sorting out his wardrobe.

Cynthia reached inside and pulled out one of her granddad's favourite jackets; one that he wore every weekend. She held the jacket to her nose and took a long, hard sniff. The jacket had the smell of her granddad which was strangely comforting and she held the jacket close, hugging it to her. After a while, Cynthia put the jacket back in the wardrobe to continue with her search and finally found what she was looking for. Cynthia kissed the key to her granddad's shop as if she was planting a kiss on her granddad's cheek.

Cynthia held the key tightly in her hands as she made her way to the shop. She was now running a little late and, although she knew people would understand, she was determined to have the door open to the locals at 9am.

It turned out to be a busy morning with regular customers flocking in and out, each offering their condolences and almost all taking time to tell Cynthia a story they had about Nobby. It was like it was therapy for them and they just wanted to share with her. Cynthia stood there all morning feeling extremely proud and honoured to have known her granddad.

That evening, Cynthia had arranged to meet Sandra on their bench. She still had the Butlin's programme with the article and picture of Ringo to give to her. Things had been so upside down since her granddad's passing that Cynthia had forgotten all about the programme.

For the second time in the same month, Sandra was waiting for Cynthia, and it wasn't even that Cynthia was running late. She was glad Sandra was there though; she had been feeling terribly lonely all week.

'How are you Cyn?' Sandra asked as she Cynthia fell into her arms.

Cynthia pulled a face that tried to explain the hurt she was feeling and Sandra pulled her in close and hugged her again.

'Do you want to go to The Moka? Seeing people and listening to the jukebox might help cheer you up?' Sandra suggested kindly.

Cynthia shook her head, 'No, I'll leave that Sand if you don't mind.'

She had no intention of going there and to have to be around people like Danny the King Mixer. Cynthia told Sandra she was happy to just sit on their bench and talk. And that is what they did. They spent the next three hours talking about the good times Cynthia had had with her granddad, and they talked about what they had done throughout July. It certainly had been an extraordinary month for a lot of different reasons.

'You know Sand,' said Cynthia as they were giving each other a goodbye hug, 'I'm not bothered anymore about things that were once important - you know the autographs and that. Granddad dying has put it all in perspective. There are more important things to worry about.'

'I know,' Sandra replied, 'I know. We had a laugh trying though didn't we?'

Cynthia nodded and they laughed as they hugged goodbye.

***

On the morning of the funeral, Cynthia's mum and dad presented her with her granddad's old clock, which they said he would have wanted her to have. Cynthia didn't really know whether to laugh or cry, but she hugged that clock for all her life.

Cynthia's dad drove his family to the Gap Road Cemetery. Cynthia sat in the back with her two brothers either side of her; both had bought new suits for the occasion. When they arrived, there was already a decent-sized crowd gathering around the modest chapel. Cynthia recognised plenty of customers from her granddad's shop and that made her feel warm inside.

The service itself was short and, by most standards, sweet. Cynthia's dad got up and made a speech, as did Tommy, one of her granddad's old friends whom he had served with in the forces. He spoke kind, loving words about his pal Nobby and it was evident that her granddad had lived a full life. He was much loved and Cynthia suddenly didn't feel so sad, which was a relief.

Hymns were sung and the vicar said his bit. Cynthia didn't really hear any of that to be honest and, throughout the service, had kept glancing over her shoulder to look at Sandra. On more than one occasion Sandra simply stick her tongue out and Cynthia had to stop herself laughing. When it was time to place Cynthia's granddad in the grave, she asked Sandra to stand beside her. She was glad to have her friend there to support her.

Once the funeral was over, the majority of the congregation retreated to 'The Jolly Gardeners'. It was quite near her granddad's shop and he was known to have had a swift half or two in there some lunch times or after the shop had closed. He had been well liked in there, so the landlord made everyone very welcome.

The 'afters' was very well-attended, which pleased Cynthia and her family. Even James and his family arrived, including Old Man King. Cynthia waved at James and he made the sign of a phone at his ear, which she took to mean he would call her. She nodded his way and mouthed the words 'yes please'.

Kenny also dropped by and Cynthia was pleased to see him too.

'Come on, let's get some fresh air,' Cynthia said to Sandra and Kenny. They made their way out into the pub's beer garden and each sparked up a fag.

'I know what's happened is terrible Cynthia, but you shouldn't let it stop you, you know. That's not what your granddad would want is it?' Kenny said.

'Stop her? What you talking about Kenny?' Sandra asked.

'The Beatles of course. I thought once you two had made your appearance at the wake, you'd be off to London Airport.'

'London Airport?' Cynthia asked.

'Yeah, London Airport is where The Beatles fly into on the way back from their recent concerts in Stockholm,' Sandra added.

'Yeah, I thought that would be an excellent opportunity to try and get your LPs signed, especially if you hang around the lane which the car carrying The Beatles will use to exit the airport,' Kenny said, proud that he had done his homework.

Cynthia looked at Sandra, and Sandra could tell what Cynthia was thinking.

'Shall we Sandra?' Cynthia was now smiling from ear-to-ear.

'No Cyn, you can't. It's your granddad's wake.'

'It's what he would want Sand. He did tell me not to give up, didn't he? It won't take us long to go and get our copies of *A Hard Day's Night*,' Cynthia replied.

'But Cyn, we'd never get there in time; they land in just over an hour or so. I know, I checked this morning. The buses and tubes would never get us there on time,' Sandra added, blushing a little.

'But you would if I drove you there,' Kenny said, pointing to a battered old Morris Minor he had recently purchased.

Sandra shook her head laughing. 'Okay, only if you can drop by our houses on the way so we can get our albums, then piss it…let's do it!'

No sooner had Sandra stopped speaking, then all three of them raced toward Kenny's motor. After the necessary pit stops to collect the prized vinyl, they were flying down the street and on their way to London Airport. Kenny drove like a lunatic most of the way; he was like a man possessed and was determined to help Cynthia and Sandra get their LPs autographed.

As they approached the airport perimeter fencing, they could see thousands of Beatle people pushed up against them waving flags and banners. The Beatles must have already landed because a thousand girls were screaming their heads off. There was also increased security because on the very same day, the Prime Minister and the

Queen Mother were flying out. There was even some rumour that Ed Sullivan was in the airport too. Kenny had worked out exactly where he needed to park the car. He drove through an industrial estate area and skidded the car into a gravel ditch.

'Go on, get out. Run. You'll need to stand over there,' Kenny shouted at his two pals, pointing to a large metal gate.

Cynthia grabbed Sandra, and Sandra grabbed the records, and they made a run for the metal gates.

'Look,' Sandra cried, pointing to a black Rolls Royce that was speeding its way along a path towards the gate.

'Faster...Run...Faster,' Cynthia called out.

Both girls ran as fast their legs would carry them, managing to reach the gate at exactly the same moment as the Rolls Royce. The Roller slowed to a halt and Cynthia and Sandra stood beside it. The windows of the Rolls were tinted so they couldn't see inside. For all Cynthia and Sandra knew, it could be anybody in that car, or it could be acting as a decoy and The Beatles were already far away by now and possibly heading for their next gig.

Other than the sound of the Roller purring away, and the two girls breathing heavily after their run, there was complete silence. Cynthia and Sandra struggled to regain their breath and stood frozen to the spot, unsure what their next move should be. Sandra turned to Cynthia for an answer, but she could see that Cynthia was as lost as herself. And then, finally, there was a buzzing sound and the rear window nearest to them started to drop down. A hand revealed itself and it had a ring on two of the fingers. Sandra instantly recognised the rings.

Slowly, Cynthia and Sandra crouched down so they could look inside the car and four faces grinned back at them. Both girls started to visibly shake at the sight of Ringo sitting next to George, with Paul sat next to George, who in turn sat next to John.

'Alright there girls,' George said, ''Ere I recognise you,' he said pointing to Cynthia. 'You have that bright yellow dress, don't you?'

Try as she might, Cynthia just couldn't speak. She was so shocked, she couldn't utter a sound and could only just manage a nod. She also couldn't take her eyes off George, but still managed to prise the copies of *A Hard Day's Night* from Sandra's firm grip. Her best mate was in a hypnotic state, her face frozen with a shocked expression which was locked onto Ringo, who was now smiling back at her.

Cynthia handed them to Ringo, who accepted them.

'Blimey, they're a bit grotty ain't they ladies?'

It's...it's ...been...ages. We've...been trying to get them...to you...' Sandra finally stuttered.

Ringo laughed as he passed them around to the others, who all signed them.

'There ya go girls, all done. You only had to ask,' joked a very jovial Ringo passing them back to Cynthia and Sandra who now couldn't form any words. They just sighed and smiled.

The driver of the Rolls began to cough, getting impatient after spying a large group of girls running in their direction.

'Hold up driver, yer swine,' said John smiling whilst looking behind him. 'Listen girls, we're about to be invaded by a Beatle maniacal horde.'

Paul had also spotted them. 'He's right y'know. I think we had better get going eh? Ta-ra then girls, ta-ra then.'

All four of the Fabs waved at Cynthia and Sandra as the car window went back into its 'up' position and the Rolls Royce slowly eased away. Cynthia couldn't help feeling like she'd heard the sound of that 'tara' before.

All they could do was hold up their hands and wave back.

Just as the Roller was about to change gear and speed away, Sandra exclaimed excitedly, 'Oh piss it,' and ran after the Roller.

'Ringo! Ringo!' she cried, 'Do you want a pear drop?!'

***

29th November 2001

Cynthia walked into her lounge and found Sandra curled up on her sofa, lying under a couple of coats and still wearing the clothes she had arrived in a few hours earlier. Since then they had finished off three bottles of vino blanc which were now lying on the floor near the record player.

A Hard Day's Night had long since finished playing, but the album was still on the turntable after being played at least twenty times in a row the previous night.

The two old friends, and they knew they would be friends to the end, had drunk and talked about all the big events that had hit their lives in the intervening years since the halcyon days of The Fabs, their Fabs...

Cynthia had relived getting married at 18 to James and them being blissfully happy for 18 months or so before the cracks started to appear. It was doomed from then on. They were simply too young, far too young. Just as her mum had told her. Had she listened? No. And was she still being reminded of it on a weekly basis by her mum? Yes she was!

Sandra was actually sad she had never married if truth were told. She had failed miserably to find the right bloke and somehow always picked out a wrong 'un. If there was a bloke to avoid, she'd end up going out with him; it was like she had wonky radar which never failed to find the target. She said she somehow knew it would all be downhill from her Ringo.

But, despite all the heartache and pain which it brought their way, last night they had mostly laughed. They had delighted in reliving their days of chasing four blokes around parts of London and the rest of the UK for that one month in the summer of 64, in one last flush of youth before life got serious and, in some ways, frightening.

And they had never forgotten that day when they finally met their heroes and got those flipping albums signed.

As she now continued to tidy up, Cynthia picked up the *A Hard Day's Night* record sleeve along with the empty wine glasses, the clinking of which now finally woke up Sandra.

She rubbed her eyes and then farted.

Cynthia smiled whilst Sandra tried to style it out. She then glanced at Nobby's old clock on the wall of his granddaughter's rented flat and groaned.

'Blimey...is...that the time...? Piss it, I'll have to throw a sickie Cyn. I'll never get to work, not in this state anyway...'

'You do that Sand mate. You tell 'em...,' said Cynthia as she looked at the face of George Harrison smiling back at her from the second line of that iconic album cover.

'You tell 'em we've had a death in the family...'

273

About the Authors

Mark Baxter photo © Tony Briggs

Mark Baxter: Lives in South East London and likes Millwall, red wine and Tubby Hayes. His previous books include 'The Fashion of Football' 'The Mumper' 'Elizabeth, Peter and Me' 'The A-Z of Mod' 'Ready Steady Girls' and 'The Beatles Footprint'.

His films include 'Outside Bet' 'A Man in a Hurry - Tubby Hayes' and 'John Simons - A Modernist'

Ian Snowball – Born and raised in Kent. Ian has an admiration for music and cult writers such as Pete McKenna and John King and tends to read any books with musical connections. An early fascination with music kicked off after having bought his first 7 inch record That's Entertainment by The Jam. From here on there was a musical discovery that included Northern Soul, Reggae, Ska, Punk, House music and such bands as The Jam, The Small Faces, The Prisoners and The Who. Ian began writing books in 2008 and had his debut novel Long Hot Summer published in 2009. His next project was a book about British youth cults called Tribe: Made In Britain, which he co-wrote with Pete McKenna. Ian and Pete then collaborated on a crime fiction novel about Mods and East End gangsters that was set in 1967. The book called In the Blood was published in 2012, the same year as Thick as Thieves (Personal Situations With the Jam)-co-written with Stu Deabill, of which Paul Weller said was 'the best book on The Jam and its audience I've ever seen'. 2013 then saw the publication of Supersonic (Personal Situations With Oasis) and From Ronnie's To Raver's (Personal Situations in London's Clubland) which were also co-written with Stu Deabill. And in November that year Ian and Pete had their northern soul fictional short stories book called Nightshift/All Souled Out published. In 2014 Ian had three books published. His book about Ocean Colour Scene called Soul Driver was published one month after his book on Dexys Midnight Runner's called The Team That Dreams in Caffs which he co-wrote with Dexys band member Geoff 'JB' Blythe was published and finally that year Ian's other published book about the Medway garage and punk scene was called the Kids Are All Square. In 2015 Ian co-wrote That's Entertainment (My Life In The Jam) with The Jam's drummer Rick Buckler. 2016 also saw the publication of Ian's book Keith Moon: There Is No Substitute with an introduction by Pete Townshend and a foreword from Clem Burke. This was Ian's third best-selling book.

Recommended reading

Ian Snowball & Pete McKenna

Black Music White Britain by Ian Snowball and Pete McKenna. It has often been quoted that if you can remember the 1960's then you wasn't there. Sure enough the 60's was a time packed full of exciting cultural, political and musical change. This in turn impacted on the youth of the day, a youth that was really still finding its steps having found itself breaking away from its post war teenager cocoon into something which at that time was unrecognisable. But, then some might say so were the 50's. Gradually youth was finding a voice…and it was backing it up with a sense of style and new sounds. Jazz music was always going to be cool. But for many teenagers Jazz was also 'dug' by their older brother and parents. The 1950's teenager was ready to embrace something new. That was when the first Modernists appeared on the streets of Soho and, it wouldn't be long before the black artists, many who had been previously, to the larger part ignored, would be embraced and welcomed in Britain and, every note and drum beat lapped up.

Publisher: New Haven Publishing Ltd
ISBN: 9781910705667

The Who: In The City by by Ian Snowball is an exciting new book that has never been attempted before. The book tells the unique story of one of rock and rolls greatest bands and their personal history with the city of London. All four original members of The Who were born and grew up in London and this book documents the facts and figures of this time and then adds to the story further by taking the reader on an amazing journey through all of the bands London concerts and gigs across a fifty year period. The story is further brought to life with contributions from friends and fans of the band and these include Kenney Jones (Small Faces and The Who), Jim McCarty (The Yardbirds), Steve White (The Style Council/Paul Weller) and Peter 'Dougal' Butler (Keith Moon's PA). The book also includes other London places of Who related interest, such as their hang-out's, homes and where they got their hangovers. Additionally there are features, that serve as a walking tour for any serious Who fan visiting London and these include locations relating to the band like the Goldhawk Club and Quadrophenia (the movie) and many more from around city.Ian Snowball is the author the best-selling Keith Moon: There Is No Substitute, That's Entertainment: My Life In The Jam (Rick Buckler of The Jam's autobiography) and Thick As Thieves (Personal Situations With The Jam). Ian is also donating 50% of his royalties for this book to the Teenage Cancer Trust, a charity that Roger Daltrey is a patron of.

Publisher: New Haven Publishing Ltd
ISBN: 9781910705452